S*The* tolen Girl

Renita D'Silva

bookouture

Published by Bookouture

An imprint of Storyfire Ltd.
Carmelite House
50 Victoria Embankment
London EC4Y 0DZ

www.bookouture.com

Copyright © Renita D'Silva 2014

Renita D'Silva has asserted her right to be identified as the author of this work.

All rights reserved. No part of this publication may be reproduced, stored in any retrieval system, or transmitted, in any form or by any means, electronic, mechanical, photocopying, recording or otherwise, without the prior written permission of the publishers.

ISBN: 978-1-909490-54-3
eBook ISBN: 978-1-909490-53-6

This book is a work of fiction. Names, characters, businesses, organizations, places and events other than those clearly in the public domain, are either the product of the author's imagination or are used fictitiously. Any resemblance to actual persons, living or dead, events or locales is entirely coincidental.

The Stolen Girl

ACKNOWLEDGEMENTS

Thank you, as always, to Oliver Rhodes for his continued belief in me and for another stunning cover, to Lorella Belli for her guidance and tireless efforts in making my books reach a wider audience, to my wonderful editors Jenny Hutton and Claire Bord whose amazing insight I am indebted to, to Debbie Brunettin and Helen Bolton for their scrupulous eye for detail, and to Kim Nash – the best book ambassador any author could wish for.

This book would not have been possible without the help and advice of Tom Beynon, who gave up so many of his Sunday afternoons listening to me hash out fictional legal scenarios and talked me through what was feasible and what was not, who put up with my phone calls and texts brimming with questions and patiently answered every one, who talked to lawyer friends in other disciplines and read up on legal texts outside his field of criminal law to give me solutions. Thank you SO much, Tom.

Thank you to Margaret Ilori for her time, for providing answers to my questions even though they weren't related to her field of law.

Thank you to Vineeta Goveas Giles, who patiently explained the difference between a child psychologist and child psychiatrist and gave her input into my fictional scenario.

Any oversights and mistakes are my own. I have taken some liberties with the prisoners' visits and the Visits Hall. Most prisons do not allow more than one visit/ visitor per day. I have also taken liberties with social workers' duties – in some boroughs, some of the things that Jane does would have been done by a child support officer.

I am incredibly lucky in having amazing neighbours who also, coincidentally, work in crime enforcement and family support. A huge thank you to Peter McKay and Monika McKay for answering my many questions at all hours, for their support and wonderful friendship, and for understanding when I did not have time for cups of tea. Thank you to Alex McKay, for her lovely smile which never fails to cheer me up. And a big thank you to David for always, without fail, telling me stories.

Thank you to the Tharumanayagams and the Ponweeras: Niluma, Noel, Sunanda, Dillon, Rochelle and Samara, for adopting Tanya while I was writing, picking her up and dropping her off when I asked and when I didn't, for feeding her and making her a part of their family.

A huge thank you to the Strudwicks: Amelia, Dave, Eloise, Jacob, Lily and Keira for their love and support.

Thank you to the Ahadis: Evelina, Karina, Alex and Abs for all their help and for taking Tanya to fun things, especially the Summer Ball which she is not likely to forget.

I am grateful to the mums at the school, and all my friends, too many to name individually, for their support.

A huge thank you to my lovely sister-in-law, Levin D'Souza for asking around and getting answers to questions related to Indian law. And to my wonderful mother, Perdita Hilda D'Silva for her advice, her inspirational quotes, her support and love.

Thank you to my family for putting up with a mum and wife on a deadline.

And last but not least, thank you, reader, for choosing to buy this book and read it. Enjoy.

For Tanya Ayesha D'Souza
My burst of sunshine, my delight, my muse.

PART ONE

Present Day

Popped Bubble of Truths

Chapter 1
Diya

Mother

Mother

Noun: a female parent.

Verb: to be the mother of; to assume as one's own; to care for like a mother.

Related forms: motherless, unmothered.

❄ ❄ ❄

The day my mother is arrested I have a roaring spat with her.

Friday the eleventh of February. Cold and grey, my breath escaping in smoky wisps like spilling secrets, the brush of icy air like the caress of a ghost, the white taste of winter in my mouth. School has finished for the day and there is the delicious anticipation of no school next week to look forward to. It is half term – yippee. Five whole days of freedom from the taunts, the jeers, the constant dodging of bullies.

Shadows dance to twinkling lights reflected from other flats onto the windowsill when Mum comes in from work, smelling of curry and smoke and other people's sweat, bearing that flighty look she gets when she is worried, her lips pulled down into a grimace, her eyes flitting this way and that as if they long to escape the boundaries of her face. They remind me of Lily's hamster, they do, with their constant scrabbling. She wrings her hands and picks the tissue she is holding to shreds.

'What is it, Mum?' I ask when I am unable to take her restlessness any longer, even though I know what's coming. I can read the signs; I am not stupid. She is already in the bedroom we share, pulling clothes into the suitcase which hasn't been up long enough to gather dust. I've been at Fernhill Secondary only a term and a half, the same amount of time we've been here in Kenton. This is the fastest we have moved anywhere, the smallest time we have stayed in one place.

Usually I don't mind this constant moving. I really don't. I like that it's just Mum and me against the world. I like moving just when the bullies are starting to get particularly vicious; it is thwarting them, isn't it? I like the thought that they will turn up at school having dreamt up new names to call me, a new form of torture, only to find that I am no longer there.

I can't say I like starting at a new school, identifying immediately the same old bullies in new guises just a tad before they identify me. It is wearying having to endure new bullies calling me by the same few names, having to suffer the same regurgitated pranks.

And now, finally, I have reached my limit. I do not want to move again. Because, for the first time in my life, I have a friend. I have Lily.

I know. It's sad, isn't it? It's taken me thirteen years to find a friend. It hasn't been that bad though. I didn't know what I was missing. Anyway, if I had had friends all this while, I would not properly appreciate what Lily means to me, would I? And I have always had Mum, the two of us against a world that is cruel to me, a world that judges me on how I look, not bothering to see inside. And so far, Mum's been enough.

'I'm afraid we have to leave, sweetheart,' she says, trying to shut the overflowing suitcase, contents spilling out like M&M's from a burst bag.

Normally, I enjoy the excitement of moving to a new flat – the new smells, the fresh layout of the same few rooms. I do a quick reconnaissance of the shops close by, the cafes and the chip shops where I can while away some of the hours waiting for Mum to come home from whichever job she is currently doing. Funnily enough, I like winter evenings best. I have books and food to keep me company while I wait.

I like sitting in the chip shop and doing my homework, the mouth-watering smell of battered fish, the sizzle of potato hitting hot oil, the vinegary crunch of steaming, freshly cooked chips making my brain cells spark and fizz into producing some of my best work. No matter how many times we move, wherever I find myself, the owner of the local chippy becomes my friend.

'Ah, there she is,' they'll say, be it portly Dave, Turkish Ali or cheerful Jen, looking out for me once I've been round two weeks in a row after school; the scratch of my pencil on paper harmonising with the cooking sounds, the reassuring banter of the chef with the customers reverberating in my ears like music.

I'll watch their tired faces crease into grins as I walk in, beads of moisture glistening on their upper lips like droplets sticking to leaves after a shower, wait for them to say, 'And what homework have you got today?'

I will shrug off my bag and sigh, 'History and maths.'

They will bring me crispy golden fish and fat chips oozing oil into the foil packet they are wrapped in, steam escaping the corners, along with a smile as warm as the fryer in which they cooked their offering. 'You work hard for your mum, now, so when you are older, you won't have to slog long hours in front of the cooker like her, like us.'

On busy days, I help behind the counter and earn a few quid which I then spend on chocolate and crisps. Mum doesn't know, and what she doesn't know won't hurt her, I tell myself. I love the feel of food filling the gaping hole that yawns in my stomach, always wanting more. The explosion in my mouth from a burst of chocolate or the salty kick of crunchy peanuts from a Snickers bar instantly wipes out the horrors I've had to endure that day – the name-calling, the jeers. When I am eating, I can forget. The warm feeling in my stomach afterwards is comfort, like my mother's hug. It envelops me, makes me feel safe, loved. And the thought of the food awaiting me at the end of the day gets me through long afternoons at school, when the desks on either side of me are conspicuously empty, when people move to sit two benches away, sniffing loudly, complaining that I stink. The thought of the lunch I carry in my bag, a tuna salad baguette that my mum has packed, plus the KitKat I bought on my way to school and the cheese and onion Walkers I will buy in the cafeteria along with a can of Coke, tides me through the morning when my classmates call me lard-arse.

The other activity I love, which provides solace from the realities of daily life, is reading. When I read, I can escape to diverse, happier worlds, I can be a different person, a person other than the fat girl my schoolmates, no matter where I move to, seem to despise and be repulsed by. I revel in the joy of discovering a new word, trying it out, the feel of it in my mouth, the way it rolls off my tongue, a gift to the listener.

Mum loves my pronunciation. 'You speak English like the British who invented the language,' she says proudly, her eyes shining.

'I am British, Mum,' I laugh.

'You are,' she says, her voice awed as if she cannot quite believe it.

Mum makes me say new words that I have learnt again and again, watching my tongue shape the word, her eyes screwed up in concentration. She tries to repeat after me but she pulls the word every which way, stressing the wrong syllables. The more she tries, the more she gets it wrong, until finally she gives up, with a 'Pah!' in that way she has, rolling her eyes and shrugging and thrusting her arms out at the same time, and I give in to the laughter that has been bubbling in my throat and we fall about laughing.

When I was little, just as I was beginning to make sense of the world, Mum realised how much I loved words by the way my face lit up when I learnt a new one. I would clap with delight and repeat the word again and again, fascinated by the way it sounded, the way it tumbled out of my mouth. She fetched a notebook and asked me to write down any words I did not know the meaning to; any new words I found in the books that I was reading. The first word I jotted in that new book – we called it 'Diya's Vocabulary Book', written painstakingly in my just-learned-to-join-up-letters writing – was 'mother'. I knew the meaning to that one of course, but I wanted to write it anyway. Mum had me write out the full meaning, the verb, noun and related forms. 'Mother': such a simple word, encompassing so much.

'You,' I had said, cupping her face in my palm, and she had looked at me, her eyes filling up in that familiar expression of love and joy and wonder, that expression I can never get enough of, her eyes shimmering like chocolate buttons melting in the sun.

'Yes, me,' she said, smiling and swiping at her eyes.

'Why are you crying, Mum?' I asked, puzzled.

'They are tears of joy, darling,' she smiled. 'I am so happy to have you for my daughter. Do you want to write "daughter" in there? Shall we look it up?'

Since then, I have amassed quite a few of those notebooks. I think I am onto my seventh or eighth one now. Nerdy I know, but who's to care? I haven't had any friends up until now to make fun of the books that I lug with me everywhere. Not all of them at once, of course, only the one I am currently using. I read such a lot and I'd much rather be prepared when I come across a word I don't know.

My vocabulary is brilliant thanks to these books. I hardly ever need to refer to the earliest ones now – I know all of those words by heart, have used them many times. I make a point of using a new word that I have learnt as many times as possible. My record is twenty in a day; it was the word 'schadenfreude' – even the teacher did not know what it meant. She had to look it up. It is not a very nice word; it means 'pleasure derived from the misfortune of others'.

Food and words are my best friends, or have been thus far, after my mum and, more recently, Lily.

I like coming home from the chip shop, dragging my school bag behind me by its strap, my clothes smelling faintly of oil and the outdoors. I let myself into the dark flat wherever we are staying, the noise of countless televisions blaring, arguments erupting, dinners cooking and children yelling filtering in. The soft buttery glow of reflected light from the lamps outside oozes into the flat like caramel from a Creme Egg and envelopes me in comfort. The stale, slightly desperate smell of the empty flat is masked by the overpowering odour of spiced grilled meat wafting from the Kebab shop, which inveigles in on a burst of nippy air through the open front door as I enter, and the thick cloud of trapped air sighs as it is displaced, huffing like a spurned lover.

I am not scared to be on my own. In fact, I feel safe, cocooned in the collective warmth of the hundreds of people living in these flats, above, below and around me. I like to imagine what an alien zooming past on his spaceship sees when he looks down on us mortals. Will he rocket into each flat and wish he was part of the lives being led there rather than trapped in a machine ogling a culture he longs to own? And what will he think of me, sitting in the dark on the sofa with a bag of crisps, a can of Coke and a pack of Skittles, reading my book by the mellow gold light of the lamp beside the sofa as I wait for Mum to come home with leftovers from the restaurant where she's been working? The smell of chocolate and adventure, the gooey brown taste of sweet escape, the crunch of teeth working overtime, the rustle of the foil pack gaping wider to dislodge the last of its contents, the wistful sigh of pages turning, my mind transported, no longer in the room but in a world created by the author of the book I am reading, beige crumbs swilling like confetti, blending into beige carpet.

When I hear Mum's tread on the stairs, I quickly dispose of the wrappers – she doesn't approve of my choice of snacks, what mother does? – and sweep the crumbs under the sofa. (I always know it's her. I know by the rhythm of her footfall, the way she favours her right foot more than the left, the sigh of exertion she releases after each step. The last flight of stairs is always the hardest for her. 'They get me every time,' she laments. 'It doesn't matter if we live on the second floor or the fifth, I cannot handle the last flight of stairs after a long day at work.')

When I hear her key in the door, I am propped up again on the sofa with my book, no evidence of offending snacks. She will smile, the lines on her face crinkling, her eyes glowing, the tiredness leaving them briefly as she looks at me.

'Hungry, miss?' she will ask and we will sit together in front of the television, still in the dark, the reflected light from other flats and the flicker of the telly basking us in a warm glow. She will save all the pieces of meat from the vindaloo, and the paneer from the saag for me and she will throw her head back on the cushion, swivel her gaze towards me and ask, 'How was your day, sweetheart?'

'About the same,' I will reply.

And she will say, 'That bad, huh?'

'That bad.'

She will smile softly at me then, her eyes shining with care. 'We both need a bit of a lift, don't we? Look what I got for dessert.'

I love moving into a new place and getting used to the smells. Every flat in every town smells different. Some smell of escapades, others of pain, yet others of anger, danger, fear. I like to wander through the rooms, usually two plus a tiny kitchen and bathroom, and imagine the lives of the people who lived there before us and wonder where they are now.

This flat, the one we currently inhabit, though not for long if Mum has her way, smelled of new paint and old despair when we first arrived. Now, to me it smells of hope and new beginnings. Not so, it seems, to my mum.

She tries to pull the suitcase closed but it won't shut. Both sides are full to bursting, blouse sleeves waving out of the edges like drowning arms in the sea after a shipwreck. She manages to pull the top to and tries to sit on it to squash the clothes together. 'Here, help me,' she says, looking up at me for the first time.

'No.' I fold my arms together, my legs planted apart: my warrior stance.

'Diya, don't be difficult now, please.' Her voice is desperate, laced with panic. Her eyes plead with me, eyeballs moving frantically again, as if she can pierce the wall, see past it to some peril only she can imagine.

'Mum, I'm tired of moving. I want to stay here.'

Her shoulders slump and she doubles into herself. Unlike me, my mother is tiny. At thirteen, I am almost as tall as her and twice as big. I bet she could fit into that suitcase she is trying to close. 'I thought you liked moving,' she says in a small voice.

'Not anymore. I have a friend now, Mum. You know that. I have Lily.' My voice is accusing. I don't care. She knows what a big deal finding a friend is for me. She was so happy when I told her. She baked a cake to celebrate. 'You said I could have her round for a sleepover this half-term, remember?' With each word, my voice has been getting louder. I try to mask the hurt I feel but it is hard.

My mum has never been one to go back on her promises. And I was so excited that, for the first time, the very first time, I would be doing stuff other girls did routinely, that for them was a matter of course. Sleepovers, staying up late sharing secrets, midnight feasts, giggling after lights out. 'You said we could have the bedroom and you would camp on the sofa. What happened to your promises, eh? I don't know why you keep insisting on moving all the time. I've had enough. I'm not going!' I shout.

When she looks up, her bottom lip is trembling. That makes me mad. She's going to use tears against me – talk about cheating!

'I'm sorry,' she says softly. 'So sorry, Diya. We have to move, sweetie. We have no choice.'

'Why?' I yell. 'Why do we have no choice?'

'I've lost my job.'

A lie. She is a rubbish liar, her face flooding crimson every time she swerves from the truth. First tears and now a lie.

'Nonsense,' I say. 'And anyway, the kind of jobs you do are a dime a dozen.' I say this deliberately, aiming to wound as much as I can and, just as I thought, she flinches. 'You could ask the chip shop owner, Ali. He'd give you a job in an instant. He fancies you anyway,' I scream.

She doesn't say anything, just allows the tears to keep on coming, making no move to wipe them. She fiddles with her pallu, twisting it into knots, the way she does when she is nervous and upset.

'Why do we have to keep moving when we've barely settled? I'm not coming. You go.'

The neck of her sari blouse is soaked now. Her nose is running. I cannot bear to stay in this room, tainted by her anguish, any longer. I walk to the door, opening it so fiercely that I almost pull it off its hinges.

'Wait,' she yells. 'Where are you going? We have to leave tonight.'

'Have you not heard a word I've been saying?'

'Please.' Her voice is urgent, begging. 'Please don't, Diya.'

I slam the door shut with a satisfying thud on her teary face and clatter down the stairs, the smell of burgers and overcooked rice, the faint yellow tang of urine, the reek of feet and angst trailing me. I hear our door open and close as she attempts to follow me, but she has no hope in hell of catching up. I hear her breath coming in laboured gasps and after a flight of stairs, I do not hear her at all.

A police car idles half on the curb, half on the pavement, just outside the front door, blocking the entrance to the flats. I have a good mind to slap it, ask what they are doing obstructing people when they are supposed to set a good example, but I rush past instead, wanting to get away, not get in trouble with the police, and to put as much distance between my mum and me as possible. The anger is a hard ball in my chest, fiery and red, propelling me forward. I want to douse it with a chocolate bar or two, I think. I dig in the pockets of my sweatshirt. Damn, I ran out without my coat – it has some change in the pockets. And it's freezing – even though, as the bullies said last week, snatching my coat and stuffing it in the toilet bowl, I have plenty of padding to keep me warm. Lily had found it for me, and together we cleaned it the best we could. I ran a load of laundry before Mum came home and she had been inordinately grateful; she'd kissed me and said, 'What would I do without you, my best girl,' her eyes shining, soft as chocolate-coated marshmallows. I'd pretended to blanch, pulling away.

Goosebumps, teeth chattering, the breeze smelling of battered fish, tasting of ice, nippy on my cheeks. I rush back to the door. The police car is still idling, though now another car plus a police van have joined it. I am not surprised or unduly bothered; there are often police cars idling by our block of flats. I'm annoyed though. If the front door was blocked before, when there was only the one car, now access to it is even more constricted. I know they have to make their arrests or whatever, but shouldn't they be more considerate of the residents? I have a good mind to write a letter of complaint. I make a mental note to discuss the pros and cons of this with Lily at the sleepover – I've been a tad nervous as to what we'll talk about, seeing as we'll be spending almost twelve hours together. I worry that she might get bored with me, even though I have two movies lined up that we could watch and a choice of three more. I have been collecting topics we might talk about all week, just in case conversation lags. Then I remember that if Mum gets her way, there will be no sleepover, that we might be moving this very evening, and the orange ball of fury, temporarily doused by the icy breath of winter, sparks and blazes again.

The police vehicles are empty except for one of the cars. The driver's face freezes, going as white as the breath escaping my mouth in heaving puffs, when he sees me running back, our gaze meeting for a brief second, his eyes the dark blue of regret. He opens his mouth and I wonder if he's going to say something, but he only looks stricken. Oh well, no time to worry about that now. I clatter up the stairs without pausing to take a breath, run up to our door and screech to an abrupt halt.

It is wide open, a cluster of policemen forming an impenetrable wall around it in a semi-circle, enclosing my mother as if they are a rugby scrum. Mum's face is devoid of colour, pale as the pristine pages of a new notebook, her orange sari garish in contrast.

All those police cars – they came for Mum? Do they think she's a terrorist? I feel a giggle building inside and threatening to burst out of me at any minute. What a laugh we will have about this later, Mum and I!

Her eyes close when she sees me and she sways on her feet. A phone beeps, the radio one of the policemen is wearing crackles loudly.

'Vani Bhat, I am arresting you on suspicion of the abduction of Rupa Shetty from Bangalore, India, thirteen years ago…'

Abduction? Ha!

'…and on suspicion of obtaining leave to stay in the United Kingdom by deception, on suspicion of remaining in the United Kingdom beyond time limited by leave and on suspicion of being in possession of false identity documents. You do not have to say anything. But it may harm your defence if you do not mention when questioned something you later rely on in court. Anything you do or say may be given in evidence…'

I am reeling from the assault of the words the policeman is uttering, the tableau being played out at the door to my flat, when I hear a clattering on the stairs behind me. I turn to see the driver of the police car who had caught my eye running up towards us. The door to Flat 3A opens and a small face peers out, two curious eyes the green of pond water. A sound from within and the door is slammed shut.

'What's going on here?' I ask and my voice is reedy, wobbly as tentative notes being played by amateur fingers on a piano.

The group of police gathered outside our door turn as one to look at me and I squirm under the scrutiny of so many eyes. They look shocked, wearing the same expression as the man running up the stairs, the driver of the police car, who is breathing loudly and noisily behind me.

'Sorry, we didn't mean for you to be privy to this. We waited until you'd left. We didn't think you'd be back so soon,' one of the women says gently.

'I forgot my coat,' I say and immediately I think, *why am I telling them this?* The laughter is still bubbling in my chest in anticipation. I'm disbelieving. There is a mistake.

There must be. 'Why are you here? What's going on?' I ask once more.

There must be some quiet unspoken agreement among them as it is the policewoman who speaks again. 'We couldn't risk waiting any longer as she would have fled, given us the slip again, like she's been doing for the last thirteen years.' Her voice is soft, apologetic.

I feel the laughter morphing into tears, the taste of salt in my throat, at the sight of their serious faces, grave as headstones lining the cemetery, my mum's closed eyes, her face blanched as if someone has taken an eraser to it and wiped it of colour and expression.

'I'm sorry, I still don't understand.' Why am I being so formal? Why is my mum standing there rocking on her feet, her eyes shut, her face blank? 'There must be some mistake. You tell them, Mum.'

She opens her eyes when I say 'Mum'. 'Diya is my daughter,' she says, her voice high and scared but unwavering. 'I am her mother.' She is speaking to them but looking at me. There is apology in her gaze, and love, all the love she feels for me, the melting chocolate-button gaze. She is telling them she loves me with her eyes.

I realise with a start that she might be saying goodbye, that this was why she wanted to move, this was why she thought she had no choice. The first tendrils of fear bloom, creeping up from the pit of my stomach, taking a hold of me. 'What did you do, Mum?'

The policewoman who spoke earlier looks at me and her gaze is tender, remorseful. I hate it. I hate her.

'No!' I shout, 'please, no,' babbling, desperate as the policewoman restrains me, her arms gentle yet surprisingly strong, as my mother is led away by the posse of officers, as flat doors open and heads peek out, as my whole world turns upside down on a February evening while shadows steal up the walls and night sneaks in via the back door and takes up residence.

'I love you, Diya. I love you so much,' my mother says, softly blowing kisses into the air around my face and, even though she leans close, she can't quite touch me, and even though I lean in towards her, I am being held back by the policewoman. I struggle, I kick. I want my mother. 'You are my daughter. Believe me. You are.' Mum looks right at me as she says this, as if conveying a part of herself. 'Nothing can change that. Nothing. I am sorry it had to happen this way. At the time…' Her sigh is immense, catching on a sob. 'Perhaps there was some other way, but at the time… I will explain everything in my letters. I will write. I love you, Diya.'

My mother's words float up the stairs, echoing up the stairwell like dispatches from a ghost, propelled by the deflating air from the popped bubble of the truths I took for granted and believed up until now, the purple smell of horror, the scarlet taste of pain, the icy white grip of shock raising goosebumps.

'I am your mother, Diya. You are mine. I love you, Diya, my darling girl, light of my life,' are her last words to me, as she is led away.

Chapter 2
Aarti

Crinkled Orange Rind

Breakfast: 1 slice of toast (wholemeal from a 400g loaf). No butter.

Mid-morning snack: Banana.

Lunch: Tomato Soup. No croutons.

Afternoon snack: Apple.

Supper: Mixed salad. No dressing. No croutons.

❉ ❉ ❉

Aarti twines the salad on her fork, around and around, the leafy green reminding her of fields gleaming in the sun. She aches to be home, where there are people hired to look after her, to cater to her every whim. She brings the fork to her mouth but her stomach recoils, nausea threatening to get the better of her. She welcomes the familiar feeling; it comforts her, even as she rushes to the bathroom, is sick over the bowl, heaving until there is nothing left inside to purge. How many toilet bowls in how many bathrooms has she heaved over? How many years of her life spent like this, bent double over a cistern? The dirty yellow smell of vomit and hurt. The feeling of being cleansed, of floating on air. She has missed it, she thinks as she rinses her mouth, the mouthwash tart, stinging. It's been a few years.

The reflection staring back at her from the mirror confirms this assessment. Lips sagging like the drooping belly of a portly woman who's lost weight too quickly. Tired skin the colour and texture of crinkled orange rind. Lines radiating from sunken eyes – no money left for Botox injections anymore. None of the so-called 'age-defying' creams do what they promise. Not one. Age has crept up on her when she has not been looking, not been watching. It has crept up and taken residence while she has been busy hunting for her daughter.

Her daughter.

Nausea threatens again. She grips the sink hard, closes her eyes. A silhouette swims in front of closed lids, the shadow gradually taking definition and shape, growing from baby into young girl in a matter of minutes. The face she has imagined so many times, each feature chosen carefully, created lovingly from her fantasies. This is the curse of never having seen her child in the intervening years since she held her as a baby. Her profile changes with each conjuring. Will her daughter be like this for real? She doesn't know. All she has is this: an illusion fabricated by her yearning, painted by her imagination. Aarti pictures young honeyed skin radiant with the first flush of youth. Soft, liquid eyes the colour and texture of warm sunflower oil, curving upwards tantalisingly at the ends. Her whole life ahead of her, her best years to come.

What was she, Aarti, doing when she was her daughter's age? Photoshoots, ads, television appearances. Well on her way to becoming the top model in India.

Eyes still shut against her reflection, she turns away, out of the bathroom, avoiding looking at her supper, greenish yellow leaves wilting and tired-looking on the chipped blue plate. She counts the number of steps from the wall of the bathroom to the wall at the other end of the room. Fifteen. Her world reduced to fifteen steps, fifteen spans of her – admittedly long – feet. This her life now, for the foreseeable future.

She has done this so many times that she has lost count. Her life measured by the span of a room. Living out of a suitcase. Futilely following leads. The impersonal, generic smell of hotel, metallic air freshener and draining hope, raw despair.

That woman, Vani – her name causing a finger of bile to tickle Aarti's throat, threatening nausea again – is going to prison for what she did. And she, Aarti, is in a prison of sorts herself. Has been for the last thirteen years. Imprisoned in her head by thoughts of that woman with *her* daughter. Imprisoned by the passage of time, the lost years. Imprisoned by each day her daughter grows without her. Imprisoned by the changing image of her daughter conjured by her imagination, which may not even come close to the real thing. Imprisoned by myriad hotel rooms in myriad cities in foreign towns, following wasted leads.

But this time, it is different. This time she is assured of a happy ending.

She cannot sit still. She walks to the window, looks out onto the grey desultoriness of a deserted car park. It has started to drizzle. No surprise in this cold, miserable country. Rain spatters, an oblique hazy curtain visible in the murky yellow light of lamps dotting the car park, ricocheting off cars the smoky blue of unending night. She has deliberately chosen this view. Has been doing so for the past ten years. She does not want a repeat of what happened that time. Her lawyer has warned her that he won't be able to get her out as easily if it happens again…

And so she avoids temptation, eschews hotels by city centres. Books rooms without views, which look out onto a land devoid of people, except for the solitary figure, valiantly making his way towards a car, hunched against the weather, fighting the pull of icy wind, hood turned down over his head, covering his face so he looks furtive, up to no good. The car, one of many moody grey silhouettes wearing darkness like a frown, briefly flashes gold and red as it is unlocked. Orange brake lights sweep over the desolation as it reverses out, fleetingly exposing forlorn rows of slumbering cars like the sudden flash of a camera catching a woman unawares. A spurt of noise punctuates the thick navy silence which settles like a sigh after the roar has subsided, as suddenly as it started.

Aarti looks out onto a landscape as bleak as the inside of her head feels most of the time. All the time, really, with the exception of today. Today she should feel triumph. Today she should feel joy at the culmination of thirteen years of pursuing leads in the quest for her child. Happiness that Vani is being punished for what she did to Aarti, for what she has taken from her. And yet, all she feels is drained. Empty. Tired beyond belief. She stares at the narrow functional hotel bed; white sheets, three pillows, a stain in the shape of a heart at the right-hand corner, the bedstead chipped in three places. She looks longingly at the bottle of sleeping pills beside it. She will take one; she will nod off, soon. As soon as she hears.

She peruses her phone, sitting on the table beside her solitary dinner, the flaccid leaves forlorn, dejected. Any time now, it will ring to say that the witch has been apprehended. Any time now. After all these years of waiting, searching. All these years of grief and heartache and loss. All these years... *Give them back to me, bitch. Give my life back to me.*

She gives in to impulse, to the invitation of the bed, the sheets smelling of starch and carrying within them the imprints of all the people who have lain on them before her. The memory of sweat and semen. She closes her eyes. Waits for the phone to ring, to puncture a silence so heavy that it threatens to drown her in its depths, and wonders, as she often does these days, how it is that her life, which held so much promise, is reduced to this, how it is that she is here, in this lonely room in this impersonal place. Waiting. Alone.

It is a sensation as familiar as nausea, as familiar as spewing her insides into a toilet bowl. The two constants in her life: being sick and being lonely. She loses them for a bit and then reunites with them like old friends. There was that brief, glorious time, those few wonderful years when she wasn't lonely – when there was Vani. But after what Vani did, how can she trust that memory? She cannot rely on it. She would much rather welcome the loneliness than the illusion of trust and happiness and friendship that Vani supplied only to betray her so completely and thoroughly. No, at least loneliness never promised anything different. Loneliness did not trick her or show her the promise of a delightful, befriended future only to take everything – *everything* – from her and leave her more wretched than ever, a wreck of what she once was.

She has always been lonely.

Chapter 3
Vani

A Million Pieces

My darling Diya, light of my life,

I am sorry, so very sorry. I wish I could have spared you this pain, this horror.

The look on your face, like you were being broken, shattered into a million pieces. Oh, sweetheart, I wish I could have held you, comforted you. Remember when you were little how you used to jump into my arms, wrap your legs behind my back, your arms around my neck and bury your head in the curve of my shoulder? I wanted to hold you like that again, hold you close to my heart until I erased that look from your face, until the smile that habitually inhabits your face made an appearance. I wanted it to be just the two of us against the world, like we were for so long. But the world butted in, didn't it?

Diya, I know you are lost at the moment. I know you are confused and hurting. But know this: you are loved. So very much.

I have regretted not being able to give you more, to give you material things, the buttress of a family. I have yearned to shower you with gifts; to take you on holiday instead of running away with you to a new place every six months just when you were settling into the old one; to provide you with a mansion in which to live instead of a poky little flat where you have to share a room with your mother; to give you a big family instead of just me, a pale facsimile of a woman afraid of her own reflection.

In lieu of all that I wished to give you but couldn't, I showered you with love, all the love I had, and hoped, prayed that it was enough. And it seems to have been. You have been happy, haven't you, my sweet? After that very first smile you flashed just for me when you were a baby, you have never really stopped smiling. And seeing you happy has made even my darkest days endurable. Seeing you smile, seeing your trust in me, has made everything worthwhile.

Diya, I know that what you are going through must seem intolerable, and I cannot bear the thought of your pain, but what gives me courage is the knowledge that you will be looked after, that all your needs will be met. I have done my research into this eventuality. I know you will be assigned a social worker; you will be put into foster care. I pray that you will go to a nice home, that the woman there, a mother like me, will look at you and see a child who is desperately lost and hurting, and take you under her wing.

I pray.

Diya, my precious, I know also that you will be beside yourself worrying about me. Please try not to. I assure you, it is not that bad here. This is a wonderful country, populated with kind people who care about human rights, even those of prisoners like me who have stayed here illegally, abusing their hospitality. After they took me away from you, I was briefly held at the local police station where I asked for a solicitor. (I have been reading up, preparing quietly for this.)

'Do you have any kids?' was one of the first questions I asked my solicitor, a gentle, balding, bespectacled man.

'Two,' he said. 'A boy and a girl. Nine and seven.' He showed me their pictures.

I could not help the tears that graced my face then, Diya. 'I do not have a picture of my daughter to show you,' I said. 'She's mine,' I said.

He nodded. 'Since an Extradition Arrest Warrant has been issued, we have to attend the initial hearing. We can set about preparing your defence once that is over.'

The solicitor accompanied me to Westminster Magistrates' Court. At the preliminary hearing, I was denied bail and the judge served me with papers and set a date for my extradition hearing, which is four weeks from now.

I ache to see you, Diya my darling, I desperately do. I want that more than anything else in the world, but my solicitor tells me that he doubts the family lawyers assigned to your care will allow you to visit me before the extradition hearing. You see, my darling, in the eyes of the people who are looking after you right now, in the eyes of the world, I have committed a crime by claiming you for myself and compounded it by staying here with you without permission, in this country that has been so good to us so far.

Diya, you will hear the word 'extradition' with regards to me sooner or later. You like your words, but I don't think you know this one. How could you? Extradition means that I will be deported to India to be tried for the offence of abducting you – 'abduction', such a harsh word for what I did out of love for you – as I committed it there.

You will hear the word 'extradition' with regards to me, and you will panic. Please don't. Words are just that, my darling, mere scribbles on a page. You think they have the power to hurt, but they only will if you let them. Just because it is jotted on a legal document, an arrest warrant, does not make 'extradition' special.

There is no way I am going to be extradited, sweetheart. You are my daughter and I am going to prove it. No judge in any court can keep a mother from her daughter.

I will fight for you. I will.

I have had to fight for you all your life. Fight to keep you, fight to own you. But this is, by far, the most important fight. And I will win it.

We will be apart for a while, my sweet, just until this is sorted. Not forever, that is a promise. And I have kept all the promises I made you, haven't I? Except for the sleepover with Lily. That was beyond my resources. But this is what we will do: when I come home, which, I have to warn you, may not be soon – you see, even though I am your mum and the judge will see it my way, we have been living here with false documents, under false pretences, you and I, and I do not need my lawyer to tell me that I have broken many laws and I will be punished for it. But when I do get out, I will invite Lily round. I am sure you will still be friends with her.

She gets you, Diya, doesn't she? She loves you. Who wouldn't? But then I suppose I am biased. It is because of love for you that this situation has happened in the first place. Too many people loving you, claiming you for their own.

I know you are floundering now. But know this: you are a survivor, Diya, like me. I never thought I was capable of doing what I did. But being a mother changes a person, transforms them. You transformed me. You made me into a stronger person, a person who would do anything for her child, including break the law over and over again.

You will come through, I know. I have to believe that, if I have to get through each day without you. I have to.

You used to pester me, 'Tell me about my dad.'

So many questions and I used to scrabble around for answers, for lies. Now, in these letters, I will tell you the truth. And I will begin at the beginning. And for me, everything begins in the village in India where I grew up, where I lived the first few years of my life.

You know, Diya, my dearest wish has always been to take you to my village in India one day. Remember I showed it to you on the map once?

'Why don't we go back, Mum?' you asked.

I suppressed my yearning; I did not allow the insinuation of what had happened to paint my face the crimson of guilt. Instead, I said quietly, 'We cannot afford it, Diya, not right now. Perhaps one day.'

You had sighed then, like an old soul. You had said, 'Mum, if you listened to me and worked in Tesco or something instead of those Indian restaurants where they pay you a pittance and do not even give you proper holidays…' This was your particular bugbear. And you were off, lecturing me as usual.

I had smiled at your earnestness, had ruffled your hair, had said, 'Don't you have any homework?'

'Mum, I was doing my geography homework when you came in and disturbed me, searching for your hometown on the map,' your voice was rising in that way it does when you are exasperated.

My lovely girl. I miss you so.

'Tell me about your village. Don't you yearn to go back, Mum?' you had asked, after a bit.

'I do,' I replied.

And you cupped my face in the palm of your hands, very gently, like handling a fragile ornament. 'A shadow invades your face when you think of your village, Mum. Does it hurt? Do you miss it that much?'

How could I tell you why I couldn't go back? How could I tell you what I had done in order to have you, the bridges I had burnt?

'Let's save, Mum,' you had said then, eyes shining. 'I will save my pocket money too, and we'll go. I would like to.' Your beautiful hands tracing the path, the distance between England and India on the map. That distance, deceptively small on the map but unfathomable, unbridgeable because of what I had done.

Your hands, that's what I focused on – chubby and perfect, the hands that held mine with such trust. What would you do if you found out? Would you turn against me? Have you turned against me now? That look on your face. No, I cannot bear to think that way, I won't.

'Perhaps one day,' I had said to you then and you had looked up at me, and something in my voice had made you stop chasing the issue. You were, you are, so understanding, Diya, so much more than I deserve. You have been such a treasure.

I love you, Diya, and I hope that, despite what's happening now, you don't doubt this. I love you and miss you and will come back to you; that is a promise. And I will tell you in these pages why I did what I did.

All my love, my precious one,
Mum

Chapter 4
Diya

Despair

Despair

Noun: the complete loss or absence of hope.
Synonyms: disheartenment, anguish, desperation, distress.

❄ ❄ ❄

Soft arms enveloping me, leading me inside. I am shivering. I want to lose myself in the comfort of these arms, to forget, to disappear into before. I want these arms to be my mum's, to smell like her: sandalwood and sweat – not of a strange flowery perfume that assaults me, bringing tears to my eyes.

I am led to the bedroom and when I spy the suitcase, spilling its contents like a gossip's mouth dispersing confidences, I am undone by yearning. I want my mum, desperately, urgently. The ache is so deep and all-encompassing that I crumple. The arms support me, they heft my considerable weight. They lead me to the bed which doesn't house the suitcase – my bed. I ignore it – I do not want to look at the suitcase open on the other bed or think of the argument I had with her just before... *Before.*

I walk instead to the kitchen, the path learned by rote, my feet guiding me even though my vision is blurred. The flat does not smell of hope and new beginnings anymore. It never did – who was I kidding? It smells of despair, the old overlapped with the new.

I remember writing 'despair' in my vocabulary book, realising what it meant, that it was very different from sadness, much deeper somehow, more hopeless. I remember wondering what would prompt someone to be in such despair as to be desperate. What sort of circumstances? Now I know. Now I feel it. Despair that starts in the pit of my stomach and escapes out of my mouth in a thin sound, strangely like that produced by a child blowing tentatively on a shiny new recorder for the very first time. I am keening, I realise, finally understanding, fully, the meaning of the word we used in English the other day.

I say 'keening' softly, concentrating on the feel of the word on my tongue and it is as comforting as a hard boiled sweet that softens in your mouth, releasing scrumptious juices that trickle down your throat, caressing it with their gentle sweetness. The word works its magic as words always do and I feel a tad calmer.

I love words almost as much as I love food. I always sit in the front for English, a fine target for paper rockets and pencils, but I don't want to miss a thing. I am the best in English in my class no matter where I find myself, no matter that the school is new, my classmates new. I am not boasting. It is a statement of fact.

And yet, now, I have no words to describe what I am feeling. This numbness that has taken possession of me, this complete blank, this gaping chasm opening up inside of me. It allows me to think of words to describe the strange sounds I am suddenly making, to muse on how good I am at English, to think of anything but what just happened.

Because I don't want to know. I don't want to know.

Footsteps behind me. I turn, hopeful. *Mum?*

But it is just the policewoman, the owner of the soft arms and flowery perfume, the one who restrained me when I wanted to go to my mum… Anger, hot, stinging like Deep Heat spray. I welcome it. Better, much better than the strange emptiness I was feeling a moment earlier.

'You could have let me touch her or go to her,' I say, my eyes smarting.

'She committed a crime. Against *you*.' Her gaze liquid, watery; her expression so tender I want to hit her.

I will not accept it. I will not.

I make my palms into fists to hold in the rage that threatens to bubble out of me, and turn to face the fridge. I root around in the back of the vegetable drawer where Mum never looks and find what I'm after. A Dairy Milk bar. I had hidden it there the day I found a two-pound coin behind the sofa cushion, eating two of the chocolate bars I spent it on and saving the third for a rainy day. And if this doesn't qualify as a rainy day, I don't know what does.

'Diya is the only person in this school who can use idioms in context,' Mrs. Reid, my English teacher in Year 6 had announced to the whole school during assembly. I was bullied twice as hard that day but it did not detract from the warm feeling I carried around in my heart that whole afternoon, replaying Mrs. Reid's words in my head, imagining the expression of the bullies when she said it, their faces tightening in anger, and perhaps jealousy.

When Mum had got home, I told her what Mrs. Reid had said and she had taken my hands and we had danced around the living room. 'I am so proud of you,' she had said. 'Here,' she had taken a twenty-pound note from the emergency jar and given it to me, 'get some books, go on. Get ones that will challenge you, mind.'

And I had not spent even fifty pence of that twenty on sweets or crisps – had instead browsed second-hand book stores and amassed a treasure trove of books, which I then lugged to every single flat we moved to and which were the first items I packed whenever we moved.

I look towards the corner of the living room where the box of books sits. The pile of paperbacks has grown, multiplied. I use libraries for the most part, registering the day we move to a new place, but once in a while, when I like a book so much that I want to own it, I haunt second-hand stores and charity shops until I find it and, failing that, treat myself and buy it new, forgoing chocolate for a week or two to pay for it.

I sniff and pull the Dairy Milk bar out, tear off the wrapper and stuff the whole thing in my mouth. A profusion of chocolate and yet, it tastes salty, of sorrow. The sobs come around the chocolate and I almost choke on it. The policewoman puts her arms around me, but I shrug them away. I don't want her useless comfort.

I bite and chew and swallow and sob and taste snot and hurt and regret and guilt. Did I cause this somehow? Why did I fight with her? Why did I refuse to move? If I had agreed, perhaps… I think of the police car idling on the curb when I ran downstairs. No, we couldn't have escaped. They were watching, waiting.

'Your *real* mother has been searching for you for the past thirteen years,' the policewoman says softly.

I choke on the last chunk of chocolate and the policewoman rubs my back gently. I jerk away.

'Shut up!' I yell when I can breathe. 'Shutupshutupshutup.'

My mum would be shocked at my language. I am quiet and well behaved for the most part, preferring to bury my angst in food and books. I am never intentionally rude and yet here I am yelling at a policewoman of all people – I could be arrested, for God's sake. Good. I want to be. At least then, Mum and I will be in the same boat.

I open the freezer. Root around in the back of the fourth cabinet. Panic. Only when my fingers close around the tub I know is hiding behind the frozen spinach do I release the trapped breath. I pull it out – Häagen-Dazs Cookies and Cream – grab a spoon and eat standing up, stuffing my mouth even though I cannot taste a thing, even though I'm pretty sure I am ingesting my own tears with each gasping mouthful. I keep going until the hot flare of panic is doused by the cool ice cream, until the tub is scraped dry, until all I can feel, all I know is full, the heaviness of my limbs, the sigh of air as it travels down into my numb lungs, the drum of blood trying to make its way to the extremities of my dumbstruck body.

I think of Lily, wonder what she's doing now. Probably watching television, worrying the cuddly toy she is never without at home. She misses it at school but wouldn't dare bring it in – that would be issuing an invitation to the bullies who never leave her alone anyway on account of her thick glasses and frizzy hair, her timid demeanour, the habit she has of chewing her lower lip and bursting into loud, noisy tears at the slightest provocation. But these are the very things I love about her. They are what make her Lily. Underneath it all, she is incredibly kind, extremely generous and loving. Like me, she lives with just her mum, but her mum does not work all hours like mine.

I have told Mum so many times to apply for work somewhere with reasonable working hours. But no, she will only work at Indian restaurants recommended by the owner of the previous place she worked at. She works long hours for less than the minimum wage, no holidays, no sick leave. And we move every eight months or so, like clockwork. I do not want to accept what just happened; I do not want to acknowledge it – but it makes sense. I can see now why she didn't work at other places like normal people, like I urged her to so many times.

And even though I don't want it to, the memory of the time I was selected to represent my school in an interschool essay competition inveigles in with the accompanying hot sting of hurt and loss. The representatives from the various participating schools were to be whisked away to Switzerland for a week, where they would take part in a host of competitions and debates. I had been so excited, so pleased, had waited up for Mum even though she was working the late night shift, even though I had to go into school early the next day on account of a trip to a museum, and had shown her the letter. I hadn't been prepared for her face to fall, her eyes to water, not with joy but with dismay.

'What is it?' I had asked. 'Mum, I was selected – *me* – from everyone in the whole school,' I had said.

'I am so very proud of you, sweetheart,' she had replied, her expression that of a wounded puppy, 'but you can't go.'

No amount of persuasion would make her change her mind. I had begged, cajoled, promised to save up my pocket money, but she said we just couldn't afford it.

Siobhan, who wasn't even very good, had gone instead of me and had come back bursting with stories of the fun she'd had, taking care to recount them, always, in my presence.

I had sulked for six months, had saved every bit of my pocket money, had lost quite a lot of weight as I was not eating any snacks, and earned enough for the trip.

'See, we can afford it,' I had yelled, shoving the money at Mum, but by then it was too late.

Tears had oozed out of her eyes and dropped down her cheeks, her face frozen, a study in hopelessness. And I had stormed off and sobbed in our not-so-private shared bedroom, not bothering to smother my sniffles.

The same thing happened when the whole class went to France for a week – the whole class, that is, with the exception of me. That time I did not even bother to ask Mum. My classmates came back with tales of the wonders they had seen, the fun they had experienced, and I pretended I didn't mind, that I had had a brilliant time monitoring the Reception kids the whole week.

Somehow, now that I've let one memory in, more clamour for attention. I remember the time the head teacher of the school before this one asked to see Mum. When I had relayed the message to her, she had been shocked, terrified.

'Come on, Mum, it's nothing bad. I'm a good girl,' I had said. 'Mum, normally it is the other way round; I should be the one worrying, not you,' I had laughed.

We went together, she changing her outfit ten times, finally wearing a sari too grand for school. I knew people would tease me when they saw her decked out in a sequinned sparkly creation as if she was going to a wedding, but I hadn't cared. I had felt proud walking up to school with my mum, showing her the lab, the gym, the music hut. She had been too panicked to see properly, wringing her sari continually, but her eyes had widened and she had said that it was all very grand. I put down her panic to the fact that she hardly ever interacted with anyone outside of the restaurants where she worked.

On that particular occasion, the head teacher had called her in to praise me, to tell Mum that I would be getting a special prize for my writing. Once she got the hang of his speech, the anxious expression had lifted from her face, the creased lines had ironed out, and she had beamed. Her whole face had transformed and even the headmaster had been gratified when she held his hand and said, 'Thank you, thank you,' over and over again.

'It's not me,' he had said. 'It's all your daughter's hard work,' winking at me.

Mum had been so proud of me that day. She had wiped her eyes with the pallu of her best sari and skipped out of school, her face glowing.

I can see now why she only used to go shopping late at night and was always looking over her shoulder when we were out together. I can see why she never went to the doctor, even when she was desperately ill that one time, preferring to self-medicate, picking something from the pharmacy at Asda. She always said she was shy because of her accent and that she never understood what the doctors were saying; they spoke too fast for her. It occurs to me now that her behaviour was strange, but then I never knew any different. I did not have friends to compare it with. It was what defined my mother, who she was.

'If you worked at Tesco instead of an Indian restaurant, if you mixed more, you would understand their accent,' I had said, mock exasperated.

'I don't need to mix; I have you,' she had said, cupping my face fondly, planting a kiss on my nose.

'But what about after I go away to uni, Mum?'

'*Then* I will mix,' she had said.

And now, *she* is gone.

Don't think about it. Don't.

I push these thoughts away and concentrate on Lily. I wish I was with her, snuggling on her worn sofa, she at one end, me at the other, basking in the soft pink glow of friendship, the heating cranked up to high, the stuffy amorphous cloud of blue-grey air, smelling of Glade and beef casserole, punctured every once in a while by our shared confidences and our laughter. Watching music videos on television and munching on chocolate, me cuddling one of her soft toys, as she says she doesn't want me to feel left out.

'Here, take this one. He'll keep you company,' she said the first time I visited, shoving a bedraggled beige teddy at me. 'His name's King. He's my second favourite.'

Even though she's only six months younger than me, sometimes it feels like there's a world of difference between us. She feels so much younger somehow. She's still into soft toys whereas I have begun having crushes on boys, although they don't look twice at me, even the ugly ones. But she's sweet and kind and gives me great big hugs and imparts secrets. She tells me her mum has a new boyfriend and that she doesn't like him. She tells me she caught Shania making out with Toby, Alanna's boyfriend, in the girls' toilets and that is why Shania has been so mean to her recently. She sits with me at lunchtime. She shares her pocket money, her chocolate and her crisps with me. She shares my fantasies of the horrible fates that we wish would befall the bullies. She understands why I haven't invited her back to my flat yet, even though I have been to hers like a million times. She gets it without me having to explain that I am embarrassed, that I am shy because I have never done it before.

I so want her to like it. That is why I was going to invite her in the half term, *this* half term that has, in the space of a few measly hours morphed into a nightmare. Our plan, Mum's and mine, was to clean it thoroughly, to get rid of all the cobwebs and the lingering smell of stale curry, replacing the bed sheets and mopping the floors, before having her over.

All my life, I never felt the lack of a friend. I had my books, I had food, I had Mum. But even though my mum is my best friend in all the world, now that I have a friend my own age, I find that it is different. For example, I cannot tell Mum about the gigantic crush I have on Bhim, who sits in front of me in maths. That even though he hasn't looked at me once, I entertain this wild hope that one day he will see *me*, see past my overweight exterior to the person I am beneath. I like his studious appearance, the thick glasses and the tucked-in shirts and pressed trousers. I like that no matter how much the bullies rile him, it never affects his calm reserve.

When I told Lily, she laughed, and punched my arm fondly. 'Bhim? But what about Alex or Jacob or Raj?' But she went along with it, excited, getting into the spirit of things. 'Why don't you write him a note?' she asked. 'Why don't you…' Each suggestion more outrageous than the last.

I couldn't do all this with Mum. I just couldn't. She doesn't know Bhim, for one, and secondly, she would be angry with him for not taking notice of me.

I am thinking of everything except what happened. I have shredded the wrapper of the Dairy Milk bar to bits and it is littering the floor, silvery blue slivers on beige, like the reflection of water on mud. The policewoman is still here, sitting at the little table in the corner of the living room, watching me, worrying about what I will do next.

I do not want to think about how the only person I have in the world has been arrested for kidnapping me when I was just a baby, from India at that. I do not want to think about what will happen to me now, without her. I do not want to think of what the policewoman said, of someone searching for me for thirteen years. Not someone. My real mother. *No, no.* My real mother is the one I have known all my life. And she is gone. What will I do now? Where is she? What are they doing to her?

Her face flashes before my eyes, her eyes anguished when I refused to move, her voice, 'Diya, wait,' following me down the stairs when I ran away in anger, her shocked expression when she saw me running back up, the wall of police between us, her words, 'I am your mother, Diya. You are mine. I love you, Diya, my darling girl, light of my life.' Echoing up the narrow corridor in a blast of panic-scented, sorrow-tinged air.

My stomach hurts. I hurt, everywhere. I put my head between my knees and I rock, my mouth producing those weird keening sounds again. The policewoman pats my back, 'There, there.' She tries to hold me.

I push her away and rush to the cupboards, rooting around inside until I find the pack of Haribo Starmix I shoved in the other day when I heard Mum's key in the lock, and the six-pack of crisps I keep with the spare toothbrushes that we never need to use, but if we do, it is my responsibility to find them as Mum always forgets where she puts them.

I sit on the sofa and eat my way through the pack of Haribo and some of the crisps, dropping wrappers and crumbs everywhere, not offering any to the woman who I am pretending isn't there. Even though I am partial to sweets and crisps, I do not usually eat in this uncontrolled manner, without caring how much junk I am stuffing into my body. Normally, I am careful, rationing my treats, saving them for when I really need them, for when the bullying has been particularly bad, say. And if this doesn't qualify as an emergency, a time when I really need the sustenance, the comfort of junk food, then I don't know what does. Food is the only thing I can think of now that can tide me through this nightmare, bite by bilious bite.

I crunch and chew and swallow and these sounds drown out the clamour in my brain, all those questions and worries and hurts spilling out and demanding answers. I eat without tasting a thing; everything is dark blue, the colour and texture of grief. I eat until there is a knock and I jump up and rush to the door on wobbly legs that refuse to move fast enough. I push it open and begin to say, 'Mum. I knew they would let you go. I knew they had made a mistake…'

It isn't Mum. I knew it. I did. Somewhere deep down I knew.

As if from afar, I hear the policewoman say, 'This is your social worker,' her voice incredibly gentle, like a glass vase that might break from too much pressure.

My ears are ringing. I am swaying on my feet, like my mum did when she saw me, that moment when the world as I knew it imploded in my face. I picture the globe that represents my world shattering, the confetti of iridescent, dancing particles, the million shards sparkling and glittering and winking up at me. So beautiful and yet so deadly, each little piece fit to draw blood. I picture myself stepping on the tantalising, inviting shrapnel, each shimmering pearl topped with a perfect vermilion globule of my blood, round like an Indian woman's bindi, like the bindis my mother likes to wear…

The woman standing in the doorway is stout, bespectacled, with greying hair and kind eyes. Someone's mum. Just not mine.

I turn around and rush to the bathroom, making it just in time. I am violently sick, again and again, and the feeling is welcome. It is much better than shock and numbness pierced by pinpricks of hurt, stabs of pain, incisions of grief and, worst of all, notches of acceptance. In a corner of my mind, I know.

I know because of the way my mum looked at me, the resignation in her eyes as she was led away. I know because of the way her eyes were constantly flitting everywhere, forever checking, only ever at rest when it was just her and me in the confines of our flat, the curtains drawn, phone off the hook: 'So no one will disturb us; I need it after the day I've had.'

I know because of the way her hand used to grip mine tight sometimes when we were out, how she used to whisper, 'Come on,' and lead me down this alleyway and that, urgently, her little feet making huge strides so I struggled to catch up, her palm locked in mine, gaze darting like a startled fox in search of cover, until we were completely alone. Only then would she stop, making sure, once again, that there was no one about. Then we would bend double catching our breath, having lost our bearings, standing in a deserted road in the middle of nowhere. She would laugh a fake laugh that sounded more like a sob and say, 'That was fun, wasn't it? An adventure. Now, let's see where we are.'

I know.

And I don't want to. I don't want to.

Chapter 5
Aarti

The Cavernous Emptiness
of a Wasted Life

Breakfast: Cereal: Bran Flakes – 30g, with a dash of skimmed milk.

Mid-morning snack: Orange.

Lunch: 1 boiled egg, 1 slice of wholemeal toast (400g loaf) – no butter, and a banana.

Afternoon snack: Apple.

Supper: Mixed salad. No dressing. No croutons.

❄ ❄ ❄

Writing in her food diary comforts Aarti. She started the habit in the clinic as part of her programme, when she was hospitalised, after…those terrible, black days after.

She still finds it hard to force food down past the barrier in her throat, but she makes sure she eats something at the requisite times; she makes sure she eats enough so she can pen it down in her diary, her lifeline. There is an entry for every day, going back thirteen years. So many books, charting what she has eaten each day of her life for the past decade and a bit. So much unsaid; the gaps in between breakfast, lunch and dinner, speaking of longing and yearning, hurt and loss, the cavernous emptiness of a wasted life.

She has not binged since her interlude at the clinic and she has not made herself sick. She was sick the other day of course, retching and welcoming that long-lost feeling, the comfort it gave her, but that was nerves. She is proud of how she got to the very edge and bounced back, how she has survived despite the devastating blow that life, via Vani the traitor, has dealt her.

And now, the culmination. Vani, that bitch, the very thought of whom is like harbouring a burning, stinging mouthful of raw chillies, is in prison where she belongs. And Aarti's child, her child… This part she doesn't understand. This cold, grey country with its incomprehensible laws. *She* is the mother; surely her child should have been brought to her once her kidnapper had been apprehended? But no, not here apparently. Instead, *her* child has been shipped to some stranger.

'Because she doesn't know you, you see,' her lawyer had explained patiently. 'And she's undergone a lot of…'

'And she knows them, the people she's currently with?' Aarti had asked, unable and unwilling to control the rising shriek in her voice.

'She has been through so much; she needs to come to terms with what's happened. The trauma… She will come and see you soon. Give her time.'

'What about me? The trauma I have suffered?' Aarti had yelled. 'I have been waiting thirteen years for her. *My* child. Mine.'

Silence at the other end.

And so, she is waiting, walking the fifteen paces from one end of the room to the other, waiting for her daughter to deign to visit her, giving her time.

Chapter 6
Diya

Strategy

Strategy

Noun: a plan or method for obtaining a specific goal or result.

Synonyms: approach, manner, system, technique, way.

❆ ❆ ❆

I have a strategy. I am not going to think about it, any of it. As strategies go, it's not the best. But I do not have the energy to think of something else. I am drained. It will have to do.

I stick to my strategy, ignoring the stinging in my eyes, the vacuum in my heart, ignoring the social worker who talks me through what will happen, in her soft voice that washes over me like water tripping over stones and makes me think of marshmallows, pink, fluffy, melt-in-the-mouth.

I stick to my strategy until she says, 'She is here, staying at a hotel nearby. She would love to have you stay with her, of course. Or, we could arrange for emergency foster…'

'Sorry,' I say, 'who?'

The social worker blinks, startled by my sudden input, and then she smiles, her eyes tender as she looks at me. 'Your mother.'

My weighted heart perks up, does a tango in my chest. 'Mum is at a hotel?' Was this all some sort of giant hoax?

Her smile disappears, a desperate anguish taking its stead. 'I am so sorry, Diya. I should have made it clear. The woman who gave birth to you. She's staying at…'

I do not, cannot hear any more. I put my hands to my ears to shut out her words but they reverberate inside my head, going round and round like a hamster in its wheel. *The woman who gave birth to you.*

'I am sorry,' the social worker is saying, her eyes shimmering. 'So sorry.'

She reaches a hand out to touch me. I jerk away.

'I do not want to stay with her. I do not want to see her,' I yell. 'She is not my mother. My mother is… She is…'

I cannot say any more. I rush to the toilet, heave my agony into the bowl. I heave and heave even though nothing comes. I am empty inside. Wrung out. Bare.

'When can I see her?' I ask when I stumble out of the loo and have to face the social worker sitting on the little foldable dining table the previous owner left behind, gazing at me with her tragic eyes. The drone of the policewoman's radio crackles from the sofa. This flat has never seemed smaller that it is now. There is no escape.

The social worker attempts a smile. 'You've changed your mind? We could go now. Or do you want to have the tests done first and I could take you after we've been to the hospital?'

The rage comes from nowhere. I feel like grabbing this woman and shaking her until her teeth chatter so much they fall out of her insensitive mouth. 'I do not want to see that woman. I want to see my mother!' I yell, so loud that the policewoman looks up from the perusal of her phone, swivelling towards us so that the sofa creaks.

We used to giggle about the rude noises that sofa made, Mum and I. She would twist and turn, the sofa emitting all sorts of funny sounds that sent me into peals of laughter. I close my eyes and sway on my feet. I yearn for her, for her arms around my body, for her mouth to whisper endearments in my ear: 'Just a nightmare, Diya. Go back to sleep.' I wish…

'We… I'll check with the team…' the social worker says.

'What team?' I screech, hardly recognising the high-pitched shriek produced by my vocal chords.

'The team responsible for your care.'

I make my hands into fists. 'Why do I need permission to see my own mother?'

The social worker squeezes her eyes shut and speaks softly, as if each word hurts. Why does she hurt when I am the one who is suffering? I am the one bereft. I am the one lost. 'She is under arrest as we speak. It is highly unlikely that you will be allowed to see her until her hearing is over and she has been moved to a more permanent…' She stops but I know what she was going to say. Prison. My mother is in prison. My sweet, loving, anxious, fearful mum. No wonder her eyes were never at rest, no wonder she was constantly worried. *Be careful what you worry about, it might just come true.*

I hug my stomach tight to hold in the pain that threatens to burst out of me in never-ending howls. I cannot fathom my mother in prison. I cannot fathom any of this…

'How can you decide what's best for me? I will tell you what's best. I want my mother. I want to see her,' I manage before nausea overtakes me and I rush to the bathroom again.

I stick to my strategy during the interminable car ride to the hospital, looking out of the window at nothing in particular, chewing on one of the caramel toffees from the pack I brought with me, clutching it tight on my lap. We pass a cramped street of similar residences, narrow, squashed-looking buildings. I picture a giant plucking the houses and pulling them lengthways to give them some height before gently setting them down again. I sympathise with the houses. This is exactly how I feel too, like a giant hand is orchestrating my life, pulling it this way and that at whim.

We are passing along the high street now, the shops closed for the night, bleak ghosts, formless shadows of the selves they are during the day.

Lights twinkle inside restaurants, reflecting off cutlery shiny as New Year resolutions, picking out faces, some happy, some contemplative, some with mouths open mid-conversation, revealing the mush the expensive food is reduced to once it's chewed. They eat merrily, knives and forks performing an intricate dance between plate and mouth, and I wish I was one of them, although how could we afford it, Mum and I... Ah... The pain is a flower blooming in my stomach. A huge flower whose petals reach outwards into all my body's many crevices and organs. *Stop, stop. Strategy, Diya, Strategy.*

A girl waits by the bus stop, dark brown hair, droopy face, pulling her raisin-coloured coat close around her. Her bruised eyes meet mine, a fleeting communion, and they are expressionless, empty. That is how I should be, I decide. That is the root to not feeling. *Empty yourself, Diya.* I swallow the toffee, stuff a couple more in my mouth, close my eyes and concentrate on drowning out the marshmallow voice of the social worker, the screaming in my brain, the pain in my insides. Instead I allow the smooth caramel sweetness to talk to me, the only sounds I hear being the bite, chew, swallow, bite, chew, swallow, until the car judders to a halt and the social worker gently takes my arm.

I shrug it off with more force than necessary as it brings to mind comfort, the security of a hug from a loved one. *Don't go there.*

'Well, here we are,' she says and I follow her stubby legs clad in sensible black trousers into the blinding light, the bustling busyness, the moaning patients, the argumentative relatives, the ringing of phones, the bleeping of pagers, the pain-filled eyes that I recognise, that could be mine reflected back at me, the long-suffering voices of receptionists, the harassed nurses trying on smiles that are in short supply, the screech of beds, the staccato beat of doctors' feet dancing on lino as they make their way to the next emergency that needs tending, the bitter smell of medicine and desperation, of agony mingling with fragile hope.

I am subjected to all sorts of tests, so many people examining me, kind-hearted nurses sneaking in sweets with reassuring smiles like bolstering a building that has no hope of standing up on its own, the slightly metallic smell and icy feel of machines nudging my body like phantom fingers making contact. Can the machines detect the numbness inside me, the flower of pain that ruthlessly seeks to gain control?

The doctors smile gently and a tad wearily as they prod and probe, their wan faces creased into lines that give testament to the long hours they have spent here, circles shadowing their eyes like ghosts at a funeral come to claim their own. They entertain all my endless questions, a ruse on my part to get my mind thinking about anything but what she might be doing now – where she is, is she scared? – to try and ignore the fact that I feel hopelessly lost. I am falling, like Alice, and the fall is endless and I haven't quite reached the ground yet.

I do not want to think of what is going to happen to me, what I will do when I am eventually left alone, not surrounded by a dozen well-meaning strangers, and I cannot keep the horror at bay any longer. I do not want to think about the fact that I am terrified. I do not want to face the question that needs answering. Without her, without the truth that she is my mother, who am I?

A stolen baby found thirteen years later, that's who you are, a voice in my head screams, slinking out the door in the recesses of my mind that keeps it reined in. *Someone who has been living in a false reality in a false world,* it yells before I push it back into place, bolt the door and lose the key.

But the damage is done. *Perhaps that is why I did not mind the moving,* I think. The constant upheaval suited my mindset, which was never quite settled in one place because I didn't belong with the woman I believed was my mother. *No. No.* She is my mum. She is. Her face, that look, like she was being broken, her voice overflowing with all the love she feels for me, 'I am your mother, Diya. You are mine.'

I am doing it again. Thinking of her. *Force everything out of your mind. Strategy is the key.*

'What is it?' the nurse helping me into my clothes asks, her voice the soft pink of dawn.

'Nothing,' I say, willing myself to flash her a watery smile.

And suddenly, surprisingly, I am folded into her arms, into the haven of her soft body that spills all around me, enveloping me into its folds, smelling, weirdly, of dog. I want to stay here forever, sheltered in these unfamiliar arms, warm in the cave of this woman's embrace. Eventually, I pull away, look up into eyes the dark blue of shadows dancing on water.

'Do you have a dog?' I ask.

'Now how did you know that?' she laughs and we spend the rest of the time chatting about Bugbear, her schnauzer, and his antics.

The social worker accompanies me through all the interminable tests. She knows when not to speak, when to leave me alone with my thoughts, and for this I am grateful. I think of Lily. I will have to tell her sometime that the sleepover is cancelled or postponed indefinitely due to 'unforeseen circumstances'. I blink away the moisture staining my eyelashes and think of her reaction. She will, I know, burst into tears, hug me, offer comfort, want to talk about it. I close my eyes, weary. I am glad I am here, away from everything, everyone I know, glad that I do not have to say anything or do anything; just allow myself to be taken care of by all these kind-hearted strangers.

Finally, the social worker says, blue rings hugging her brown eyes, 'That's it for today, Diya.'

The nurse, 'mum' of Bugbear the schnauzer, confers another warm hug and an assurance that I look after myself until tomorrow when she'll be back with more stories.

'What a day it's been, huh?' the social worker says wryly as the cold grey air, punctuated by pulsing lights and punctured by sirens, tasting bitter, of medicine and gasoline and smoke, hits us outside the sliding double doors of the hospital. We both shiver and pull our coats closer around our bodies.

Assorted smokers pace up and down, wearing the cobblestones thin as they take urgent puffs of their cigarettes, their haggard faces relaxing briefly, drawing succour before going inside to offer some. An ambulance lounges beside the A&E entrance to our right. As I watch, another ambulance drives up, sirens blaring. Paramedics jump off, unload a stretcher – a bloated, bloody face, eyes glued shut and weeping, body wrapped in sunny yellow blankets. I shudder.

What are you doing now? Are you okay? I miss you, Mum. The thought is there before I can chase it away. *She committed a crime against you,* the policewoman's voice, inveigling in. The policewoman who rushed off as soon as the social worker came, as if she couldn't get away soon enough. No, that's not quite right. I am not being kind or fair.

The policewoman had tried to squeeze my hand, had sounded apologetic as she said goodbye. Her radio had crackled several times while she was waiting with me, but she had ignored it. 'I am needed elsewhere. You take care now,' she had said, and her eyes had shimmered, leaking moisture. I had looked away from the naked emotion shining in there, afraid that it would start me off. And I had decided that I couldn't, I wouldn't cry. Because that would mean accepting what had happened, colluding in it. I had pulled my hand away from her grasp and refused to look at her as she left, as her footsteps echoed down the stairs just before the door closed and I heard, once more, my mum's voice floating up to me, 'I am your mother, Diya. You are mine. I love you, Diya.'

A woman, high heels, navy blue dress coat, perfectly made-up face, blonde hair in disarray in complete contrast to the rest of her, comes running out of the doors we just exited, pressing buttons haphazardly on her phone, her polished scarlet nails dancing on the keys. 'Jake, please come at once,' she sobs into the phone, mascara running, her fragile composure dropping like a discarded mask.

'Where are we going now?' I ask before I can stop myself.

I do not, absolutely cannot countenance going back to the flat. Anywhere but there, climbing up those stairs which echo with her footfall as she was led away by a cavalcade of officers, shackled, handcuffed like a common criminal. The woman I still think of as my mother. The only mother I have known.

Your real mother has been searching for you for the past thirteen years. The policewoman's voice reverberates in my ears.

I need to eat. I need food – chocolate, crisps, anything at all.

'Since you didn't want to, um…stay with the woman…' the social worker has the grace to blush.

I am glad she didn't say, *your mother*. I cannot think of that woman, whoever she is, as my mother. My mother is Vani, and she has been taken, cruelly, from me. *Don't think of that… Concentrate on your strategy, Diya.*

'We have arranged emergency foster care for you. We are going to your foster carers now. Farah and Sohrab Khan. I showed you pictures and told you about them, asked if you'd rather go straight to theirs or the hospital first and you chose the hospital, remember?' she says gently. 'They have two boys, five and seven. Do you want me to show you the pictures again? I will in the car.'

Her voice washes over me, soothing. Marshmallows, that's what I want.

I grab her hand. 'I want something to eat,' I say.

She smiles at me, her expression tender. 'Oh, darling, of course. Come on.'

On the way to the hospital café, I try one more time. 'When can I see my mum?'

She chews her lower lip and I notice, once again, the bluish black circles ringing her eyes. 'It's difficult. You're here at the hospital because we want to make sure she didn't...' She doesn't complete the sentence, she doesn't need to.

'My mother...' I begin, daring the social worker to challenge me, '...wouldn't harm me. She cannot bear the thought of me being hurt.' And yet, she has. I am hurting, right now. I push away the thought, angrily swiping at the tears I thought I'd exhausted which are beading my eyes. I remember the time she found out I was being bullied, the raw agony in her eyes, the way she had bunched her hands into fists and said she would come and fight the bullies herself, and I had known that she would too, my slip of a mother who was, who is, scared of every little thing, especially people. 'She *loves* me,' I yell and a passer-by shrouded beneath his coat cringes as if slapped. He turns and I see his eyes, red-rimmed. He has lost a loved one too, I think, the flower of pain blooming.

'In the eyes of the law, she has wronged you,' the social worker's voice is tender as the whisper of silk on skin. 'Look, it's complicated, Diya. This case, your case…there are not many precedents. Family lawyers are right this minute poring through legal tomes and going over past cases to try and find out what is allowed and what is not.' A deep sigh. 'We all want what's best for you. I know you desperately want to see her, but…'

'You think seeing my mum is not in my best interests?' I yell, venting all the anger I feel at this situation I find myself in, all the hurt, the helplessness, the anxiety rendering my voice a broken squeal.

She sighs once more, sounding as helpless as I feel. 'I will talk to the team in charge of your care, put forward your case. Okay? I cannot promise more. And even if we do go to see her, and that's a big "if", mind you…'

My heart lifts at the thought.

'…it will not be for a few days yet, until she's been charged and moved.'

It sinks again, my somersaulting heart, at the sudden vision of Mum in prison. I blink it away. I try.

The café looms, a tired woman manning the counter, sorry-looking cakes and sandwiches drooping in orange light.

'Ah, here we are.' The social worker's voice falsely cheery, both of us relieved.

She buys me a sandwich, apple juice, a packet of crisps and some oat biscuits, and I eat to fill the Mum-sized hole in me, to allay the fear, to douse the worry. I cannot taste the food and the Mum-sized hole refuses to be filled by anything other than Mum herself, and yet I eat. I chew and swallow, because at least it is something to do. My stomach roils. The flower of pain flourishes. This is too big a loss, too huge a pain for food to comfort, to soothe; too wide a chasm to fill. For the first time in my life, even the one thing usually guaranteed to ease the pain is not helping.

The social worker watches me eat, her eyes soft as the sky at twilight, and I am reminded of Mum watching me those evenings when she brought back my favourite dishes from whichever Indian restaurant she was currently working at. I turn away from the social worker's gaze and freeze momentarily, almost choking on my juice at the sight of us reflected in the glass window of the café, a chubby woman gazing affectionately at a chubby girl who could, in this shadowy light, be her daughter. My stomach churns. My body hurts, the flower of pain running riot inside.

'Let's go,' I say, not able to finish the food for perhaps the first time in my life, binning the rest instead of saving it for later, knowing it will not help, not relieve me of the incessant ache of missing my mother.

In the car, the social worker, Jane – such a solid, dependable name – says, for at least the third time since I've met her, 'If you need to talk about anything, anything at all, I'm here. Okay?'

Like all the other times, I pretend not to hear, staring resolutely out of the window at the blackness outside.

'I mean, I may not physically be there if it is, say, the middle of the night, but you have my number. You can call anytime. Even if it's four in the morning.'

She smiles. I don't.

'You cannot take me to see my mum.' My voice sullen, tinged purple with agony and yellow with tiredness.

She sighs, defeated. 'Not now. But I will try and find out what the legal constraints are, I promise.'

The foster carers' house is in a quiet residential street a twenty minute drive away. *Good*, I think, *the further away I am, the better.*

The door is opened by a slight woman wearing a salwar, her hair pulled back in a bun.

'Hello, Diya. I am Farah. Welcome,' she says, enveloping me in a hug before I can move away, her gentle fingers stroking my hair.

She smells of sanctuary and of detergent, with a slight hint of curry. She smells of home, of Mum after she's come back from the restaurant and had her shower. This woman's smell, the feeling of being in her arms, brings it all back, threatens to undo me and I push her away, hard.

I cannot trust anyone. How can I, when the person I love most in the world has betrayed me? I believe my mum and yet, all the evidence points to her guilt. I think of her, just standing there meekly, her gaze apologetic.

Allowing herself to be led away like a criminal. 'You tell them, Mum,' I had pleaded. And she had done nothing, hadn't denied the accusations. All she had said was that she loved me, that I was her daughter.

I close my eyes, push these thoughts away, try to get my bearings. I cannot trust anyone. Not even myself. Not when I betray myself every time I think of her, miss her, ache for her. I have to be strong. I cannot afford to get close to anyone. This woman is just a foster carer, paid to look after me for a few days.

At least she didn't kidnap you.

My eyes sting, a feeling fast becoming as familiar as breathing. When I open them, I spy two heads peeking from behind a half-open door, one stacked on top of the other, the hint of a pyjama bottom, stripy blue. Identical bug eyes, identical shocks of unruly hair. One of them is wearing glasses, the other has a mole right at the centre of his nose. They look curiously at me, unblinking, assessing. I stare back. Finally, one of them attempts a smile.

'What are you looking at?' I yell, but my heart isn't in it and it comes out weary, barely louder than a whisper.

'Affan, Zain, what are you doing up? To bed, both of you,' their mother clucks and they disappear in a swish of pyjamas.

'I am tired,' I say.

'Of course,' the woman, Farah, says. 'Have you eaten?'

'Yes.'

'Come.' She holds out a hand, then drops it to her side when I do not make a move to take it. She motions me to follow her up the narrow stairwell, echoing of the boys' hurried footsteps, their conspiratorial giggles, the lemony scent of fabric conditioner and mischief settling in the displaced air crowding the stairwell in the boys' wake.

'Bye, Diya, I'll be back for you tomorrow bright and early. Sleep well. You've earned it,' my social worker, Jane – I must remember to think of her as that – calls up the stairs.

I do not bother to reply.

Farah points to the little bathroom sandwiched between two other rooms, the door of one of which is just closing, a flash of pyjamas, a shock of hair, a red fire engine overturned onto its side, Lego blocks scattered everywhere. A piece of paper flaps on the door, stuck with Blu-Tack that is curling at the edges, a legend inscribed on it in haphazard writing, in a jumble of capitals and small letters: 'No GaLs aLouD'. The door to the other room is shut. A landing and then, tucked into a little alcove, another door.

Farah opens this one. A bed with a sky blue coverlet, yellow flowers dotting it in buttery splotches, a cream IKEA wardrobe glowing dirty yellow in the light pouring in from the street lamp just outside the window, a small table with a bedside lamp and some books. The artificial smell of flowery air freshener masking something else, the stale odour of a room not in use, no memories associated with it, the grey taste of dust and emptiness.

I go to stand by the window. A tiny garden hosting a trampoline and a plastic goal post. The grass blue in the darkness, black shadows dancing across it merrily, laying claim. A tumbledown shed, the door swaying in the wind. The silvery silhouette of a cat perched on the fence, tawny eyes glowing. A road, abutting the fence, cars whizzing past, eager to get home. Footsteps in the alleyway beyond, the sound of a match being struck, the hiss of drawn breath.

'It's not much,' Farah says. 'Spare towels and bed linen are in the cupboard here. If you need anything, just shout. Our room is the one beside the bathroom, next to the boys'. We put you in here because the boys tend to wake up in the night – we wanted to give you a little privacy.'

A pause.

I do not move, do not turn, force myself to stand still as a beacon, a lighthouse in the darkness guiding my mother home. My mother… That flower blooming again, encroaching, entrapping me from the inside. *I want you, Mum. I miss you.* I open the window, breathe in the heady scent of ice and night and cigarette smoke.

'Sohrab is working late, an emergency. Hope he doesn't disturb you when he comes upstairs later.' She waits again.

I do not respond.

'If you need me, at any time of night, just knock. I am a light sleeper, you will not be disturbing me – chances are I'll be awake anyway.'

Why is she being so kind? Why does she sound like my mother? If she doesn't go away now, I will break. I want to bend as far as I can go out of this window. How does it feel to fall, be weightless? Will it match what I am feeling inside?

As if she knows what I am thinking, Farah comes up to me, puts her arms around me, draws me into a hug.

I jerk out of her embrace.

She pulls the window shut. 'It's too cold to leave it open, isn't it? Look, you are blue.'

She takes my hands in hers and rubs some warmth into them. I retrieve them roughly from her warming grasp.

'Goodnight,' she says after a bit, and walks away, quietly shutting the door behind her.

I do not inspect the books. I turn off the light and lie on the bed, on top of the sheets and duvet. I lie there and stare at the ceiling, white, undulating, unwavering until my eyes hurt and the tears that I have been holding back so desperately come in unstoppable waves.

Chapter 7
Vani

Master Puppeteer

My darling Diya,
 How I miss you! Here are just a few of the things I yearn to see again:

1) *The way you scrunch up your nose when you are thinking.*

2) *The way you know just when I am hurt or upset, and you crack a joke, cheer me up.*

3) *The apple and strawberry scent of your hair.*

4) *The way your head fits snugly in the curve of my shoulder, the way you throw yourself at me with abandon, the feel of your arms around my neck.*

5) *The way you wait for me to get home from work, curled up on the sofa with a book, your eyes lighting up when you see me reflected in the glass of the window as I let myself in.*

6) *The way your smile starts as a twinkle in your eye which then spreads outwards, your lips inexorably lifting like they have been pulled by the string of a master puppeteer. Your eyes crinkle and your face folds into itself as giggles of mirth escape your lips, like birdsong heralding dawn.*

7) *The way when you open your eyes in the morning, they search for me and when they alight on me, they are inundated with contentment, awash with happiness.*

8) *The way you bite the end of every single pencil or pen you use.*

9) *The way you always misplace your keys.*

10) *The way you eat Maltesers, licking off all the chocolate until only the crisp centre remains, biting into the kernel last, allowing the sweet crunchiness to explode in your mouth. The way your tongue sweeps the outskirts of your lips after, aiming for any chocolate you might have missed.*

11) *The way your face runs the gamut of expressions when you are reading.*

I could go on and on, my darling. The thing is, I miss everything about you. You are growing without me, eating, sleeping, talking without me and I resent every single minute of our time apart.

How are you?

'A stupid question, Mum,' you would say, were you here with me, rolling your eyes, that expression in them that says it all.

What wouldn't I give to see your animated face, to hear your voice now! But, my darling, I genuinely would like to know. You see, Diya, for the first time in your life, I don't know how you are. And it is killing me, the not knowing, the not seeing, the not being with you. I hope you have kind people taking care of you. I pray for that. I dread to think of what you must be going through, how you must have felt that first morning when you woke up and searched for me and I wasn't there. I am sorry, my sweet, so desperately sorry.

I have told my solicitor everything in full detail. He is asking for a DNA test to be actioned. He has set the process in motion, the first step being to check if we are eligible for legal aid as I cannot afford to pay for the test.

Diya, I know you will be worrying about me, but I am all right here. I am. I hope, my darling, that you forgive me for what I am putting you through now, for what I did then, for everything I took away from you. I suppose this is why I did not tell you the story of your past, our past, the whole sordid truth – one, because I thought you were too young, and two, because I was scared. Scared as to what you might think. Scared that you would ask to go back. You who were always so happy, so content with me and with what life threw at you. You who packed at a moment's notice when I said we had to move, picking up your box of books and your bag and saying, chirpily, 'Let's go'. You who have made me so very proud. You who deserved so much more. So much that I *couldn't give you but* she *would have.*

I love you, my darling. I hope you don't ever doubt that.
Yours,
Mum

Chapter 8
Aarti

Accusatory Finger

Breakfast: Cereal: Bran Flakes – 30g, with a dash of skimmed milk

Mid-morning snack: Why hasn't she come to meet me? Why? Don't you want to meet your mother, eh, daughter? Why aren't you here?

❉ ❉ ❉

Aarti has taken to sitting downstairs in the lobby with her food diary for company. She does not want to go out, walk down to the High Street. It is too cold, for one, the chilly air that tastes of ice permeated with the smell of frying chips and junk food, making her nauseous. And much as she likes the feeling of being sick, she'd rather do it in the comfort of her own bathroom or the bathroom of her hotel room as is currently the case, and not in a public loo reeking of other people's urine.

And two, well… 'Please do try and stay away from crowds. If it happens again, I won't be able to get you out as easily.' Her lawyer's voice resounding in her ears.

And so she sits in the sofa in the lobby, breathing in the creamy scent of vanilla air freshener mixed in with a faint whiff of orange cleaning liquid, the crinkly leather squeaking in complaint every time she moves. From behind the cover of her diary, she peruses every face that enters: the tired families, the old couples, the new lovers. Hoping to find her daughter's face amongst them. Hoping to recognise her instantly, even though all she has in her mind's eye are hazy snapshots of a wispy-haired, dimple-cheeked, almond-skinned baby and fantasies of how her daughter might look now.

She needs to be careful, she knows; it is all too easy to slip into depression like she did after…those dark, ceaseless days after her daughter disappeared. It is monotonous, this waiting, this ache to see her child. Anger wars with hopelessness and she is tired of feeling out of control. At least before, when she was looking for her child, she was in charge, *doing* something. Now, she is waiting. And waiting. An interminable stretch of empty time gaping bleakly until she meets her child.

She had imagined that once Vani was in prison, she would be reunited – immediately – with her daughter. She had actually entertained the hope that she might be involved in the arrest, had imagined driving up in a police van, accusatory finger aimed at Vani's chest, the look of utter shock on Vani's face before it disintegrated into fear. She had pictured Vani begging her for mercy and she, Aarti, ignoring her, turning instead towards her daughter. She had imagined opening her arms and her daughter falling into them, their reunion as effortless as their separation had seemed endless. She would pat her daughter's back and say, 'There, there, everything is all right now,' and they would walk away, arm in arm into a new life while a protesting Vani was led away in shackles.

She has to admit that Bollywood movies have had a big part to play in the origin and nurture of these fantasies.

Frustrating, this waiting. How bloody long is her daughter going to take?

A woman walks in the door; small, slightly stooping, weighted down by bags. Watching from the corner of her eye, Aarti does a double take. No, it cannot be. Vani is in prison, isn't she?

She stands up, dropping the diary. Walks towards the woman. The woman looks up. Petite, wary, her eyes not the deep brown of pools of water sparkling in potholes after the rains that Aarti was expecting, but the stormy blue-black of the sky besieged by heavily pregnant monsoon clouds.

'Sorry,' Aarti mumbles, cheeks burning, and backs off from the woman's puzzled gaze.

'Excuse me,' someone says and Aarti turns. A young man, holding out her diary. She thanks him, sits back down.

The years have a habit of folding back like the pages of a book, she thinks, chewing the end of her pencil. She blinks and she has lost her bearing, the book of her memories has opened out to another page; she is back in the days before. When she was a young girl living with her parents. Fawned over by the entire country and yet, alone. Friendless, unhappy. She was lost and drifting, she was bulimic and struggling, until…Vani entered her life.

PART TWO

The Past

A Curtain Ripped Open

Chapter 9
Vani – Childhood
Dhonihalli, India

Fish Food

Vani is crying, open-mouthed. She has been for a while. Her face is wet, her nose is running. She can taste salt and slime as the tears mix with snot and run into her open mouth. She doesn't know why she is crying, the reason for her tears long forgotten, and yet she is unable to stop. She sits at the base of the hill, in the shade of the mango tree, at the very edge of the field, her legs dangling in the stream below.

The stream is just as happy as Vani is sad. It babbles and coos, and deposits wet cuddles onto her bare legs. Birds warble and whistle high in the trees above and the air smells of bruised mango, a haunting scent that makes her even more melancholy, if that is possible. Her stomach feels hollow.

Silvery fish dart past her feet, scales iridescent, and she is beset by the sudden craving to catch one, tears momentarily forgotten except for the residual taste of salt at the corners of her mouth. She bends down to try and grab one as it swims past, tantalising, and her hand inside the water looks huge, broken, separate from the rest of her arm. She lunges at the fish, makes a fist and she is sure she has caught it. She can feel its slimy body flutter helplessly inside the prison of her palm; she can feel her lips moving upwards in a contented smile, even as the sun dries the few straggly tears on her face. She opens her palm gently, her heart in her throat, but it is empty, wet, water trickling down it in sorry, silvery drips.

She screams, she rants. A leaf falls into the water with a plop, a shimmering ripple, iridescent blue.

And then, without warning, the water is dark, no longer glinting. A monster, blocking the sun. She looks up, mid sob, heart thudding in the enclosure of her chest. And there is her father, standing in front of her, across the stream, tall as a giant, single-handedly obstructing the sun, casting the stream in shadow. He drops the tiffin box he is carrying beside him with a thud, not caring that the gleaming container is now tinged muddy brown. He bends down and ties his lungi higher, above his knees, and Vani watches transfixed as he wades across the water, mastering the stream in two big strides. And then he is beside her, his finger, cool, wet, on her chin. He lifts up a corner of his shirt and wipes her nose.

'What's the matter?' he asks.

'I want to fish,' Vani sniffs.

'That's all? Why are you crying then?' His voice is gentle, deep as the well in Charu aunty's courtyard that Vani has been warned against. 'Come, we'll do it together,' he says, rubbing his hands.

He puts his arms around her and hoists her up the hill, her legs dangling like the cat's tail when it has stolen fish and escaped to the rafters. He sets her down gently by the loamy soil underneath the recently watered coconut trees.

'First,' he says, 'we have to make a fishing rod. For that, we need a stick. Will you find one for me?'

Her tears forgotten, Vani flies around collecting twigs, showing them to her da.

'Not that one, too small. Nor that. Ah, that one's perfect,' he says and she grins.

'Next, we need some thread. I'll get that, you wait here,' he says, winking.

He disappears into the house via the front door so Vani's ma, who is in the kitchen, doesn't spy him. For a minuscule second, Vani is worried that he might not reappear again. Her chin wobbles, but before a sob can escape her lips he is out again, holding up a spool of thread.

'Shh,' he says, 'I stole it from your ma's sewing box, don't tell.'

And she giggles happily, glad to be in on the conspiracy, sob forgotten.

Her da asks her to bite off a length of thread and when she does, he says, 'How strong you are!' His praise makes her chest puff out with pride, dries any straggling tears right up.

'Next,' he says, 'we dig for worms.'

They dig and dig, the late afternoon sun plastering Vani's hair, which has escaped the tidy plait that her mother had combed it into just that morning, onto her back in wet, lank strands. The worms wiggle and twist and when she pokes them with a stick, they curl up into Kannada alphabet shapes. Da finds half of a coconut shell and they lure the worms into it, the brown ropy interior writhing slimy pink.

Finally, when the shell is half full, Da declares them ready.

Vani and her da carry their makeshift fishing rod and the booty of wrigglies down the hill to the stream and position themselves on the bank. Da's tiffin box lies forgotten in the mud on the opposite bank and Charu aunty's stray comes up and sniffs it. Da shoos him away.

Suggi's cow, tethered to the post for grazing, ventures as close as her rope will allow, looking askance at them with curious almond eyes. 'We are fishing,' Vani tells her, marvelling at her shiny brown nose, those liquid expressive eyes.

'Now, Vani,' Da says, 'first we have to bait the fish.'

He picks a worm with his finger and ties it to the end of the thread. It wiggles its pink body at Vani, pleadingly. 'You are fish food,' Vani tells it, 'fish food.' She grins. Sweat dribbles down her back and collects in the waistband of her knickers. The air smells orangey red, of dust and worms and excitement.

'Now,' Da says, 'once you have tied the worm, hold the stick like this.'

Da helps her cast the rod. And they sit there as the afternoon fades to evening, trying and failing to catch the fish slinking past.

But Vani doesn't mind. Her heart is full, despite her stomach growling, despite her arms sticking to her sides with sweat, slick and slippery, and later, years later, she will identify that warm, replete feeling as happiness.

They sit there until the sun travels down the sky and dips behind the trees flanking Chinnappa's house at the edge of the village. They sit there until Vani's ma calls out for them, saying she will come and whip them, even Da, with the fat stick she uses to scare the crows that steal the grain meant for the chickens, if they don't come to the house *at once*. They sit there until blue-grey wisps from kindling – burning as water is heated for their evening wash – stain the darkening sky.

The air tastes of wood smoke. It smells charred with a spicy undertone. With all their worms gone and no fish to show for it, Da takes the coconut shell and tries to scoop up fish with it.

And just when Ma starts coming down the hill, stick in tow, just when she yells, 'Where have you been? I've seen neither hide nor hair of either of you. And is that my spool of thread lying half-buried in the dirt? And what on earth is your tiffin box doing there, Ganesh?' Da lets out a victorious cry of, 'Vani, I caught one.'

Ma stops mid-rant to squint at the cloudy water overflowing from the brown shell. Vani watches the silvery scale streaking around the muddy orange water and she screams with joy. She jumps on the bank and loses her footing, falls into the stream, and Da drops the coconut shell and bends down to pick her up.

She is wet, soaking, yelling, 'We caught one, we caught one!' and there is a rueful look on Da's face as he mumbles, 'Um...we did, but...' and Vani spies the coconut shell lying upturned at the bottom of the roiling stream and Ma starts her yelling all over again, just as Da picks up his tiffin box with one hand and Vani with the other and they race up the hill to avoid Ma's stick.

Later, after washing themselves in hot water scented with coconut husks, red rice and fish curry warm in their stomachs, they squat beside each other as Ma tries to scrub the tiffin box free of grime by the light of the lantern.

The trembling light casts shadows on Da's face and dances patterns on his body and Vani says, 'Tell me stories, Da.'

And he does, stories of princesses and giants and ghosts and monkeys.

Just before she drifts off to sleep, a thought occurs to Vani. 'I think the fish smelled the curry bubbling and thought they would be in it,' she mumbles. 'Tomorrow Ma is not making fish curry so they will not be wary and I am sure we will catch loads. Shall we try again tomorrow?' and Ma looks up sharply and Da laughs.

In the coming years, whenever events threaten to get the better of her, when the hard bumps of life make her stumble and trip, Vani will pull out this particular memory from the recesses of her mind and it will soothe her, tide her through the difficult times. And this is what she will remember most: the infectious crackle and boom of her da's laugh like the fizzing fireworks lighting up the night sky at Diwali, the salty taste of drying tears, the silvery water gleaming rose and gold as the afternoon faded to evening, the coconut shell full of worms writhing muddy pink, elusive fish glinting like sequins, the smell of kerosene from the flickering lamp colouring her dreams and painting them all the hues of the rainbow.

Chapter 10
Aarti – Childhood
Bangalore, India

Deflated Skins

Aarti runs through the endless rooms of her house, populated with irreplaceable artefacts and dime-a-dozen servants who address her as 'Madam' and look at the floor while talking to her. She is calling for her mother. She suspects her mother is in her room, but the door is shut and she will not come, even though Aarti knocks and knocks. Frustrated, she flings a statue onto the floor and watches dispassionately as it shatters. It is expensive, she knows. Everything in her house is expensive.

Servants stop what they are doing, the mopping and the polishing, the sweeping and the dusting, to gawp, flabbergasted at the waste, thinking, she knows, that the statue – before it was smashed to smithereens – could have fed their entire family for two days at least. The smell of shock and fear permeates the air-conditioned, sandalwood air freshener spiked air.

The servants look away when Aarti catches them staring. They think she doesn't know what's going on behind their meek faces, their servile demeanour, and that makes her mad. Do they take her for a fool?

One scurries up with a dustpan and brush to sweep the sorry remains at her feet. The taste of anger in her mouth, flaming orange.

'Leave it!' she yells and flings another statue right at his face.

He flinches.

Blood erupts, bright red droplets oozing out from between lips of bruised brown skin and she bursts into tears. Loud, frantic sobs.

The door to her mother's room flings open and she strides outside, her face like a *Rakshasa*, a monster, all scrunched up and scary, her hands squeezed into fists. Aarti knew her cries would bring her mother to her. Her mother hates the sound of Aarti's sobs like nothing else.

'What is this racket?' her mother yells, her face contorting, morphing into something even more frightening.

Aarti feels warm, wet liquid oozing down her thighs, forming a dark creamy puddle on the floor. The dirty yellow smell of urine and shame rends the air.

'He did it,' she says, surreptitiously pulling her legs together, feeling her bare feet slipping on the mess, pointing at the servant with a wavering finger, wanting to draw her mother's attention elsewhere.

The servant has tried to wipe away the blood with the back of his hand, scarlet drops staining the light russet skin of the inside of his palm, but more droplets keep on coming, oozing out of the wide-lipped gash on his face in horizontal slashes.

Aarti is transfixed; she is repelled. She wants a wash, she wants her mother's arms around her, telling her it's all right, it's okay, even though she cannot recall her mother having ever done that to her in her life.

'How dare you?' her mother is screeching at the servant while he cowers silently, fearfully, dustpan lowered, the debris of the statues around him. 'Get out. Now. And don't come back.'

The other servants are pretending to work, but from their too-straight backs, the way they cringe ever so slightly at every word her mother utters, Aarti knows they are listening, paying heed.

Her mother turns on her heel and goes into her room without a second glance at Aarti and the door slams shut, the loud bang reverberating in the horrified, doleful silence with the finality of a chapter ending. The servant who has just been sacked slinks away, blood still pouring out of the wound on his face, dustpan left behind, forlorn amidst the ruins of the statues, like relics left behind after an earthquake. The other servants avert their eyes.

Aarti steps away from the puddle of her own urine, the bitter green aftertaste of guilt and hurt and fear and yearning in her mouth, the tang of ammonia assaulting her nostrils, inducing nausea. She walks away, gingerly at first, her wet feet slipping on the cool mosaic floors, and then she is running. She is running from room to room, her damp thighs stinging, her sodden knickers chafing, her face wet and her heart heavy from the weight of her tears. She is running the length and breadth of her huge house and she is alone.

❉ ❉ ❉

It is the evening of the party. Aarti's seventh birthday celebration. A festive atmosphere invades the house, the rich smell of frying spices and condensed milk, coconut roasting in ghee and gulab jamuns doused in golden syrup. She is laughing excitedly, shouting, 'Come! Come!' to the woman who looks after her – Tara – tugging at her hand and trying to drag her along. Tara is laughing as well, the sound like bells tinkling, and Aarti knows somehow that Tara is just as thrilled as she is.

The rooms of the mansion are polished and sparkling, speckled mosaic floors so clean that Aarti's naked feet slip and slide on them and she can see her reflection smiling up at her from within the mauve and ginger spotted depths. Some servants are putting up fairy lights which twinkle and shine, others put up banners, yet more bring in platters of samosas and spiced nuts, poppadum and aloo bhujia.

Vats of curries in varying shades of orange, turmeric and cream bubble in the kitchen. Harassed-looking cooks – sweat pouring off their faces like water from a tap, their aprons tinged the deep red of curry powder – stir and chop, fry and boil, with the panicked frenzy of people on a deadline.

Aarti stuffs a samosa in her mouth and continues with her exploration. She stands on tiptoe and peeps out of the window on the landing. Gardeners have strung lights all along the drive and onto the jacaranda trees. The garden looks transformed, a multicoloured, twinkling paradise, silvery blue, green and orange lights winking and dancing, blinding and dazzling. A gazebo is being erected on the lawn near the fountain which dispenses first turquoise, then emerald, then vermilion water. Excitement bubbles up inside Aarti, an excitement so huge that it bursts out of her in giggles that she cannot control, and her hands start clapping of their own accord.

She skips downstairs and stops short on the bottom step in amazed wonder. A veritable feast of balloons in all hues of the rainbow flood the hall, nearly taking over the huge space. She blinks once, twice, unable to believe the miracle of the floating, colourful world in front of her, unable to accept the evidence of her own eyes. One servant is stringing some balloons onto a banner. The other is blowing up even more.

'Give,' she says imperiously to the servant blowing, unconsciously imitating her father's tone, knowing even at such a small age just how to speak to the servants, how to put them in their place. 'One blue and one pink and one yellow. I want them now.' She stamps her foot.

Her parents come in at that moment, just as she holds the coveted balloons in her hands, the rubbery, magical feel of them, all weightlessness and light, inundating her heart with colour.

'Aarti, what are you doing? Why are you not ready yet? Tara, why haven't you dressed the child? The guests are arriving soon. Put her in that pink choli, it highlights her fair skin. We want you to be on your best behaviour, Aarti. Mr Ramlal, a scout for Divas, the leading child modelling agency in Bangalore, is coming.' Her mother scrutinises her closely, 'What's that in your mouth? Not eating are you? Do you want to end up fat? No modelling for you then. You'll ruin all your chances.'

Aarti's stomach feels hollow. She rushes to the bathroom and rinses the remains of the samosa from her mouth. She tries being sick but nothing comes. The balloons are dropped on the carpet and forgotten, the air escaping them in a hopeless sigh as they lie there reduced to mere deflated skins. Blue, pink and yellow tongues that have lost their puff.

Tara washes her; she scrubs Aarti's face until it glows. She dresses her in the pink choli that emphasises the fairness of her skin. At the party, Aarti glides amongst the adults with a poise she didn't know she possessed, instinctively imitating her mother. Even though this is a celebration for her birthday, there is no other child present. She is not sure which of the men she is introduced to is Mr Ramlal, but she is polite to everyone, answering all their many questions. She laughs along with the adults, she says amusing things which make them smile, she clinks her glass of soda against their glasses filled with wine and beer.

At the table, she is so tired that her head is in danger of falling into her plate a couple of times. Her mother pinches her lightly both times and she startles awake, smiles at the guests. She pushes the food around on her plate, not eating a thing. She talks slightly louder than normal to hide the rude noises her hungry stomach makes. She thanks everyone graciously for her gifts.

And she thinks it has all gone splendidly, but when the last guest leaves, her father turns to her and the look on his face tells her she has done something wrong. 'Mr Ramlal said to wait a year,' he huffs.

Her mother is assessing Aarti, her expression grave. 'You really must stop eating between meals, Aarti. I will have to tell those servants to stop feeding you.'

Her father's voice is tight, clipped. 'We'll find another agency. We'll prove him wrong.'

Aarti retreats into her room, allows Tara to take off her clothes, dress her in pyjamas and tuck her into bed.

'Am I fat?' she asks and Tara looks startled for a brief minute and then her face softens.

'Of course not, madam, you are perfect,' she smiles.

Aarti's stomach rumbles loudly in the soft silence of the room and Tara asks, 'Have you not eaten, madam? Shall I get you something?'

Aarti's mouth waters as she imagines eating the paneer kurma that she loves – the sweetness of coconut mingling perfectly with the delectable richness of the cheese, with rasgullas for afters, juicy syrup oozing and dribbling down her chin. Her mother's face floats before her eyes, her expression hard: 'You should stop eating between meals.'

'Can you sleep here tonight?' She asks Tara instead, holding her hand, not letting go.

Something crosses Tara's face, an expression that Aarti cannot name but has seen before, on the security guard's face when he shoos away the beggars who congregate at the gate, their worn lungis and concave stomachs, their scrawny hands poking through the bars, palms outward. The security guard lifts his stick and says 'Shoo', but Aarti can see that his heart is not in it. And the beggars know it as well. It is the expression on his face, like he is about to cry, like he is hurting deeply inside, hurting on behalf of the beggars.

Aarti has seen the security guard sigh and dig in his own pockets for change to give them.

'Listen, I shouldn't be doing this, encouraging you lot. I could get into serious trouble,' he has said, looking furtively around and Aarti has surreptitiously squeezed deeper into the rose bush from whence she is spying on him, the sharp tingle of being pricked, blood sprouting as red as the roses on the shrub, the heady fragrance mixed in with the tang of rust filling her nose and reminding her, longingly, of rose water flavoured Rooh Afza, making her already parched throat sting more than the naked skin of her arms which is being punctured in a thousand places sporting tiny, perfectly conical droplets of blood, like she is wearing polka-dotted sleeves, red on brown.

Aarti knows somehow that whatever Tara is feeling for her now is the same feeling the beggars arouse in the security guard. A flush of shame blooms scarlet on her food-starved skin. A servant feeling like that about *her*, the mistress of the house. How dare Tara have the temerity, when Aarti has everything! Everything.

Rage bubbles inside her, briefly, blessedly pushing aside the hunger pangs she has kept at bay all evening which are even now gnawing away at her insides, making her yearn for another samosa, a ladoo, a piece of her birthday cake: chocolate and cream, so light and melt-in-the-mouth, it is like eating chocolate-flavoured air. She pulls her hand away from Tara's.

'Get out,' she says, coolly, imperiously, using the same tone of voice her mother uses on her, Aarti, most of the time.

And as she watches Tara leave, Aarti makes up her mind to never again put herself in a situation where a servant feels anything at all for her except envy.

The next morning, after a night spent tossing and turning, equal parts hunger and anger warring with a roiling shame, she goes downstairs and informs her parents that she doesn't like Tara anymore. She does not give a reason and her parents do not ask for one. Tara is sacked, another servant brought in her place. Aarti does not allow herself to get close to this woman and after six months she makes sure she is replaced.

Aarti forces herself to eat nothing at all between meals and the bare minimum at meal times. She gets used to the aggravating pangs of her stomach, the growling and the complaining, grows to welcome it. She is snapped up by the second best modelling agency in Karnataka barely weeks after her seventh birthday and, thanks to her success, this agency shoots straight to the top, displacing the agency that rejected her.

Aarti's face is everywhere, smiling down from billboards, grinning from body lotion tubes and baby powder cartons, cough medicine bottles and posters advocating fairness creams. She is voted the cutest child in Karnataka, the best, the most loved. She haunts the rooms of her silent house, stopping at mirrors to check her reflection for any offending ounces of extra fat, assessing herself, critically, like her mother does. She pauses at the steadfastly shut door to her mother's room, willing it to open. She dares to enter her father's empty study to which she's denied entry when he's present, and breathes in the musky, officious smell that lingers, a phantom presence in lieu of her father. She has servant after servant replace Tara until of course, until…Vani.

Chapter 11
Vani – Childhood
Dhonihalli, India

Spinning Eddies

Vani wakes as usual when their neighbour Charu's cock crows intermittently and Dodo butts his head against the kitchen door, wanting breakfast, whining all the while, a funeral dirge. Her da's snores erupting in fits and snorts every so often travel down to Vani from the wooden bench, which he tops with blankets and old saris and has used as a bed ever since the floor became too much for his complaining back to handle. Her ma lies beside Vani, mouth slightly open, lips twitching in a half-smile.

In the years to come, Vani will look back often on this moment, and she will wish with all her heart that she had held on to it for longer, savoured it, relished the succour, the comfort of being bracketed by the soft, warm commas of her parents' bodies, instead of wanting to get up, get on with her life, impatient in the way only a child can be.

As if she can sense that Vani is awake, her ma stirs and then, yawning, smiles down at Vani, her eyes crinkling, affording Vani a glimpse into the dark cave of her mouth, her red tonsils, her spotted pinkish-white tongue.

'So, you know what to do today?' Ma whispers, so as not to wake Da.

Vani's parents are attending a wedding in the village across the river. They will be late back. Vani is to go to Charu's after school and wait for them.

'Yes, Ma,' Vani sighs and her ma puts a warm finger smelling of sleep to Vani's lips.

'Shh…You'll wake Da. He doesn't have to work today. Let him sleep.'

Later, Vani will try to recall what sari her ma was wearing that morning. Somehow it will be of utmost importance to her to remember that one fact. She will wish with all her heart that she had taken the time to notice.

Her mother turns to her, brushes the hair off Vani's face and smiles down at her, but Vani impatiently swipes her hand away. She wants the day to start. It is going to be exciting, different. She is looking forward to it.

And so, she stands and stretches. Dodo scratches the kitchen door. Suprabhatam Bhajans start playing in Charu's house, the tinny sound drifting in through the open windows on air scented with night jasmine and a hint of rain.

Da's snores sputter to a halt and he opens his eyes, sees Vani looming over him, and smiles. 'Up already?' he asks.

She is their only child. Everyone in the village bemoans this cruel twist of fate. They wail to Vani's parents, 'You should have had a son to carry on the family name,' and her parents bristle, pull Vani close, their voices sharp and designed to discourage further chat as they say, 'We would have Vani over a son any day.'

'Your daughter is the one who stays by you; you lose a son to his wife,' her mother is fond of telling anyone who will listen.

Their little family is happy; they are content even though they don't have much. Vani's father ploughs other people's fields, coaxes other people's crops to grow for a living. His burning ambition is to own a field one day. He is a quiet, softly-spoken man, a rarity in their village where they are all so loud, where they compete with each other to be heard. He loves Vani and he loves her mother and is not afraid to show it, again unlike the other men who hit their wives and children regularly, yelling at them at the slightest provocation.

That morning, as her da wakes and smiles bleary-eyed at her, Vani hears the thoo of Charu spitting just outside their house. Charu stands beneath the coconut tree which demarcates their compound from hers every morning, scrubbing her teeth with mango leaves.

'So do you want dosa or idli for breakfast today?' Ma asks, but Vani's reply – masala dosa – is drowned by a scuffle outside. A sharp scream. Dodo's frantic barks. The agitated rustling of leaves. A swish and a thud.

'Aiyyo Devare,' Charu's anguished voice drifts in above the wails of the Suprabhatam Bhajans. 'Aiyyo, I have been bitten by a snake! Help!'

Charu must have stumbled into that nest of leaves underneath the guava tree, the favourite haunt of the snake that resides there, snuggling in the wet mulch. She must have inadvertently stepped on it, it must have struck.

Ma runs outside, closely followed by Da who is frantically knotting his lungi, Vani hot on their heels. Charu is prone amongst the leaves, sobbing, holding her leg, bent at the knee, the snake long gone. Da carries Charu inside and Ma rushes down the hill in her nightie, unkempt morning hair flying behind her, a brown dot amongst the emerald fields, to fetch Dhooma, who owns a rickshaw, to convey Charu to the hospital in Udupi.

Her ma and da hurriedly wave Vani off to school, telling her to stay with Nagappa's wife until they return home from the wedding, if Charu is still at the hospital when school is finished. They carry an ashen-faced Charu up to the waiting rickshaw and Vani skips off amongst the fields, waving a quick goodbye, not even bothering to note the colour of her mother's sari, her father's lungi.

When she goes to collect her tiffin box for lunch, Sister Carmelita comes for her. Like all the village offspring, Vani attends the local convent school, the only school for miles around, operated on the charity of the nuns. Sister Carmelita's face is grave, her eyes struggle to keep a lid on the emotion that is threatening to erupt out of them and explode onto her visage. Vani's giggling, shoving classmates go silent, wondering who is to be called up. Sister Carmelita's eyes shine, they glisten, and for a brief minute, the leather-skinned, pimpled nun looks almost beautiful. Sister's voice is as soft as Vani's mother's arms when she says, 'Here, Vani, come with me.'

Fear makes a stranglehold of Vani's chest and she frantically goes through her movements of the morning, wondering what she has done wrong. She does not want to be in trouble with the nuns, nobody does. It means whacks with a wooden ruler on naked palms, instantly sprouting blisters, and kneeling on cold cement floors for the better part of the day, subjecting bare knees to torture, and reciting Hail Marys and Our Fathers from the worn prayer book – never mind that you are a Hindu.

Vani hops to keep in step beside Sister Carmelita, her mind taking an inventory of her sins of that morning. During Kannada lesson, she was told off for talking but so were Dinesh and Radhika. Is it the compass she 'borrowed' from Sunaina without asking perhaps? She was planning to give it back that afternoon. She watches the nun's long strides eating up the ground, her habit whispering around her legs, swish, swish, almost like the sound a cane makes as it whooshes through the air just before it comes into contact with flesh. Vani bites her lip and tastes rust, the black roiling flavour of dread. Salty sobs threaten.

Together, Vani and Sister Carmelita enter the nun's hallowed office where pupils are allowed only if they have done something very good or very bad, and there stand Father Vincent *and* Mother Rita grouped in front of the statue of the Holy Family, their faces sombre. Now Vani *knows* she has done something horrible. The tears she has been holding back explode, ignoring the admonishment from her sensible self that she is too old for them, and they cascade down her face in briny gashes.

'Does she know?' Mother Rita asks, her voice loud in the heavy grey silence.

'I didn't tell her,' Sister Carmelita whispers.

Mother Rita comes round the barricade of the table, kneels beside Vani and envelops her shuddering body in her arms. 'Why are you crying?' she asks softly.

'I was going to give the compass back,' Vani gulps out between sobs.

'Oh, darling, it's not about the compass,' Mother Rita whispers, sitting herself down right there on the floor with a creaking of knees and a swooshing of voluminous skirts. 'You have done nothing wrong,' she says, smoothing Vani's hair.

And Mother Rita holds Vani in the nest of her arms as she imparts the news that is to change Vani's life forever in a voice weary beyond words, and after, Vani will always associate these things – the musty aroma of sweat and mothballs, the hefty arms encircling her, the taste of salt and the memory of a borrowed compass, Mother Rita's rosary, the harness of the beads, the sharp ends of the cross poking into Vani's cheeks as she holds Vani's rocking body, as she sobs right along with Vani – with unfathomable, unendurable grief.

Afterwards there is a conference. All the elders of the village meet to decide Vani's fate. She is not aware of this. She is suffering nightmares from having been taken to look at the bloated, fish-nibbled bodies that she is told are her parents. She yells and screams so much that she is not taken to the cremation. But she can imagine how it happens. She can see it in her mind's eye. So clear. Even though she does not attend.

She sees the crematorium nestling snug beside the river that stole her parents, the expanse of calm sapphire giving no indication of the carnage it perpetrated just days before. Two wooden pyres, side by side, flanked by the desolate huddle of villagers. The swollen effigies that masquerade as Vani's ma and da sandwiched between the stacks of wood that make up her parents' last bed on this earth. She sees the chief village elder, Nagappa, walking towards the pyre, pouring kerosene over the two mounds. A match is struck, and doused instantly in the brisk wind that has started up. Nagappa strikes another match, which flickers but does not die. He holds it to a stick whose mouth is tied with white cloth smothered in kerosene. A flash, staining the air golden yellow as the stick catches fire.

It is evening, that hour just before twilight, the sky the dusky pink of newborn skin. Gulls circle. Crows cackle. The air smells of death and sorrow, of wasted lives and abandoned hope. A cloud obscures the setting sun, a sudden shadow cast on the mourning crowd swathed in the white of woe.

A breeze roils the mud, it swirls red and accusing. It almost extinguishes the light. Before it can go out, Nagappa touches the makeshift torch to the twin pyres. They are alight almost at once, the flames licking and dancing, bright orange and gold. The pyres slowly disintegrate, auburn flames pirouetting towards the rainbow-hued sky now obscured by thick, blue-grey clouds. The mourners shiver as the clouds shed tears bemoaning lives plucked at their peak, a weak rain trying and failing to douse the flames. A dog barks somewhere, mournful, punctuating the eerie silence that has fallen over a village that is never quiet.

It is dusk when the villagers leave, in clumps of twos and threes, propping each other up, husks of exhausted grief, their white mundus flapping like ghosts, shimmering in the darkness, the sky the exact shade of the soggy mess of charred ash and the couple of half-burnt twigs which is all that remains of Vani's parents.

While the villagers are at the cremation, Vani hides. Amongst her mother's saris and her father's clothes. Breathing in their smell, imagining their arms encircling her, the feeling of safety, of being anchored, cushioned by the opening and closing brackets of their bodies. She refuses to acknowledge that the bloated bodies the boatmen dragged out of the river, gorged on by fish, are her parents. They are coming back, they have promised. And so she hides from the truth, hides from herself. She breathes in the faint whiff of their smell which lingers in their clothes and she remembers, memories engulfing her, enveloping her, warming her.

Cremation – take the *M* away and it becomes creation. Years later, when she has learnt English and is proficient in it, she will wonder how those two words, life and death, could be separated by just one letter. Because it is that easy to lose someone, she supposes. Blink and they are gone. When you go to school, you have parents who love you, whose life revolves around you, and by lunchtime, you are an orphan.

Sitting among their things, she pictures their last moments. Chattering to the boatman – her mother was never silent. The boatman laughing, his smiling visage morphing into a grimace as the boat jerks suddenly and he falls backward from standing, almost losing his grip on the wooden paddle. The boat dizzying as it is trapped in the throes of a whirlpool, sucked into its spinning eddies. Turning and tossing like a little plaything. Vani's parents' eyes meeting, the distress in them. Both of them, thinking, at that minute of Vani. The smell of fear; feeling the years they will not live slipping through their hands; the sound of everything they have yet to experience reverberating in their ears. The flavour of water: as pure as lives unlived, as fresh as decades unsullied by experience. The taste of lost moments, of all that remains unsaid choking them as water floods into their mouth, as it insinuates everywhere, laying claim; the swirling vortex that will choke the breath out of them, dragging them into its depths, their last breath a desperate prayer for the daughter they have left at home.

Vani huddles into her mother's saris and hopes it was quick. She wishes. She prays.

Afterwards, she is swaddled in myriad arms and learns to identify from the different shades of sweat, the textures of skin, the bones digging into her, which of the village matrons is holding her. She does not understand – or chooses not to – when they hit their heads and murmur,

'Aiyyo, what to do with this one? They had nothing. The house is not theirs. They own not a pie.'

Vani knows, even though she wishes she didn't, that although she is related to every single person in the village, none of them can afford to keep her. How will they provide for her when they struggle to provide for their own? How will they get her married, with whose dowry? She is a girl, a burden that even the most well-meaning do not want to shoulder.

And so, while they try and locate distant relatives, hoping to find someone who will assume responsibility for Vani, she shivers in a corner enduring the women cosseting her. She chokes on the rice gruel they feed her, trying to squeeze it down past the constriction in her throat, the swollen, nibbled bodies of her parents floating before her eyes. Whose idea was it that she should look at them, those bodies? She cannot remember. It is custom for loved ones to pay their respects. And, blindsided by grief, she obeyed custom – the disbelieving part of her wanting to prove everyone wrong by yelling jubilantly, 'These are not my parents! You have made a mistake,' – not knowing then that what she would see would taint the image of her parents that she carried within her, would haunt her for the rest of her life.

She doesn't think she can sleep. Yet she must do. For every morning she wakes as usual when Charu's cock crows and Dodo butts his head against the kitchen door. For a blessed minute, she is stuck in that dreamy state between sleep and waking and all is well in her world. She fancies that she can hear Da's snores, his mouth wide open, a welcome receptor, she's always joked, for lizards which lose their balance on the woodlice ridden beams above. She imagines she can hear her ma's soft breaths escape from between pursed lips, phut phut phut. Eyes still closed, she feels beside her for her ma's comforting arm and is nudged instead by the twig-like shoulders of Aunt Shimy. And memory nudges in as dreams are chased away by her conscious self; wakefulness arrives and with it, sorrow. The heavy weight of it sitting tight on her chest, robbing her of breath. And even before she opens her eyes, shut tight to block out the honeyed light which inveigles under closed lids, a mellow turmeric glow warming her eyelids, she knows. Her ma and da are not here. She is alone, bereft.

A month after their death, the village elders come visiting. They look grave and they arrive en masse, and she figures something has been decided. In a way, she is relieved. She knows that she cannot live like this. She does not want to live here, constantly bombarded by what was, haunted by the very last image of her parents floating in front of her eyes. She wants to go away. Far away from this place of her birth contaminated now by grief, steeped in loss.

And so, when they tell her that they are sending her to Bangalore, that her distant relatives there have agreed to take her on as a servant, she is relieved.

'You will be staying in a mansion,' Nagappa, the chief village elder says, trying to sell her their plans for her future, not knowing that she has already made up her mind.

The elders desperately want to feel that they are doing the right thing by Vani, she knows, but she understands also that they are relieved to be rid of the terrible burden and responsibility of looking after her. By listing all the points in favour of this opportunity, they are convincing themselves as much as they are Vani.

'These people are millionaires, the elite of Bangalore. You are very distantly related to them.' Nagappa clears his throat; he is obviously saving the best for last. 'And you know the Fair and Lovely model?'

She doesn't know and doesn't much care but she nods by rote and her head feels heavy as it moves up and down, up and down.

'She is their child! Your second cousin twice removed.' Enthusiasm colours his voice. He pauses, looking askance at her and Vani realises he is waiting for her to say something.

'Great,' she says and her voice is as dry as the river during the drought. At the thought of the river, a wall of pain assaults her. She shuts her eyes, rocks on her feet, a desolate involuntary keen escaping her mouth as she waits for the wave of hurt to pass. Waves, rivers, she is battered on all sides. Not for the first time, she wishes she had drowned with them. She has wished for this ever since she heard. As it is, she is drowning, drowning in the hurt that wells up within her, that cannot be assuaged except by the tangible feeling of being enveloped in her parents' arms.

Nagappa is looking desperately to his band of followers for help. One of the women comes forward, puts her arms around Vani. Padded shoulders, the smell of fried onions, and, she is sinking, like her parents did that fateful morning. Unlike her parents, however, for her there is no oblivion as she suffocates in the press of unfamiliar arms.

Nagappa clears his throat again as his cue to continue. 'You are to leave the day after tomorrow. I will take you there. They will look after you well. There are a lot of servants, so what is required of you will be minimal. In return, they will feed you, clothe you, give you a place to stay. They are very kind; the lodging servants stay *inside* the house, with them and not in a separate outhouse. And, I am told, their house is so huge that each of the servants gets a room to themselves – talk about generosity! But you will never want for company – as I said, there are plenty of servants. And when you come of age, they have promised me that they will find you someone suitable to marry. Don't you worry about that.' He says all of this in a rush as if to forestall another keening, rocking session from Vani.

She listens through the whooshing in her ears. She is conscious of a feeling of relief when she hears that she will have a job to do where she is going. This way, she can keep busy as a means of keeping the sorrow at bay, and at the same time she will not feel too beholden to her benefactors – the only ones amongst her hordes of relatives who have agreed to take her on, albeit as a servant.

'Their daughter, the model, is not much older than you in fact.' Vani watches Nagappa's mouth form the words, the little drops of spittle that collect at the edge of his lips, tinged red with the remnants of paan he must have chewed before coming here. He stops, gathers his breath, lowers his voice an octave. 'Her name is Aarti Kumar.' His voice full of awe. His eyes gleaming as if he expects the entire world to have heard of her.

The name means nothing to Vani except, now, an escape route.

Aarti Kumar, Vani thinks, *here I come.*

Chapter 12
Aarti – Childhood
Bangalore, India

Weighty Procession

Aarti has just completed her first ever photo shoot and it has been a huge success. She has been pampered and praised, her every whim indulged. Her bone structure has been declared exquisite, her eyes divine. She has drunk fizzy Coca-Cola until she cannot take a breath without a bubble escaping her mouth, and she has been very good and not eaten even a bite of the feast of sweetmeats and chocolates brought in just for her. She is so animated she cannot sit still, bouncing on the polished leather seat of the car that is conveying her home, bouncing free of the restraining hand of the servant who has accompanied her to the shoot. The car smells new, of wrapping paper and the promise of presents, she muses as she tries desperately to keep a lid on the excitement that threatens to fizz up out of her along with the treasure trove of bubbles from all that Coca-Cola.

Once home, Aarti stands in front of the closed door to her mother's room, polished walnut with figures of deities carved onto it, breathing in the tangy smell of varnish. Her father is not home, as per usual. He is always out working. She experiences a moment's brief hesitation as she remembers her myriad previous attempts to get her mother to come out of the room, to notice her. They always, inevitably, end in disaster. *Not this time,* she convinces herself, as she has done all those other times, hope triumphing over futile reality as ever. This time she has done something that will surely please her parents. After all, isn't this what her parents have always wanted for her? And the photographer at the shoot said she was a natural, one of the best child models they had ever had.

When her mother hears about the shoot, she will flash one of her rare smiles, Aarti decides. She might even say, 'Well done!' The thought gives her courage.

She tries the doorknob, as she has done hundreds of times before, unsuccessfully every time. This time, by some miracle, she finds it unlocked. Taking it as a sign that her mother wants to see her, has been waiting to hear her news, she rushes inside and flings herself at her mother where she is lying on the bed, curtains drawn. 'Amma, I was a great success! They loved me, said I was the…'

The icy look on her mother's face makes her words dry up, causes her lower lip to wobble.

'How dare you enter without knocking first and asking permission?' her mother snaps, each word a grenade. 'Go back, close the door and try again.'

She does as she's told, walking on jelly legs, closing the door quietly behind her. She knocks timidly at first and then louder.

Her mother denies her entry. 'I am busy now – try again later,' her mother calls in that tone of voice she uses for servants.

And Aarti's perfect day is spoiled, irrevocably and completely. She is sick over the toilet bowl – the bilious taste of bubbles and deflated excitement and unappeased hurt, the acrid stink of rejection – trying and failing to purge the feeling of being unwanted, unloved, a nuisance.

❅ ❅ ❅

A year later. Her mother is in the garden, taking tea with a friend, hibiscus flowers nodding in the perfumed air, fragrant jasmine bushes dispensing secrets along with nectar to the gossiping bees. The servants have carried a table and some chairs down from the house and have set up an awning in the shady west lawn in the shadow of the jackfruit and mango trees. They have brought a pot of tea, a jug of milk, ladoos and Mysore Paks, soan papdi and doodh peda, onion bhajis and kachoris – freshly prepared, oozing steam and invitingly spicy scents – from the kitchen, and arranged them on the table along with a vase of flowers; a profusion of red, yellow and pink roses, the heady aroma wafting up to Aarti's hiding place.

Aarti has given the servant looking after her the slip and crept downstairs. She is crouching amongst the aboli bushes, breathing in the zesty scent of fruit ripening in the sun, flies noisily flitting around her, turquoise butterflies with red spots alighting on the orange flowers, dragonflies with translucent wings humming. Tucked cosily inside her hiding place, eavesdropping on the murmur of leaves nodding in the soft yellow breeze, the conversation of insects, following the weighty procession of ants to their anthill under the banyan tree a world away, basking in the drowsy afternoon as it tilts towards evening, the reddish brown haze of dust in her eyes, her head propped on the tray of her drawn, bony knees, spying on her mother and her friend, she is happy.

Somewhere in the bowels of the house, the servant in charge of Aarti is searching for her. Aarti can just hear her cries, faint as water gurgling at the bottom of the well, 'Madam, Aarti madam, where are you?'

Aarti swallows down a giggle. Her stomach rumbles and the bushes whisper reprimands as she crawls closer to where her mother and her friend are sitting, shrubs closing ranks around her, the green smell of burgeoning life and the brown earthy odour of mud assailing her nose. Aarti stays very still and she listens.

'She is the top model in Karnataka now. Next, she'll conquer India.' The hint of pride in her mother's voice makes Aarti's chest swell with joy. Her mother's voice drops to a whisper and Aarti leans closer. 'You know, I didn't really want kids.'

Aarti sits still as the Buddha statue on the mantelpiece in the drawing room, the stones in the mud digging into her feet, the thorns from the bushes biting into her. She thinks that is the reason why she feels the prickle of tears stinging her eyes.

'Dev was okay with that?' her mother's friend asks.

The hiss of tea being poured, the clink of tea pot, the chatter of china. 'Shall I send for more tea?'

'No, I'm fine.'

From the house drift faint cries like the jangling of temple bells floating on the wind, 'Aarti ma'am,' a sing-song voice. 'Time for your tea.'

But Aarti's hunger is gone, replaced by a different hunger, a hunger that quivers with fear, afraid to hear more and yet wanting to.

Her mother's voice lowers to a growl, 'I told him I couldn't have kids.'

'No!' The friend's voice shocked.

'No need to sound so upset. He loved me, wanted to marry me anyway. And I relented didn't I?'

'Why didn't you want kids?'

'Oh.' Aarti watches her mother pat her flat stomach, the stomach that housed her not so very long ago. 'The havoc they cause to a woman's body. As it is, I have never gone back to the way I was before,' her mother's voice, martyred.

'You look all right to me.'

Her mother laughs, pleased. Silvery tinkle of wind chimes. 'It's been a lot of work. I must admit, I was so disappointed when the only child I conceded to having turned out to be a girl.' A pause and then, 'Want a peda? This new cook makes the best pedas in Bangalore.'

'No thanks. Any more and I'll explode.'

A bee buzzes close to Aarti's face. She bats at it and it swoops. A prick, sharp as a nail gouging into a wall in an explosion of plaster. The pain is excruciating and it takes every ounce of strength Aarti possesses not to cry out. Tears fall silently down her face, insinuating themselves into the gap between her closed lips, tasting of salt and mud.

'I almost died after she was born, you know. Lost so much blood. I was right: kids didn't agree with me. After that, Dev didn't pester me again. He – we – had to be happy with what we got. At least she's pretty; we could have done a lot worse. But she does like her food. We are constantly curbing that. She cannot be doing any modelling if she's overweight. Takes after my mother. Fat as the Mysore dam, my mother.'

Somewhere a dog howls, a mournful whine of complaint. Aarti's hand is fat and getting fatter by the minute, swollen with the poison of the bee sting. She sniffs as quietly as possible, the taste of snot and salt. She spits on her palm, trying to ease the pain, bubbly saliva sluggishly spreading, frothy cream on exacerbated red skin. The tears, hot and enflamed as a gaping wound keep on coming.

'Aarti's thin as a runner bean – what are you saying?' her mother's friend exclaims.

'Yes, well. She has to maintain it. The servants spoil her; I am constantly having to yell at them to not give her fried food and all those snacks they keep shoving down her throat.'

Aarti's legs are cramped. She moves them surreptitiously and the leaves swish. She freezes in place, worried her mother might catch her out. If the women hear a rustling in the bushes behind them, they ignore it, sipping their tea and not eating the snacks.

Aarti's face is wet. Her hand throbs. She sits there while her mother and her friend move on to other topics. She sits there until the cries from the house die down. She sits there until her mother and her friend move away and servants come running behind them to clear away the tea things and transport the chairs and table back to the house. She sits there until the sun's buttery rays, which filter through the canopy of trees, morph from scorching gold to mellow orange, until the fragments of blue visible above the green leafy awning darken to an uncompromising navy spattered with grey, like smudges in a child's painting. She sits there, cradling her sore hand until blue shadows dance upon her brown body and stain the red dust the dark black of dried blood.

She does not eavesdrop on her mother again. And she does not enter her mother's room with or without permission, or rush to greet her when she gets home again either. Except the once…

She is a teenager – just. Thirteen and a bit, long and gangly, her arms and legs out of proportion with her growing body. She has long since accepted that her mother is not one for hugs. And as for her father…tall, moustachioed, a big man with a personality to match. Always working, never there. He rarely smiles, the upward lift of his lips barely displacing the displeased frown that has taken up permanent residence on his face.

'The papers declare Anjali the new up-and-coming model, dubbed to be the Face of India. Why not you?' Looking at Aarti over the top of his glasses, his gaze disappointed as it so often is where she is concerned.

Aarti is a sum total of her achievements for her parents. A plus for every good thing she does, a minus for everything she doesn't do or has yet to do. The minus side always, without question, trumping the plus, so she is permanently striving to redress the balance.

She has long since learned to wrap her arms around herself when she feels the urge for human contact. And yet, today that doesn't suffice. She has been feeling ill and out of sorts all day and when she visits the loo, she discovers that she has started her period. And even though she knows to expect it, has been waiting for it in fact, the sight of all that blood gushing out of her freaks her out. Her back aches, her head hurts. She needs reassurance, a kind word from someone close to her, not an impersonal massage from a servant paid to heed Aarti's every request, doing what is needed by rote while escaping in her head, a faraway look in her eyes.

All of the servants are the same. They do not like Aarti because she bosses them around, is strident with them and sacks them without fail after six months. After the debacle with Tara when she was seven, Aarti will not make herself vulnerable, open to a servant's pity. She cannot fathom anything worse. And so she cultivates her reputation and sticks to it. It hasn't done her any favours, especially now when tears threaten and she aches for someone to talk to, someone to listen, someone to care.

She waits, endures her loneliness until she hears her mother's car. Then she runs downstairs, uncharacteristically, and when the door is flung open and her mother enters smelling of her expensive perfume and the outdoors, two servants following hefting her many shopping bags, Aarti flings herself at her.

A look of intense distaste crosses her mother's face. 'What are you doing, Aarti?' she screeches, pushing Aarti away.

But Aarti resists, holding on to her mother, crying her heart out. 'I am aching, Amma, I hurt. I started my period today.'

If anything, the distaste on her mother's face is even more pronounced. She shoves Aarti away roughly. 'There is no need to make such a scene,' she spits out, her mouth set in a line, 'especially not in front of the servants. And you are creasing my clothes.'

And with that, Aarti's mother storms upstairs, her entourage of servants following, and locks herself in her room without another word to Aarti, never once looking back at her.

Aarti vows then, standing shattered at the bottom of the stairs as servants scuttle around her, carefully avoiding her gaze, that if she ever has children, she will strive to have a loving relationship with them, even though she has not had much experience with either giving or receiving love. She will show her children that she cares for them. She will let them know that they are *wanted*, that they are the *most* important thing in her life, not the *least* important. She will.

Chapter 13
Vani – Arrival in Bangalore

Dispatches from an Inferior Universe

Bangalore is throbbing with noise, swollen with people. It assaults Vani's senses; it crowds out the pain and emptiness yawning inside her, which is a good thing.

Hawkers thrust their goods at her, aggressively wanting her to buy dusty flowers, multihued glass bangles with gold engravings, garish plastic toys. The smell of earth and hot oil competes with the odour of decomposing vegetables and rotting blossoms. A woman sits behind a little stall displaying vibrant yellow piles of turmeric, mounds of greenish brown coriander powder, a tower of chilli powder the shiny crimson of the kumkum her ma used to wear… Her mother's beautiful face, her eyes shining with love, floats briefly before Vani's eyes only to be replaced by the bloated caricature the villagers dragged out of the river.

Grime swirls, dirty red, noise crescendos, vehicles honk and threaten to run Vani over, a rickshaw almost scraping her leg, and Nagappa, who has accompanied her to the city, yells, 'Lo!'

The rickshaw is long gone, careering over potholes, the driver turning back to grin lasciviously at Vani. Nagappa shakes his fist at him. 'Keep your eyes on the road in front of you,' he shouts in Kannada before resuming squinting at the address from over the top of his spectacles which sit awkwardly on his nose and gleam with a coating of dust, his face shiny with suspended sweat globules. A lone shimmering globule wobbles off his chin and is absorbed into the twirling dirt.

People urinate by the side of the road, standing companionably side by side, their lungis hitched up, chewing paan and gossiping as they do their business. Cows join them, lifting their tails with a swish and depositing warm brown spatters of dung right onto the middle of the rutted road. An auto drives over the dung droppings, sketching coffee patterns upon the dust.

'Not much longer,' Nagappa says, his voice weary with the effort it is taking to find the house. 'Must be right here.'

He has asked two or three people for directions since he and Vani got off the bus and each one has given a different answer. He looks tired and flustered, sweaty and in need of a cool drink and a seat.

Vani is assaulted by a sudden pang for green swathes of fields billowing in the sun, the quiet gentleness of the village that has been home all her life, punctuated here and there by the cawing of crows, the barking of dogs and the laughter of people who have known each other since childhood. One dust road runs through the village, dotted by a smattering of huts on either side and flanked by the river where the villagers wash their clothes and bathe and fish, that fateful river that turned on them, claiming Vani's parents for its own…

All at once a high compound wall, topped by glinting blue and auburn shards of glass put there to deter burglars, materialises up ahead. There is an imposing iron gate which Nagappa rattles, and a khaki-clad watchman appears, looking at them appraisingly. Vani looks away. Nagappa gives him the letter, points to Vani, tells the watchman that she is the new servant they are expecting. Another assessing look. Vani makes herself very small, hides away in the confines of her mind.

Then the gate is opening with a deafening screech and they are inside and it is as if the noise and bustle have melted away and they are in paradise, a completely different world to the mess and chaos just beyond the wall.

A wide expanse of garden looms, dotted by gardeners who douse the greenery, which is as stridently uniform as the fields in Vani's village are cheerfully haphazard, with pumps gushing silvery waterfalls. Like the watchman, the gardeners too assess Vani curiously as she walks past.

The grounds are endless, the sun bakes her head, the quiet is uneasy, forced, as if it is levied against its will. Sounds drift in over the high wall from outside every once in a while, dispatches from an inferior universe.

Just when Vani opens her mouth to ask Nagappa if they can stop for a bit so she can gather her breath, the mansion emerges ahead. Daunting, huge like a prison, she thinks and immediately shoos the thought away. And yet, even though the house looks grand and beautiful, like something one might find amongst the pages of books, it gives her the creeps. She shivers as Nagappa reaches up, rings the bell and an incongruous nursery rhyme reverberates within the bowels of the house.

A servant opens the door, leads them into a room huge enough to house all the inhabitants of Vani's village. Chandeliers sparkle, ornaments gleam; everywhere there's evidence of great wealth. It is like being in a museum, or a palace where nobody lives. The servant moves noiselessly, disappearing somewhere inside the house.

Nagappa and Vani exchange glances. He looks impressed, awed.

'This is where you will be living,' he says, and there is envy and self-congratulation in his voice.

Take me back, Vani thinks. *This place scares me.*

The woman who comes down the stairs is regal and has a brittle, inaccessible beauty, the kind that one sees but does not experience. Unbidden, her mother's smiling face rises before Vani's eyes and she sways on her feet as it is immediately replaced by the bloated effigy. It is only when Nagappa nudges her that she realises the woman is addressing her.

'So you are Vani,' the woman says, her voice making Vani feel as if she is being steeped in icy water.

Her gaze evaluates Vani, taking her in, from top to muddy toe, and Vani is ashamed of herself; her dirty, dust-encrusted clothes, the grime on her cheap chappals which has stained the pristine floors of this hallowed room, her dishevelled appearance.

'Hmm...you are younger than I expected, but you can help look after my daughter. Come, let me take you to her. She needs to be up and ready for her shoot.' The woman's voice is as cold as her looks, and just as distant.

Nagappa waves goodbye as Vani follows the woman up the intricate, winding staircase. Vani is trembling inside, very aware of how alone she is as the ornate front door closes silently behind Nagappa and all connection with her previous life is severed, just like that. She is now at the mercy of this woman and her famed daughter, the supermodel, Vani thinks, the reality of her situation, until now lost in the haze of missing her parents, dawning on her as she follows the woman's clackety heels up the stairs.

Vani has forgotten the daughter's name. Will they expect her to know? She shivers as she follows in the woman's wake along an endless corridor, beautiful sculpted wooden doors leading off either side.

At last the woman stops in front of a room and knocks. There is no answer from within. In a fit of impatience, the woman pushes open the door.

The room is huge and dark, and Vani blinks, trying to make out shapes in it. The woman clicks her tongue and walks up to the curtains, pulls them open. There is a sound, a whimper. Vani makes out a vast bed in the middle of the room, a mosquito net draping it gracefully. There is movement from within.

'Wake up, Aarti,' the woman huffs, her voice impatient.

Oh, her name is Aarti, Vani thinks, relieved. Though of course she cannot call her that. What *will* she call her? Ma'am? Yes, that sounds respectful. If she doesn't like it, the girl can correct her but at least this way she will not be insulted.

The girl mumbles. Even through the impediment of mosquito net, Vani can see that she is stunning, although perhaps a bit too thin. Her face looks flushed. She can barely open her eyes.

'You'll help her get ready for her shoot, won't you?' the woman asks of Vani and without waiting for an answer, flounces out of the room.

Chapter 14
Aarti – Meeting the Help

Sliver of Blue

Aarti wakes with a headache, sore throat – the works. Honeyed sunlight trickles in despite the barricade of curtains, assaulting her head, inflaming her face. She opens her mouth to yell for a servant but her throat is too raw. She is used to the soreness of course, it comes with being sick last thing every night, but today, along with it, she seems to have misplaced her voice. She has two photo shoots scheduled; she will have to cancel both she thinks, her head heavy. She closes her lids, which feel weighted down by hot bricks, and drifts in and out of a shallow, nightmare-infested sleep.

She is startled awake by the sound of a voice that is somehow out of place, the noise like cymbals clashing in her brain. She blinks, and the effort it takes to move her eyelids is immense. She is hot all over and yet, she is shivering inside. Is she dying?

'Wake up, Aarti,' the shrill not-in-the-right-context voice reverberates in her head. It jars and jolts as if someone is juggling hot bricks in her skull. 'Don't you have a photo shoot to go to? Do you know what the time is? 9:30! If you don't turn up, they'll give the contract to Nidhi. You know she's been angling for the top spot, don't you?'

Her mother. In her room! When was the last time her mother had deigned to enter her room? A year ago? Two? She cannot think. Her head feels heavy, too heavy. She just wants to sleep.

The curtains are drawn back with a screech that echoes in her hot, ailing head. Sunlight dances on her face, demanding entry behind weighted lids. She manages to lift a sluggish hand, scrabbling around blindly for a pillow to cover her face.

The next moment, golden orange spots of light abuse her closed eyes as the pillow is pulled away, hard. She is shaken harshly, rough fingers bruising tender skin.

'Wake up; you have to leave *now* if you are to make it. Oh, and here's the reason I came in search of you. This is Vani, your new servant. I have sacked Bhanu; she was useless that girl. Vani, make sure Aarti's up and ready for her shoot, won't you?'

And with that, she hears the swish of her mother's skirts, the bang of the door as it slams shut behind her – her mother never leaves a room without making a hell of a racket – Aarti experiencing the reverberations like a physical blow, her sore head screaming, feeling like there's an elephant sitting on it, crushing it.

She can sense the silence in the room settle like a soft sigh in the wake of her mother's departure. Once more, she gropes around for the pillow to pull back down over her aching eyes, bruised sorely, despite being shut tight, by the light streaming in through the window.

Soft hands cool on her face. A gentle voice filled with concern, 'Ma'am, you've got a fever, you are boiling.'

Tell me something I don't know, she thinks. 'Curtain,' she manages to whisper.

The feel of air in the room shifts, becomes cooler, lighter somehow, as the curtains are drawn.

'I'll see if I can get you some medicine, ma'am,' the voice says and she hears quiet footsteps exit the room.

'Wait,' she wants to say. 'Please. Stay with me. I need you. I need company.'

But it is too late. The door is opening with a quiet whine, a burst of noise – one of the servants calling for another – drifting in on a gust of air smelling of the imported coffee her father favours and the sandalwood air freshener the servants spray liberally through all the rooms of the house on her mother's orders. Somehow all her senses are on super alert; she can experience every ache in her sickly, throbbing body that feels like it has been battered, run over by a lorry.

She is afraid to fall asleep, to drift into that heavy state she has been flitting in and out of, pursued by dreams she cannot quite remember but which leave her terrified, gasping, her heart a living thing trapped in her rib cage, thundering for release.

She wants the person back, the new servant, anyone at all. She doesn't want to be alone. She wants her mother. A part of Aarti had imagined, hope blooming like the first rose of summer in her ailing chest, that her mother had come into her room because she somehow realised, with that instinct mothers are supposed to have, that all was not well with her daughter. That she had come to hold Aarti in her arms, nurse her better.

Why does she keep doing this to herself? Setting herself up for rejection over and over. When will she learn, she chides herself, her head and heart aching.

Just as she is drifting into a heavy stupor, Aarti feels a cloth, blessedly cool on her heavy forehead. She feels gentle hands cupping her face. And she marvels, her traitorous heart lifting joyously in the beleaguered prison of her chest, that her wish has come true. Her mother is here. Her mother has finally come when Aarti has needed her. Her mother loves her.

And then a soft voice says, 'Ma'am, open your mouth please, just a tiny bit, for me to slip these pills in.'

Aarti does as she's told, even though it hurts to move her jaw. She almost gags on the bitter pills. She savours the water that swiftly follows, deliciously cold on her hot, parched tongue. She swallows, pushing the medicine past her enflamed tonsils and tells herself that the scorching tears squeezing out from between her eyes and mingling with the wetness dripping from the cloth is because she is ill, that is all. Because she is so ill.

The new servant tends Aarti through her illness. She stays with her through the unending nights, when Aarti wakes up from nightmares wheezing and terrified, and is grateful for the shadowy figure beside her bed, offering comforting words and the warmth of her presence. The new servant bears witness to Aarti's ramblings and delirious mumblings, her soft hands administering medicine and cool cloths.

Aarti's mother does not come to check on her again.

On the third day of her illness – or is it the fourth? – Aarti opens her eyes which, blessedly, do not feel like paperweights any longer, and gets a good glimpse of the angel who has cared for her all this while. The girl is slumped on a chair beside her bed and is staring fixedly at the chink of light streaming in through the tiny gap in the curtains which dances on Aarti's bedspread, creating cream patterns in the dark stuffiness enveloping the room. The girl does not realise she is being watched; she is lost in her thoughts, her head inclined towards the window, eyes angling for a glimpse of sky as if she wants to escape into the heavens.

A slight shadow of a girl, long messy hair, dark circles under sunken eyes that reflect a torment that seems strangely familiar. Something about this girl speaks to Aarti. She too is hurting, Aarti realises suddenly. She too is lost, like Aarti. Somehow, looking at this girl's eyes, which gaze wistfully at the sliver of blue visible through the chink in the curtains, is like seeing herself – her pain, the turmoil that she keeps hidden so carefully reflected back at her. But how can this servant girl have anything in common with Aarti? Her illness is making her fantasise, spin stories out of nothing, make connections where there are none. She cannot get close to a servant. She cannot allow herself to be vulnerable in their eyes, in the eyes of anyone really. She is a supermodel, adored and envied by millions; she will not have anyone pity her, no.

'Who are you?' she asks, wincing internally at the coldness, the imperiousness in her voice.

The girl startles, her gaze jolting away from the perusal of the window to settle on Aarti's face.

'My name is Vani, ma'am.' The voice is soft and seemingly meek, but with a hint of iron in it.

'The cloth on my head is hot.' Aarti says, coolly.

Without a word, the girl starts sponging Aarti's forehead. Her expression hasn't changed but a hood has dropped over her eyes, like a door closing. They are empty now, devoid of emotion.

The room smells of stale air, heavy and weighted down with illness, thick, porous and swilling with germs. It tastes muddy brown, of remorse. Why is Aarti like this? Why can't she talk normally, without upsetting those around her? And since when did she start worrying about distressing a servant girl? This illness has made her soft in the head. First, she imagines connections that aren't there. And now she's feeling bad for asking the girl to do what she is paid to do!

'Open the window,' she commands, and the girl stands up to do as she is told.

Her new servant is petite and very young, Aarti notes. But she walks with the hunched bearing of a much older person, her shoulders stooped as if from years of carrying the weight of the world on her slight frame. She flings open the windows and honeyed golden light floods in, instantly dispersing the pall, the gloom that has settled in the room like smog. Fragrant early afternoon air, smelling of roses and earth, tangy and sweet, floats in, enveloping Aarti in its soothing warmth, voices drifting in its wake.

Aarti knows that if she walked to the window and peered down, she would see the head gardener squatting on the dry red mud, lungi hitched up, sharing paan with the driver, the two of them surrounded by the green, manicured lawns which the gardener's minions have just finished watering, the crimson heads of hibiscus nodding in the breeze, flies buzzing and dust swirling in a thick reddish-brown cloud, pink and yellow bougainvillea bursting down the wall, singing in riotous colour. She knows that they will be sitting where they have a good view of the kitchen and can stare at Gangamma and her posse of girls as they chop onions, grate coconut and grind masalas for the evening's dinner. Gangamma will come out in a bit when she has set the pot of curry to boiling and has made sure the girls are occupied; she will then reprimand the gardener and driver for distracting her girls. The gardener and driver will fake surprise, asking how they could be accused of distracting anyone when all they are doing is taking a much deserved break from their duties and minding their own business.

'You know exactly what you are doing,' Gangamma will yell. 'Those girls do not need an excuse to shirk their duties. All they've done for the last twenty minutes is simper and blush, thanks to you.'

Gangamma will continue her tirade without pause for a further ten minutes until finally, when the men's eyes have acquired a glaze, she will inhale a huge gulp of air and, on the expelled breath, ask them to come inside and have a cup of tea and some bondas. They will smile and follow her into the kitchen, mission accomplished, and Gangamma's girls will giggle and nudge each other and avert their eyes as they serve them.

'Why are you here?' Aarti asks Vani who is standing at the window, silhouetted by amber light and a sky the bluish white of eggshells.

'Pardon, ma'am?'

Vani's face is in shadow, her hair haloed by sun, gleaming around her face. She could be pretty, Aarti thinks idly, if she took a bit more notice of herself, if she was a tad more animated, if her face was not so empty, expressionless. As soon as the thought takes root, Aarti wonders, *why am I thinking like this? What do I care?*

She remembers Tara, the servant who had the gall to pity her and the vow she made to not get too close to anyone, to not let anybody feel anything for her except envy. It's worked a little too well, of course. She has no friends at all, no confidantes. But she likes it that way. Doesn't she?

I should sack this one, she thinks. *I'll give her a couple of days, though. After all, she's just nursed me back to health.*

But she knows she will give this girl more than a couple of days. The burden this girl lugs speaks to Aarti. She is a kindred soul.

'I said,' Aarti says, raising her voice ever so slightly, steel entering into it, 'why are you here?'

Something crosses the girl's face. A shadow. For a fleeting moment, it takes over her face, envelops her, snuffing out what life there is in that forlorn visage. Then it is gone. The girl speaks and when she does, her voice is steady, monotonous as if she is discussing the weather. 'My parents died. I was sent here because your family is distantly related to mine and you needed a servant.'

That is what it is, the load this girl is hefting. Her parents are dead. And Aarti's might as well be for all they care about her.

'Were they nice?' She asks and this time her voice is soft, a yearning note entering into it without her meaning it to.

The girl turns away, her back to Aarti, but not before Aarti sees her face crumple. And somehow that sight arouses something in her. She wants to go up to the girl, comfort her, she is galvanised by the impulse. Before she can think of what she is doing – *Vani is a servant, for God's sake,* a voice in her head yells – she pushes aside the bed linen and tries to stand up. She tries. But she is too weak, she has no strength left after days of illness and she falls to the floor in a jumbled heap, a shocked, involuntary cry escaping her mouth. In an instant, Vani is beside her, helping her up, her soft hands easing Aarti onto the bed.

Aarti lies back on the nest of pillows too tired to do anything except close her eyes. But before she drifts into a healing sleep, Aarti looks up into her new servant's eyes, empty again, and yet behind that blank screen she can spy glimpses of shimmering hurt, and says, 'I am sorry. So sorry, about your parents.'

She is asleep within seconds but not before she feels drops of something hot land on her hand like offerings – the girl's tears escaping from between eyes squeezed shut against the flow.

Aarti sleeps. She dreams of a curtain ripped open by wave upon wave of water, salty and tasting of sorrow.

Chapter 15
Vani – Life in Bangalore

The Tang of Cow Dung

It has been sixty days since Vani's parents passed away, days in which she has gone from being the only child of loving parents to an orphan; from being a free soul going to school every day and dreaming of a future to being a servant, a nonentity, her future decided on the whim of her employers; from only having to take care of herself to trying to satisfy this notoriously hard-to-please girl she finds herself being at the beck and call of.

Even the smells are different here. No earthy scent of wet grass and freshly ploughed fields, the tang of cow dung, the tart spiciness of mangoes maturing in the mid-afternoon haze, the fruity whiff of jackfruit being sliced open on Charu's veranda, the sizzling aroma of gossip and excitement, the laughter of women nattering in the meadows, the grumble of men as they urge the buffaloes on, the shriek of boys playing cricket, the shout of Gauri's son as he is chased by Ganganna for stealing ambades, the yelps of Dhomu's dog as he is whipped for stealing the scraps meant for the cows.

Instead the sandalwood air freshener scent of yawning emptiness, of bubbling anger and roiling injustice. The windows forever closed to keep the dust out. The chilled, artificial air inside the house seethes with the suppressed rage of servants who outwardly look biddable but inwardly fume with loathing towards their employers; it swarms with things left unsaid, little hurts which gradually grow into big wounds; it agitates with the absence of love and affection.

When Vani wakes – very early as she hasn't been able to sleep, not really, since her parents died – she likes to stand on the landing and look out of the window at the garden. Dawn is only just staining the grey horizon the soft pink of budding hope, and the gardens are shrouded in mist, an ethereal cloud that she aches to touch, that she wants to live in, melt into. She fancies it is her parents come to say hello and she tries to make out their faces in it.

She does that sometimes in the middle of the day too, when she has a moment; looks at the sky and tries to identify the silhouette of her parents' faces amongst the frothy clouds. She knows that they are looking down on her. She knows that there is a plan in all of this. She believes this because the alternative – that her parents are but a smattering of ash scattered across the village, breathed in and sneezed out by the stray dogs that roam the streets, that Vani is stuck here in this life of servitude for the fathomable future – is too hard to countenance.

And so she searches for signs – a fluffy white feather found while doing Aarti's bed that has no reason being there, the sun parting storm clouds and bestowing a golden smile just as she looks out the window – and she believes it is her parents looking out for her, sending their love her way.

Some days when she is the recipient of an unexpected kindness, when one of the other servants puts her arm around Vani and says, 'You all right? You are looking a bit peaky. Have a sit down, why don't you?' and the warmth of human contact after days of loneliness makes her want to heave, bend over with the effort it is taking to contain her grief, hold it in, she imagines her parents whispering, 'Shh, it's okay, it's all right. Our darling girl, you will be fine.' She hears them and that gives her hope.

Vani was in awe of the daughter of the house, Aarti, when she heard of her, when Nagappa described her. But after Vani nursed her back to health, after she saw Aarti at her most vulnerable, calling out for her mother and getting Vani instead, a mere servant paid to look after her, all she felt was an overwhelming pity. Vani noticed how, when Aarti came to after her illness, the light dimmed from her eyes when she realised it was Vani sitting beside her and not her mother. Vani heard Aarti call out for her parents in the depths of her delirium and her cries went unanswered. And sitting there tending to the ill girl, Vani understood how lucky she had been, how blessed, to have been loved so thoroughly and completely by her parents. Yes, she lost them and she would miss them forever, but they had loved her, celebrated her. She was the apex around which their lives gravitated, the sun to their earth. She had been adored, wanted, indulged. Even in the midst of her grief, the throes of her anguish, Vani had those memories to hold on to.

Aarti had the run of a huge house and myriad servants at her bidding; she was the darling of Karnataka and set to be the Face of India; her every material need was met, catered for. And yet, she didn't have love.

How must it be to have parents who do not care for you and to live with that knowledge? No wonder Vani hears her retching in the bathroom after every meal. Aarti is trying to disgorge that knowledge, Vani knows, but she cannot regurgitate it out of her body, however hard she tries. It will be there in Aarti's mother's empty eyes the next time they sweep over her, not really seeing her, the next time she makes a casual, cruel comment, 'Are you wearing that? It makes you look fat. Go change.' In Aarti's father's complete indifference to her except when someone else has won a contract he thinks Aarti should have.

And so, despite Aarti's ordering around of Vani, despite her vitriol and her impatience, Vani feels sorry for Aarti, understands where she's coming from. Despite Aarti's superior status, she and Vani are not that different – they have both lost their parents, albeit in different ways; they are both denied the love they desperately yearn for.

On the second month anniversary of her parents' death, Vani cries herself to sleep. The sobs keep on coming. She smothers them with her pillow, glad that her room is at the very end of the attic – which has been given over to servants' quarters – and quite isolated. She mourns and heaves as she lets it all out. All her regrets: not remembering much of that morning, how she is beginning to forget the contours of her mother's face, the sound of her father's laughter, how she cannot for the life of her remember where exactly the mole was in her father's face. She does not have any photographs of them, no one in the village owned a camera and the notion of paying Sumesh the photographer to have their picture taken when there was no occasion for it – no wedding or other celebration – was preposterous when they couldn't afford to buy fish and meat, milk and eggs.

She is giving herself over to the tears when she feels a cool arm on her shoulder. For a minute, a brief, joyous minute, she wonders if it is her mother, come for her, come back. She turns, not bothering to wipe her streaming eyes, her mouth open and gasping, shuddering for breath.

It is Aarti!

Vani blinks and sits up in shock. Of all people, Vani did not expect her.

Hurriedly, she wipes her eyes and manages to speak between heaves, 'Sorry, sorry, did not mean to disturb you, ma'am.'

Aarti's eyes harden briefly; there is a flicker in them. Even in her desolate state, Vani understands that Aarti is deciding what persona to wear – the impetuous mistress, the concerned girl? How does Vani know this person so well? How can she read the workings of Aarti's mind?

The hard look disappears. Vani sees that Aarti has given up affecting and decided to be herself, to give in to the same impulse that made her walk into Vani's room. Didn't Vani lock the door when she retired for the night? *Fool,* she admonishes herself, even as her breathing struggles to calm down, remembered sobs bursting out of her in occasional hiccups.

'I hear you every day you know. Your room is directly above mine.' Aarti's voice is wry but there is something soft in her eyes, an expression Vani has never seen before. It makes Aarti look even more beautiful than she does when she dresses up to go to her shoots, Vani thinks. Her hair is down, she is wearing a nightie and no make-up and she looks so much younger, a lost little girl. Like Vani herself.

'I am so sorry for disturbing you, ma'am. I did not realise,' Vani manages between hiccups.

Aarti fiddles with the end of her nightie. 'What is today? It is something, right? Normally your sobs stop after a while. Today they just...'

'I am sorry,' Vani says again.

Aarti stamps her foot, clicks her tongue. She is used to people doing her every bidding, answering her every question, anticipating it even before she opens her mouth to query. 'What is today?' She asks again.

'Two months since they died.' Saying it out loud makes it more real somehow. It is out there now, the knowledge that Vani has lived two whole months without her parents, absorbed into the miasma haunting this room, smacking of grief and whispered secrets.

Aarti comes and sits at the edge of Vani's narrow, hard cot. They could be two girls talking about ordinary things – movies, boys.

'How? How did they…?'

Vani is surprised by a sudden burst of affection for Aarti because she is sensitive enough not to say 'die', even as fresh waves of grief assault her.

'Drowned,' she manages, and the bloated visions of her parents loom before her eyes. She tries to blink them away, to will the smiling faces of the parents she knew and loved to grace her head instead.

Aarti's slender, perfectly manicured hand snakes along crumpled bed sheets seeped in sorrow and reaching Vani's scuffed, work-callused palm, rests on it. 'I am sorry.'

The tears start again, Vani cannot help them. It is all too much.

And Aarti, her mistress, the notoriously hard-to-please girl, the one all the servants have warned her against, does something even more out of character than entering her servant's room to check if she is okay, more out of character than sitting on Vani's bed and laying her hand on Vani's, something so out of character that Vani almost chokes on her tears.

Aarti opens her bony arms and holds Vani as she shudders and sobs. She comforts Vani like Vani comforted her when she was ill, nursing her like she nursed Aarti through her fever. Aarti holds Vani as she exhausts her grief, the back of her expensive nightie getting soaked just as much as the back of Vani's tattered one. She cries right along with Vani, until Vani doesn't know who is comforting whom, both of them giving in to the exquisite release of tears, both of them wishing the other holding her was her mother.

Chapter 16
Aarti – Friendship

Nugget of Joy

Aarti doesn't know what she was thinking but once she hugs the servant girl, comforts her, a line is crossed. She cannot go back to treating Vani like a servant again, she cannot keep her distance.

And now, the two sides of her are at war. One side desperately wants Vani for a friend, someone to share with, someone to talk to. The other thinks, *Why her? She is nothing. A servant. Remember Tara and the vow you made not to get close. If you must have a friend, why not a fellow model, someone the same class and status as you?*

The side of her that wants friendship with Vani counters: *I could never make myself so vulnerable as to admit my loneliness to a fellow model. But Vani… Vani knows. She understands. She is going through the same thing.*

And what would your parents think if you got so pally with a servant?

What do they care? All they want is for me to be the top model in India and once I achieve that they will want me to conquer the world. Even then, they will not be happy. Even then, they will not be satisfied.

Aarti has never felt the need for friends before. She is above all that. She sees girls talking, laughing, sharing secrets and she is apart. Alone. Always. She doesn't *want* to be one of them.

One of her classmates at the ridiculously expensive school populated by the children of Bangalore's elite that she used to attend had accused, once, 'You think you are better than all the rest of us, don't you? You look down your nose at us.'

'I do,' Aarti had replied, 'and I am. Better than all of you.'

She's always been single-minded in going after what she wants. She's always been ruthless. But now, for the first time in her life, she feels protective towards this servant girl. Why? She cannot explain even to herself why she feels compelled to treat Vani differently, to talk to her as a friend would. She wants the camaraderie she experienced briefly the previous night, the sense of some weight she did not even know she carried easing when she comforted the servant girl.

And so, the two parts of her are at war until finally the one tells the other, *The fact that she is your servant is to your advantage. It is her duty to please you. She can be your friend if you so wish. It will be on your terms. After all, you can sack her at any time. It's entirely up to you.*

And so it begins. A friendship that shouldn't happen, a relationship that is doomed from the start.

In the evenings, after all Vani's other work is done, while she brushes Aarti's hair, they chat. Aarti drinks in the stories of Vani's parents, the love they showered on their daughter, the love Aarti wishes she had had. And then, Vani goes upstairs to bed and Aarti listens for the sobs that do not come. And something blooms in her heart, a little nugget of joy. Talking to her is helping Vani sleep. For the first time in her life, Aarti discovers the joy of doing something for others, instead of it being, always, the other way round.

One day, she asks Vani to answer her phone. She watches Vani blink, once, twice, then pass the phone to her.

'What's the matter?' she complains, irritated. 'I asked you to take it.'

'I don't understand it, ma'am.' Vani says, softly. She still calls her ma'am, even though Aarti has asked her not to, several times.

'You don't understand English?'

Vani is briskly cleaning the dressing table, putting lipsticks and mascara back in their containers. 'No, ma'am. Never learnt it.'

'I'll teach you,' Aarti says, surprising herself once again. She seems to be constantly doing things she's never done before in Vani's company. The girl has that effect on her.

And so, in the evenings, after Vani's jobs are done, Aarti teaches her English. They laugh, and they gossip, Aarti filling her in on the latest antics of some of the more notorious models as Vani practises her letters, and over the ensuing months, they morph into friends, sisters even.

By the time Vani finishes practising her reading, it is very late, so Aarti asks Vani to sleep in her room, on a mat on the floor and they talk late into the night, sharing experiences and stories. Aarti learns of love, the self-sacrificing kind. She hears of how Vani's father was bitten by a rabid dog and rushed to the hospital in the nearby town because he stepped in front of Vani to protect her from the dog. She learns of how Vani's parents scrimped and saved to buy chicken once a week and how they made sure she ate it all, only sucking on the bones after. She hears of how Vani's parents bought 'damaged' eggs – eggs with cracks and blemishes on them – and watered-down milk, which was all they could afford, so Vani could have the requisite proteins and nutrients. She listens to how Vani's father walked everywhere without sandals so his feet were forever blistering and sore, so Vani could have textbooks for school.

Aarti looks at this plain young girl, her dishevelled hair, her salt-stained face, her sorrow tainted eyes, her thin body hunched with pain, her perfectly ordinary features transformed into something special by the glow on her face as she talks about the parents who had loved her, adored her, for whom she had been their world. She looks at this girl who has nothing, who is beholden to Aarti for her food, her bed, the clothes she is wearing, and *envies* her.

Over the course of the next few months, it gives Aarti immense satisfaction to see Vani's face light up as she learns to read, to spell, to speak English, first hesitantly, then passably fluently. When Aarti's phone rings and Vani answers in English, 'Yes, of course, I will give her your message,' and puts the phone down, beaming, Aarti is blindsided by the surge of sheer joy that courses through her.

'Don't get ideas into your head,' Aarti jokes, trying to tamp down the emotion bubbling in her.

'I won't, ma'am,' Vani laughs. She has long since dropped the 'ma'am'. She is teasing.

Somehow in this little orphaned servant girl, Aarti finds a kindred spirit, someone she doesn't feel threatened by, someone she can share with, be herself with. And as her friendship with Vani develops, she is no longer beset by the need to please her parents, to court their approval like before.

One day while Aarti is at breakfast, her mother says, squinting at her suspiciously, 'You look too happy for this time of the morning. Have you been drinking? Are you in love?'

Normally, Aarti would have been thrilled beyond belief that her mother had condescended to speak to her instead of perusing the society pages of the broadsheets for pictures of herself. She would have been grateful that her mother had *noticed* her instead of looking right through her like she usually did, so much so that Aarti used to wonder when she was very young whether she was invisible. This time, though, Aarti just smiles secretly to herself and says, 'None of your business.'

The look of shock that crosses her mother's face like a fleeting shadow before it is masked by cool indifference and her mother's trademark shrug and an icy, 'Suit yourself,' gives Aarti immense pleasure for days afterwards.

Vani is almost like a little sister to Aarti. She bosses over Vani, orders her around, like she imagines an older sister would do. Almost. Their relationship is unequal, of course it is. Vani will always be deferential to Aarti; her livelihood depends on Aarti, however much they both delude themselves otherwise.

'I need someone who will tell it like it is,' Aarti says to Vani often, but she knows that Vani won't. She wouldn't dare.

Truth be told, Aarti likes this inequality, she enjoys this relationship because the balance is tipped in her favour; she is smug in the knowledge that Vani is her friend, but it is according to *her* rules, *her* say.

Sometimes, late at night when her stomach yawns with hunger and she cannot sleep, it occurs to Aarti that her relationship with Vani is very much like her parents' is with her but she immediately banishes the thought. How could it be so? She *cares* for Vani. Her parents do not care for her, only for her achievements.

And you, don't you care only for what Vani can give you? A little voice asks.

No, of course not, the other part of her protests. *Vani is my friend. She holds my hair while I am being sick and...*

She holds your hair when you are being sick, mocks the first voice. *She combs your hair. She listens to you talk. She laughs when you want her to, she doesn't when you don't. Exactly my point...*

I am teaching her English.

So you can feel happy, feel good about yourself.

At that, she quiets the annoying voice in her head, denies it entry even late at night when she is at her most vulnerable, when unappeased hunger chases away the blessed oblivion provided by sleep, when visions of food goad her empty stomach into rebellion and thoughts like these are a welcome relief. Even then.

Chapter 17
Vani – Visiting the Village

The Caress of a Peacock Feather

A year after Aarti held Vani when she cried, a year into Vani's friendship with her employer, a letter arrives for Vani, the first that she has received. She holds it to her nose when one of the other servants hands it to her and fancies she can catch a whiff of the hauntingly familiar scent of the village, which for her is the smell of churned mud, gossip and emerald fields basking in the sun.

They do not like Vani much anymore, the other servants, now that she is 'in the inner circle' – their taunting moniker, now that she is sleeping on the floor of the young mistress's room, now that Aarti has optioned Vani to herself.

'Be careful,' they tell Vani, eyes flashing, words dripping with vitriol. They cannot hide the glee from their voice, the pleasure of anticipation as they regale her with stories of how Aarti has sacked other servants, mercilessly and thoroughly, refusing to give so much as a letter of recommendation, just because they did not iron her dress to her exacting standards, or because they hurt her hair while combing it.

'She's mercurial; she can turn on you, like a pet tiger which has developed a taste for human flesh,' they say, spitting the paan they have been chewing loudly into the basin.

Vani is a defector now, no longer one of them.

'What we talk about stays here, understand?' they warn, their voices sharp, their gazes flinty.

She nods, the churmuri she has been eating tasting of earth in her mouth. The banter, the including her in their conversations is gone now. It stops the moment she enters the kitchen where they all meet up after their work is done. She is the drop of ink seeping through milk, turning everything murky and unpalatable in its wake. She clutches the letter which the cook, who sorts through the post, has thrown at her, and she runs away to the relative safety of her room.

Why didn't I lock the room that day? Vani laments for the hundredth time. Because she did not think anyone would enter, more fool her. Aarti has the run of all the rooms in the house; she can enter anywhere, anywhere at all. And even if she had locked it, Vani tells herself, Aarti would have knocked in that imperious way she has and Vani would have had to open the door. *Why didn't I sob softly?*

Vani misses the company of the servants, their sympathy and their small kindnesses – the giving of extra ladoos with her tea because she is 'wasting away', the regaling her with jokes to make her smile – little acts that had warmed her right up. She does not belong anywhere; she is balancing precariously between two worlds.

And yet a part of her is pleased that *she* has been taken into Aarti's confidence. Vani understands Aarti, feels a strange solidarity with her employer. She is able to see beyond Aarti's facade of stern, brittle woman to the child beneath. The girl who yearns for love, who is lost, lonely. Vani can identify with that because she feels the same.

Ensconced in her cot, door locked this time, she holds the letter close. She fancies it smells of the village despite the distance it has travelled – the fresh green of the fields, the soft milky white of burgeoning paddy, the raw red of muddy earth, the sparkling silver of monsoon rain. She slits it open.

The voluptuous Kannada script is neat, careful as if someone did a few drafts and this is the best version, to send to the 'big house'.

'Vani,' it reads and she sees her name and aches for the tiny house that was her home, the small garden that was her mother's pride and joy, the gurgling stream, her mother's arms, her father's shoulders from the top of which she fancied she could see to the edge of the village and beyond. 'Charu aunty is very sick and asking for you. Please come.'

Aarti doesn't want her to go but Vani begs and entreats, pointing out that it will only be for a week, promising that she'll be back before Aarti notices she's gone.

Aarti gives in finally, after making sure that Vani will, under no circumstances, stay away for longer than seven days and Vani sets off for her village. It is like coming home and it is like visiting a different continent. The coconut trees waving in the sun, the dust swirling on the mud road, the rows of huts, they tease her with their familiarity, they revel in their nonchalance. The village is the same, lounging indolently beside the twinkling river that glimmers and winks in welcome.

That river.

As soon as she enters the village, the images she has kept at bay, the bloated, unrecognisable visages of her parents swim into view. She blinks them away, walks briskly to Charu's house the long way round, so as to bypass what used to be her house – her parents' and hers.

Charu is a shadow of her former self. Her room smells musky, of disease, with death hovering close. She smiles weakly when she sees Vani, cupping her face with trembling fingers, her touch light as the caress of a peacock feather. 'My, how you've grown. You look beautiful. They would be so proud.' The ghosts of her parents linger between them, shimmering within the curtain of their tears.

Afterwards, Vani cannot help it; she walks past her old house, now occupied by another family, children playing hopscotch in the courtyard, raising an avalanche of reddish gold dust, the hibiscus flowers her mother had planted in full bloom, the bright purple of regret, the cashew tree replete with yellowish orange fruit, bees buzzing, pineapples ripening, guavas turning yellow in the late afternoon sunshine, the smell of ripe fruit and rank sorrow. Vani cannot picture her parents in that house. She cannot see herself there either. Vani runs. She runs into Nagappa's wife's arms and is anchored by them while she sobs.

Later, Vani goes to the crematorium. She stands there as the pink-spattered twilight sky darkens to red, sun setting in the horizon, a mellow crimson-dusted gold ball. Rats scuttle amongst the half-burnt wood; stray dogs hunt for scraps. Mosquitoes whine and feast on flesh that has become inured to the city. She stands on that desolate ground, seeped in mourning, tainted by grief, smelling faintly of smoke and something else, something ethereal, not quite animate, the air swirling with particles of ash, a black cloud thick with the organic matter of hundreds of bodies that have been cremated here over the years, and asks her parents for a sign.

A lone bird swoops, black wings silhouetted against pinks and golds. Another bird joins it and they plunge down, so close that the air from their beating wings brushes her face, whispering solace. The birds look at her, once, before they fly away. She gazes into their glittering opal eyes, their wings flapping in unison as they blend with the darkening sky, and she feels at peace for the first time since she set foot in the village. A part of her has been worrying that her parents were stuck here, in this bleak crematorium while she waited in Bangalore, hunting for signs of them in the clouds. But now, she knows. They are at peace. She felt it in the flutter of the birds' wings, read it in the look in their eyes. She understands that her parents are happy wherever they are and the knowledge soothes her.

She spends the next day at Charu's side. Charu recounts for Vani in her halting, laboured speech, the story of how Vani's parents came to the village as newlyweds, how they wanted many children but were so happy and excited when, after many miscarriages, Vani came along. And as Charu talks in her gasping voice, weighted down with illness in that room smelling of impending death, Vani can hear her mother, as clear as if she is in the next room. She sounds happy, her lilting tone threaded through with laughter, as she replies to something Vani's father has said.

Vani does not walk past her old house again, preferring to take the long way back to Nagappa's house, where she is staying. She pretends not to hear the delighted shouts of the children who now live in her old house, playing lagori in the dust, the smile in their mother's voice as she calls them in for a snack. She makes out that she does not hear the children launch at their father when he gets home from the fields, telling him stories about their day in breathless voices, his laughter as he asks them to slow down. She pretends not to see the lives being led in her old home. *I belong there, not you,* her head screams and her heart feels drenched with longing for the past.

Vani has mixed feelings about being back. She has no place here, in this village, anymore. She doesn't belong. She is lost, more so than in that big house with the hostile servants and the inscrutable girl who is her employer and also, oddly, her only friend.

On the third day, one of the elders comes running, panting, to Charu's house where Vani is sitting, holding her hand. 'They want you back. You have to go at once, an emergency.'

Vani was meant to stay a week at least. But she leaves on the overnight bus bound for Bangalore, panicked, worrying the whole way, unable to sleep. Has something happened to Aarti? Aarti's parents? What emergency would warrant Vani having to go back immediately when they have at least a dozen other servants catering to their every need?

The noise, bustle and dust of Bangalore welcome Vani like an old friend and the village is a bittersweet memory. An alien family creating memories in *her* home, trampling on the ghosts of her father and mother and her childhood self. She cannot bear to think that those children she saw playing in the mud will have the same house colouring their reminiscences as she does, the same house as gatekeeper to their recollections, as the backdrop to their dreams.

And so she returns, to the servants and their hostile stares warring with pity. To the mansion furnished with every luxury but lacking in warmth and love, which nevertheless feels more like home than the village. To her little room at the very top where she does not sleep anymore. To her prickly employer, whose deepest secrets – her bulimia, her insecurity, how lonely she feels despite her fame, how all she wants is to be loved – only Vani is party to.

Aarti is not at home when Vani arrives. Neither are her parents.

'Are they at the hospital? What has happened?' she asks the other servants and they laugh in her flustered face.

'She's fine, gone to her shoot,' they tell her.

'But...' Vani stutters, 'something must have happened. She summoned me back urgently.'

They look at her pityingly and do not deign to grace her question with an answer.

Aarti's room is in a state. Vani clears it up. And waits for Aarti.

When Aarti comes, after four long, agonising hours, she looks fine. She bursts into the room, her face lighting up when she sees Vani. She throws her arms around Vani, holds her close.

'I missed you,' she says at last, releasing Vani, holding her at arms' length. 'I couldn't sleep without you beside my bed, telling me stories. I couldn't do *anything*.' Her eyes are shimmering.

'Is that why you called me back?' Vani asks. She is exasperated. She is touched.

'I couldn't function without you,' Aarti moans. 'I couldn't eat at all, not a morsel. Which is not a bad thing, mind you.' She stands in front of the mirror and peruses herself critically. 'I might have lost some weight actually.'

If you lose any more you will disappear, Vani thinks. Out loud, because Aarti is clearly expecting a response, she says, 'I missed you too.'

Her employer's face beams. She comes and puts her bony arms around Vani again. Aarti has to bend to do this. She is so much taller than Vani.

'You are like my sister. I do not want to lose you ever again.'

'You did not lose me,' Vani says.

'Let's make a pact,' Aarti's eyes shine with enthusiasm.

In many ways, Aarti is such a child. Even though she is some years older than Vani, she feels like a much younger sibling.

'Okay,' Vani says, sighing inwardly. Knowing she does not have a choice.

Aarti has written it out already. 'Read this,' she says. 'It is in English. I looked up some of the wording on the internet. We will both sign and I will keep it in a safe place.'

'We, Aarti Kumar and Vani Bhat, declare that henceforth we are sisters, bound not by blood, but something even stronger: the immense and unbreakable bond of our friendship. We are family now and we will never willingly break this tie that is stronger than blood.'

This sounds like something a seven-year-old would write, Vani thinks. She knows that this is not so much a pact as a ploy to keep her tied to Aarti. *She can and will break it but I can't and won't dare,* she thinks. She is annoyed that Aarti called her back from Charu's bedside just because she was missing her. She does not want to participate in this childish charade.

But Aarti's eyes are glowing as she says, 'Shall we?'

And so Vani signs it, thinking, *It's just a game. A silly, innocent, kids' game instigated by a girl who's never really grown up and who's never had much of a childhood – for which she's making up now that she has a friend*, carefully printing her name in English like Aarti has taught her and then doing it again, joined up, for her signature.

After, Aarti makes three copies, one for herself, one for Vani and one spare, to keep safe with all her other documents.

Vani signs it, and she does not realise at that time what she is getting herself into. Or perhaps she does. But she is at a weak point. The village she yearned for has moved on without her; even the house she will always think of as hers is now occupied by someone else. This woman is all she has. She is beholden to her. And so she signs the pact, intertwining her destiny with Aarti's.

Aarti does not send Vani back to the village again, citing the pact, citing how much she missed Vani the one time she went, telling Vani that she cannot manage without her. Not when Charu dies and the letter comes to invite Vani to the funeral, not when Vani's other relatives pass away.

Life expectancy is not high in the village. People work too hard for very little return, the crop dependent on the whim of the monsoon. And there isn't enough food to go around.

Vani looks at all the food squandered in that mansion, the food Aarti regurgitates after every meal, and she cringes at the wastage. In the village, nobody diets, they are all naturally thin. 'You should stay a spell in our village; you wouldn't have to be sick at all then,' Vani said to Aarti once and she laughed, her sunken eyes meeting Vani's in the mirror, a bubble of dribble staining her left lip. Vani tells Aarti these truths and she thinks she is joking.

When Nomu, the boy Vani grew up playing cricket in the fields with, dies of a snake bite, she begs Aarti. 'Please,' she says, 'I want to go. I want to say goodbye. I will be back in two days.'

'Vani,' Aarti sighs, 'I can't cope without you. You cannot leave me. Why don't you understand? Why are you putting me through this?'

'It is just for a couple of days.'

Aarti's face hardens. 'I don't see why you are so attached to that village. *I* am your family now. If you go, I will die. Remember the pact,' her voice sharp as venomous fangs stabbing tender skin. 'Now, where is that shirt I was going to wear? Have you ironed it?'

That is the first time Vani thinks of running away. The pact, Aarti's intense dependency on her, is becoming a noose around Vani's neck.

She thinks of running away countless times after that. Whenever she is tempted to escape, the thought that holds her back is: where will she go? Vani knows nobody in Bangalore; all the people she knows are in the village, most of them dying or already dead. And she doesn't fit in back in the village, not anymore. They cannot keep her. That is why they sent her away in the first place. And if Vani does escape, what if Aarti actually kills herself like she is always threatening to do? Aarti is neurotic, highly emotional. Vani wouldn't put it past her to wilfully take her own life.

And despite everything, despite Aarti's stifling need for Vani and her maddening superiority, despite her ordering Vani around and her bringing up the pact at every opportunity, despite her not allowing Vani to return to the village, her keeping Vani imprisoned almost, Vani *understands* her neurotic, highly insecure employer/friend. She feels sorry for Aarti.

And so Vani stays with Aarti, even though her every instinct warns her to flee. She casts her lot in with her.

PART THREE
Present Day

King Solomon's Judgement

Chapter 18
Diya

Heartache

Heartache

Noun: deep sadness especially for the loss of someone or something loved.

Synonyms: grief, heartbreak, woe, sorrow.

Related Words: agony, torment, dejection, desolateness.

❈ ❈ ❈

I wake to mellow morning light streaming in under tear-glued, salt-stained eyelashes, dancing a tango upon closed lids, demanding that I open my eyes. I refuse to acquiesce to the request of soft February sun, creating dappled figures that cavort beneath my lids and, eyes shut tight, turn to my right, facing my mother's bed. I know she'll be sitting up in bed, her hair, which she normally ties back into a rigid bun, free to cascade down around her shoulders, a soft blue-black cloud with the occasional grey thrown in. She will be praying, mumbling whispered endearments and entreaties to a God she desperately, persistently believes in, her lips moving intently, her eyes closed. Her shift doesn't start till ten and she allows herself this luxury until I wake, her mouth moving quietly in prayer.

'God has been good to me thus far, very good,' she likes to say when I ask her what she is doing, her eyes softening like ice cream sitting too long outside the confines of the freezer. 'He has given me you and I am thanking him for it.'

'So why don't you go to the temple then?' I tease, knowing it is the hordes of people milling there that puts my timid mother off.

'I don't have the time,' she mumbles.

'Don't have the time for God? How could you, Mum? He might smite you for that – beware!'

And she will turn round in distress as if God is standing behind her, looking over her shoulder, hand raised ready to smite. Easily alarmed, that's my mum.

I open my eyes to smile at her, spy the wardrobe where her bed should be. Have we moved sometime during the night? The night… And memory comes flooding back, in aching waves of pain, and I close my eyes and burrow under the bedclothes, pulling the duvet up around my head, tasting salt. The flower of pain that has taken up residence inside me throbs out a scorching scarlet greeting. It seems to have encroached everywhere, laying claim to my unresisting body. I lie there, trying to delude myself that the cocoon of darkness, the smell of my own sweat and hurt, is my mother's embrace…

I could not get to sleep the previous night. Every time I closed my eyes, her face careered across closed lids, eyes pleading, 'I am your mother, Diya. You are mine. I love you, Diya, my darling girl, light of my life.'

Where was she? What were they doing to her? Was she comfortable? And then, even though I fought it, the policewoman's voice inveigled in, 'Your *real* mother has been searching for you for the past thirteen years.' *No, No, No.*

I did not want to think about it, any of it. But I couldn't think of anything else.

'Mum,' I heard, a plaintive cry. And my heart ached. It literally ached. And I understood, finally, fully, the meaning of the word 'heartache'. Food. I wanted, *needed* food to drown out another, different kind of hunger.

The soft padding of a little boy's unerring footsteps, the creaking of a door, Farah's voice, 'Shh, Zain, it's okay, Mummy's here.'

Heartache bloomed, it reigned supreme. I ached for the arms of the woman who had loved me, looked after me for thirteen years, who had been, who is, my world, my life.

I stood up, I paced the small room. I switched on the bedside lamp, perused the books, but my mind wouldn't rest, wouldn't settle, and reading didn't calm me or transport me like it usually did. How could I lose myself in someone else's story when mine was taking centre stage?

I remembered the time we saw a little boy fall into the road. Mum had rushed to him while everyone else stood helpless, horrified. She had careened straight into oncoming traffic, disregarding the groan of vehicles, the distressed whine of car horns, the yelling of strangers, the police car drawing up, pulsing blue lights dancing. She had helped the boy up and wiped away his tears gently with the hem of her sari and handed him to his mother across the road, a look passing between the two of them, a look party only to mothers, a grateful look which encompassed a whole dialogue, completely wordless, underscored by glistening tears in both pairs of eyes. My mother had done this despite the fact that she did not like crowds, that she was afraid, illogically I had always thought, of the police.

'We have done no wrong, Mum, committed no crime. They are not after you, you know,' I would laugh when, every time a police car whizzed past, siren blaring she would tense, making to run away, convinced they were coming for her, her eyes wide and distraught.

She had flinched when I said that, her grip tightening on my arm, and I had smiled and patted her hand, 'It's okay, Mum. I was only joking.'

Oftentimes we were more like friends than mother and daughter. She made me laugh, brought out my protective instincts because she was afraid of everything. At thirteen, I was almost as tall as her, and far more worldly wise I thought, having commandeered and belonged to this world that she was still not quite a party to, because of her hang-ups and her many worries and fears. She watched from the outskirts, happy that I had fit in, and when I was with her, I felt accomplished, basking in the glow of her approval, her pride, and the bullies, their harsh words, the ribbing I endured at school was forgotten.

We had fun together, despite the fact that she was always working and exhausted when she was not. When she was with me, her face would radiate contentment, pleasure, pride.

'You make my world complete,' she liked to say. 'You are my light, Diya, you are my world.'

And I knew I was, completely, unequivocally.

And now, my world is shattered and I don't know who I am, where I belong.

I shake my head. No, I cannot erase all that went before because of one silly accusation. There must be some mistake, there must.

Where are you, Mum? I will come and find you, I will.

Somehow the thought gives me the courage I need to fling off the duvet, open the door, and poke my head outside. The house is quiet, still. No boisterous shouts, no noise, no laughter.

I make my way to the bathroom, stare at the pudgy-faced, swollen-eyed girl in the mirror and tell her to get a grip. 'You are going to sort this today,' I tell her sternly. 'You are going to ask the social worker to take you to your mum, and you are not going to budge until she says yes.'

I pause then, the word 'mum' opening up a cavernous hunger for her arms, her touch, and I peruse my face in the mirror as I have done a million times before trying to spy in this fleshy visage my mother's delicate features. Her face blossoms before my eyes and I think, her nose? No. Her eyes? No.

'You look like your father,' she's said when I've asked. 'He died when you were a baby. He loved you so, absolutely adored you. Who wouldn't?' her face shining.

'How? How did he die?'

And her eyes would fluster, they would flit to the chair, the table, her hands frantically working the ragged ends of her sari. 'An accident.'

I used to think she was a terrible liar. Now though, I wonder.

I thought her agitation was because of the fact that she had lost him, because memories of him were too hurtful, too raw. Now, I wonder.

No, Diya, no. She is your mum.

But I can see nothing of her in me, nothing at all. Nothing at all.

A flash of anger at her, the purple-red of a heating coil. *Why, Mum? Why?*

My eyes fill with tears. I furiously blink them away. Recall her words as she was led away, her sigh so immense, 'Perhaps there was some other way, but at the time…'

What do you mean, Mum? What do you mean? I am so angry at you. When I find you, I will give you a big hug, just to revel once again in the feel of your arms around me, and then I will fight with you. A big roaring wallop of a spat. Like nothing you've ever seen before.

Tears threaten again and I resolutely stride out of the bathroom and make my way downstairs, deliberately making a lot of noise on the stairs to alert everyone to my presence just in case they have forgotten I am here.

All the three rooms that comprise the downstairs – the living room, dining room and kitchen – are empty. Buttery golden light pools in through the windows, dances on the surfaces, fawning on the curtains, lending a sheen to the worn black sofas, shining on the silent telly. It is one of those sunny yet extremely cold February days.

I walk to the kitchen which smells of stale curry and raw onions, and see the note on the table: *Taken the boys to their swimming lesson, will be back at 11:00. Sohrab had to go into work – another emergency! You were asleep, didn't want to wake you. Milk, juice, butter, marmalade, cheese in fridge, bread in bread bin, cereal on top of fridge. Make yourself at home. Farah. xxx*

I look at the clock, 10:15 a.m. I know my social worker's arriving at 11:00 as well. I will be ready by then. I will have plenty of questions for her. She will be shocked and wonder where the quiet mousey girl from yesterday has gone. Good.

I open the fridge, pour myself a glass of milk, down it in one gulp and then start my quest. I systematically go through each drawer, find lentils and pulses, rice, atta for chapattis, three different kinds of pasta. I open and close each cupboard and drawer, disturbing nothing until, in the last set of drawers, tucked into the corner, I find an open pack of Chocolate Fingers, a six-pack of Walkers containing only three packs – two cheese and onion and one ready salted, and a four-finger KitKat.

I take my haul upstairs and eat my way through the loot, tasting nothing except the sallow yellow tang of grief. Once again, the food does nothing to ease the pain, to keep the sorrow, the desperate ache for my mum at bay. The taste of chocolate and salt, invoking nausea, summoning heartache. Like in the hospital cafeteria the previous evening, I cannot finish the food. It hurts too much, brings back memories of how, lost and desperate, I had raided the kitchen of the flat that I had, until the previous evening, shared with my mother and munched my way through all the junk food I could find and yet… it hadn't helped. It could not assuage the anguish, could not douse the pain of missing my mum, could not quieten the voice shouting in my head that she had lied to me all my life, betrayed me. *No, no, no, no.*

Food is not helping anymore. In fact, if anything, it is exacerbating the wound, rubbing against it, chafing it.

I throw the half-eaten KitKat, the dregs of the chocolate biscuits and the crisps in the bin just as I hear the key in the lock, the high-pitched voices of the boys bringing noise on a blast of freezing air into the house and Farah asking them to shush. I sit there, one of the books from the bedside table open on my lap, staring at nothing, the words blurring before my eyes.

How is it fair, I think, *that they have their mum with them while I don't?*

Stop, I tell myself, just as a car pulls up outside, making a racket on the gravel. There is a soft knock on the door and the musical voices of the boys calling 'Mum' in unison drift upstairs. I ignore the ache in my heart as I hear Farah's gentle footsteps making their way to the front door, as another blast of ice incites the warm fuzzy cloud of air that has just settled inside the house into disarray like a cockerel among chickens.

❇ ❇ ❇

'Where is my mum?' I ask Jane as soon as we are seated in the car.

She does not look away from the road and her soft voice undulating brings to mind the honeyed sweetness of tender pink marshmallows exploding in my mouth, belying the harshness of the words she is uttering, 'She has been taken to the Westminster Magistrates' Court and she will be served papers for extradition today I imagine.'

Extradition. I roll the word around in my mouth. A word I don't know – one that qualifies for my vocabulary book. Hard, uncompromising, like the plum stone I bit into by mistake once and nearly broke my tooth on. 'What is extradition?' It drops out of my mouth like a cold, ruthless bullet. I hate the word, I decide.

Jane sighs and I know immediately that whatever is coming is not good news. 'Since she committed…uh… the crime in India…she will have to go back to India for the trial…'

The panic comes from nowhere, enveloping me, swallowing me whole. 'No!' I yell, dropping my head onto my lap, screaming my pain out, 'No! No! No!'

The car swerves and stops. I feel cool arms around me. Jane doesn't say anything, just holds me, and for that I am grateful, even though as soon as I am able to breathe I shrug off her arms. Every hug I receive, however welcome, only makes me miss Mum more, only shows how inadequate other arms are when I am attuned to that one pair, the arms that have raised me, that have played with me, that have carried me, held me countless times, have nursed me through childhood illnesses, that have always, always been there. Until now when I need them the most.

'There must be some mistake,' I say when I can talk. I will not be able to live knowing she is in another country, thousands of miles away. I can't bear it. I cannot.

'The Indian police had to submit a request for a warrant of arrest and extradition to the Secretary of State here, Diya,' Jane's voice is softer than usual, like a very fluffy, warm pillow I could sink into. Despite how much her words have the power to hurt, her voice takes the edge off them. 'It was all checked, double-checked and approved.'

I ignore her words, let them wash over me and away, like a stream gurgling over pebbles on its meandering journey to the river. 'Can I see her?' I ask once again, knowing what her answer will be and yet unable to bear the thought of Mum being so far away, separated by an unbridgeable distance. They cannot do this, isolate me from the only mum I have known, surely? I have to see her. I have to. Now. I will only find the comfort I am seeking in her arms. This cannot be happening to me, to us. This is some sort of joke.

'Um…I know you want to…' Jane begins and I explode.

'I hate you!' I yell, channelling all the futility I feel at being a child, a pawn, all the hurt, at the one person who is here, beside me.

I yank open the car door and walk out onto the hard shoulder, the roar of vehicles, the cold air slamming me in the face. *At least I am feeling something,* I think, shivering, as my extremities gradually go numb, *something other than pain.*

Why, Mum, why? Explain. Explain this mess to me.

I want to see her. 'I want to see you, Mum, right now!' I yell and my words are lost in the whoosh of cars racing past on the motorway, the smell of smoke and petrol exhaust and ice.

Up ahead the warning, 'No service station for 18 miles', is obscured by the legend 'Tom loves Diane' painted in fluorescent green graffiti right across the sign. I picture Tom, half his body hanging over the bridge, blond hair slick on his forehead, tongue poking through teeth in intense concentration, painstakingly painting those letters upside down, declaring his love to the world. I want to do that, paint 'Vani is my mum and I want her back here with me', up there for all to see.

'I know you do,' Jane says.

Did I just speak my thoughts out loud? I don't know when Jane has come to stand beside me and I don't care. She is shivering, pink goosebumps dotting her chubby white hands.

'Why are you here and she isn't?' I scream, my words lost in the hiss and roar of the cars zooming past.

The February air envelops me like a ghost, creepy fingers chilling my spine. A sleety drizzle falls, quiet as the world outside a shut window. Cars whine and whoosh, groan and complain as they whistle past. Fog hangs in the distance, an ashen blanket. I imagine its icy embrace obliterating the sign, the bold proclamation of Tom's love for Diane. I wonder whether he still feels that way or if he's moved on, found someone else, and there are other signs further along, his fickle love given away like sweets to whoever is next in line. The dull silvery curtain of rain matches my mood, matches how I feel inside, and I think, good, much better this than the brightness, the clear, cloudless morning I woke up to.

Jane has been speaking but I haven't really been paying attention. I only catch the last bit of what she is saying: 'She is here.'

Mum, my heart declares and I whip around instinctively, even though my brain tells me there is no way. 'Where?'

My heart has always been much faster than my head, which I have been told is quite sensible. My heart doesn't pay heed to my head though; it is impatient, quick to rise in hope, to jump to conclusions. I suppose that is why it keeps breaking.

'I am sorry,' Jane's voice is like the fog. It creeps up on you, surrounds you, fools you into believing everything is okay. 'The woman who gave birth to you, who has been searching for you for thirteen years – she desperately wants to see you, Diya. Would you consider meeting with her?'

A high-pitched keening. An anguished wail. After a bit, I realise that it is coming from me. My own alien throat. Something is wrapped around my shoulders. A coat. A whiff of unfamiliar perfume. Flowers. Spring. Warmth. I'm cold. So very cold. Nothing can warm me. Not anymore. Except for the one embrace I am denied.

Arms guide me to the car. The door closes slowly, shutting out the wind, the chilly slice of outdoors. Jane starts up the engine. I turn away from her, to the window. It is misted over. I draw a ghostly figure in the condensation, and I hear her laughter. Mum's infectious laugh like silvery bells chiming. 'What have you drawn now?' Whenever she boiled rice or potatoes, I would be at the kitchen window, etching symbols in the condensation. She refused to rub them away and there they would remain for a few days, the faint outline of them taking shape and form every time the kitchen steamed up. 'They are your creation – how can I bear to wipe them away?' she would smile, eyes shining.

The pain is a physical thing eating my insides. Not a flower, no, not anymore. A monster.

I have to eat, drown out the monster.

'I am sorry,' Jane is saying. 'I cannot begin to imagine how hard it must be for you, Diya.'

No, you cannot. 'Do you have something to eat?' I manage.

The sound of a zip being undone, a swish, a rustling, then, 'Here.'

An Aero bar. I rip it open, swallow. Chocolate floods my mouth, travels down my throat, pushing past the salty lump that has taken up permanent residence even though I cannot recall having granted it permission. And yet, the pain doesn't budge. If anything it intensifies, reminding me of the day before, stuffing chocolate into my mouth to placate the abyss of loss gaping inside. As if I need reminding! Chocolate used to help, it used to at least sugar-coat my insides, if not make everything better. Not anymore.

'The woman who gave birth to you…'

'Stop saying that, calling her that,' I yell.

'She is here,' Jane continues after a pause, 'she's come from India to be with you. She has been travelling here for the last thirteen years, on and off, searching for you.'

Somehow, Jane saying this does not hurt the way the policewoman's words did. Perhaps it is Jane's voice, a waterfall, soothing, washing away my hurt. Or perhaps I am getting inured to pain. After all, how much ache can a human being endure before they begin to shut down?

'She was even arrested once, briefly, for snatching a child on the street. She thought it was you,' Jane says.

Despite myself, I am interested. The heating cranks up with a groan of complaint. The condensation on the pane runs down in streaks. The figure disintegrates.

'Really?' I ask.

'Really,' she says. 'Are you up to meeting her?'

Panic. It grips me once more. 'Not quite yet,' I manage.

'You have more tests at the hospital today. You will likely be given the all clear this evening. Tomorrow, I will take you to meet with a psychologist. Perhaps after that? Let me know.'

I look out of the window, sparkling clean now the mist has steamed away; no evidence of my drawing of earlier.

'I'm fine. There is no need for all these tests.'

'We just have to make sure you're all right, you know? That she did not mess with you...'

'She *loved* me. She loves me.'

I close my eyes and shut out the world as Jane drives, the flowery, slightly chemical smell of car air freshener, the taste of chocolate and sorrow and panic and loss and, nudging for a place amongst these feelings, a tiny burst of curiosity about this woman who has been searching for me. The rhythmic rocking of the tiny car, buffeted by vehicles speeding past on either side, is comforting. I wonder if when I look at her, I will recognise her, see reflected in her face some of my features: the slightly upturned nose, the too-far-apart eyes, the flabby cheeks, the wide forehead. Will it be like looking in a mirror and seeing an older version of myself, like those computer animations where you enter a number and they age you by that number of years? Without warning, pity for her because she lost a child blooms, even though I can't quite connect that child with *me*. If I feel sorry for her, then do I believe her? If I do, then that means my mother...

Mum…the woman I have loved and looked up to all my life…the woman who is facing extradition…

And my mother's face blossoms in front of my closed lids: her soft, small face, her constantly moving eyes, glowing as they look at me, her button nose, her weary chin, her bow lips. Guilt sears, chocolate and salt, as the tears that roll down my cheeks slip past the barrier of my lips, as they make their arduous way along the slope of my mouth and inveigle underneath my chin.

Chapter 19
Vani

Borrowed Time

My precious Diya,
  These are the little details other mothers take for granted, but I never did, knowing that I had you on borrowed time:

1) *The way you grow every single day. A minuscule amount, not quite noticeable perhaps. But I noticed. I noted every little aspect of you, stored it away for the time when I would need to pull it from memory, for times like today.*

2) *The way your eyelashes splatter your cheeks like a fan when you are asleep and your lips part a little, dreams escaping via soft inhalations. I would love to get a peek into your dream world, Diya, to see what you think about when you are lost to the world and to yourself, if only to ease my constant worry that what I did has unconsciously affected you, that it will manifest itself somehow, some day.*

3) *The way you sigh sometimes when you are thinking, the long-drawn-out lament of an old woman with years of experience wrinkling her skin and lining her face.*

4) *The way you wear your hair, in a messy ponytail, most of the strands having escaped the confines of your hairband by the end of the school day, fanning across your face like shadows swaying on the russet bed of leaves in the heart of a forest.*

5) *The way you chew the ends of your hair when you are thinking, when there is no pencil end left to bite, a bad habit that I have warned you against but would give anything to see you do now.*

You will have outgrown your skirts and trousers, and most likely your shoes. You are growing an inch a day nowadays and I am so proud; soon you will be taller than me and I will look up to you. I will let you in on a secret here, Diya – I do already. You are admirable. Everything I hoped you would be and more. You inspire me every day with your innate goodness, your generosity, your happy demeanour, your sunny smile.

You will be needing a new wardrobe. Your hair will need a cut soon. I so wish I was around to nag you, to take you shopping, get your hair cut, give you a hug, a kiss, breathe you in, be rewarded by your smile, that twinkle in your eyes…

I wish.

So, we – my solicitor and I – are waiting. Waiting for the funding for the DNA test to come through and for it to be sanctioned. And while I wait, I write these letters, these missives to you.

Diya, I thought I would send these to you via my solicitor. But… You see, if this case, my case, goes to court, you will be on the side of the prosecution. And this case is very complicated and does not have many precedents, my solicitor informs me. While your lawyers and your care team go through the few cases on record and try to work out if any contact between you and me is allowed, they are erring on the side of caution. They fear that us meeting and even my letters to you might somehow influence you, bias you towards me in court.

I understand. I do, although it is torture to live without you, Diya, much harder than I anticipated. I cannot bear to think it, but it must be worse for you, to have to find your bearings without your mother by your side, especially now, when you need me most, when you are desperately hurting and lonely and lost. I am sorry, Diya. So very sorry.

I will stop now, my darling. Shadows are creeping down the wall and dancing on this sheet of paper. More tomorrow. Until then, sweet dreams, my heart.

Sending a goodnight kiss and all my love your way,
Mum

Chapter 20
Aarti

The Taste of Longing

Breakfast: Cereal: Bran Flakes – 30g with a dash of skimmed milk. Tastes of longing.

What is taking her so long? Why doesn't she want to see me? What have I done except wait for her, spent thirteen years searching for her, missing her?

I am tempted to go to her, rather than wait for her to come to me, but I don't know where she is. I am back to square one. I still do not know where she is. A small consolation is that at least now she is not in Vani's clutches.

With each day that passes I am more inclined to hire the private detective who found her for me, but I have run out of funds to pay him. Anyhow the real reason is that I am afraid. When I do find her, what if she doesn't want to see me?

Isn't that why she hasn't come yet? Isn't that why I am still waiting?

What if she shuts the door in my face and I lose her all over again?

❄ ❄ ❄

Aarti is running, running through the empty rooms of her house, listening for the sounds of a child's laughter, a child's cries and met only by silence. She is running like she used to when she herself was a child in search of her mother. She is running like a woman possessed, convinced that if she runs fast enough she will find her child, panic owning her body like an accomplished lover, sending thrills of fear up her legs and down her spine, manifesting itself in shuddering, soundless sobs that burst out of the void of her mouth. She is running from room to room, her face wet and her heart heavy from the weight of her tears. She is running the length and breadth of her huge house and she is alone.

Aarti wakes up gasping, grasping at air, wanting, yearning, aching…coming up empty. Always coming up empty. She blinks, tries to orient herself. A palm tree swaying, lurid green. The soft murmur of voices. The fruity scent of air freshener not quite masking the stale whiff of overcooked vegetables. She is in the lobby, tucked into the sofa behind an artificial palm – it is that sort of hotel – where she can spy on people without them noticing. She must have dozed off and been visited by the nightmare again, the same one that has besieged her repeatedly over the years. A nightmare that she lived through thirteen years previously and, as if once wasn't horrifying enough, one that she relives over and over again.

Aarti has not been sleeping well at night, too keyed up, worrying about why her daughter hasn't contacted her, worrying if, when she does, will she bond with Aarti, thinking of what to say to her daughter when she finally meets her.

She shrugs away the last vestige of the lingering nightmare and watches guests arrive, young families, old couples – the hotel is near the town centre and yet not that near. It is one of those 'affordable' ones. In the early days, Aarti would have balked at staying anywhere other than a four-star hotel at the very least. But now the money is dwindling, along with any work she had hoped to find. She is the skinniest she has ever been but the industry has always been fickle, geared towards younger, prettier women.

To tell the truth, she hasn't really been interested in work for a while now, thirteen years to be exact. Everything has taken second place to the urgency of finding her daughter.

Aarti closes her eyes, a headache looming as memories of that awful time after claim her. All those years of searching, leading up to this point. And somehow, despite all the years of not knowing, the lonesome hours bleeding into each other, these last few days are taking the longest.

The waiting. The yearning to see her daughter, to touch her, talk to her. She puts both arms around her stomach, hugs herself close. She is nervous. Afraid. Will her daughter like what she sees? She is a far cry from the model she used to be once. Age has caught up with her; there are lines around her eyes, lines tugging her lips downward, spidery strokes that no amount of make-up can hide. Lines etched over the years of searching, bearing witness to her degradation, her despair. Lines that mark the ravages Vani has inflicted on her. Vani has a lot to answer for, she thinks, as she closes her eyes and imagines her suffering in jail, the thought calming her nerves. A hell of a lot to answer for. *I hope it is hell for her in there.*

Chapter 21
Vani

The Echo in the Room

Dearest Diya, my darling girl,
  Do you remember:

1) *That time you decided to teach me to swim because you had read somewhere that everyone should know how to swim and you were shocked that I didn't? You coaxed me into the water of that freezing outdoor pool.*

You said, 'Come on, Mum, it's not that bad.'
You were so patient, even when I kept on crying, the tears mingling with the chlorinated water of the pool.
'You are doing so well,' you cheered.
And I smiled through my tears, splashed some water on you and said, 'I am.'
I was afraid of the water after what happened to my parents, but for your sake, because you so wanted me to learn, I got in. I was terrified, and yet, I was so proud of you. As

you held my hand and persuaded me on, I was thinking that when I was old and no longer able to take care of myself, a little senile perhaps, this was how you would look after me. With the perfect blend of gentleness and firmness.

But all the while I was also thinking, as you led me across the pool, admonished me to, 'move your legs, Mum, move your legs', not caring about the other swimmers gawping, the older ones smiling softly and meeting my eye, awe and envy mingling in their expressions, the younger ones hiding their smiles, all the while I thought, will I get to see you grow into a wonderful adult? Will I be with you when I am old? Will you want to know me at all after you find out? What will the knowledge do to you?

2) *The one and only time we went on holiday? You wheedled and sweet-talked, and said, 'Everyone goes, Mum, why not us?'*

But the thing that clinched it for me was when you said, in a huff, 'Why don't we ever do normal things like other normal people?'

And so, I gave in and we spent many excited evenings, me swept along on the wave of your enthusiasm, researching holiday cottages, circling the ones within our meagre budget, planning how to get there.

I smiled along with you, while worrying about the hazards of a new place, the people we might encounter – all it took was one person to make a connection, place a phone call. I tried to shut out images of police ambushing the holiday cottage, dragging me away, your shattered face, the enthusiasm and excitement replaced by fear and heartbreak.

'Relax, Mum,' you told me on the train, barely able to sit on the seat, that's how excited you were, as I surreptitiously checked out every single person in our compartment and the people walking up and down the train, the people getting on at stops, the people I locked eyes with at the stations.

We had rented a small caravan by the beach and we had the perfect two days. We bought burgers and kebabs at the local Tesco and cooked them on the tiny grill. We shivered under the blankets – the heating was not working, and we laughed ourselves to sleep telling each other funny stories. We built sandcastles replete with moats. We ran into the icy water and ran right back out again. We sucked on sticks of sickly sweet rock and let the wind whip our hair into a tizzy. We window-shopped and won 20p on the slot machines at the pier.

Somewhere around the afternoon of the second day, I relaxed. We sat on the beach and you played in the sand and gambolled in the water, your hands bunched into fists as if to grab hold of the miraculous waves, and I watched you and revelled in you, the magic, the miracle of you.

I took plenty of pictures. You see Diya, I never had any photos of my parents and I regret that more than I can say. You sputtered when you tasted salt and I have a picture of that. I have one of you sitting cross-legged in the water, still as Buddha, my golden brown marvel surrounded by all that bobbing blue. And there is one of the two of us, smiling into the camera, the one we asked a passer-by to take, our hands occupied by newspaper cones of chips, the salty oily smell of them, the smacking vinegary taste, seagulls swooping, sand winking honey-yellow and the sea surging and ebbing behind us.

You slept on the train home, your hair smelling of salt and dotted with sand, long black strands flecked with gold framing your face. Your arms around my neck, soft snores escaping from between half-open lips, a smile flitting across your mouth like a frisky butterfly alighting on a nectar-bountiful bush.

3) *That time you were eleven and starting to grow breasts and I decided it was time for a talk? I sat you down and tried to tell you what would happen. You laughed as I stumbled over the words, as I tried and failed to meet your eye.*

'I know it all, Mum. I know what will happen to my body,' you said.

'You do?' I asked, shocked, finally looking up at you.

'They've told us in school.'

'They've told you in school?' I repeated, not able to process the information fast enough.

'There is an echo in the room, don't you think?' You asked, eyes twinkling.

'There is an echo in the room?' I said and we fell about laughing.

Afterwards, I tried talking about boys and you sighed, impatient, and said, 'I'm not stupid, Mum. I read a lot you know; I can put two and two together. And anyway, nobody's interested in me.' You had blinked and fiddled with your jumper then and I had cupped your chin, cornered your gaze with mine.

'Have you looked at yourself, Diya? Really looked at yourself? You do not see what I see, do you? The caramel eyes one can lose oneself in, the straight nose, the lovely lips that actresses pay huge amounts to have pumped up? I know you are worried about your weight, but that is puppy fat, darling. You will lose it as you grow into your adult body. And even if you don't, you are beautiful, just as you are.'

You had blinked away the tears beading your eyes. 'To you, perhaps, Mum,' you said and I wished with all my heart that I could show you what I saw when I looked at you.

I had led you to the mirror, asked you to look at yourself.

'You are beautiful,' I said. 'Repeat after me.'

'You are beautiful,' you said and we laughed, your tears dispersing like rain drops.

'You know what I mean, silly girl,' I said.

'You know what I mean, silly girl,' you repeated.

And once again, we were laughing, laughing until tears – happy ones this time – rolled down our cheeks.

We had some good times, didn't we? All we need in this life, I have learnt, Diya, is to know we are loved. We want to be loved and cherished and to be the centre of someone's world. You are the centre of mine. I hope you know that, sweetie. I hope you do.

I hope that today you pull out a memory of the good times we had and it soothes you like a hug.

Night night, my love. Sending kisses, the sweetest of dreams and all my love your way,

Mum

Chapter 22
Diya

Friend

Friend

Noun: a person attached to another by feelings of affection or personal regard.

Related forms: friendless, friendlessness, non-friend.

❄ ❄ ❄

'Oh my God, Diya, I am so sorry,' Lily says, engulfing me in a hug so tight it knocks the breath right out of me.

I inhale her smell: milk and vanilla, so familiar in the unfamiliar world I am still finding my bearings in that my legs almost give way right there in the school corridor.

'Friend' was one of the first words I wrote in my first ever vocabulary book. I think it came right after 'Mother'. I knew the word, its meaning and usage long before I actually understood what friendship entailed, what being a friend meant, many years before I experienced friendship with this wonderful girl standing next to me, her eyes shining with empathy, her arms feeling like home. I have first-hand knowledge now of what being a confidant means, the giggling and sharing of secrets, the making of promises. The only first-hand knowledge I had before Lily was that of being friendless, experiencing the state of friendlessness.

I met Lily, on my first day at this school, when she came up to me and said, 'Hi, I'm Lily. Nice to meet you,' her hand outstretched and her grin wide.

No child in any of the other schools I had attended had done that. They had just ignored me and I had ignored them back, a defence mechanism on my part. It didn't work though. They didn't leave me alone for long, the bullies. And ignoring the jeers and taunts required gargantuan effort on my part. I learnt the hard way not to flinch when they called me names, to wipe my face clear of expression, to bury my nose in a book, risking being labelled a swot. After all, what was one more label to add to the many I seemed to amass no matter what school I went to?

I had thought Lily was making fun of me, that this was some new kind of prank. I had been afraid to take her hand. She had sensed my hesitation and she had put her arms around me, surprising me because, once again, no one had ever done that before and also because of how good it felt, how natural. We were just two girls greeting each other, two *friends*. That was the first time I allowed myself access to the word in the context of me, allowed a sliver of hope to nudge in.

'Oh come on, I'm not that scary,' she had laughed into my stiff, unused-to-hugs shoulder.

And I had breathed in her smell, that curious blend of milk and vanilla, reminiscent of ice cream, and relaxed, feeling comforted.

And after all those years of not having a friend, it was that easy. That was Lily. She openly and disarmingly chose me for a friend and stuck with me, stuck by me.

Initially, I found it hard to confide in her, afraid she would mock me, laugh at my silliness. I had no experience of sharing. But she taught me how. She gave and gave and waited until I could give back. She is a blessing and now, standing here, I appreciate just how much.

'I have missed you,' I say, realising as I say it that it is true. I have, even though everything I feel has been masked and taken over by the incredible flower of pain that flourishes within me, binding my insides in a stranglehold.

Her eyes sparkle while mine are dry as skin inflamed by eczema. I have exhausted tears this past week. I am empty, numb. It is so nice to see Lily, a familiar face after the jumble and upheaval of the week off school for which I had had such high hopes: the various tests; the different doctors; the pungent smell of chloroform and bleach, mixing with the purple, sickly sweet aroma of illness and death lingering in the corridors of the hospital; the psychologist with her big eyes and thick glasses which somehow make her eyes look even bigger; the gooey taste of chocolate and the comforting crunch of crisps forever ruined by the briny tang of guilt and hurt and loss so that now I cannot eat a chocolate or a crisp without feeling sick with the ache of what I have lost, without that flower, the weed stirring in my stomach, burgeoning.

'I am so sorry. I didn't know where you were, Diya. I tried asking around. Nobody in your block of flats knew. If I had known, I would have been round in an instant.' Lily's voice is high-pitched with pain; she is hurting for me.

'I am sorry about the sleepover,' I say.

'Pshaw…' she says, a jumble of discordant sound bursting out of her mouth as she is surprised mid-sob. 'That's the last thing you should worry about,' she hiccups.

'I was so looking forward to it,' I say, and even as I say it, I feel the pain bloom in my stomach and I want to double over. I manage to stay still, and even though my eyes prickle, they are dry.

'Yes,' she says, launching herself at me for another hug.

'Hey, Diya, Lily,' the boisterous throng of classmates pushing past call and Lily pulls back to stare at me, her eyes wide with shock, tears glinting at the corners, sticking to her eyelashes like glitter in a child's painting, the sequins on my mother's sari.

No, don't think about that.

'Did you hear that?' she asks.

Did I just speak my thoughts out loud? I think.

'They talked to us, the coolest gang in the school actually said hello to us!' Lily is smiling and at that moment, with her sparkly eyes and her glowing face, she looks stunning.

'You look beautiful,' I say. 'You should cry more often.'

She stares at me for a minute and then links her arm through mine. 'As if I don't cry enough already, silly,' she says good-humouredly. 'As it is, everyone calls me a cry baby.'

I quickly discover that I am a celebrity. At lunchtime, Lily and I are invited to join the cool table; they move over to make space for us.

'How *are* you?' they ask me. And, 'Is it true?'

'What?' I say, looking at a point above their heads, thinking of nothing. My strategy is finally working. My mind is blank.

'That your mother was arrested for kidnapping you?'

I flinch, I cannot help it. Epic strategy fail.

'Leave her alone,' Lily stands up, picking up her tray and mine with one hand and tugging at my arm with the other, 'Come on, let's go.'

'No, wait. Sit, please.' The girl who asked the question – I don't know her name, I was practising my strategy when she told me – has the grace to look embarrassed, two spots of colour dancing high on her cheeks which make her, for one brief moment, look less like her friends and more like herself, a tiny bit of personality shining through. These popular girls all look alike, clones of each other. Long blonde hair, long black boots, endless legs.

Lily looks at me. 'You want to?'

I shrug.

She sits back down.

I admire her courage, the way she holds her own in that gaggle, the way she is happy to give up hanging with the cool crowd if it means I am spared being a target. *She is a true friend,* I think. *I can trust her,* I think and the pain starts again. *I trusted my mother and look what happened,* a voice inside my head whispers. I want to double up. I ignore it, will it away.

All around me there is chatter. My classmates talking about who fancies who, who has put on weight and who they are convinced is anorexic. They talk about *X Factor* and the latest band to make number one, they prattle about clothes and phone apps and I think how far removed I am from all of this. I think, why did I ever feel nervous to come here? Why was I scared of these *kids*, once upon a time?

I eat my sandwich but I cannot taste it. I cannot taste anything anymore. I have stopped craving chocolate and crisps, have gone off them. I eat because I have to, because Farah does not let me leave the table unless I finish what's on my plate – 'This is one of the rules in this house, Diya, and you have to abide by it. I haven't given you much, look, just the same as the boys.'

The joy I used to derive from food is not there anymore. It does not comfort like it used to. I am blank inside, numb, except for the times the flower blooms, taking over. Mostly this happens late at night, the darkness as unrelenting as the images that scroll under closed lids. My mother keeping vigil when I was ill, her worried gaze fixed on me, her gentle hands ministering cool cloths to my blistering forehead. My mother taking a hold of my hands, dancing me around the flat when she read my report. My mother cooking, her hair escaping in flustered tendrils around her face, beads of sweat trembling on the top of her upper lip as she stirred and sprinkled and fried. My mother holding me, her arms administering the comfort I always took for granted. My mother's soft, love-filled gaze, the way her whole face transformed when she looked at me. My mother being led away, between a posse of police officers. My mother's voice, drifting in a ghastly echo up the stinky stairwell, 'I am your mother, Diya. You are mine. I love you, Diya, my darling girl, light of my life.'

Ever since Jane told me about her impending extradition – I have looked the word up, know now what it means, although I stubbornly have *not* written it in my vocabulary book, the first ever word I needed to look up that hasn't gone in the book – I have been consumed with a desire to do something. I cannot just let her go. I cannot. She is here, in this country, close by for now. But she may not be soon. She will be taken to India and charged with… *No. Nononono…*

And then, despite myself, I think of another woman, searching desperately for the child she lost, looking into every little girl's face and seeing her daughter, recognising some feature of hers. Thirteen years of searching, waiting, longing, hoping, while I was being loved and looked after by another woman.

I ache for my mother, I miss her. And yet, I feel sorry for this other woman, I feel upset for her loss. I cannot equate the girl this woman lost with me. I cannot see my mother as a villain – the woman who loved me so much that she endured thirteen years of being afraid of her own shadow, scared to look behind her in case the shadow pounced and snatched her child away as she had, once long ago, appropriated another woman's.

I feel guilty, I feel torn, I feel terrified, out of my depth. The flower runs riot inside my body, my head aches and I do not want to think, to feel. I want the luxury of an empty mind, I want the anonymity, the welcome respite of dreamless sleep, but both evade me.

I have read every single book on the bedside table in that little room in Farah's house that is temporarily mine, but I couldn't recount the stories in them to anybody even if my life depended on it. I know at what time of the night Zain calls for his mother, at what time Sohrab stumbles to the loo. I know when Affan runs to his parents' room on padded feet and when he is led back gently by his mother and eased into bed. I know when they cry out in their sleep and when Farah rushes over to comfort them. Those times I curl into a foetal position, smothering my sobs with one pillow and the pain in my stomach with another.

On the rare occasions when I do sleep, I dream. I see a woman and a child. Then I see another woman who says the child is hers. The women fight, they pull the child, they break her in two. I wake up with my head pounding, my heart trying to crawl out of the stranglehold of my chest. I open the window and breathe in big gulps of freezing air, startling the fox who looks up from his dominion of the bin and peruses me curiously with tawny eyes. I watch the couple making out under the lamp post in the alleyway and wish for the blessed relief of an ordinary life.

I taste the sweet night air and I talk to my mum. 'Mum, it is 2:30 in the morning. Are you awake? In another life, my life of less than a week ago, you always, without fail, no matter how tired you were, used to fall asleep after me. You once told me that you never let yourself give in to the persistent command of your droopy eyelids until mine closed, until my breathing settled into the regular rhythm of deep slumber. You would always fluster awake if I so much as moved, remember? It comforts me, Mum, to think that you are awake somewhere thinking of me, while everybody else sleeps, the soft blue blanket of air in their rooms populated by their reveries, punctured by their sighs, perforated by their dream-coated mumbles. Wherever you are, you will be worrying about me, I know. I am fine, Mum. I am. I hope you are comfortable. I hope you are okay. I love you, Mum. I miss you so. I wish…I wish you were here. If you were, I would drift off to sleep content in the knowledge that all was well in my world. You are less than fifteen miles away and yet it feels like eternity, an immeasurable, unbridgeable distance. And soon, you will be gone. To India. I cannot contemplate that, Mum. I will not accept it. I cannot just sit here, helpless, and let you go. I will do something – that is a promise, even though I feel powerless, like a mere pawn in this game being orchestrated by players who do not know me and yet hold my fate in their hands. At times I am angry with you, Mum, for doing what they say you did, for getting us into this situation. But then your face looms and I cannot stay angry with you any longer... I love you, Mum. I hope this kiss I am blowing to the stars makes its way to you.'

I close the window before the nippy draft invades the whole house and Farah wanders in bleary-eyed to check on me. Goosebumps have sprouted on me like sores, my hands are blue as sorrow, my teeth chatter like unruly children. I cannot bend my fingers. And yet, I don't feel the cold. I don't feel anything except the weed of pain which has taken me over.

The fox has disappeared inside the dustbin, only bushy tail visible, waving like a hand at an airport. The lovers have disentangled themselves from each other's embrace and are making their separate ways home, turning to look back at each other from opposite ends of the alley. A car zooms past. A drunk sings loudly, slurring on the words as he stumbles home. Where is my home? Who am I? Rupa Shetty? Diya Bhat? Who am I?

'Diya?' I startle into the present at the sound of my name. For now, I think wryly, I am Diya Bhat. 'You and Lily want to hang out with us after school? We're going to Crazy Joe's for milkshakes.'

Lily is looking at me hopefully.

'You go, Lily. I have...Jane, my social worker, is picking me up. I don't want to make her wait.'

My classmates wait for me to say more, qualify the statement with an explanation. I fiddle with my juice carton. 'My foster carer lives quite a distance away, you see, and she cannot pick me because she's got two boys of her own at primary school and they finish at around the same time as us.' I am babbling but I cannot seem to stop. 'This is just for the first few days. I'll start taking public transport soon; I think I'll have to take three buses to get here.'

I swallow, look down at my plate littered with the remains of my sandwich. It feels like this is the longest I have spoken since it all happened. I sit quietly in front of the psychologist, answering her questions in monosyllables, and she has taken to giving me a piece of paper now to depict my feelings. She has encouraged me to keep a diary. She has said she understands why I might be feeling tongue-tied. I had snorted then, in exasperation, I couldn't help it. But I feel for her too, this woman with her thick glasses and owl-like, kindly eyes who is trying to do her best by me. But what can she do? What can anyone do?

I haven't taken up Farah's or Jane's offer of a chat, to talk about anything, anything at all. Jane has not brought up the woman who has been searching for me since she mentioned it that day in the car – I cannot bring myself to say 'my mother', I cannot think of her as my mother even though I feel sorry for her. It would be a blatant betrayal of the woman who has looked after me and loved me and lived for me for thirteen years. Whatever she did, there must have been good reason behind it. 'I am sorry it had to happen this way. At the time...' she had said, her sigh immense, as she was led away. I ache for those easy days together, just the two of us, happy in our little bubble, nothing else intruding upon us, no outside world, no people laying claim.

The week's gone by in a haze of tests, all of which came back fine. 'They cannot find anything wrong with me; my mother loved me,' I said to Jane fiercely in the car when she drove me back from the hospital for the last time, after I had said goodbye to the doctors and the kind-hearted nurse, Eileen, who gave me a picture of Bugbear, her schnauzer, and a million hugs and asked me to visit sometime, though not in similar circumstances. Eileen had smiled softly, her eyes shining. 'You are a lovely girl, Diya,' she had said. 'I would take you home in an instant.'

That, there, is the problem, I had thought. *I have one too many people demanding me for their own, and I was taken home by a person who perhaps shouldn't have.* But she must have had a reason, I had thought immediately, knocking the previous thought away, angry at my mind for having betrayed my mother even for an instant. She must have had a reason.

Jane has not mentioned the woman again but I know she will. It will come. The woman is here, somewhere close by. She has been looking for me my whole life. She will want to meet me, I know. I just…every time I think of it, of her waiting patiently to meet her daughter – *me!* – my stomach cramps, my head aches.

It is not fair that my mother is in prison while this woman is here. I am angry at this woman for turning up, for causing all this mess. Without her claiming me, my mother would be with me and all would be well in my world.

If Mum hadn't taken me, there wouldn't be a mess. I squash the thought. I cannot fathom another life with another woman as my mother. I cannot.

'Isn't there anything I can do? Anything I can say that can help towards her release?' I had asked Jane on one of our journeys to the hospital. She had sighed deeply, eyes meeting mine briefly before concentrating on the road, something akin to pity shining out of them.

I don't want your pity, I had thought, anger flaring.

'No, Diya, I am so sorry. It is out of our hands now,' she had said.

'How?' I had yelled. 'How can it be out of my hands? *I* am the one affected by all this. How can I not have a say?'

She had pulled over, stopped the car, put her arms around my shaking shoulders briefly before I shrugged them off.

Jane is waiting in the car park when I come out of school, the new gang I find myself a part of giving me elaborate hugs. I extricate myself, encourage Lily to have a milkshake for me and walk slowly to the car.

Jane smiles at me as she starts the engine. 'How did it go?'

'Fine,' I say, fiddling with the clasp of my bag, not looking at her.

When we get to Farah's, dusk has settled like a curtain announcing winter's last act before spring takes centre stage, mellow golden light pooling underneath street lamps with heads ducked down like chastised children. The curtains are not drawn in the front room. I can see Farah, Affan and Zain sitting at the table; their heads bent together, their hair haloed by soft light bathing them in a supernatural glow. As I watch, Affan places his hand, palm outward on the table. Farah reaches out, lays her palm on top of his. Zain, not to be undone, lays his hand on top as well, the boys' palms sandwiching their mother's. And suddenly, I know what I must do.

'Jane,' I say softly.

She has just switched off the engine, is scrabbling about for her purse.

'Yes?' Her eyes, the colour of sea-splashed gravel, shining in the gloom.

A dog howls somewhere, mournfully. A car pulls up in the garage next door and a besuited man jumps out, loosening his tie, running a weary hand through his hair. The door opens and a little boy launches at him. He drops his bag and lifts up his son. The boy's delighted laughter, his cries of 'Higher, Daddy,' rend the evening air, stained blue by the sorrow of the dying day and infused with the heady promise of impending night.

I never felt the lack of a father, never missed him. You were enough, Mum. Was what you told me about him, that he had died in an accident, a lie? It will be like this from now on, won't it, me questioning every truth you ever told me? 'You tell them, Mum,' I had said that fateful evening when they took you away from me, but you stayed silent. One moment, one unacknowledged plea and thirteen years of truths collapse, topple around us like a house constructed of paper blown away by a child on a whim. Thirteen years of trust, destroyed as easily as an elaborate sandcastle washed away by one unruly wave. Can I believe anything you say ever again?

'This woman you mentioned, the one who has been searching for me, she brought the charges against my mother?'

Zain tickles his mother and then both the boys are jumping on their mother, tickling her. I see Farah's head fall backward, her eyes crinkle in laughter.

'Yes. But, Diya, she did it out of love for you. I know it is hard, but try not to blame her.' Jane's voice is gentle as the breeze that whispers through the bare trees, soft as the murmur of the wings of crows flying to their nests to roost.

'Yes, yes,' I say impatiently. 'She still wants to see me?'

Farah pulls the boys close, plants a kiss on each of their heads.

'Of course she does.' The car smells of dying engine, exhaust, Jane's perfume mixed in with sweat, her tiredness.

'I would like to meet her,' I say. 'Tomorrow.'

Farah stands up, turns and looks out of the window. The car is dark, headlights off, and yet I have the feeling she is looking right at me.

I will meet this woman and I will reason with her. I will tell her how much I love my mother. I will bargain with her, I will promise to be a wonderful daughter; I will promise her anything, anything at all, as long as my mother doesn't have to be in prison, as long as she is not extradited and charged, as long as I know she is safe and free. So simple. Why didn't I think of it before? I wonder as we get out of the car and walk towards the house as Farah opens the door, a little boy on either side of her, sheltered under the awning of her arms. Is she holding them or are they propping her up? When she sees me, she disentangles herself, steps forward and pulls me into a hug, even though I resist and escape at the earliest opportunity.

And for the first time since that nightmarish evening, I sleep. I dream that my mother is free, that she is smiling at me, her butterscotch eyes glowing, that we are dancing together, she in her sari, me in my jeans and sweatshirt. We dance and we laugh, her sari pallu swirling, trailing a rainbow in our wake, and our joy rings out like pealing bells and we are happy.

Chapter 23
Aarti

Lightheaded

Breakfast: While I was eating my slice of toast (from a 400g wholemeal loaf – no butter), I thought once again of my girl, as I have taken to doing all the time now.

What is keeping her? If it was me, if I was told my mother was waiting to meet me, had travelled all the way from India for the privilege, I wouldn't dally.

I have railed at the lawyer, asked him to do something. Surely I should have access to my own child? He keeps going on about how the child is undergoing huge trauma, to give her time...

'Time! How much longer do I have to wait? Thirteen years isn't long enough?' I yelled.

'There are procedures,' he mumbled. 'She's had a shock, been cruelly separated from the only mother she's known...'

'I am her mother!' I screeched.

Cruelly separated. Ha! Doesn't she want to meet the mother she was cruelly snatched away from when she was a baby? What has Vani done to her to make her so...so reluctant to meet me? Has she filled my child's head with stories, tall tales about the woman whom Vani's always known would one day reclaim the child she stole? Did she think she would get away with this? She must have thought I would give up, sink into despair and let it claim me, like she claimed my child for her own…

❈ ❈ ❈

Aarti sighs, shutting the book with a frustrated thud. The food diary, which has given her such solace over the years, is not helping. She cannot concentrate on anything, cannot settle. She is so keyed up. She wants to walk to the high street, but in this present state, it would not be a good idea, she knows. Her lawyer's voice echoing in her ears, 'If it happens again, I will not be able to get you out as easily…'

It happened on her third trip to London. The investigator had phoned to tell her of a possible sighting in Harrow – a woman matching Vani's description seen entering a kebab shop in Wealdstone with a three-year-old child, a little girl. Aarti had booked into a hotel near the kebab shop which was, thankfully right on the high street.

Aarti had sat glued to the window of her room looking at the flow of people below, waiting for news. It was early April and a weak sun graced the sky, casting the colourful shop awnings and the pavements glittering with the previous night's rain in a mellow gold glow. People milled about, all colours and races, most in shorts. Just looking at them made Aarti shiver and she pulled her shawl closer around her neck, revelling in its warmth, the heating in the room turned to high, nose pressed to the window.

Teenagers pushed each other into the puddles glistening on the road. Cars moved at ants' pace, hindered by traffic lights and speed bumps, the drivers' eyes glazed with boredom. Near the flower shop a girl idled, checking her phone. Tall, thin, effortlessly stunning, her long blonde hair falling down the sides of her face like a shiny waterfall, iridescent in the sun. She must be a model, Aarti thought, struck by a sudden pang for bygone days, when she used to be feted and loved and admired. At the time, she had been pleased, but irritated by the constant spotlight of devotion dogging her. Now, she mused wryly, some of that dazzling adoration, the feeling of being the centre of attention, basking in the limelight, wouldn't go amiss.

Aarti started to turn away, to ring for a pot of tea, when she saw her. A little girl holding on to a woman's hand. About three years old. The right age.

From where she was sitting, by the first floor window, Aarti couldn't see the woman's face. She was turned away, haggling with a vendor who had set up shop under a blue and white striped awning, plastic containers of onions, peppers, marrows, aubergines and tomatoes jostling for space on a narrow table that took up most of the pavement. The woman was slight and stooped, clad in a sari, her head covered by a pallu like married women commonly wore in India, incongruous here. Aarti knew without a doubt that she was hiding her face, that when she whipped the pallu away Aarti would see Vani, fear glowing in her eyes. Heat rushed through her, the thrill of rage, the adrenalin-fuelled buzz of discovery. One of the few positive feelings she had felt in a long time, like the sheer blast of hope when her investigator had phoned to tell her about the lead.

Her eyes were drawn to the little girl. Huge eyes, almond, flecked with gold. A round, dimpled face, curly brown hair. Adorable. The girl looked up, and for a moment, Aarti was sure she saw her sitting there, her nose pressed to the window. The cherub held her hand out palm up, opened her little fist as if she was offering something and Aarti was convinced that the little girl *recognised* her, knew her for who she was – her mother.

And then she was running, clattering down the stairs, not bothering to close the door to her room, not bothering to wait for the lift. She was flinging herself into the street, undeterred by the blast of wind that insinuated itself around her, wrapping her in its icy embrace, chilly fingers tickling her spine which was clad in only a thin jumper.

She took huge gulps as she ran, tasting excitement and joy. She sprinted past the rush of people, her elbows digging into flesh, running on strength she didn't know she possessed.

Please God – she was praying to a God she had forsaken long ago, at around the same time she forsook her parents – *please*. And it seemed God listened to her prayer, because as she came to a panting, heaving halt, the little girl was still there.

The child looked up at Aarti, her expression curious, and then she smiled. Aarti squatted down right there on the wet, rain-slicked pavement and pulled the girl into her arms, breathed in the soft baby smell of her, talc mixed in with the sweetest of dreams. A brief moment of bliss, before the woman turned.

'Hey, what are you…' she began.

But that is as far as she got before Aarti, who had gathered the last of her resources, stood up and, with all the strength she had left, slapped the woman hard across the cheek and then, promptly, fainted.

It had taken several lawyers and several lakh rupees to get Aarti out of that one. She had apologised over and over, the circumstances had been explained and the court ruled 'lower culpability' and 'isolated offence' and 'mitigating circumstances'. She was let off with a fine.

Afterwards, her lawyer had sat her down and warned her that this had better not happen again. 'Would you consider stopping this? Do you have to come over every time there is a sighting?' he had asked, his eyes soft.

In another world, at another time, she would have flirted with him, knowing there was something there, that he liked her. 'I can't, I can't stay away. This is my life now. I have to know.'

He had nodded once. He understood. 'But please,' he had said, 'no repeat of this. I cannot get you out as easily next time. And you cannot help anybody, cannot find your daughter if you are in prison.'

Her phone rings, startling her out of her reverie.

'Ms Kumar?' A crisp English voice.

'Yes?' she blinks, trying to get back to the present.

The lobby of the hotel, the chemical smell of bleach and artificial flowers, phones ringing in reception, a woman laughing, high-pitched, the laughter fading to a tinkle.

'Your daughter is ready to meet you.' The voice softening on the last word.

'Leave that this minute, Henry, and come here at once,' a male voice yells sharply, somewhere behind her.

She breathes in, trying to rid herself of the lightheaded feeling that seems to have swamped her, clutching the diary to her chest like a talisman. *Your daughter.*

'Shall I bring her round tomorrow after school?'

Aarti nods before realising she is on the phone. She clears her throat.

'Yes,' she says. 'Yes, please,' and floats up to her room on legs that seem to glide on air – past Henry who is still giving his tired, beleaguered father the slip – to decide what she will wear when she meets with her daughter for the first time in thirteen endless years.

Chapter 24
Vani

The Snake of Apprehension

My darling Diya,

1) *When you were seven months old, you fell ill. You had a temperature, diarrhoea, the works. Your cry reverted back to being the mewl it had been when you were just a few days old. Your cheeks were flushed and inflamed.*

I was beside myself. I hadn't registered at the surgery. We had fake papers but I did not want to put them under scrutiny just yet. It was early days. I told myself that if you did not get better within the next two days, I would take you to the doctor, risk being damned.

That night, you wouldn't settle; you kept opening and closing your mouth, chomping on my hand, and I could feel the hot, desperate heat of your tender gums. I held you in my arms and prayed to a God I hoped had not forsaken me after what I did. I bartered and bargained with him — what I did, I did out of love for you, you see, and it would be fitting punishment if God took you away from me.

As dawn chased night away and light inveigled itself into the dark room, the air weary and thick, weighted down with illness and fear, I made up my mind. I was going to take you to the doctor. If we were caught, that was fine. Your life was, had always been, more important than what would happen to me, to us.

And then, as I stood up, you opened your mouth and I saw it. A sliver of white poking from between the sore red gums at the centre of the bottom palate, looking like the moon trying to part the curtain of sky at twilight.

I laughed, I cried. I held you close, rocked you and then rushed out with you to buy a teething ring. You improved as soon as the tooth pushed through and after that, with the other teeth it was easier, perhaps because I knew what to expect.

2) *You walked when you were one and a bit, tottering steps – your goal: me. I had put you down on the mat in the living room, where I could keep an eye on you as I cooked. I was frying onions for our supper, the smell of spices and busyness, sweat plastered to my face, the sheen of steam, and I felt this grip on my sari. I looked down and it was you, standing upright and smiling at me! You had walked across the room and into the kitchen, all on your own and I had missed it!*

I screamed with delight, lifted you up, twirled you around. 'Show me,' I said, setting you down, kissing your fragrant cheek.

And you had toddled on jelly legs that managed to hold you up, just; you had teetered like a haphazard stack of books and you had stumbled like a cute little pygmy, drunk on exhilaration, right into my arms. Drunk on love and happiness, that's what I was. And pride. I was so proud of you, my love. So very proud.

I still am.

3) *When you were two, the gibberish you were speaking, which always, nevertheless, made absolute sense to me, transformed by magic into words. And once you started speaking, once you discovered the marvel of words, you were off and there was no stopping you.*

It was a time of miracles, the first and foremost being that we had done it. We had run away to a strange country, breaking so many laws, and we had survived beyond that crucial first year. You were now officially a toddler and you seemed content. I used to watch you all the time, right up until the inevitable happened and we were separated, to see if what I did had affected you. Everything you did, I compared with what literature was available. Was it normal? Were you happy?

If you had a nightmare, I would worry that perhaps it was the trauma that you had experienced manifesting itself in your sleep.

'What was the scary dream about, darling?' I asked as I rocked you in my arms, trying not to let my worry colour my voice, your breath coming in gasps of remembered sobs.

'A snake.' You hiccupped.

My heart stilled. A snake? Definitely something about India, then. What did it represent?

'Huge one. And it came close, opened its fangs, hissed at me and then swallowed me whole.'

I closed my eyes, the snake of panic gripping me and swallowing me whole. 'I know it is hard, but try not to think about it, Diya,' I said, thinking, the blind leading the blind. I was trying to reassure my daughter and I was terrified, possessed by the snake of apprehension. 'There are no such snakes in England, I promise.'

I held you until you fell asleep out of sheer exhaustion in my arms.

Afterwards I spent ages looking up references about snakes in dreams, obsessing about what your nightmare meant, what your subconscious was trying to communicate to you. I couldn't settle, convinced that the trauma you had experienced was taking its toll; that this was the beginning.

Sometime in the early hours of dawn, I stumbled to the loo and found, lying open beside the seat, the book you were reading. It was all about snakes! And it was open to the page on pythons, replete with pictures, fangs wide open. I sobbed in sheer relief, sitting there on the toilet seat for what seemed like hours.

You had so many nightmares. You were prone to them. I suppose that comes from reading everything in sight; it fosters an overactive imagination. I painstakingly researched every single nightmare, searching for evidence of what was going on in your subconscious, worrying about whether you were really as happy and as settled as you looked.

4) *My next test was enrolling you in school. I would miss you terribly, but you were ready.*

That first day, you cried, holding on to my sari. But you came back out skipping happily. You had had such fun, as I knew you would.

For days, I waited for a phone call, for the police to turn up, but the false papers did their job. I breathed easier after that.

You enjoyed school. You loved studying. The other children – not so much. They made fun of your weight and of the fact that you loved to learn. But you took it in your stride. I did not even know you were being bullied until some years later when I was called in because of an essay you had submitted in which you described what you were going through.

When the head teacher called, I thought, this is it. They've found out.

They had – not about what I had done but about what was being done to you. 'Please always let us know if you have any concerns, Ms Bhat. We're here to help.'

I went home on teetering legs, unable to stomach the thought of you hurting, of you going through so much and me not knowing. And I thought I had been observant. What else had I been missing? What kind of mother was I?

I waited all day, not going to work, pacing up and down, and you were shocked to see me home so early when you walked in, the shock replaced almost instantly by joy.

You had flung yourself at me and I had held you in my arms, relishing as always the feel of you, breathing in your scent, chips and that flowery deodorant you had taken to wearing and something musty, uniquely you.

'You didn't go to work?' A question in your voice.

'The head teacher called me in,' I said. 'I didn't know you were being bullied. How long has it been going on?'

A shadow fluttered briefly across your face. 'Oh that. Mum, it's nothing.'

'Really? The teachers don't seem to think so and neither do I.'

We had talked late into the night. You assured me you were fine. You said you were happy and I believed you. I had no recourse. You seemed happy, content with your lot. But the guilt that was always hovering reigned supreme. Would you have been bullied if you were brought up in India? Perhaps you wouldn't have been overweight there. You would have had people to look after you, feed you when you came home from school, proper food, not a lone mother who worked long hours to make ends meet, who wasn't around enough.

Lord, I thought for the hundredth time, what have I done?

You had turned then, in your bed. 'Mum?'

'Diya, why aren't you asleep? You have school tomorrow.'

The thought of school and what it would bring for you petrified me.

'Go to sleep, Mum. Stop fretting. I am fine.'

'I love you, darling, you know that?'

Someone banged on the door of the flat opposite.

'I do, Mum. I love you too. Now sleep. Go on.'

Was my love enough? Had I done the right thing? I asked myself that every single day and I asked it again that night, as the door being slammed shut in the flat opposite reverberated through our flimsy walls. And as usual my heart said yes. If I had not done what I did, you would not have been mine. You would not have looked at me like you do, with love singing out of your eyes. You would have loved me, perhaps, but not like I wanted you to. And yes, I was selfish, incredibly so, but for once in my life I did what I wanted, what my heart was urging me to do.

The question I am afraid to ask is, are you the one who has paid the price, Diya? Have you been paying all your life? This is the question that has kept me awake many nights and still does. Have you? I hope not, Diya. I sincerely hope not. I hope my love was, has been, enough.

5) *Sometime in the first year of school, your accent changed. The words that fell out of your mouth were perfect, polished, like precious stones tinkling against glass. You spoke like they did on television and on the radio. And I was glad. Now, you couldn't be claimed by another country, another life. You were English; if people couldn't see it, at least they could hear it.*

Even though I can read and write competently in English, I speak in that slow, careful way people with English as a second language do. I thought you would be ashamed of me, ashamed of this woman, with her frayed saris and her long drawn out vowels. But you never once corrected my pronunciation, my darling, like the other Asian mums at the restaurants I worked in grumbled that their children did.

You accepted me as I am. You seemed just as proud of me as I was, as I am, of you.

Diya, this sanctioning of the DNA test is taking longer than I expected. The legal wheels are taking their time to turn but they are turning and this will be sorted and we will be together soon, I hope.

I love you more than you can fathom. You are my life.
Mum

Chapter 25
Diya

Love

Love

Noun: a feeling of warm personal attachment or deep affection, as for a parent, child or friend.

Verb: to have a profoundly tender affection for (another person).

❈ ❈ ❈

I stuff Maltesers and pretzels mindlessly into my mouth, the saltiness of the pretzels counteracting the bittersweet explosion of chocolate and the memories associated with it. This car, Jane beside me, tired eyes fixed on the road ahead, the familiar smell of sweat mingled with flowery perfume, is like a second home now. I chew and crunch and swallow and try to think of nothing. It is difficult.

I have armed myself with snacks for the car journey to battle the nervousness, the queasiness I had been feeling all morning, that persisted after lunch and built up to a crescendo by the last class of the day. I had purposefully walked to the vending machines and used up the last of my change on any rubbish I could lay my hands on, punching in any code, not really caring what dropped down the machine into the slot.

I didn't know what else to do, except to turn to the one thing that used to offer comfort up until recently. I needed a crutch to while away the long agonising minutes of journey eating up the distance between me and the woman, until now a shadowy figure looming in the wings, like the threat of a monster used to scare an impressionable child into good behaviour.

I don't really want the snacks; my dependency on food has disappeared sometime during the week. No amount of food can fix the broken bit of me, the bit that tore irrevocably when my mother was taken from me and the certainty of who I am was destroyed.

I stare out of the window at the landscape hurtling past and feel the rush of bile flooding my mouth, the bitter green taste of envy making me nostalgic for a life that isn't mine. What wouldn't I give to be one of the teenagers congregating outside the corner shop, smoking and messing about; the dog walker whistling, the dog straining at the lead; the young girl conversing with the old woman outside the grocery store; the woman texting while waiting at the bus stop, her fingers flying over the keys; the group of girls laughing and nudging each other at the sight of a fit young man.

I take a sip of the milkshake Lily brought in for me, and the comfort I have been after, elusive as the glimpse of the moon on a stormy, overcast night, floods through me, calming my insides. It allows me to think of school and it is a relief to settle my nervous mind on that rather than on what will happen at the end of this journey and the woman waiting there for me.

I never thought I would say this but school was wonderful today, a release from the oppressive atmosphere at Farah's house, in Jane's car. Not that Farah and Jane aren't nice, but being with them is like eating chocolate and being transported instantly to the evening my mother was taken away from me. Both are very kind, caring people and yet…they are there in place of my mother and that makes all the difference.

I woke up this morning after a restful sleep, happy dreams about Mum and me, and for the first time since that horrible morning after, I thought I was waking up in my own bed in our flat. I turned to smile at Mum and of course she wasn't there, the pallid, soulless wardrobe standing in her stead. I was ready in two minutes flat, downing cornflakes mindlessly, and was waiting outside when Jane's car pulled up in the driveway in a screech of tyres on gravel, the sound, I imagined, like the nails of a monster gouging soft human skin.

When I got to school, Lily was waiting with the posse of friends I seem to have attracted because of my notoriety. As I approached, she held something out to me. A Rolo milkshake.

'I couldn't have a milkshake without getting one for you. I know this one's your favourite. We can ask the dinner ladies to keep it in the fridge for you to collect when you leave.'

I was so overcome I couldn't find the words to thank her so I gave her a hug instead.

Nobody bullies us now or calls us names, but even if they had, I wouldn't have cared. Nonetheless I must admit that it's nice to be one of a group and not singled out. Of course some of them talk about me, whispering into their cupped hands, stopping and eyeing me curiously when I walk past – after all, I am the kid who was stolen as a baby – but it doesn't bother me as much as it would have done before.

And for a brief while today, in English as we read *Macbeth*, I was able to forget myself, despite the butterflies, the flutters of anticipation at meeting with this woman, despite the worry of whether my plan would work. I was able to absorb myself in the story, to lose myself in the woes of Lady Macbeth and overlook, for a brief moment, my own woes.

'Well, here we are,' Jane says, switching off the engine, and I realise that, as I have been lost in my musings, the car has pulled to a stop in front of a Holiday Inn.

I stare at the steps, the awning, the polished amber of the reception desk, the glinting lights shedding pools of gold, applying a gilded sheen to even the most ordinary of things – the wooden arm of a chair, the sour face of the porter – and I am ambushed by panic.

I look up at the twinkling illuminated squares of windows and wonder if the woman is standing at one of them, a dark silhouette, her gaze piercing the darkness, seeking the daughter she is meeting after thirteen years, the daughter I am still hard-pressed to believe is me.

I busy myself brushing the crumbs off the skirt of my unflattering school uniform, gulp in several breaths of the stale air inside the car. It tastes bitter, of flowery car freshener and nerves.

A soft hand on my shoulder, like silken cobwebs brushing. 'It will be okay. She just wants to see you, Diya. She loves you, remember that.'

I brush away the sudden tears, glad I am looking down at my lap. I swallow past the lump in my throat. *You love me too, Mum. You love me but you are in a prison somewhere and I am here, sitting in a strange car that in the past week has morphed into the most familiar thing in the world, the little puppet dancing from the front mirror my friend. I am afraid to get out of this safe cocoon, Mum, afraid to meet her. What if I get one glimpse and I recognise something in her, that elusive, intangible something that binds us to each other? What if I am drawn to her and go to her arms and forget all about you, about my plan to save you? What if I change into a Diya I don't recognise, transform into Rupa, perhaps, the Rupa I was meant to be in another life with her as my mother? I don't want that, Mum. I love you. I am doing this for you. I am going to plead with her for you. That terrible evening, Mum, you said that you wish there had been some other way. I wish that too. I wish it was you I was meeting. I would run out of here in a heartbeat then, run straight into your waiting arms. I wish it was you.*

Jane gets out, a blast of freezing air invading the warm car. She walks round to the passenger side, opens the door for me, holds out her hand. I look at her soft pink skin, framing nails bitten to the quick, and I jump out without taking it. I walk swiftly towards the entrance without looking back as she shuts the door, locks the car and follows.

I am shaking in the elevator, like the last leaf clinging to a denuded tree at the fag end of autumn, trembling as we walk down the cramped, dark, endless corridor reeking of trapped smoke and a faintly medicinal odour reminiscent of hospital.

Jane comes to a stop in front of number 214 and knocks twice. I resist the urge to hide behind her. 214 used to be my old locker number. Is that a good sign?

As we wait for the door to open, I stare out at the gloomy February evening framed by the scratched glass of the window at the end of the corridor. Black clouds frown from an irate thunderous sky that wears an inky purple frown, cars shiver in the car park, frosted windows gleaming. Street lamps shine wearily, their dirty yellow glow not nearly enough to pierce the darkness, silhouetting unsteady slants of weak grey rain drunk on sleet and ice.

Soft footfalls on the other side of the flimsy door, painted snowy cream, paint peeling at the hinges. I picture the soles of the woman's shoes whispering secrets, exchanging confidences with the tired hotel carpet, trying to perk it up with gossip.

And then, while I am still trying to prepare myself, the door is swung open.

The woman standing there, her hand on the doorknob, her gaze flitting past Jane, settling on me and away again, is tall and extremely thin, so slender as to be insubstantial. She reminds me of a naked winter tree stripped of the protection of foliage, sans the willowy grace afforded by branches. A horizontal, colourless stalk. I worry that if she so much as sighs, or if Jane opens her mouth and blows, she will disappear. Skin stretches over the bones of her face, like a dress a size too small straining over a body unwilling to be contained. High cheekbones, sunken cheeks, a small pursed mouth, worn-out black eyes, thin lanky hair falling in a listless dark cloud around her gaunt face. Nothing in her features I recognise. Would her nose be mine if it was fleshed out a bit? Do I see myself in her weak brown eyes, in the shape of them, wide at the centre and tapering upwards at the ends? She would have been beautiful once, I think, when she was a bit more filled out perhaps, with some flesh to give substance to the bones, some curves to soften the harsh angles.

Her gaze swoops on me, then darts beyond as if she is looking for someone else, and then, slowly, almost unwillingly it seems, flutters on me again. A puzzled expression haunts her eyes. They look trapped, the pupils agitated, and she keeps looking beyond me as if she is hoping for someone else to appear in my stead. Something flashes across her face, an expression I cannot read. Her gaze shifts to Jane as if she has wearied of looking at me. I have the feeling I have disappointed her in some way. I suck in my stomach, push my shoulders back and stand straight and tall like my mother taught me. My mother…

She raises one hand to her cheek, pats it as if she is offering comfort to herself and I notice a slight tremor to her fingers. I realise she is nervous and that gives me courage. She still will not look at me, perusing the floor instead, watching her feet as they shuffle and scuff, the soft whisper of heel on carpet.

She stands there nervously, not saying anything, not inviting us in, the three of us clustered around the door to number 214, a little tableau – two squat, chubby shrubs and one tall twig – until at last I ask, 'Am I not what you expected?' and she startles at the sound of my voice.

Chapter 26
Aarti

Caramel Depths

The girl standing in front of her, the girl Aarti has spent the best years of her life looking for, is *fat*. Rolls of fat jiggle from under her chin, her face is so puffed up that it is hard to make out her features. Her arms wobble; they tremble as she leans against the doorjamb, watching Aarti watch her, taking Aarti in just as meticulously as Aarti takes her in.

'Am I not what you expected?' she asks at last and Aarti looks directly at her daughter's burnt sugar eyes that shimmer with hurt. She tries to wipe the shock from her face, ironing it clear of expression like she once used to with her parents. How can this girl know just what she is thinking? Is she that transparent?

Her daughter's voice is clear, like the ringing of bells to signal meals served at the clinic she had checked into when recovering from her breakdown after Vani disappeared with her child, *this* child, standing now in front of her, less than an arm's length away. Aarti looks at her daughter's face and finally, she is able to see past the weight, the expanse of her body and focus instead on her eyes. She finds reflected in the nervousness, the anguish in their soft caramel depths, an echo of what she herself feels.

She recognises those eyes. They hark back to a past when she was happy, to that blissful decade when she had both friendship and love, that delightful time sandwiched between the heavy, lonely doorsteps of yawning years on either side. And Aarti is able to see, at last, the girl hiding in there, lost amongst the folds of flesh.

She leans forward and extends her hands, manages to encircle her child in them. She holds her close and breathes in the apple and strawberry scent of her hair. She realises as she rests her cheek on her daughter's head and breathes in her smell, as her heart shifts a little, thaws a little, the melting manifesting itself as a wetness on her cheeks, that it has been years since she last held someone or was held by someone. It has, in fact, been exactly thirteen years.

What do you say to a child you have hankered after, missed and longed for for more than a decade? To the child who stands looking at you with the eyes of the man you loved and the body that you have tried all your life to stay clear of, a body that repulses you. What do you say first?

Yes, you are not what I expected. All those pictures I conjured up, images of you at various stages of your life, none of them were…like this. It feels like a double betrayal, like she, Vani, has won again. She stole you once and now it is as if she has stolen you all over again – my vision of you.

All her life, Aarti had sworn to herself that if she ever had children, she would not behave like her parents, delivering barbed comments and thoughtless jibes, hurtful admonishments that would scar for life. And so, she stops the references to excess weight, the advice to eat healthily that seem to be stumbling over her mouth in their eagerness to come out against her will, and says instead, shyly releasing her daughter from her grasp, 'Come inside.'

Her daughter enters hesitantly, makes for the little table beside the bed and lowers herself down onto one of the chairs. Aarti looks at her daughter – *her daughter!* – here, in this hotel room, and is struck dumb by nerves, nausea churning, inciting her stomach to riot, even though she has been unable to eat anything since the phone call informing her that her daughter was ready to meet her. She bites down the sudden urge to be sick, as if by purging herself, she will get rid of all the things that have already gone wrong, start again.

How does one fill a silence of thirteen years? How about the words I practised over and over in front of the mirror: I missed you, sweetheart, every single day you were away, I missed you. But you are here now. You are here and everything is going to be all right.

She opens her mouth to say these words as the stranger who is her child spills out of the chair opposite and regards Aarti with familiar eyes. Her daughter is playing with her skirt, alternately bunching and loosening it. *She's nervous too,* Aarti thinks.

Instead, the words that tumble out of her mouth are, 'You look just like your father.'

Her daughter flashes her a half-smile, a gentle trembling upwards of her lower lip. She could be beautiful, Aarti thinks, if only… *Don't go there. Look past the weight. Don't say anything you might regret. You've already lost thirteen years. You have begun on a shaky footing. You do not want to spend the rest of the time you have with her, the time she has afforded you, the time she can refuse, saying things that will be hard to take back, harder to undo.*

'Tell me about him,' her daughter says.

'He misses you. He sends his love,' Aarti lies. *He doesn't know I am here, meeting with you.*

'And you?' Her words a challenge. Her eyes shimmering. 'I am not what you expected, am I?'

That question again. She is just like her father, Aarti thinks, both of them stubborn, not giving an inch once they get an idea into their head.

No, darling, you aren't. You are nothing like I imagined. Even your name is different from the one I chose for you and I cannot get my head around that. The words falling out of your mouth are accented; you sound foreign. You are foreign to me.

She aims for a bit of truth and a bit of evasion, 'I did not know what to expect, after thirteen years. I created so many images in my head. Of course the reality of you was always going to be different from the picture in my head, Rupa.'

Her eyes flashing, 'I am not Rupa. My name is Diya.'

Aarti is exhausted. She does not know what to say, how to go forward. She did not expect this meeting to be quite so difficult, so hard, like cycling uphill when you have no strength left to carry you onward. She tries for a smile. She knows it doesn't quite make it to her eyes. 'We called you Rupa. Your name is Rupa on your birth certificate.' Her voice sounds brittle as a twig on a dying tree.

'My name is Diya,' the girl repeats.

Aarti gives in. What else can she do? *I hate you, Vani. I will not let you win. I will concede this to you, but I am not going to let you win.* 'Diya…' she says and her daughter smiles, properly this time, and it is like the first marigold of the season, blooming joyous and hopeful, and Aarti reaches across spontaneously and cups her daughter's face in her palm and her daughter flinches and the smile disappears and the moment is lost and Aarti's hand falls back down, forlorn, to hug the side of her body.

Outside, darkness has fallen, not with the aplomb with which darkness arrives at home in Bangalore, always with the prelude of twilight, the sky mutating through myriad hues like a woman changing saris, unable to make up her mind. Here, in this frigid, sunless country, the sky just switches to a darker shade of grey. Now, it is a tempestuous bluish black – the exact shade, in fact, of the eyes of the girl looking back at her.

Aarti clears her throat, makes herself say the words she has practised all day in front of the mirror, the words she has decided on after countless tries, the words she has learnt by heart. 'I missed you, sweetheart, every single day you were away, I missed you. But you are here now. You are here and everything is going to be all right.' Her voice sounds artificial to her ears, as if she is saying the words by rote, as if she doesn't really mean them.

But her daughter nods and her eyes sparkle with sudden tears, and the social worker stands and says, 'We must be going,' and her girl looks at her and says softly, 'Goodbye,' and Aarti takes her daughter's hand in hers and this time her daughter doesn't flinch and Aarti is gratified; she is emboldened and she pulls her daughter in for another hug.

And then she is leaving and it is over, and Aarti is disappointed and she is reassured that the awkward first meeting is done and, even though it began badly, it has ended well, and that is all that matters.

Chapter 27
Vani

World of Reveries

My darling Diya,

I have been moved to Bronzefield prison.

'It is one of the best prisons around,' my lawyer informed me with a pleased smile – and he is not wrong.

It is like a big, communal house but with very high walls and doors which are locked on the outside. The other women here are mothers, sisters, daughters. We share stories and relive memories of our loved ones and it gets us by, makes sluggish time pass that little bit quicker.

Some of the women are elated after a visit from their families. Others cry, their sobs rending the walls, making us weep in reciprocal pain. Much as I miss you, Diya, I do not want you to visit me here, darling, even if you were allowed to meet me. I do not want you to see me like this.

Have you grown? You must have. I miss seeing you off to school, miss your voice, your smell. I miss your arms around me. I miss your smile, your repertoire of expressions, that wist-

ful look you get sometimes when you are chasing a thought in your head. I miss seeing you asleep an arm's length away when I wake first thing. I miss falling asleep listening to the sound of your dreams. No matter how tired I am, I have always stayed awake until you have fallen asleep. Once I hear your even breathing, signalling deep sleep, I let myself go, escape into the world of reveries. When I wake up in the night for the loo, I plant a kiss on your cheek smelling of slumber and the sweetest of dreams, soft and malleable and growing and precious and mine.

When you were little, I used to wake many times to check on you, just to make sure you were breathing. It was my fear of losing you, I guess. I have never quite given up that habit. Over here too, I wake countless times during the night, and it takes a moment always to register that you are not there. And then the pain, that had been napping briefly, awakens. Thirteen years with you by my side and now I am alone again. It is like missing a limb, missing the best part of me. It is like losing my parents all over again, except much, much worse.

It is always after you have put your book away and turned off the light, just before sleep claims you, that you share your innermost thoughts with me. I cherish that time. I wait every night for it.

Your voice thick with impending sleep, you will say, 'Mum, have you fallen head over heels in love?'

Your questions almost always have something to do with the book you are reading currently. How do I answer that question? What do I say? I deflected it that time you asked, darling; I can't remember what I said, but you were very good at deciphering unspoken messages and you did not pester. You left it and asked instead, your voice wistful, 'Do you think I will find love one day?'

'Of course, my sweetie,' I said, and I was thinking inside, my baby's growing up. *'You will find someone who will sweep you off your feet, who will cherish you and adore you, who will love you like you deserve to be loved. You will.'*

You fell asleep that night with a smile on your face and I knew that you were dreaming of love.

Here's what I wish for you, darling. I wish that when love finds you, you will recognise it, you will recognise him. I didn't, you see. I didn't see love until it was staring me in the face. And I only realised what I had after I had lost it.

Diya, the lawyer just paid me a visit. The DNA test has been sanctioned. They will be contacting you soon and once the results come through, this nightmare will be on its way to resolving. I cannot wait, sweetheart. I cannot wait.

All my love, my darling,
Yours,
Mum

Chapter 28
Diya

Biological

Biological

Adjective: related through birth; being such by blood and not by adoption or marriage.

Synonyms: birth, consanguineous.

❊ ❊ ❊

Jane's phone rings while we are driving back from meeting with the woman who claims to be my mother.

'What shall I call you?' I had said to the woman.

'Uh…' she had faltered.

Jane ignores her ringing phone. It beeps a couple of times and then rings again. She looks at me apologetically and mouths, 'Do you mind?'

I shake my head no. She pulls into a parking spot just being evacuated in front of a post office and bakery.

'What is your name?' I had asked the woman.

'Aarti,' she'd said.

'Shall I call you Aarti then?'

She had flinched. I knew my voice sounded angry, interrogative, but I couldn't help it. The whole thing seemed staged, felt unreal.

Somehow the visit did not go as I expected, or, I gather, as she expected it to. She clearly had been imagining someone else, had probably nurtured this romantic idea of a daughter, skinny like her perhaps.

In the car just now, before her phone rang, I asked Jane, 'So this girl she snatched from the street because she thought she was her daughter, did she look anything at all like me?'

Jane's eyes had faltered; they had skipped away from the road for a brief moment and settled on my face, her gaze like being sheltered from the storm on a freezing evening. 'She loves you, Diya. Give it time.'

I worry the loose thread on my skirt, which I realise is a bit short for me. I must have gained height in the past week, well, since before half-term anyway, since before it all happened. I might even be taller than Mum now. She will have to look up to peer at my face, gaze at it as if she is drinking me in, like she does of an evening when she has just got home from work. She will be so pleased. She used to chart my growing height, my developmental milestones with delight and awe in equal measure. She will joke that she doesn't recognise me when she sees me. When she sees me. If she sees me…

I blink and look out of the window. Cream buns, chocolate éclairs, doughnuts and cakes in all their delectable glory line the bakery window but I do not feel a smidgen of desire for the appetising confections. Before, in those innocent days when I had no idea all this was looming, I would have scrabbled around for some change, jumped out of the car and into the shop, stuffing éclairs and doughnuts willy-nilly into my mouth.

A little girl skips out of the bakery on her mother's arm, clutching a gingerbread man. Pink Smarties for eyes, a chocolate button nose, blue iced grin. She takes a huge bite. Crunch. His head disappears.

How can that woman that I just met be my mother? I do not recognise her. I do not feel anything for her, anything at all. She could be anyone as far as I am concerned. My mother is somewhere close by, staring at the oppressive walls and thinking of me as she waits to be extradited to India. In this strange woman's bony arms, smelling of pain and discomfort and something else, something medicinal, I was uncomfortable. I didn't quite fit. I worried that if I moved I might break her. Her skeletal arms were like brittle cord encircling me, keeping me captive, her hip bones jutting into me. I felt disproportionately large, the excess weight bulging out of me, making contact with her insubstantial bird-like bones. In that scrawny prison, I was lost, at sea. I did not know what to say to her. Even the impassioned plea I had prepared on behalf of the woman who will always, in my mind, be my mother, the words I had been rehearsing, flew out of my head.

Jane walks up and down in front of the post office, head bent against the cold and sleet that has thickened into a proper downpour, performing an intricate dance of politesse as she dodges people who trudge past. Customers entering the post office freeze on the step as they shake off the drops clinging to their coats. Jane pulls her cardigan tight around her with one hand and holds the phone with the other. Her greying hair whips about her face, lank blonde-grey strands hugging the contours of her round, kind visage. I am overcome by a sudden rush of affection for her.

I had been expecting to like the woman, I realise now. I had expected to feel *some* recognition, some tug of an inner bond, perhaps the calling of the umbilical cord that had once bound us together. I had imagined she would look more like a mother, like Jane perhaps, cuddly and comfortable, or Farah, petite but real, not this scrawny emaciated husk of a woman. But then, she hadn't expected me as well. I have a suspicion she was repulsed by the excess weight bursting forth from the contours of the person she had been waiting thirteen years to acknowledge.

Well, tough. We disappointed each other.

Jane is gesturing into the phone, looking at me, trying to avoid a man clutching a sheaf of envelopes encased in thin plastic close to his chest. Her hair and cardigan gleam with moisture. Rain drips down her face, a stealthy drop hanging at the tip of her nose, shining silver before blending into the grey sheath of rain that blurs everything, an amorphous curtain.

A posse of teenage boys stumble past, clutching beer bottles, pushing each other, yelling, laughing. One of them catches my eye, winks. I blush, look away, down at my hands sitting primly on my lap, pudgy fingers drumming my skirt like a woodpecker's incessant tapping.

'You look just like your father,' she had said.

And I had thought, *of course I do since I am nothing at all like you.* Guilt bloomed, a purple bruise, warring with red splotches of anger. Guilt at disliking this woman who had spent the better part of the last decade and a half looking for me, who was possibly this emaciated because of the worry and pain of missing me. Anger that *this* was my mother and not the one who had loved me and looked after me all these years, who was even now languishing in some prison missing me. Anger that, because of this woman, the mother I loved was in prison. I was in this situation because of this woman. I did not like her. In fact...

The woman had sighed then. And the purple bruise had nudged out the red splotches, spreading right over them, incorporating them into one giant bruise, guilt winning over anger.

'Tell me about my father,' I had said softly.

And she had. I had watched her thin mouth, pursed and tiny as a newborn kitten's, moving as she told me about my father, and I had waited patiently for the moment when I could come up with my passionate plea. Somehow, I couldn't bear to interrupt her. She was too fragile; I was afraid that if I said anything she would break, disintegrate before my eyes, become a heap of silky powder, the silvery colour and texture of bone with bits of leathery skin thrown in.

And then, just when she stopped and looked at me with hope shining out of her dull brown eyes so that for a brief moment I could see that she had been beautiful once, Jane had placed a gentle hand on my arm and said it was time to go.

A blast of rain, yellow dribbles, tasting of ice and salt and impending night gusts into the car as Jane squashes into her seat. The squelch of wet cotton making contact with leather, the musty whiff of moist sweat. Jane looks at me and there is something in her eyes.

'What?' I ask, wary.

'That was Vani's lawyer,' she says softly.

It is suddenly too hot in the car. I cannot breathe. I cannot find words to speak; my throat is constricted, my chest hurts.

'He wants to know if you will consent to a swab being taken for a DNA test.' She reaches across and lays her wet hand on top of mine. The brown tang of damp leather drying too soon, her hand warm on mine, moisture dotting white wrinkled skin like sequins on a bride's veil. For once I let her leave it there, taking comfort, not pulling away. 'Vani insists that she is your biological mum. It took this long to get permission from the judge, to procure legal aid to sanction it, et cetera, et cetera.'

As her marshmallow voice washes over me, I can breathe again. In fact I have to tell my racing heart to slow down, to take it easy.

'Of course,' I manage to squeeze the words past the great big lump in my throat, a salty protuberance that tastes of relief, joy even. 'Of course. When does he want it done? When will we get the results? Once it is proven that she is my biological mother, can she come home?' As soon as I have squeezed the words past the plug, they trip over themselves in their urge to come out.

Jane's eyes are as soft as my mother's cotton sari, chocolate brown like my mother's skin gleaming after a shower. 'I do not want to dent your excitement, the first bit of enthusiasm you have shown in days,' she says, her voice like flowing water whispering soft lullabies to the pebbles in its path. 'What I am trying to say is…the extradition order wouldn't have been issued and she wouldn't have been arrested if they didn't have incontrovertible proof…'

'Stop.' I don't let her finish, pulling my hand away from under her grasp, turning away from her to stare out the window. The rain drips and drabs, it surges in the drains, collects in the gutters, soaks pedestrians with its icy tears. The wind whips the dustbin lids into a bizarre dance and they gallop down the street like charging horses, they dance like desperate debutantes.

'She wouldn't do that to me, subject me to the DNA test, if she wasn't sure. Don't you see?' I yell, glaring at Jane's shadowy silhouette reflected in the window.

'I'm sorry. I just…I don't want you to get your hopes up, Diya.'

'Are we going to sit here freezing to death or are we going to get back at some point?' I ask coldly.

The engine sputters into life, Jane sighs. 'I…' she begins.

'When am I giving the swab?' I interrupt, my voice chillier than the gale sweeping outside.

'I could take you tomorrow lunchtime?'

A woman in a yellow raincoat stained grey by the stormy evening is battling the wind and trying to move forward. For every step she takes, she is pulled back two by the force of the wind. 'And how long will the results take to come back?'

'Three to four days. A week at most.'

'Well then.' I lean back in my seat and close my eyes. Images swirl before them. My mother, eyes shining, liquid like molten caramel: 'Diya. My light. The light of my life.' She is not lying. *She has been lying to you all your life.* No, my mother would not willingly set me up for disappointment, allow me to hope if she didn't know for sure. This much I know.

So why is that scrawny slip of a woman lying? Why has she put me through this agony? Why would she go through with this, searching for me for thirteen years, snatching the little girl she thought was me and almost ending up in prison on a kidnapping charge – the same crime she has accused my mother of – if she did not believe I was hers? Is she mad? Her face, those weak eyes, that brittle embrace swim before my eyes. She could easily be. I need to know. I need to find out.

'I will visit with this woman, Aarti, again tomorrow.' Her name unfamiliar on my lips, bitter as the seed of an apple bitten into by mistake. 'Can you bring me?' I ask and Jane's eyes gravitate away from the road toward me again and she smiles, the smile soft as vanilla cream cake.

'Of course, sweetie. I will rejig my schedule so I can take you.'

I am swamped by a wave of affection for Jane, despite the concerns she's raised about the DNA test. She is only looking out for me, after all.

'I'm sorry,' I mumble, chewing the inside of my lip. 'All this, it's hard for me.' The closest I have come to admitting what I feel within.

Jane's eyes leak as, with one hand, she pats my hands which lay joined on my lap, demure as nuns.

'Hands on the steering wheel, please! I don't want to die just yet,' I yell, mock angrily and she beams me a watery smile.

'I cannot begin to imagine, sweetie, how hard all this must be for you,' she says, taking my admonishment to heart, her brimming eyes firmly fixed on the road ahead. 'For the record, I think you are one of the bravest people I have ever had the pleasure of knowing. I admire you immensely.'

I sniff, something warm blooming in my heart, pushing at the cold weed of pain that has already been dislodged a tiny bit by news of the DNA test.

Out on the rain-battered pavement, a little boy is being coaxed along by his mother. He digs his feet in and refuses to move, his small face set in a determined frown. She pleads with him, both of them wet and bedraggled, soaked to the bone. He shakes his head, shivering a little. She bends down, picks him up, holds him close and battles the wind as, together, they make their way home.

Chapter 29
Aarti

The Suggestion of Curves

Breakfast: Fruit salad.

I haven't heard from the social worker. I don't know how the visit went. Last night, I was feeling positive. Now, I feel like a failure. I think she hated me. I think she will not want to see me again.

Mid-morning snack: Kiwi Fruit.

The social worker just called! She's coming to see me again. My daughter. That means the visit went well, doesn't it? That means it did.

She wants to see me again. She wants to come back to visit.

Lunch: Two helpings of happiness and a serving of excitement.

❄ ❄ ❄

Aarti cannot wait. She cannot sit still. She paces up and down, up and down, fifteen strides each way. She paces and she rehearses what she will say to her daughter.

Aarti does not want to call her Diya, the name Vani gave her, but her child will not answer to Rupa, having inherited her father's stubborn streak along with his eyes. Should she call him, tell him she has met his daughter, their daughter? Not just yet. For now, Aarti wants to hug the reality of her daughter close, savour the fact that she has found her, met her, is going to meet her again, before sharing her around.

She stands in front of the wardrobe, open and spilling its contents, deliberating on what outfit to wear. Something voluminous, in case her daughter feels threatened by how slim she is. Something that gives the suggestion of curves.

Her daughter is like a delicate butterfly which will fly away at the slightest hint of movement. Aarti needs to take her on her terms. As she is already doing. Aarti is so proud of herself for not asking the question that had bloomed on her lips the whole time she was meeting with her daughter, 'How did you get so fat?' For not bursting out with, 'That woman abused you! Look how you've turned out.' She did not say anything, but the thought hovered, the elephant in the room.

After not losing anything in her life, to lose her daughter, her most precious heirloom, to Vani was devastating beyond measure. And now is the time to even the score. To better the score. Already she is winning. Her daughter has come to visit once and is coming again. Aarti has that to look forward to. Vani has nothing but the prospect of long years in jail.

Aarti sits on the bed – the room does not feel like prison anymore; it has pleasant connotations now. This was where her daughter sat yesterday, worrying her school blazer which was too short for her by the looks of it. At this age they are always growing, shooting up overnight almost, she knows. Vani will not get to see this but *she* will. About time.

She smiles.

Chapter 30
Vani

Rollercoaster of Emotions

Diya, my darling,

Do you remember that Mother's Day when you were ten?

As soon as I pushed open the door to the flat, you ambushed me. You had made me the most wonderful card: a woman wearing a shimmering, multi-hued sari, vermilion kumkum and a wide smile fashioned from red fabric.

'That's you, Mum,' you said, beaming at my expression of awe.

For her skirt, you had painstakingly pinned actual sequins. The card glittered and shone. It was so beautiful it took my breath away.

And then, you produced a bouquet of the most exquisite roses. 'Because nobody gives you flowers and a woman should be given flowers,' you said, repeating a line you had memorised from one of your books.

You must have saved your pocket money for a week at least to get me those flowers. I was humbled, overcome, floored by your love.

Afterwards, while we were eating, you said, completely out of the blue, 'Mum, we learnt about King Solomon's judgement in RE today.'

'Huh?' I asked.

'You don't know the story?' Your eyes lit up. You loved educating me.

'No,' I said, smiling quietly to myself.

'Mum! How could you not?' You rolled your eyes in that way you have and launched into the story. 'King Solomon was approached by two women both claiming a little boy for their own. Each said she was the mother of the child.'

I choked on my rice. Had to take a sip of water while you waited, impatiently, to continue. I nodded weakly when I was able to recapture my breath. The roses grinned at me from the bottle masquerading as a vase; pink, red and yellow smiles of daughterly love.

'So what do you think King Solomon did?' you asked.

You were waiting for my cue, so I said, my voice shaky. 'What did he do?'

'He called for a sword.' You paused for dramatic effect.

The smell of roses mingling with curry assaulted my nose.

'He said the child must be split in two and one half given to each woman.' You looked up at me to assess my reaction.

'Mum, why on earth are you crying?' You rolled your eyes. 'It's just a story! And he didn't even hurt the child because the real mother cried, "Please don't kill my child. She can have him." And that was how King Solomon knew who the real mother was.'

You came and put your arms around me, kissing my cheeks and very gently wiping away my tears, your touch silky and delicate as butterfly wings. 'Mum, you cry about the silliest things.'

I held you close, breathed in the apple scent of your hair and murmured, 'Why do they have to tell you such gory tales anyway?'

And you laughed, the sound like the spring in the village of my birth gurgling at the height of summer, and I laughed right along with you.

My sweet, you must have heard from the lawyer by now. Your heart would have jumped in your throat when you heard of my request. Was it joy? Or fear? I am sorry to have to subject you to this constant upheaval, this rollercoaster of emotions.

I asked the lawyer if they would need to take your blood for the DNA test and he said no, just a swab of your mouth. I was relieved. I do not want you to hurt any more than you are already.

All my love to you, my sweet,
Mum

Chapter 31
Diya

Guilt

Guilt

Noun: a feeling of responsibility or remorse for some offense, crime, wrong, whether real or imagined.

Synonyms: contrition, regret, self-reproach, shame, compunction, qualm, chagrin.

❈ ❈ ❈

'Why did you lie to me?' I ask the moment the door is opened and I see the emaciated woman who claims to be my mother looking back at me.

She flinches, takes two steps backward as if she has been slapped. Jane sighs and squeezes my hand gently as if to say, 'is this necessary?' The room smells of old secrets and fresh regrets, a musty achy smell. A trill of feminine laughter drifts in from outside, obscene in the charged silence.

This time I did not take snacks for the journey to visit this woman. I did not need any buttress. I was alert, prepared. On the way here, the list of questions I want answers to was making circuits of my head like a racing car driver rehearsing his laps before the race.

She lifts a tremulous hand up to her cheek and rubs the papery skin as if I have slapped her and it is smarting. The bed is made, the little table beside it laid out with tea things. A pot of tea, a selection of biscuits: bourbons, custard creams and Jaffa Cakes arranged on a chipped saucer, shades of brown and white on blue. Two places set. A pang assaults me, I feel winded as if someone has punched me in the stomach, knocked the breath right out of me.

'Tell me why,' I say, my voice softer, less aggressive than before.

Tears are shining in her lacklustre eyes, highlighting them, giving them definition and much needed gloss. She looks glamorous, transformed.

I think of my mother, languishing in prison, of the pain this woman has put her, put me through. I have had to get used to living without the one person in the world who has always been there for me. I have had to deal with losing the one person in the world who is *mine*. I have had to depend on people I don't even know, have had to bunk with strangers.

It hasn't been too bad – I like Jane and Farah. Affan and Zain are cute and mischievous; they are obviously awed by me – I quite enjoy making them blush when I catch them spying on me, two pairs of huge brown eyes peeking from between the tiny gap of a barely open door. I have hardly seen Sohrab to form an opinion about him one way or another.

I don't miss food like I used to which is a good thing as my jeans and skirts are loose on me now; I think I am losing weight. I do not need food as a crutch. I am realising that I do not need anything at all. I can endure, I can get by. I am strong. Stronger than I gave myself credit for, stronger than I thought I was.

But…there was no need for any of it; there wouldn't have been this turmoil, this upheaval if not for this woman.

I feel a hundred years old, so far removed from the silly problems haranguing teenage minds. I even feel distant from Lily. I have no time for crushes. Seeing a girl hanging on Bhim's arm yesterday, looking up at him adoringly, did not break me, only caused a tiny niggle of hurt. Compared to the huge pain that lives within me all the time, this was but a negligible scratch, mostly to my ego I suspect.

But I *want* to care. I want those silly concerns to be my life. I want to be an ordinary teenager and not someone carrying the weight of the world on her shoulders, skipping lunch in the cafeteria – the jokes and banter, the discussion of who loves who, the rating of boys based on looks and 'wow' factor, the making fun of teachers – to give a swab for a DNA test. I want to have fights with my mother, hang out with my friends, get a tattoo, practise snogging in front of the mirror. I want to be normal.

And I cannot be. Because of her, this woman standing here in front of me, her hands hanging defeated by her sides, an expression of intense hurt on her face. I cannot let her off quite this easily just because she has set a place for me at the table, because it looks like she has waited all day to see me.

She has been waiting to see you for thirteen years.

'What is your story?' I ask. 'Why are you here?'

She is silent, looking at me, her eyes huge in that emaciated face. Voices raised in argument drift in. A car sputters, once, twice, dies.

'I had to give a swab for a DNA test this lunchtime,' I say, holding her gaze. 'My mother…' she cringes as if I have hit her again, '…says I am hers.'

She shakes her head vigorously. 'No. Nononono.' Her voice is shrill.

Why is she acting like a petulant child? Why do I feel like I am the adult here, like I have to take control of the situation? For God's sake, if anyone has been wronged, it is me.

'I know my mum,' I can hear my voice getting louder.

She shuts her eyes, sways on her feet.

'She wouldn't put me through this if she wasn't sure, if I wasn't hers.' My voice wavers at the last.

She opens her eyes and walks up to me. She abruptly kneels down next to me and I can hear her brittle bones shift audibly, the sound like the crack of a whip. She leans close, her breath on my face and I try not to flinch, to move away. Her breath smells fusty, of mouldy onions with a slight tang of mint. Her eyes flash.

This close I can see the droplets clinging to her lashes like children reluctant to let go of their mother's skirts. Lines emanate upwards and outwards from the corners of her eyes. I catch a whiff of lavender mixed with something lemony. The cream powder she has caked on her visage has dried and cracked; it has seeped into the lines of her face affording glimpses of leathery brown skin beneath.

'You are mine,' she hisses. 'She stole you from me.'

She closes her eyes, rocks on her knees. Tears snake out from beneath closed lids and create runnels in the powder, which, when wet, looks like pink sludge. 'You have no idea what I have been through. She betrayed me. She hurt me so much. She was my only friend in the world.'

I don't want to hear this. I don't want to know. But… she seems so impassioned, so convinced. Suppose, just suppose she is telling the truth… Guilt sears, hot, laced with pain. Why would my mother put me through the agony of a DNA test? Why would she get my hopes up only to have them crushed? No, Mum wouldn't do that to me. She wouldn't. But what if her lawyer forced her into it? What if the DNA test proves that my mother is not actually…? No. No. I will not entertain that option. I will not.

Aarti stands up all of a sudden with another creaking of fragile knees. Her hand brushes mine and I look at it, bony, old. I don't know what to think, what to feel. I am so weary. I just want all this to end.

Instinct takes over and I reach out, stuff a bourbon biscuit in my mouth, then another. The bilious, acrid taste of fear, of guilt. I rush to the adjoining bathroom, spit the biscuits out, gargle.

'Here,' Aarti is holding out something when I come back.

A crinkled piece of paper. I am afraid to take it, worried as to what I will find. But she is thrusting it at me and there is no way out.

I look down at the brownish yellow sheet in my hand, worn like the age-scarred skin of an ancient man, each line mapping out the years he's lived, the experience he's amassed. What am I about to discover?

A birth certificate. Father's name: Sudhir Shetty. Mother's name: Aarti Shetty. Child: Rupa Shetty.

It's amazing how much a wrinkled little slip of paper smelling of mothballs and secrets has the power to hurt.

I do not know that child, I think. I cannot identify with a girl called Rupa Shetty. I am Diya Bhat. The girl on this sheet of paper, who is she? What could she have become? I imagine growing up in India, answering to the name of Rupa, walking to school with my hair tied up in two plaits on either side of my head, weighed down by a satchel of books like the children I have seen on television. I cannot. I imagine calling this needy, twig-like woman in front of me 'Mum'; a masculine version of me, an unknown entity, 'Dad'. I cannot. All I know is the life I have lived as Diya, with the woman the very thought of whom unleashes a flood of yearning in my heart.

I plop myself into a chair, holding my stomach. The piece of paper flutters with a soft sigh onto the carpet, an incriminating brown patch on creamy beige.

'Tell me about her,' I say and my voice is wounded. Soft. Like snow falling on a winter's day, swirling and settling with a gush and a sigh, turning the whole world white like lies. 'You said she was your friend.'

And sitting there on that hard wooden chair that bites into my back, in my school uniform that is a little too short and a little too loose, I listen to this woman recount tales of the young girl who came to work for her, who was her only friend and confidante, with whom she made a pact of everlasting friendship.

'She was my servant. And yet, I loved her. I loved her with all my heart.' Hurt and accusation creep into her voice. She sounds whiny, like a child with a complaint.

'She is very easy to love,' I say softly.

Her eyes well with tears. Silvery-blue like baubles. Like the sun shining on my mother's favourite cream sari, making it glimmer and twinkle. How can the manifestation of grief look so lovely? So unabashedly beautiful.

Her sorrow overflows onto her face. Her make-up, which has collected in grey splodges on her cheeks, dissolves and regroups into flat little cakes when she wipes her eyes roughly with the back of her hand.

She reaches across and I baulk. I cannot help it. I see the hurt bloom in her eyes, and more tears squeeze out and join the others. I move closer to her and she touches a tentative finger to my cheek. Her finger comes away with a shining drop like a pearl balanced on the tip. I did not realise I was crying.

'I was so shocked. I felt so betrayed. She was my friend, my confidante, my family. What she did…in one fell swoop, I lost all the family I had.'

'Do you miss her?' I ask softly, choking the words out past the lump in my throat.

'Every day,' she whispers. 'Every single day.'

'Then get her out. You can. You have that power. She is your friend, your family. How can you let her fester in prison?'

Her expression hardens; her gaze loses its shine. She wipes her eyes, smudges the grey splodges and looks at me, her countenance rigid, uncompromising. 'Was. She *was* my friend. Not anymore. Not after this…'

'She's the only mother I have known.' My voice ruptures. 'I love her. Please.'

She stands up, looks towards Jane, wrings her hands. 'I can't. I cannot forgive her. Ever. You don't know what she put me through.' Her voice is cold as the blue-veined stones in that quarry we visited with my previous school, brittle as her bones. 'I was a model, an actress, at the top of my game, one of the best in India. She took that from me. Afterwards… I couldn't do anything, I had a breakdown. She ruined my career. She ruined *everything*.'

She looks at me and her eyes are like bullets, little black stones that glare at me. 'Look what she's done. My own daughter will not acknowledge me. My own daughter loves her, calls her mum, begs for me to forgive and forget.'

She slaps a hand on the table and Jane looks up from the perusal of her phone. It hardly makes an impact, though her bones crack audibly. 'I hate her. I will never forgive her. She could have had everything. Instead she took everything *I* had, even the name I chose for you.'

I think of my mother, of that kind, soft face, those tired eyes that always lit up at the sight of me. 'She loved me. She loves me. She has brought me up well.'

'Exactly. *She* has brought you up. She has denied me the pleasure of rearing my daughter. Even now, you call her Mum and me Aarti. How can I forget? Forgive? Why should I?'

'She did it because she loved me.'

Another crack on the table. 'No.' Her voice is a screech. 'She did it because she wanted what was mine. She stole my life. She destroyed it. She wanted what I had. The one thing I wanted more than anything in the world. She knew that... She knew... And yet...'

She collapses in a flood of sobs.

Jane stands, comes up to me. 'Time to go,' she says and I nod, relieved to leave that room populated by the unassuaged grief, the blatant need, the searing anger of the woman I cannot think of as my mother.

Before I leave, I pat her shoulder awkwardly. I squeeze her bony hand, not too hard, aware of its fragility, its unbearable vulnerability.

'Bye,' I say, not being able to add 'Mum', to give her what she wants to hear, the word sticking in my throat, making me want to gag, making me ache, my heart yearn for another woman, the yellow taste of longing filling my mouth, the purple stain of guilt bruising my insides.

She pulls me close and I endure her hug, the feel of her bones jutting into my surplus flesh like accusatory fingers.

'I'm sorry,' she whispers into my hair and my heart perks up, hoping she'll say the words I long to hear, hoping she'll promise to talk to the police and help bring about my mother's acquittal.

But instead she utters a jumble of words that I have to strain to catch. 'I did not offer you tea or biscuits even.'

I hide the dullness in my heart, the hurt with a bright smile.

'I will come back tomorrow after school,' I say and her face lights up, shimmering, radiant, as she smiles through her tears.

Chapter 32
Aarti

Mothers and Daughters

Today my daughter walked in the door and said, 'Why did you lie to me?'

I thought then that she knew what I had done. She knew. I was terrified but determined to stand my ground, make my case.

Turns out she didn't know. Her bluster was because Vani, that traitor, has actioned a DNA test.

I have been underestimating Vani all these years, I realise now. In my mind, she is still the meek, soft-spoken girl who was my confidante, not the woman who stole my child and kept her from me for thirteen years. I assumed that once Vani was apprehended, she would give up. But once again, she has surprised me...

I had such high expectations for who I would become. Vani stole that from me along with my daughter and my hopes for a happy family.

Sitting here, in this impersonal hotel room, whiling away the hours until my daughter comes – yes, she's coming again!

Ha, take that, Vani! – I remember. Memory is all I have left, as proof against Vani's perfidy. Memory and this girl of course. My daughter, this stranger who watches me carefully with her father's eyes, her trust and love something I have to play for, win over.

❆ ❆ ❆

Aarti doesn't know when her food diary morphed into an actual diary but at some point it has. She twirls the pen in her hand, bites the end, savouring the bitter, inky blue taste in her mouth, and thinks of her daughter, of what she will say to her when she sees her next.

Mothers and daughters. Without warning, after years of ignoring her and pretending she doesn't exist, her own mother's face looms before Aarti's eyes – that stunningly beautiful but cold woman Aarti strived to gratify for years. She tries to blink away thoughts of her mother, but somehow the memories keep on coming, like moving a boulder that has sat on the bed of the forest for years and dislodging a whole army of creatures beneath.

Aarti had yearned for a look from her mother, a smile, a kind word. She had been ridiculously delighted when her mother deigned to speak to her. She is struck by the irony of how she spent her childhood trying to please her mother and now, she is trying to please her daughter.

The last time Aarti blatantly tried to solicit her mother's attention was the day she got her period and was aching for a hug, a kind word, and her mother pushed her away. After that, whenever Aarti desired affection, she binged on food and was sick. The feeling of being sick, purging herself of all desire, for food, for love, calmed her. She learned to rein in her emotions, to hide her hurt behind empty eyes. She was distant, reserved, cool. A coolness that drove men mad.

She never flung herself at her mother again. Never touched her except in public, when photographers urged, 'Closer, closer, now smile,' and she and her mother posed for the camera, pristine pearly whites flashing identical icy smiles, cold hands cringing on contact.

Years later, when the childish contours of Aarti's face had taken shape and matured; when the promise of high cheekbones and full lips had materialised; when she was fawned over and adored more than she thought possible; when, if as far as her parents were concerned, she was the sum total of her achievements, then she had reached a pinnacle; when she no longer sought her parents' approval, no longer wanted or needed to please them, when she had been out of touch with them for a while, her mother had tried to initiate contact.

Her mother had telephoned out of the blue and Aarti was pleased to note that the sound of her mother's voice no longer incited turmoil in her like it once used to; it did not make Aarti feel instantly like a fat, ugly, unwanted child.

She listened to her mother say, 'Hello? Aarti, is that you? Speak to me, darling…' and she slammed the phone down, taking great pleasure in cutting her mother's voice off, silencing it. How dared she call Aarti 'darling' when she had been anything but?

Her mother had tried again, and each time, Aarti had cut her off without replying, and the fourth time this happened, Aarti had said, 'Please do not call me again,' in a perfectly polite, perfectly cold voice that brooked no argument, the very tone of voice her mother had used on Aarti so many times over the years.

And then, one day, her mother turned up at one of her photo shoots to try and talk to her...

Aarti is at the Cosmopolitan India photo shoot, having her make-up done, when there is a knock at the door to her dressing room.

'Tell whoever it is I am busy,' she yells to the man expertly applying her make-up.

He goes to the door, opens it. Snippets of conversation drift in; a high-pitched voice, pleading.

Then he is saying softly, 'It is your mother.'

A hush settles in the room. The oily tang of foundation.

She opens her eyes, peruses her reflection. Porcelain skin, the sheen and texture of silvery silk. Rosebud lips. Almond eyes that invite one to lose themselves in their depths, highlighted by russet eye shadow. Burnished ebony hair that cascades down her shoulders in lush waves. Hourglass figure, not an ounce of fat in evidence. She looks good even if she says so herself. Powder swirls gold in the air of the room that sits heavy and quiet, waiting.

'Ask her to knock and wait to be let in,' Aarti says coolly.

Her make-up artist stares at her.

'Shut the door!' she yells. 'What are you looking at?'

He closes the door.

After a bit, there is a tentative knock.

'Who is it?' she shouts and hears her mother's voice after a hiatus of five years, not imperious but timid: 'Your mother.'

'Go away,' Aarti yells. 'I am busy.'

'Please,' her mother begs and her voice breaks at the end.

And it is because she has never heard her mother plead before and because she herself is looking so good that Aarti lets her in.

She cannot fault the way I look, she thinks.

'Come in, but I can only spare three minutes,' she says. 'You can go,' she tells the make-up artist, who takes his kit and runs.

Aarti does not recognise the woman who aroused such mixed emotions in her, equal parts hurt and need, affection and hatred, in the shrivelled but well-dressed woman standing just inside the door. The affection is gone now, Aarti muses. It has withered to nothing, squeezed out on a tide of unreciprocated regard. Aarti does not feel anything for the woman standing meekly by the door, her famous looks gone, and along with it, her haughtiness. This woman is weak, faltering. This woman is as easy to crush as a child's willing and loving heart.

'What do you want?' Aarti asks.

'I am sorry,' her mother says. 'I am sorry for how I was.'

Ha, too little too late, she thinks. *What took you so long?* She thinks. *Now you feel sorry,* she thinks. *Now, when I am everything you are not.*

Out loud, she says, her voice cold and cutting as ice cubes clinking in a tumbler, 'Okay, you are sorry. Now go.'

'I almost died when you were born, you see. I suffered so much. I couldn't bond with you. I blamed you.'

'And I blame you,' Aarti says, the numbness replaced by hot, all-consuming rage. 'But I am justified. You were not. I yearned for love and I was spurned. Why are you here now? It is too late, far too late. Go.'

'Please,' her mother says again.

'I begged too,' Aarti says, 'I begged for an iota of affection. I got nothing. You didn't even allow me into your room when I knocked. At least I did. Now go. I don't ever want to see you again.'

Afterwards, she sobs. She cries and rages, her make-up running down her cheeks, the sheen disappearing in wet tracks, leaving behind a raw woman with a bleeding heart manifesting itself via dirty brown splotches on her skin and in the naked agony in her blotched eyes. Eyes one can drown in, choking on the waves of pain.

Enough... Aarti resolutely shuts away the memories of her mother and concentrates instead on her daughter. She did not think she would survive losing her child and

Vani in one fell swoop. But she did. She did not think she would survive living on her own again after losing her family and her best friend. But she did.

All these years there were dark times, especially after yet another sighting proved to be a dead end and she left this country empty-handed and hollow, devoid of hope once more. She survived all those, bounced back. This is the last lap. She will not, yet again, go back empty-handed.

She sits, pen and diary clutched in her fists like mascots, and watches the timorous sun of this alien country stain the grey horizon the blush pink of bougainvillea and the bright gold of the first sunflowers of the season.

Chapter 33
Diya

Family

Family

Noun: any group of persons closely related by blood, as parents, children, uncles, aunts and cousins.

Synonyms: blood, clan, kin.

❈ ❈ ❈

School is much better now than it ever was. I have a group of friends. I am not thinking of food all the time. My skirts and trousers don't fit anymore – I am used to that feeling, but this time round they are falling down rather than squeezing the breath out of me.

I like the solid comfort of Jane's reliable presence. I love the familiar smell of her car: the chemical odour of citrus air freshener, her floral perfume mixed in with something musty, reminiscent of old shoes, yellowing photographs and greying memories, tainted by time, purple with age and shimmering with the orange glow that looking through the wistful lens of nostalgia into the past endows, all the more precious for being half forgotten. I feel secure when I am sitting in there with her, the doors locked, sheltering me, keeping out the weather and the world. I like the fact that she doesn't talk, doesn't push, the way she waits for me to make conversation. I am comfortable with her.

And I like the soft familiarity of Farah's house, Farah's quiet, unassuming presence, her unobtrusiveness. She doesn't interfere and yet she is there. I appreciate, more than I can say, the way she did not say anything when I broke down one afternoon when I came in from school and saw her standing at the window. I caught a glimpse of her back and something in the way she lifted her arm to rub a stray hair out of her eyes made me mistake her for my mum. For a moment, when the foolhardiness of hope hijacked sense, I thought my mum had come home and was waiting for me, waiting to surprise me. She had turned then, and instead of the much loved profile I was expecting, I was treated to the disappointingly familiar one of Farah. To my intense embarrassment, I had burst into tears, loud, messy sobs a two-year-old would be ashamed to own. And Farah had wordlessly enveloped me in the refuge of her arms, letting me cry my angst out, vent my fury at the world, at her, passing me tissues when I needed them.

I adore little Affan and Zain. I suspect I might even be beginning to love them. They are not shy around me any longer. Their mother tells me that they stand at the window and wait none too patiently for me to get home and that they are out the front door as soon as they spy Jane's car turning into the street. They commandeer me the moment I climb out of the car and fill me in on their day, their mother laughing and asking them to at least wait until I am inside the house. They want help building their Lego, they want to show me the latest additions to their football card collection, they need assistance getting onto the next level in the newest Mario game. Ideally, they would also like me to do their homework for them or at least, as Zain petulantly put it, biting the back of his pencil to mush, 'Give us all the answers,' and added a reluctant 'please?' – but here, their mother draws the line. It is nice to have the chatter of little boys crowd out the weed of pain that is always there, making its hurtful presence felt at the oddest times. It is nice to feel wanted, to be fawned over, to have their faces light up at the sight of me.

Spending time with Farah, Sohrab, Affan and Zain has made me realise, for the first time, what I have missed out on. I was always content with it being just me and Mum. But now, having met Sohrab, noticed the way his eyes soften when he looks at his boys, the way he helps me with my homework without my having to ask, the sheer strength of his presence imparting a sense of security and love, I miss the dad I never had. I feel a flash of guilt for entertaining the thought, even briefly. My mum, she has always been enough, her love wrapped around me like a warm blanket in the middle of winter, more than making up for the lack of other people in my life. And yet…now that I have experienced briefly what having a father figure feels like, I regret that I didn't know my dad. It is like how I never realised I missed having company, friends my own age, until Lily.

And having Affan and Zain look up to me, the way they fill a room with their constant chatter, crowd out my pain with noise, their overwhelming generosity, the way they include me in everything as a matter of course, their unabashed, open-hearted affection, makes me wish I had had siblings. The first time they embraced me, I was gobsmacked. They had come into the kitchen and hugged their mum, both of them flinging themselves at her, grabbing any part of her they could. And next, without warning, they went for me. I had stood rigid as a commandment, stiff as a statute of law as the boys clambered all over me. And, though unexpected, it was lovely. I felt warm, loved; it brought surprised tears to my eyes.

'Don't cry, Didi,' they had said, scrabbling to wipe my tears, their fingers smelling of chocolate and mud. 'We were just playing. Did we hurt you?'

'No,' I had managed, 'no.'

We had all sat together with a bowl of microwaved popcorn, the heady smell of caramel and charred smoke (Farah burnt the first pack but she managed to get the timing right for the second) filling the house, and settled down to watch a movie, the boys cuddling on either side of me, and their mother had explained that I had cried because I was happy and I had said yes, I was happy because I was loved so much.

'So you cried?' scoffed Affan and he had stretched across my stomach, tugged at his brother's hand and rolled his eyes.

'They were happy tears,' I said, tickling first one and then the other, not stopping until they were crying with laughter and then, pointing at the tears streaming down their eyes, 'Like yours.'

The nights do not stretch endlessly like a bottomless cavern anymore. I can sleep now; the huge weight I am carrying doesn't threaten to crush me, dissolve me into a million pieces when I shut my eyes at night. The weight, like the weed of pain residing inside me, is familiar as my left arm, familiar as the heavy cloud of melancholic air that suffuses the room I have started to call, tentatively, my home away from home, familiar as the cat that jumps onto the roof of the shed and regards me with tawny eyes as I try to fall asleep, familiar as the fox's plaintive cry, familiar as the sliver of cloudy grey sky silhouetted purple and dirty brown by the chilly yellow glow of the drooping lamp just outside my window, familiar as the smacking sounds of lovers kissing beneath the lamp post at the same time every day, familiar as the smell of tulips from the air freshener Farah favours mingling with the fresh vanilla scent of laundered sheets barely masking the reek of sorrow and loss and guilt and hurt and betrayal that populates the room, familiar as the wardrobe that is the last thing I see when I close my eyes and the first when I wake, the thing I see in place of my mother.

Some days I can smile and it doesn't feel like my cheeks are hurting with the effort. Yesterday I even laughed at something Lily said and she gave me a tight hug, her eyes shining.

'I missed the sound of your laughter, Diya,' she whispered.

Some days I close my eyes and I cannot summon up the sound of my mother's laughter, her voice when she used to say, 'Diya, you are the light of my life.'

I am confused. I am torn. I am on tenterhooks. I am awaiting the result of the DNA test. I am dreading the result of the DNA test.

Every evening, Jane drives me to visit with Aarti. I try to call her Mum like she wants me to, gargantuan eyes in her skeletal face pleading, but the word sticks in my throat, like a bitter pill, like a lump of liquorice, and it is too much of a struggle to roll it off my tongue, push it out past the barrier of my lips. This thin, needy woman will never be my mother regardless of what the birth certificate she showed me says, irrespective of what the result of the DNA test might determine, but I cannot bear to break her by telling her so, even though I suspect she knows. She looks at me with those lacklustre eyes and I want to say something, do something to add some life, some shine into them.

When I visited the day after I accused her of lying, after I told her about the DNA test and she told me about my mother, we sat at that lonely little table that wobbled on unsteady legs. She poured me lukewarm tea from the pot and I wondered how long it had been sitting there. I took a sip and tried not to gag. It was too sweet and spiced with something. Cardamom? Cinnamon? I managed to swallow it down.

'Eat a biscuit,' she said, her eyes never leaving me, her hands moving constantly on her lap.

'I'm fine, thanks,' I said, the horribly saccharine taste of the tea roosting in my mouth like a lingering bad smell.

She smiled then, the lines around her face creasing, the bones looking to poke through skin. She was so thin, fragile like the best china you are afraid to use, to touch, to look at even, in case it breaks.

'That's good,' she said, nodding. 'Full of sugar, those things. I don't touch them. Bought them for you.'

You should touch them. If I were you, I would cram them in my mouth, ingest them in bucket loads, I thought. But I was moved. She had gone to the trouble of getting the biscuits for me.

I was pleased she was venturing out, though the thought of her thin body jolted and jogged by people's arms and elbows gave me the shudders. Yet, the thought of her pacing up and down this tiny room, waiting for me to visit, hurt too. All I felt when I was with this woman, when I thought of her, was a desperate pity, a fraught sadness and guilt. Guilt that I couldn't love her like she deserved. Guilt that she was reduced to this. Guilt and hurt at the need shining out of her eyes, at the bones dancing beneath the thin, brittle layer of translucent brown skin.

'Do you like it here?' I asked, the question bursting out of me despite my not wanting to know the answer. How could she? She was displaced from her home, confined to this tiny room, meeting with a daughter who found it hard to acknowledge her, whom she saw for an hour each evening. I knew Jane would let me stay with Aarti if I asked, and I knew Aarti would have liked that, liked the company, but I couldn't, not yet. As it was, the hour passed in a state of agony. I did not want to say the wrong thing, do the wrong thing, cause tears to shine out of those aggrieved eyes. I did not want to stay any longer than necessary in the vicinity of this woman who carried her hurt like a war wound, always on display.

With Jane and at Farah's I could retreat into myself if I didn't want to talk, they would let me be. Here, I had to talk; I had to smile, act happy to see her, be with her. I felt compelled to please her. It was too much. The effort took it out of me. It was as if I was the adult and she the child that I needed to entertain constantly. I was under pressure to produce the right reactions. Anything different from expected and her lower lip would tremble and she would turn away and I knew I had hurt her, disappointed her, not met expectations, not done what was required, yet again.

It was hard to feel sympathy for her when she bruised so easily. Guilt bloomed, damson as a plum lodging in my throat. And anger. Blossoming scarlet behind my eyes, tasting hot as the raw chilli I had once bitten into by mistake. A childish petty rage when I wished she would grow up, when I wanted to throw her emotions back at her, to speak my mind to her without worrying she would crumple, disintegrate into a million pieces, when I wanted to yell, 'You started it.'

And now, I had asked her this pointless question, asked her if she liked it here. Why? Was I a sucker for punishment?

'I do,' she replied, her eyes shining as she smiled at me, 'because you are here.'

She opened the wardrobe on the other side of the bed, pulled her suitcase out, rummaged through it.

'Here,' she said, holding something out.

A doll. Blonde hair, pink face, red cherub lips, blue eyes, long curling lashes.

'For you.' She smiled shyly. 'I got it when I came from India. I was waiting for the right moment.'

I managed a wide smile that almost spilt my face in two, held it in place.

'Thank you,' I said. 'She is beautiful. I'll call her Maeve,' pulling the name out of nowhere.

She laughed, the sound like glass shattering. 'Lovely name,' she trilled.

'Why Rupa?' I asked. 'Why did you choose that name for me?'

'Rupa means beautiful.' She smiled. 'You were a lovely baby – huge caramel eyes, dimpled cheeks, creamy vanilla skin. Very cute. As I knew you would be.'

Were. She said 'were'. *Stop being so petty.*

Her voice wobbled as she said, 'And she took that away from me too. Vani. I rue the day I met her.'

Change the topic, quick. 'What do you do here while waiting for me? What is your routine?' *Oh no,* I thought. *Another question set to trip the guilt switch.*

'Oh, I have breakfast, then go for a walk, then come back and wait for you.' Her voice was soft. 'I don't mind. Honestly. I have waited thirteen years – what are a few hours here and there?'

Why can't I love her like she wants to be loved? I thought. And as always another face swam before my eyes, the face I ached to see again, the woman I yearned for and missed.

I left soon after with the doll. It sits in my room, in the wardrobe beside the holdall Jane packed for me with all of my clothes and stuff from the flat that horrible evening. It looks at me with accusing eyes whenever I open the wardrobe to get my clothes. I just couldn't tell her I was too old for dolls. And there it sits, begging to be played with, a reminder of the mess I find myself in.

It occurs to me sometimes that I should be angry with my mother, that in many ways this is her fault, that even though she showered me with love, I did not have the best of childhoods, moving as we did from place to place. I could have had a different childhood, a different life. And yet, I never felt I was lacking in anything, never wanted for anything. I liked being with her, just the two of us. I did not mind waiting for her during the long evenings she worked to make ends meet.

When I was younger, before I was old enough to be left alone in the apartments, she took me with her to whichever Indian restaurant she was working in at the time. She would sit me in a corner with a garlic bulb to peel or a potato to chop with a blunt knife. I loved being there amidst the noise and the heat of a working kitchen, the appetising spicy smells, the steam from the pots, the dancing flames, the sounds of sizzling and frying, chopping and stirring, the easy banter of the cooks. I loved being showered with kisses, sneaked sweetmeats by workers on their break, hugged, cuddled, taken for a walk. I loved the feeling of cold air on my face after the hot kitchen, the feel of a warm hand in mine, the food I had been fed constantly, a piece of ladoo here, a samosa there, heavy in my stomach. I felt secure. I knew, without a doubt that I was loved.

I think that is why I was most at home doing my homework in chip shops while I waited for Mum to get home from work. The clatter of pots and pans, the bustle of a busy kitchen, the deliciously tantalising smells, the blast of cold air as the door was pushed open, the whisper of customers' clothing as they walked past, the rise and fall of voices in conversation, they were all as familiar, as soothing to me as my mother's embrace, the way she had of hugging me with a glance, imparting comfort with a smile.

I cannot be angry with her. She loved me. She loves me. I remember the look she gave me as she was led away, her promise to write, tell her side of the story. I haven't received any letters. Perhaps she is not allowed to write to me. I know she has a valid reason for doing what she did and I will reserve judgement until I hear it. I do get cross sometimes, but I cannot stay angry with her for long. I miss her too much.

Truth is I do not want her to have been in the wrong. Truth is it is easier to believe her than countenance the alternative. Truth is I am hoping for a miracle.

Aarti – I always think of her as the other woman – loves me as well. And yet, somehow, even though it is my mum I should be angry with, I am angry at her, at Aarti. This woman who has been searching for me for almost a decade and a half. I am angry at her for turning up, for putting me in this position.

I open the window and look outside. The air smells green, jaunty, the fragrant evening redolent with the promise of spring, evident in the buttery slivers of daffodils the colour of hope peeking out from between cupped green bulbs like a woman's face escaping the confines of her sari pallu. Shrubs are pregnant with shoots and the promise of new life, and the grass smiles its stained yellow, recovering-from-winter smile as it basks in the soft twilight glow. A bird calls from somewhere among the budding trees.

A car drives into the close and I realise with a thrill of recognition that it is Jane's familiar Ford. I am not expecting her. There must be some news. Fear grabs my heart in a stranglehold. I clatter down the stairs, past the boys doing their homework with Farah, three bent heads, a profusion of black curls. Three pairs of eyes scrutinising me as I rush past and open the door. Jane's low beams slither across the curtains, sweep a curved orange path along the wall, dance a pattern on my top as she pulls up, switches off her lights.

I stand at the front door, shivering even though the evening is mild, arms draped around myself, protecting me from whatever it is she has to say. The air is infused with the fug of dog waste and dread, sweet with a fusty undertone.

Jane gets out of the car and her gentle gaze meets mine. It is swimming, but I cannot make out the expression in her liquid, roasted almond eyes.

'What is it?' I ask, and my voice is breathless. It is plaited with fear, threaded through with panic.

'Do you want to sit down? Go to your room? The car?'

A gaggle of teenagers walk past, laughing at something, bandying the F-word about, pushing each other into next door's sprouting rose bushes. Squeals of laughter and shouts of 'Ow!' and 'What did you do that for?' rend the air which tastes of pain as I open my mouth and take huge gulps, finding myself suddenly, inexplicably unable to breathe.

'No,' I manage. 'Tell me now.'

A pizza delivery boy zooms past on his motorbike.

'The DNA test results came back,' she says.

I sway on my feet. She reaches across and cups my face in the palm of her hand. I let her.

'I don't know why she put you through this.' For the first time since I've known her, Jane's marshmallow voice is angry, tough, sounding like a hard chewy toffee, like biting into a fruit and discovering, with a painful shock, that it is not sweet but hot and spicy inside.

A burst of evening air, nippy, carrying the scent of spring and the memory of winter strokes my cheeks. My legs give way and I lean against the doorjamb.

Jane holds out a letter to me. The results of the test. My eyes take it in, deciphering the meaning before it sinks into my heart and they swim with an assault of tears. The flimsy piece of paper determining my future flutters as my hand is suddenly rendered weightless; it falls on the mat with a sigh, pffff, like the sound a secret makes as it travels from a confiding mouth to an attentive ear.

Somewhere close by, a little girl's voice, tinkling like a chorus of bells, calls, 'Mum?'

Mum… I collapse onto the mat at the entrance that says 'Welcome' in cheery red coir letters and I sob. I sob like I have not done since that terrible evening. I sob like my being is being ripped in two. I sob loudly and completely, the sobs coming in waves, wracking me, tearing me to pieces.

PART FOUR

The Past

Precious Burden

Chapter 34
Aarti – Love

One Rainy Evening in August

All her life Aarti has had men interested in her. But for her, it's only ever been a case of wanting what she cannot have. She's stolen men away from other women, ruthlessly, just because she can. She wants men to like her, adore her, look only at her. If they don't, and it is very rare that they don't, she will up her charms and set out to ensnare them. She gets everything she wants, she always has.

And then he walks into her life, casually, one rainy evening in August.

Things are going well for Aarti. She is at the top of her game, the best supermodel in Karnataka, one of the top three in India. She has Vani who accompanies her everywhere now, whom she cannot do without, who even comes along on her shoots.

Her mother has complained about this, has warned, 'You're getting too attached to the servant. She'll get ideas in her head.'

The very things Aarti herself had agonised over when she first started getting close to Vani. But she pooh-poohs her mother, laughs at her.

Now that she has Vani, she doesn't much care about trying to please her parents. In fact, she doesn't even think of them as her parents anymore. She has a secret fantasy, which she hasn't shared with anyone, not even Vani, especially not Vani. At night as she waits for sleep to lay claim, as her starved stomach growls and complains, she imagines that Vani's parents were, in fact, hers, that *she* was the little girl who was desperately wanted, who was loved and feted and adored. It could be true. After all, she and Vani are so close they could be sisters. Lying in the dark listening to Vani's quiet exhalations and her own abused stomach's loud grievances, the air drifting in through the partly open window whispering secrets smelling of night jasmine and intrigue, anything seems possible.

And so she laughs at her mother and is pleased to note the hard glint that comes into her mother's eyes, the shadow that fleetingly crosses her face. Hurt? Upset? Aarti doesn't care.

'Well, you'll learn the hard way,' her mother says. 'No good ever comes from fraternising with that class of people. All they want is what you have.' Her mother's voice brittle as peanut candy.

Many years later, Aarti will recall this particular phrase of her mother's and she will admit, even though it feels like trying to swallow a raw bitter gourd, that her mother was right. But for now, she is happy, secure in her unlikely friendship with her trusted servant.

Aarti is at a party when it happens, when love swoops down and takes hold, catching her unawares.

Outside the club where the party is taking place – a celebration for the release of a Kannada blockbuster – rain falls in slanting sheets of fury, blurring everything in sight, giving dust-swirled, grime-sodden Bangalore a much-needed sheen, working magic like the wand of a make-up artist adding definition here, shadow there, completing the metamorphosis from plain to stunning.

Umbrellas bob and pedestrians caught off guard scurry for cover, the women pulling pallus and dupattas over their heads. A group of boys run, laughing, using their rapidly wilting notebooks as shields. They will go home to see that the ink has bled onto the pages, gluing them together, depriving the boys of notes to study for their exam the next day. Their mothers will yell at them, ask if they have coconuts for brains, and they will grin through mouthfuls of steaming vadais and sweet tea, cosy in their warm kitchens smelling of oil and fried spices, watching the rain skitter on roofs and churn the mud into slush.

A little girl skips in the middle of the road, dancing amongst gurgling potholes of restless brown water, sodden tendrils of hair clinging possessively to her shimmering face, immune to rickshaws honking, bus conductors leaning on their horns, people yelling at her to move out of the way of traffic. Her mother dashes onto the road and gathers the girl in her arms, kissing her wet face again and again, which must taste, Aarti thinks, of rain and mud and little girl. She watches them standing there, surrounded by honking traffic and yet, lost in their own world, the little girl safe in the harbour of her mother's embrace, her small arms wrapped securely around her mother's soggy neck, and she feels a pang, that ache of longing that she keeps hidden from the world. *Unconditional love,* she thinks. *Vani had that,* she thinks.

'Romantic, isn't it?' a voice queries from behind her. A deep voice. Musical in a masculine way. Familiar.

A voice she's pretty sure she's heard before.

She doesn't turn immediately, just takes a dainty sip from her glass and lets the noise and bustle of the party wash over her in soothing ripples. 'Yes,' she says eventually.

'Are you always like this, weighing every word you utter, thinking it through?' There is a smile in his voice. He is standing very close, she can feel his body heat emanating from just behind her, the smell of lemon and musk, the mint and wine on his breath.

She pauses for good measure, watches a woman slip on a puddle, a man hold her arm and help her back onto her feet, watches the woman thank him profusely, her face upturned, wet tendrils of hair hugging it, even as she tries to ineffectively wipe the grime off her muddy sari.

'Not always,' Aarti says.

He laughs, waves of warm chocolate washing over her. His laughter is even more seductive than his voice.

She turns. He's tall, a head taller than her – and that's saying something as she's one of the tallest models around.

A toned body that suggests long hours at the gym. Warm golden eyes that match the feeling that hearing him laugh aroused in her. A profusion of curly brown hair. A day's growth of beard. Straight nose and lips…full and inviting. She is caught unawares by a sudden, unexpected thrill of desire. It's been a long time since she's felt like this. The last time was in high school when she had that crush on Magesh. He was already taken, his girlfriend a plump, plain girl called Shanta. Perhaps that was part of his appeal for Aarti, since he wasn't all that good-looking. Aarti had set out on a campaign to win him over. By the time she had the satisfaction of seeing chubby Shanta devastated and looking even uglier with her long face and penchant for bursting into tears, Aarti had lost interest in him. Magesh had followed her around doggedly for a year, sending notes and flowers. Spurning his advances had given her great pleasure. And it set the tone for the years that followed. She found that she enjoyed making boys and men alike fall in love with her, losing interest the moment they did.

She has always been faintly repelled by the men she's come across, by their attraction to her, their desire. But not this man. She finds she is enjoying his attention, responding to it.

'I know you,' she says.

'Do you?' he smiles, and his eyes glow charmingly.

She is blindsided by a sudden impulse to touch the dimple dancing in his left cheek. She sets her glass down very carefully on the table beside her, gathers her breath.

Where is Vani? she thinks, knowing, of course, that Vani is waiting in the car for her like Aarti asked her to. She could do with Vani beside her right now, to bolster her confidence.

'You are…' It comes to her in a flash. 'Sudhir Shetty. The Kannada movie heartthrob,' she recites, repeating what she's read about him in the papers. That is why his voice was so familiar; she's heard it on television! She stops, suddenly realising what she has said, her heart clamouring loudly, painfully in the confines of her chest. She bites her lower lip, feels colour flood to her face.

He smiles, flashing that dimple again, his eyes twinkling down at her. It is so nice to be able to look up to someone for a change, she thinks, even as her heart executes a tango. Makes a change from bending her knees to maintain eye contact with other men, who are almost always shorter than she is.

'Do continue,' he grins, a mischievous gleam in his eyes. 'I love listening to pretty women describing my charms.'

'I did say I only think before I speak sometimes,' she counters tartly. 'Obviously this wasn't one of them.'

'Ah, but when you don't think before you speak, is that your heart speaking?' he asks, winking.

'No, just the entertainment column of *The Hindu*,' she says and his eyes twinkle merrily, the dimple tantalising as he laughs.

She looks around him, behind him. 'Where's your entourage?'

All the pictures she's seen of him – and there have been many; he's one of the best-looking men to grace the Kannada film scene and rumour has it he'll be poached by Bollywood soon enough – he's trailed closely by security guards and personal assistants. But here he is, alone and talking to her. Now that she's managed to look away from him, she's aware of the eyes of the whole room on them, cameras flashing in their direction. You can never keep the press away from these dos and nobody wants to either – after all, any publicity is good publicity.

He waves his hand languidly, his dancing, flame-coloured eyes devouring her face. 'Sent them away. They deserve some time off, don't you think?'

He leans close and for a moment she is sure he is going to kiss her. She can feel his minty, alcohol-stained breath on her face, caressing her. Her heart is performing weird somersaults. She can sense her face getting hot, feel the eyes of the room on her, knowing they are craning their necks, the photographers edging surreptitiously forward, the better to capture the moment.

'I could do with a break from them, to be honest. I feel like a schoolboy doing a bunk.' He winks at her, moves back.

She realises she has been holding her breath only when she releases it in a sigh. She is disappointed. She *wanted* him to kiss her, she realises, surprising herself, spectators be damned.

Just as her heartbeat is returning to normal, he leans very close again, his breath tickling her cheek, raising goosebumps.

'I don't know about you, but I have the strangest feeling we're being watched.'

She cannot help it, she bursts out laughing. And that is the picture that appears in all the newspapers and tabloids the next day, Sudhir leaning into her and Aarti grinning, her mouth wide open in what her mother snorts is 'a very unflattering pose. No lady should reveal her tonsils to the general public.' And then, appraising her curiously, a segment of the orange that constitutes her breakfast in her hand, 'So is there some truth to the rumours?'

Aarti turns away so her mother will not see the blush creeping up her neck, the fluster she feels inside. *I hope. I wish,* she thinks.

She's spent the previous night awake, thinking about Sudhir, fantasising about the two of them together. Fantasies that had made her wish, for the first time since Vani started sleeping in her room, that Vani wasn't there, her breathing intruding into Aarti's imaginings.

'Oh, none at all,' she says airily to her mother. 'I have my career to think of.'

'Your career will get a huge boost if you hook up with the most eligible bachelor in town,' her mother muses. 'In fact, the two of you together will be a force to reckon with.'

Chapter 35
Vani – Moving House

A Divine Butterfly

Vani is happy for Aarti and just a teeny bit envious. She cannot imagine someone loving her the way Sudhir loves Aarti, with that complete and utter adoration.

One evening, Aarti comes up to Vani after she's been out with Sudhir, and Vani knows from the look on Aarti's face that something momentous has happened. Aarti takes Vani's hands in her own cold ones. She sits Vani down on the bed, her face grave.

Vani feels apprehension engulf her chest, making it hard to breathe. Has Aarti read Vani's innermost thoughts, her feeling of being trapped, of wanting to run away?

'What's the matter?' Vani asks, trying and failing to keep the worry out of her voice.

A luminous smile blooms on Aarti's face and she is transformed, a divine butterfly. She looks like a heavenly being in her ethereal white salwar kameez, tendrils of blue-black hair framing her delicate features. 'Sudhir and I are getting married.' There are tears in her eyes.

Vani flings her arms around Aarti. 'I am thrilled, so very pleased for you.'

'The wedding is in two months. Not much time to prepare, I know, but I didn't want to wait.' She holds Vani at arm's length, looks around the room. 'We have to start packing.' She means Vani has to, of course. 'Do you think two months is enough time to pack my entire life?'

'I'll try my best,' Vani smiles. Inside, she is thinking, *I packed my entire life into one little bag in half an hour when I left my village to come here.*

'I will be mistress of a castle, Vani.' Her eyes shine. 'This house is tiny compared to Sudhir's pad. Wait until you see it.'

Afterwards, Vani wonders how could she have been so thick, how could she not have seen it coming? She stands there, shocked, trying to get her bearings. She should have known, of course. But she didn't make the connection. She was reminiscing about the move here from the village, that time of intense upheaval in her own life.

'Vani, what are you looking like that for? You will not be staying in servants' quarters, don't you worry. You will have the room right next to mine. Ours, I should say, mine and Sudhir's.' A blush creeps into Aarti's voice, colouring it the red of blood oozing from flesh pricked by a thorn.

Vani's world uprooted again. To go to a new house with an already established hierarchy of servants, to have to bear their hostility… It is too much to think about. She smiles, she tries to. But the smile wobbles.

Aarti pouts, she sulks. 'I thought you would be happy for me.'

And Vani does what she has become an expert at doing. She hides her angst, her fears and says in a voice with just the right amount of cheer, 'Of course I am. So happy. Now, when do we start packing?'

Aarti is married in a breathtaking ceremony that is 'the event' of Bangalore, a wedding unsurpassed in the entire south of India, or so Vani is told via the papers which she can now read because she is fluent in English. She does not attend of course. Invited guests only. The crème de la crème of India. No servants masquerading as so-called sisters.

Vani packs both of their belongings and says her goodbyes, counting down her days in the house that has been a refuge after her parents died, while Aarti is away on honeymoon in the Seychelles. She sees the newly married couple's pictures in the tabloids, reclining on loungers, wearing shades and looking deliriously happy, holding the obligatory cocktail which Vani knows Aarti will bring up later. Has Sudhir found out yet, she wonders, and decides almost immediately that he hasn't. Aarti is adept at hiding her condition even from those closest to her. Only Vani knows that Aarti never allows anything except vegetables to stay down. Only she knows.

The day before Aarti and Sudhir are due back home from their honeymoon, Aarti calls. Vani has just finished the bulk of the packing when the cook shouts up the stairs, 'Vani, it's for you.'

She is looking at her bags – three bulging suitcases full of assorted belongings and thinking of how when she arrived she had one little bag and that hardly full. In many ways, Aarti is very nice, prickly, difficult to live with at times, but kind. Generous. Giving. The three swollen suitcases are proof.

Vani runs down the stairs. The telephone is portable but of course the cook would not deign to bring it up to her, or ask one of the others to. She is a servant, not the boss. She can jolly well climb down and take the call.

It is Aarti and she sounds breathless. 'Vani, I've missed you. How have you been? I have had a great time but it will be nice to come back, see you. I have so much to tell you.' The words tumble out in a winded rush.

Aarti had wanted to take Vani with her on their honeymoon but Sudhir had laughed at her suggestion, thought she was joking. 'There will be plenty of help over there, you know. We are staying at a five-star hotel; there will be someone to cater to our every need.'

Aarti had laughed right along with him, her lips curving upwards but her eyes spearing Vani in a panicked stare. Aarti needed Vani; she had told herself she could not function without her friend.

Vani enjoyed being so important in Aarti's life and she hated it.

'You don't know how hard it's been without you,' Aarti's saying. 'Nobody gets me like you do.' She takes a breath at last. 'Now, we are arriving tomorrow but going straight to Sudhir's place. I do not want to stay a minute longer in my parents' house. Have you finished packing?'

'Yes, but...' Vani begins.

'Okay, listen. Ram, Sudhir's driver, will be round with the car this afternoon. He'll help you load everything, and you can go to Sudhir's place with him, unpack and get our room ready for when we come home tomorrow. One of the servants will show you to our room and yours. Sudhir has briefed them. Bye. See you tomorrow. Can't wait.'

Vani stands there a minute, head resting against the wall, the smell of frying onions drifting from the kitchen, the cool feel of cement on her forehead, and then she rushes upstairs to finish packing.

At three o'clock, Vani notes the progress of a sleek black car from her vantage point on the landing, where she loves to stand and watch the sun rise, a habit gleaned during those sleepless nights in her first year here when she was desperately missing her parents and the home she had with them. Of a morning, while the household slumbers and the air in the house staggers under the weight of myriad dreams, she likes to stand on the landing and snatch a few moments of peace for herself before starting the day and giving herself over to Aarti's needs, her whims and fancies. She likes to watch for her parents' faces in the clouds, asking them permission to live another day without them, asking them to make this day a good one. This is her morning prayer, her Suprabhatam, as tantalising rays peek from the verge of the horizon, streaking the inky black the pink of a baby's smile, the orange of its laughter and the red of its wonder, staining the horizon with hope, injecting it with the promise of a brand new day.

She will miss this landing, her silent morning communion with the sky and her parents, she thinks now, as she watches the car screech to a halt just outside the front door, raising a screen of dust in its wake and startling the crows nestling serenely amongst the jacaranda trees lining the drive. She watches as a man jumps out, every bit as jaunty as the car, as he pats his hair in place and walks up to the door.

Just before he reaches the door, he stands back and surveys the mansion curiously and, even though she is pretty sure he cannot see her, his gaze lingers on the window, where she is standing, for longer than necessary. She moves backward a step and almost falls down the stairs. She rights herself and cautiously peeks out of the window again, and there he is, staring right at her, his coffee eyes twinkling, a smile streaking across his lively face.

She turns away and clatters down the stairs before Suggi, the cook's helper, opens the front door and yells for her.

'Do you make a habit of assessing every house you see or just this one?' Vani asks, surprising even herself with the aggression in her voice. She is annoyed that this man caught her out.

He grins at her, unfazed. 'Annoyed that I caught you staring?' he asks, and Vani takes a step backward again, nonplussed.

'So where is this luggage then?' he grins.

He is the most cheerful man she has ever met, she thinks grumpily. There should be a law against being this merry when the person you are meeting clearly isn't. Her emotions are in disarray at leaving this house that has sheltered her since her parents' death.

The man – Aarti did tell Vani his name but she has forgotten it and does not want to ask him – carries all the stuff downstairs and loads the car, not letting her lift a thing, which, perversely, makes her even more annoyed.

'Are you always this bad-tempered?' he asks, when she has plonked herself beside him, the back seats and the boot full to overflowing, even though the car is huge.

'Are you always this cheerful?' she counters and he throws back his head and laughs.

'Are we ever going to move?' she snaps as he fumbles with the key and he laughs even harder, pulling out a handkerchief from his pocket to wipe his eyes.

He finally manages to start the car after two tries, he is laughing so much.

'Just take me safely there,' she spits out, looking straight ahead.

On the drive over, he talks non-stop, filling her in on the servants and the hierarchy.

'Are they very annoyed with me?' she asks.

He turns to look at her and his eyes are soft, full of an expression she does not recognise. 'A little.'

He hesitates and she clicks her teeth, saying, 'Just tell me.' Somehow, even though she's only just met him, she's comfortable with this man, at ease in his company, perhaps because he's so laid-back, not riled by her bad humour, unfazed by her caustic comments.

He sighs, 'You see, the rest of us have to make do with separate servants' quarters in an annexe behind the main house – no running water, one communal bathroom, while you, the newcomer, get the en-suite adjoining the boss's room.'

Vani exhales the breath she's been holding. It is as she expected. What the servants don't know is that the en-suite bathroom is there for a reason: that Aarti will be using it to be sick, to keep her condition from Sudhir. Vani leans her head on the backrest and closes her eyes at the thought of the unpleasantness ahead.

'Don't worry, they are not that bad. And seeing as how charming you are, you will win them over in no time,' he says.

She opens her eyes at that and squints at him. He winks at her, grinning widely.

'Keep your eyes on the road,' she yells.

'Very charming,' he mumbles loud enough for her to hear.

She cannot help the smile that escapes the corners of her mouth.

'See, you look so pretty when you smile, you should do it more often.'

She blushes to the roots of her hair. 'Will you please keep your eyes on the road?' she mutters.

'If it's any consolation,' he says, his voice soft, serious, 'you have charmed me.' He looks right at Vani and she feels another blush suffusing when the first one hasn't even faded yet.

'Well, here we are,' he says and she turns round abruptly to see that they are at a very imposing gate which is swinging open to reveal a wide expanse of equally imposing driveway, surrounded by grounds even bigger, even more beautiful and well maintained than at Aarti's house.

We could be at a palace, she thinks, her heart beating wildly as the car races past pristine gardens and myriad gardeners standing in the sun, wiping sweat off their foreheads as they water the lawns. The drive goes on and on until, at last, the car pulls up at a mansion every bit as daunting as Vani expected it to be.

Chapter 36
Aarti – Marriage

Whitewashed Sky

Aarti is waiting up for Sudhir when he stumbles home, drunk, at 1:00 a.m. in the morning.

They have been married six months, a glorious whirlwind of a time in which Aarti has experienced so many highs. The high of walking into a room on the arm of her husband, soaking up the envy in the eyes of the women, basking in the admiration of the men. The high of being heralded the 'better half' of 'the golden couple'. The high of landing a part in a movie opposite her husband and discovering that she is a natural at acting. The high of her career going from strength to strength. The high of living away from her parents, not having to care about what they think or having to listen to their ridiculous opinions. The high of becoming more successful than *they* have ever been. The high of having two people, Vani and Sudhir, in her life who love her, for whom she is the most important person in the world.

'Where were you?' she asks and she tries to keep her voice on an even keel. She doesn't sound like she has succeeded. It is high-pitched, squeaky. She is tired. She is hungry, her stomach an irritable animal wanting feeding. Normally the grievances of her hollow stomach populate her dreams, the constant hunger a feeling that colours her sleep. But she hasn't been able to sleep without Sudhir by her side. Even though they have been married for just over six months, she has got used to his constant, reassuring presence beside her.

Now she is crabby, exhausted. And she has a film shoot in the morning first thing.

Vani had warned her not to stay up. 'Have a good night's sleep; you'll feel much better tomorrow,' she'd said soothingly, rubbing Aarti's back like she was a little child, the way Aarti liked, as Aarti sobbed in her arms.

Sudhir tries to focus his eyes on her, fails. She cannot see the breathtakingly handsome man she fell in love with in this cross-eyed, dishevelled caricature. His gait is measured, careful, and yet he stumbles and she quells the instinct to extend her hand to help him.

'You know where I was,' he slurs.

What makes it worse is that she could have gone tonight. But she didn't want to. She was tired.

All those parties, all that eating, all the secrecy surrounding being sick, are taking their toll on her. Thank God for Vani. She stands guard at whichever bathroom Aarti is in, warning her when someone is coming, warning people off, telling them the toilets are flooded, making all sorts of excuses. Vani accompanies her everywhere: on set and to parties, where she manages to fold herself off into a corner. Vani has a great talent for blending in, a talent that, Aarti will realise in the years to come, Vani will put to good use.

Hiding her bulimia from Sudhir is taking its toll. Aarti's mood swings upset him. She blames hormones. He rolls his eyes and tells her to get pills. She is finding it hard to keep up the subterfuge, but she cannot afford not to. Being Sudhir's co-star has afforded her a glimpse into his world of fawning females, adoring fans. Sudhir is a charmer; he flirts effortlessly with all his myriad admirers.

When Aarti confides her fears in Vani, she says, 'It's all an act. He loves *you*. You are his wife, the one he shares a life with. You are the one he cares for.' She can be very romantic, can Vani.

Aarti had told Sudhir she didn't want to go to the party and she had thought he'd say, 'Okay, we'll stay home.'

Instead he said, in his usual cheerful offhand way, 'All right, babe, I'll go then. You relax.' He smiled at her fondly.

'But…' Her face fell. 'Don't you want to stay home with me?'

'No, I'll go. I want to go.' He was still smiling but a hint of steel had entered his voice.

She did not want to protest, make a big deal. So she smiled, waved a hearty goodbye and rushed to the bathroom, was sick violently, again and again, savouring the sensation, trying to draw comfort from it. She felt Vani beside her, holding her hair away from her face and leading her to bed after. She gave in to Vani's ministrations as she sobbed.

'Nothing has happened,' Vani kept saying. 'He's just gone to a party, that's all. He's not cheated on you.'

Aarti stilled, stared at Vani, clutched her hand. 'What did you say?'

When she called him at ten, there was no reply. At eleven, he picked up and said in a voice she didn't recognise, in the slurred vowels of a drunk, as if he was searching for words and they were slipping off his tongue, tumbling around in his mouth like marbles, 'Swill be home soon.' She heard feminine laughter in the background. At twelve, he didn't pick up; twelve-thirty, the phone was switched off.

He stumbles home at one, is sick violently and crashes into bed stinking of wine. She sleeps in Vani's bed in the adjoining room and Vani sleeps on a mat on the floor. Her husband doesn't even notice. He is dead to the world and snoring in two ticks.

He doesn't mention anything the next morning and so neither does she. She goes to her shoot, comes home to find he has left sometime during the day. He didn't turn up at the set so she doesn't know where he has gone. When she calls him, he doesn't pick up. He saunters home at 10:00 p.m.

'Where were you?' she asks and this time she doesn't bother to hide the ire in her voice.

'Didn't I tell you?' he smiles, undeterred by her anger, his eyes shining tenderly down at her. 'It was Raja's thirtieth birthday. A few of us were meeting up. I thought I left you a message, darling. You were supposed to meet me there.'

She is somewhat mollified. She hasn't checked her messages. Later that evening, after he's asleep, she checks them and there is no message from him. The serpent of doubt and fear uncoils, strikes. She cannot sleep. She wanders to the window on the landing and tries to ascertain answers in the overcast sky the dark black of deep despair, relieved here and there by dots of silvery stars twinkling like Diwali lights. She is a wreck.

After that she goes to every party with him but it is not quite the same. He often gives her the slip. Tells her he will be somewhere and doesn't turn up. It is as if he *wants* rid of her. When she tells him so, he is by turns shocked, outraged and defensive.

'What if I do?' he says, every word a challenge thrown at her. 'What if I want to occasionally spend time with the lads? You and I…we work together, we sleep together… Once in a while I want to be on my own with the friends I grew up with.' These last said in a softer voice, his gaze gentle.

She doesn't notice. 'Why do you never take my calls?' she cries.

His expression hardens like milk thickening to whey. 'Because then there is no point; I might as well stay home with you,' he yells.

She cannot get the much publicised affairs he had before he met her, the feminine voice she heard that time she called him, out of her mind. And misgiving eats away at her like the constant hunger gnawing at the lining of her stomach.

And then one morning, as she is sipping tea, she asks Vani for the newspapers as usual. Vani brings them round, smiling, flicking through them as she does, choosing articles that Aarti might enjoy.

Teaching her to read English was the best thing I did, Aarti muses as she gazes absently out of the window.

The sun is just rising, casting the glittering emerald lawns in a soft yellow glow. Pink, orange and red roses sing in the arbours, and hibiscus flowers the dark purple of night wave hello to another glorious morning. A lone crow is silhouetted against a whitewashed sky. Sudhir is sleeping in, having no shoots scheduled for that morning.

'Come on, Vani,' Aarti says languidly, 'Isn't there anything at all interesting for me to look at?'

Vani's face is frozen in a grimace that she wipes clear when Aarti looks at her, replacing it with the farce of a smile, the papers slack in her hand.

'What's the matter? Not feeling well?' Aarti asks, a sliver of worry nagging at her spine.

She cannot have Vani falling ill. Not again. The last time she did, Aarti went to pieces.

'Shall I give you some of my pills to nip whatever it is in the bud?' She cannot operate without Vani. Who will ward off people barging into the loo while she is being sick? Who will come up with excuses for her not being able to attend this or that party? Who will answer her phone, comb her hair, prepare her fruit salad the way she likes it? Vani is *essential* to Aarti's well-being.

'I am fine,' Vani says and this time her smile is almost normal. 'I'll just…' She starts to take the newspapers away.

'I haven't read them,' Aarti says, pleased now all is well with her world.

'Nothing exciting happening at all,' Vani's voice is cagey.

'I will decide that for myself. Bring them here at once,' Aarti commands, her voice sharp. Vani's face is ashen. 'What is it with you this morning?' Aarti complains, snatching the newspapers, her rare good mood threatening to disintegrate.

She spreads the newspapers on the table in front of her and blinks. Once, then once again. Words swim before her eyes. She cannot, will not make sense of what she is seeing. It cannot be true.

This time, when Vani reaches for the newspapers, Aarti lets her. The teacup wobbles in her hand, the remaining tea spilling onto the tablecloth, muddy brown seeping into cream, staining it the dark russet of sin.

She runs to the bathroom and retches, again and again. But emptying her stomach does not offer the comfort it normally does. Try as she might, she cannot rid her mind of the picture that swims before her eyes, the picture that graces the front page of all the tabloids, that Vani, bless her, was trying to keep Aarti from seeing. Sudhir and the newest actress to hit the screens, an eighteen-year-old nubile beauty. They are standing too close for it to be an innocent shot. His hand is on her arm and she is looking up at him. And the look on their faces…the same look that had been captured so many times by the self-same tabloids when her husband, *her* husband, was courting her…

Chapter 37
Vani – Settling In

Naked Gaze

They are arguing again, their voices loud and harsh, Aarti's brittle, sounding like it will break any minute, Sudhir's brash and full of hurt.

Sudhir loves his wife but he cannot get through to her, get past the barrier of her insecurities. Vani catches a glimpse of Sudhir's face when he watches Aarti sometimes, the perplexed gaze mixed in with hurt. He is trying to work his wife out and failing. He cannot understand her because she hasn't told him who she is, hasn't made him party to the traits that define her.

'I am grateful you are there for her. At least she confides in you,' Sudhir has said to Vani countless times. 'Can't you tell her to ease it a bit, give me a break?' he has pleaded with Vani, his amber eyes bleeding hurt.

Vani has coaxed Aarti to confide in Sudhir. She has tried telling Aarti, showing her how much Sudhir loves her. She has gently hinted to Aarti to not read too much into his flirting.

But Aarti will not listen. She is eaten up by self-doubt, she allows her paranoia to create scenarios in her head, she does not understand Sudhir's desire for some time alone. She pushes Sudhir so much that he is pushed away.

The house is a war zone most of the time now, and even though it is big, much bigger than Aarti's parents' house, it is not big enough for all that hurt, that angst to dissipate. Whenever another argument starts, Vani escapes, even though she knows Aarti wants her close at hand. She runs down the many stairs and out of the house, into the waiting car. The car is always there, offering security like a comfort blanket, idling by the front door.

'Fighting again are they?' Ram, the chauffeur, asks, perusing Vani in the mirror, and she nods, not having the energy to talk, avoiding his naked gaze which always manages to read into the very heart of her.

Ram does not push her. He seems to know, instinctively, when she needs to talk and when she craves the quiet solace of his company. He is the happiest person she has met and also the most content. He is kind and caring; she has observed him doing myriad little favours for all the servants – helping water the gardens so Lalu, the oldest gardener can have a break, taking a thermos of tea out to the watchman by the gate, even chopping onions for the cook that time Sudhir sprung an impromptu party for twenty guests on them and the kitchen was short-staffed.

And Ram has always been absolutely wonderful to her, right from that first day when he picked her up from Aarti's parents' house and laughed at her outrage and made her blush by saying she had charmed him. He teases a smile out of her when she is grumpy, offers comfort and companionship when she is down. Even when he is not around, just the thought of him can calm her, cajole her out of a bad mood. He has even started appearing in her dreams, and lately it has been his face easing her into sleep at night instead of her parents' fading visages. He is occupying her thoughts, her parents receding from the forefront of her mind. Somehow thinking of him instead of her parents does not make her feel guilty – she can picture her parents smiling at this development. She knows that were her parents to meet Ram, they would adore him.

The other servants are distant towards her but not mean. They tolerate Vani because Ram has made no bones about the fact that she is his friend and one of them, even if Aarti, their mistress, favours her.

That first evening in this house, after Ram deposited all the cases in Aarti and Sudhir's room, he had asked Vani to come down, meet the other servants. She had hesitated, afraid.

'Come on,' he had urged. 'Where's that fiery girl I just saw?'

But Vani was cowed by the sheer grandeur of these new premises she found herself in and by the prospect of meeting people who resented her. 'I should unpack, get everything ready for Aarti,' she had said.

'You need to eat and the cook here is amazing. Since it's the last day with just us servants, before the boss and his wife arrive and everything changes, we're having a celebration. Come on.'

He had lightly put his hand on hers to coax her along and she had felt a thrill run through her at the contact. She was so surprised that she flinched and he had dropped his hand and she had felt strangely bereft.

'Come, everyone is waiting to hear how Aarti, the new mistress of the house, really is,' he had said, his eyes twinkling, and she had wondered who this man was and why he had the power to arouse such powerful emotions in her, make her behave so out of character, to yell at him when she first met him and now to render her speechless, to make her want to touch his face, stroke the stubble sprouting there, to apologise for flinching and ask him to touch her again so she could check if that thrill would manifest itself once more, to ask him if he was like this with everyone.

She had gone downstairs with him and she could hear the other servants' chatter, the laughter and banter echoing down the corridor.

'Hey, Ram,' they said, spotting him, 'come eat.'

The easy bonhomie stopped when she entered, an uncomfortable silence settling in its wake. She was scrutinized by hundreds of eyes – or at least that's how it felt. She did not know where to look.

And then, Ram had smiled in that way of his. 'This is Vani,' he had said, taking her hand again and pulling her forward, and the thrill had started at the tip of her spine and travelled upwards all the way to her heart, flooding it with something she couldn't name. 'She is going to fill us in on all the gossip about the new mistress arriving tomorrow, aren't you?'

He had winked at her then and her heart had jumped, it had responded to the warmth of his hand in hers, his soft gaze shining down at her.

After that, the servants were okay with her. The banter had started up again, softly at first, quickly reaching the pitch it had been before. Ram did not leave her side all evening, making introductions, making her feel welcome.

She sits in the car in the peaceful quiet, in companionable silence with Ram, until she can tune out Aarti and Sudhir's screams. She sits there until the fight dissolves into tears and Aarti yells for her.

And then, she leaves the haven of the car and Ram's bolstering presence and enters the chilly silence of the aftermath of the fight. She holds Aarti's hair while she is being sick, rubs her back after, like she has done a hundred thousand times. She comforts Aarti, she murmurs platitudes, she soothes. And through it all, she thinks of Ram. And it centres her.

❊ ❊ ❊

'He's having an affair,' Aarti says, her hand flung across her eyes to block the stubborn chink of light that persists in filtering in despite the drawn curtains. 'I am sure of it.' She is sprawled across the bed, the ghagra she is wearing spread out around her like the plumage of a peacock, blues and greens and golds winking and glittering, a colourful mirage festooning white sheets. 'The only way to win him back, Vani,' Aarti continues, 'is to have a baby.'

Vani stops, startled out of what she is doing. She cannot see Aarti with a baby, she just cannot. Perhaps because Aarti is such a child herself, perhaps because she needs so much mothering. How on earth will Aarti bear a child, look after it, when she struggles to look after herself? And then there is the question of her bulimia. Aarti cannot keep a meal down. How will she feed herself as well as another being growing inside her?

Vani does not voice any of these doubts of course. There is a time and place for everything and it is not just now when Aarti is so distressed. Vani resumes sorting through the wardrobe. 'Have you discussed children with Sudhir sir?' she asks.

Vani is allowed to call her Aarti, even though she doesn't. She doesn't call her anything at all. And Sudhir, of course, is Sudhir sir.

'We discussed children briefly when we were engaged. He wants to wait a few years. And I wanted to as well. In fact, I didn't really consider having a baby at all…'

That's what I thought, Vani muses in her head.

'But lately…' Aarti's voice tails off. 'If we had a baby to bind us together…'

You are thinking of bringing a baby into the world for all the wrong reasons, Vani wants to say. *You do not really want one right now,* she wants to say. *How will you rear a child in that stomach that recoils if anything solid touches it?* she wants to say. *The way to end this stalemate between you and your husband is for you to change, and by change I do not mean physically, by bringing an innocent new soul into the world,* she wants to say. Instead, Vani says nothing at all. Aarti is very agitated. Now is not the time.

'I am going to stop the pills,' Aarti says. 'I will not tell him. When I get pregnant, it will be a lovely surprise.'

Vani cannot help it. 'What about your being sick?' she asks and Aarti freezes as if only just contemplating the thought.

'I will get fat,' she shudders, recoiling from the thought of her pregnant body. And then her face sets in a grim mask. 'It has to be done, it has to be endured. I have to give him a baby before one of the other women he's seeing does and he leaves me. I cannot lose him, Vani, I cannot.'

'I think you should discuss having children with him, see if he really wants them.' Vani says. 'You are not losing him. He wants some time on his own with his friends, that's all.'

Aarti's hand comes away from her eyes. She sits up, looks at Vani suspiciously, her eyes narrowing.

'Why are you taking his side?' Her hand circles Vani's wrist hand in a vice-like grip. Her nails bite into Vani's skin and later Vani knows she will see half-moon craters in the skin, fringed by droplets of dried blood. 'Have you been conferring with Sudhir behind my back?'

'No, I haven't,' Vani says, holding Aarti's gaze. 'But he does love you, only you. I know that for a fact.'

Aarti loosens her hold on Vani and lies back down, her hair fanning the pillow, glossy black streaks on white, like crows silhouetted against the bluish white canvas of sky. Tears squeeze out from behind closed lids, glittering drops beading curly eyelashes, like jasmine buds hovering on tender stalks.

'He's a catch for all those ambitious starlets trying to climb up the acting ladder, Vani. They'll do anything to trap him and it is only a matter of time before one of them gets pregnant,' Aarti says, her voice melancholy as the song of a hermit thrush. 'There is no recourse. I need to get there first; I need to have a baby. I have to.'

And so it begins.

Aarti's periods have been very irregular due to her bulimia, but she looks up ovulation charts on the internet and, having worked out the optimum times, seduces her husband. She tries to keep food down, fresh vegetables and fruit, plenty of fish. She tries, but it is an uphill slog. It goes on for a year and in that time she is mellow, there are a lot less fights and Sudhir starts whistling around the house again.

And then, after a year, she comes to Vani. 'Why am I not getting pregnant?'

'It takes time,' Vani says gently.

Aarti is looking so good now that she is keeping some food inside her. Her skin is glowing. She doesn't have as many mood swings.

'I am getting fat but not pregnant,' she says, standing in profile in front of the mirror, pinching the skin that drapes tight over her bones, like a dress made to fit. 'I will go see a gynaecologist; I need to know what, if anything, I am doing wrong.'

Aarti avoids doctors as much as she avoids fatty food, worried they'll find out what she's been doing to her body. To decide to go to a gynaecologist takes a lot of courage and Vani admires her resolve.

And so, they go. Vani waits in the car with Ram while Aarti has her check-up. Vani looks forward to this time alone with Ram, time when she can be completely herself. She has come to depend on him.

When Aarti comes out of the meeting with the doctor, Vani knows instantly that something is very wrong. Aarti's face is swollen, she has been crying for a while.

Ram opens the door of the car for Aarti and she slides in wearily, like a person thrice her age and flings herself into Vani's arms. Her sobs rend the car, sounding as though they are being ripped from her body.

'What's the matter?' Vani asks, even though, deep inside, she has an inkling.

'It's all my fault.' Aarti sobs. 'It's because of what I have been doing.'

Vani knows where Aarti is going with this. She knows.

'Side effect of making myself sick,' Aarti hiccups. 'It's rendered me infertile. I c… c… can't have children…' she sobs. 'I can't.'

Vani guessed that this might be the case. Aarti's ruthless abuse of her body all these years was bound to take its toll.

Vani prepares to bolster Aarti as she accepts the fact that she cannot have a child. What Vani is not prepared for, what completely and utterly takes her by surprise, is what Aarti does next.

That, she does not anticipate. She does not see it coming.

Chapter 38
Aarti – Married Life

Besieged Heart

The days after that fateful visit to the doctor, after hearing his pronouncement, pass in a blur. Babies. All Aarti can see are babies everywhere. Cute babies, chubby babies, and the proud mothers holding them, showing them off. Pregnant women grin at her from magazines, waddle past in shops, their bodies swollen, and for a moment she thinks, *Thank God, thank God I am spared that* – before the pain starts. *I will never be able to give Sudhir children. I will never be able to keep him.*

Barring the love of her parents, that she has long since given up on, this is the only other time in Aarti's life that she has been denied getting what she wants. And it makes her yearn for a child all the more.

Aarti's self-doubts, which were slumbering for a while, rear their ugly heads. She looks in the mirror and she sees a fat woman. An ugly woman. A barren woman. The efforts to create the child she cannot produce have rendered her grotesque, she thinks. She is convinced it is only a matter of time before one of Sudhir's many co-stars falls pregnant with his child and he leaves her for them unless…unless she somehow produces a child, *their* child.

She starts fanatically keeping tab of Sudhir's movements again. She cannot believe now how she could have stopped watching him, been so lax this past year while she was concentrating on creating a child. She starts calling him at all hours again. The fights come back with a vengeance. Every time they are together there is animosity, yelling. He starts coming home later and later, then stops coming home altogether some nights. She cries herself to sleep. She is losing him. She cannot bear it. And she is certain beyond all doubt that the only way to keep him with her is to give him a baby before one of his mistresses does.

But how?

She doesn't want to adopt a child. She cannot live with not knowing where the child has come from and she wouldn't be able to bond with it, she knows. And Sudhir won't stay with her if the child isn't his, especially if he has to choose between Aarti and one of the starlets pregnant with *his* child. It has to be his.

There is no way I can cheat my way into having it. Or is there?

The child has to be his. She can't have a baby. His mistresses can give him babies. These facts go round and round, buzzing like a coven of bees taking up residence inside her head. And then one day she is idly surfing the web unable to focus on anything in particular, her head full of babies when she sees it. A small article. Tucked away amidst many others. *Womb for rent: the sudden rise in surrogacy.* She scrolls down to it. Reads it. Re-reads. And then her head is suddenly filled with ideas, her besieged heart blooming with hope.

Vani stops polishing the mirror. 'Why are you looking at me like that?' she asks.

'Sorry, just thinking,' Aarti replies.

The more she ruminates, the more she is convinced this will work. The two most important people in her life. The two people who love her most – well, in Sudhir's case, who used to love her the most. Yes, it can work, it will work.

It takes her a week to think it through, to make her decision. A week in which Vani keeps asking her if she is all right, keeps saying, 'Why are you observing me in that strange way? What's on your mind?'

A week in which she tries to think of any obstacles and she can see none. Her plan is perfect. It will work. It has to. It will hurt her, of course it will. But this is Vani, the girl she has been inseparable from these past few years, the one with whom she shares a bond, a pact. Vani is like her sister, she is almost an extension of her. Aarti is not threatened by Vani. Vani is…well, Vani belongs to her really. So in a way, it is natural that this should happen. And it will bind the two people she loves the most in the world, the two people who love her, who centre her life, who are her family, more tightly to her than ever.

She decides to broach the plan with Sudhir first. Vani will agree, of course she will. It is Sudhir who needs to be talked round. Sudhir who is the weak link.

Sudhir laughs when she tells him what she wants. 'Have you gone completely out of your mind, Aarti?' he asks.

They are lying in bed, having made love after what feels like ages. She cried when he was inside her and he had held her after, kissed each tear away gently and said, 'I love you, you know. Only you. I've missed this. I've missed you.'

And then she told him, hands fiddling with the sheets, brown on white, not looking at him. 'I cannot have children.'

'Is that why you've been so...'

The air conditioning came on with an angry burst. She shivered, pulled the sheets tighter around her.

'Yes.'

He'd considered it for a bit. 'I don't mind, you know. I've never really thought about kids much. I suppose I've always assumed I would have some in the distant future.' He'd noticed her face crumple, had taken her hands in his. 'It doesn't bother me. I'd rather have *you*.' His eyes soft and shiny like auburn silk shimmering gold in the sun.

She had wept then, knowing he was lying. Knowing that, even if he meant it now, he wouldn't a few years down the line.

'We are young,' he said. 'There is time. Are you sure the doctor...'

'Yes,' she had sniffed. 'There is no way I can have children.'

'We can always adopt.'

'I don't want just anybody's child. I want yours, ours.'

And then, when he was still holding her in his arms and looking at her with that indulgent gaze, mellow in the aftermath of making love, she broached her plan. And he laughed.

He sees the hot, stinging hurt welling in her eyes, rushing down her cheeks and stops mid-laugh. 'You cannot be serious.'

'I am,' she manages between sobs, knowing that tears will get him to agree faster than anything else. 'Why else would I ask you?'

He pulls his arms out from under her, none too gently, stands and starts pacing the room.

She watches him. He is so good looking, even stark naked, especially stark naked. She wonders how many other women have seen him like this. Does he hold them after sex like he holds her? Does he tell them all he loves them? *Stop this,* she chides herself. *Concentrate. This is important.*

He paces and she waits, tears drying up, impatience rushing in their stead. It has to work. This plan has to work.

After a bit, he turns and stares at her and it is as if he is seeing inside her, to her very core, for the first time. 'I have long wondered…' he says, 'if perhaps you are a little bit mad.'

She balks. Opens her mouth.

But he is too quick. 'Now I know for sure. You are. Totally.' He lifts a finger and, still holding her gaze, turns it round and round in the air in the vicinity of his forehead.

'How dare you?' she yells.

'And yet,' he says, and his voice is puzzled, 'I love you. Care for you deeply. You are the only woman I have ever loved.'

He is looking at her again as if he is trying to figure her out and she doesn't know what to feel, doesn't know if he means what he is saying or whether he is making fun of her.

'I think it is because you intrigue me. All the other women, they throw themselves at me. Not you. Your coolness, your reserve – I took that as a challenge. You were a mystery I had to solve. I fell in love with you somewhere along the way.' He sighs deeply and when he speaks again his voice is the navy blue of grief. 'And I have solved it now. I have solved you.'

He sits beside her on the bed, the mattress compressing with a sigh. His eyes are soft, a sadness in them so deep, so overwhelming that it hurts Aarti to look and yet, she cannot look away. She is mesmerised. This is the first time she has seen him cry.

'You don't love me; you never have.' The seductive voice she fell in love with oozing pain.

How can he think that? He is the one who is mad, not her.

He reaches out, and with one finger tips her face up. 'You only love yourself. Your world revolves around you and you expect everyone else to do the same.'

She recoils, pulls away.

His hand drops to his side.

'Enough,' she screeches, hands on her ears. 'Shut up.'

'Tell that poor girl what you have planned for her. Let's see what her reaction is,' he says and is pulling on some clothes and out of the room before she can say anything more.

The poor girl? Why is he calling Vani that? She will be happy to do this for Aarti, won't she? Aarti could have chosen anybody but she has picked Vani. Vani will be pleased.

And Sudhir will come round. He always does. Didn't he just say he loves her? Only her. Didn't he? Where has he gone? Who is he with? She rushes to the bathroom and retches until she feels better.

That evening, she tells Vani. The sun is dipping beyond the window as it sets, the sky a rainbow of pinks and reds and golds. Vani is combing Aarti's hair, as is their evening ritual, gently teasing away the knots. The air in the room is infused with the fragrance of the warm coconut oil with which Vani has anointed Aarti's head.

'Vani,' Aarti begins. 'I have to ask you to do something very important for me.'

Vani continues to comb, rhythmically, gently. 'Yes?'

'I have never wanted anything more than I want this. Will you do it, for my sake?'

'What is it?' Vani asks, her voice gentle.

Outside a dog barks, servants chatter as they finish for the day. Ram the chauffeur's jaunty voice yells something in Tulu and there is a burst of feminine laughter.

'Will you have a baby for me?' Aarti asks.

Vani stops combing. Her eyes meet Aarti's in the mirror. They are empty, completely blank, like shutters on a window. No hint of expression in them. 'What?'

'It is a great honour, what I am asking of you. I have chosen *you* because I trust you completely. I… He is sleeping with other people anyway. So he might as well sleep with you, give me a child. His. You are an extension of me. We are sisters, bound by so much more than blood. And, if we are to think in terms of genes, you are distantly related to me anyway. Him sleeping with you, it doesn't hurt as much as him sleeping with all those other women. It is like sleeping with me, except of course your womb is not barren. You will be able to conceive, get pregnant, have a child. His child. Mine.' She stops, realising that Vani has closed her eyes, is shaking her head, her whole body. Her hands are fisted and at her ears, trying to block out Aarti's words, the comb poking out of her right fist.

'No,' she is chanting, 'No, no, no, no.'

'Why? It is not that bad, you know. I will pay you handsomely for it. And if you are worried about doing it, well, it isn't even as painful as they say…'

Vani drops the comb, turns and stares at her, and Aarti is taken aback by the expression in her eyes, the emotion that has hijacked the emptiness of a moment before. Rage, the shimmering scarlet of fresh blood.

'Don't you ever, ever, think of anyone but yourself?' Vani spits out, and while Aarti is still smarting from the venom in her voice, she turns and runs from the room.

Aarti cannot find her voice. Shock has hijacked it, taken it captive. It is not as if Vani has a choice. It is Vani's duty to serve Aarti, and she will be serving her in the best way possible by giving her a child. How could Vani have the temerity to say what she did to her? How dare she run away?

Fury takes over and then she is shaking, she is yelling, 'Vani, come back here at once. My hair is unkempt. You haven't even finished combing it. Come back at once.'

She will come round, Aarti thinks, when the haze of rage has eased a tiny bit. *She just needs to get used to the idea. It is like that time I asked her to follow Sudhir, spy on him, and she was so shocked she stared at me, speechless, for a few minutes. She'll come back. I need to give her time.*

Aarti waits; her hair half-plaited and messy. She waits for ten minutes, twenty. Nobody comes.

How much time does that girl need? No other servant would dare to behave the way Vani does.

'Vani!' Aarti yells. 'Vani, come back.'

And her shouts, angry at first, become pained. They become choked with tears.

Chapter 39
Vani – Decision

A Cloud of Orange Mist

Vani runs madly down the stairs and out of the door, she runs into the car like she has done countless times during Aarti and Sudhir's interminable arguments. She gets in and she sits there shaking, shaking to the very core. Ram turns round in his seat and looks at her, and his eyes are as gentle as the sea after a storm, soft as the nest of her mother's saris that she used to snuggle in once upon a time in a different life when she was loved and happy and not blindsided by a preposterous order couched as a favour.

Vani has always sat in the back of this car, even when she is on her own, partly because this is where she sits with Aarti and also to maintain propriety, alone as she is with a young man.

'Are you okay?' Ram asks and his voice is like water rippling in a pond on a summer's day. 'What's the matter? What has she done?'

In all the time Vani has escaped into this car, her refuge, she has never heard this tone of voice from Ram. She trembles violently as she hears Aarti's screams drifting out via the open windows and bombarding her ears, inveigling in, despite being cocooned with the doors closed.

Aarti sounds perplexed. 'Vani.' And again, 'Vani?' The faint suggestion of tears. In a minute it is going to morph into an angry wail, Vani knows.

'Ram, drive. Anywhere. Just drive. Away from here.'

And he does. Even though he is not supposed to, even though he could get in trouble for it, lose his job. He drives Vani away, drives her around town like she is the memsahib and he is just the lowly driver.

This car is for Aarti's exclusive use. Sudhir bought it for her when they got engaged. That is why it is always idling by the front door. This is Ram's job, to wait there ready for Aarti when she needs to go out. Vani knows that Aarti will not go anywhere today. She has just returned from her shoot and she is exhausted, and this argument with Vani will be the last straw. Aarti will be sick, and then she will lie in bed with the curtains drawn and a pillow over her face, and wait for Vani to come back. Vani knows her so well. So very well. Then why didn't she anticipate this? Why did it take her by surprise?

She starts shaking again, and she catches Ram looking worriedly at her in the rear-view mirror. To calm herself, she looks out of the window at the crowds, the noise, the bustle of people going about their business. A man steps in cow dung, a little girl laughs, a woman drags a child down the road, the child digging his feet and kicking up dust. A roadside stall selling pani puri does brisk business, a group of men in lungis milling around dunking the diminutive round puris in the spicy water and swallowing them whole.

She tries to curtail her brawling heart. Tries to stem the panic, the liquid bile seeping into every part of her. The car smells like it always does, of leather and the sandalwood car freshener Aarti favours. Time passes. She doesn't know if it is an hour or two seconds. All she can hear is Aarti's voice, the sparkle in it as if she is bestowing a great honour, 'Will you have a baby for me?'

Vani thinks back to that first time when Aarti came into her room, mindlessly invading her privacy, and held Vani while she sobbed. Vani felt obligated to her after. And thus it began. Thus it began. The needy, insecure mistress. Always wanting confirmation, reassurance... Wanting so much of Vani. Wanting all of her. Her feelings, her thoughts, even her dead parents, her lost childhood, her happiness. Wanting...

'Do you want to go home now?' Ram asks, his voice like the colour cream, soothing, calm, washing over Vani.

She laughs, the sound as bitter as mustard seeds, as brittle as *her* voice. 'Home? Where's that?'

Ram pulls over onto the side of the road, almost overturning a cart brimming with flowers, causing havoc as vendors and pedestrians rush to get out of the way, yelling, 'Lo, lo,', raising an avalanche of dust which settles softly over the car, *poof*, in a cloud of orange mist.

He looks at Vani in the rear-view mirror, that naked, all-encompassing gaze. 'What's the matter? What did she do?'

'She asked me to have a baby for her.' Vani cringes as she says the words out loud. They do sound just as mad as she thought they did when Aarti spoke them to her.

She sees Ram's face reflected in the mirror, blanched clean of colour, so he looks like a pale facsimile.

So it isn't just me. He thinks it's mad too.

'What do you mean?'

An old man hobbles past, sticks his face up to the window, grins at Vani, displaying rotten teeth, a yawning cave of a mouth. He hobbles away when Ram shakes his fist at him.

'Exactly that. She wants me to get pregnant by her husband. She thinks I will be grateful for this honour. She actually said that, that it is an honour. She said he sleeps with other women, so it is fine if he sleeps with me. As I am an extension of her, it will be like *she* is having the baby. Oh, and she said that it doesn't hurt, not really.' Once she's started, Vani cannot stop. The words keep on coming, tripping over one another, a veritable waterfall of thick brown bile.

The car door slams. A burst of humid air smelling of dust and drains, rotting fruit and spices invades the car. Ram is off.

'Wait,' she wants to yell but she is sapped, all the energy having leaked out of her.

Then the back door opens and Ram slides in beside Vani. He opens his arms. She slips into them. He holds her while she cries, while she sobs out her anguish. And when she looks up, she sees her pain reflected in his eyes, in the wet shimmer on his cheeks. She feels it in the moistness in her hair.

I love him. The knowledge comes all of a sudden, it blindsides her, takes her by surprise. A part of her has always known, she realises. But it has taken Aarti's request to make her open her eyes, to see things clearly, for what they really are. She loves this man. She feels at home in his arms. The thrill his touch incites in her is love. The reason she does not sit in the front seat next to him is because she is afraid of her emotions, the feelings he arouses in her.

But she doesn't know how he feels. She is not worldly-wise; she doesn't know men, doesn't know if Ram's teasing of her, his gentleness with her, the way he looks at her sometimes, his eyes tender as the sky at twilight, is love. Does he feel for her what she feels for him? Does he love her?

'I know this is the worst possible time,' he says now, his cinnamon eyes boring into Vani's, his arms cradling her like something infinitely precious. 'I love you, Vani.'

It is as if he has read her mind and answered the question looming there.

'I have loved you from that first moment when I saw you peering anxiously down from the window, and you blustered and yelled to cover your embarrassment. I love the way you blush. I love your smile, your patience. I love everything about you. Marry me. We'll run away together, you and I.'

Outside a woman yells, 'Guavas, fresh guavas. Fifty paise only.'

She looks at this man, his liquid eyes, the way his gaze looks into the very heart of her. *He loves me.*

She has been so naïve. She did not recognise love when it smiled at her in the rear-view mirror. She did not see it shining out of these familiar crinkly cornered twinkling eyes.

'We will go far away from Aarti; we will have our own life together. You, me and one day the children we will have. You won't belong to anybody. You will have all the freedom in the world.'

She imagines going back to the village, living in the house she grew up in, with this man. She imagines sending him off to work with chapattis in a tiffin box like her ma used to pack for her da. She imagines going about her chores, waiting for him to come home. She imagines cooking for him, red rice and pickle, both of them eating while watching the hens peck at grains and cows graze in the meadow, as the sun sets beyond the fields, behind Chinnappa's hut at the edge of the village. She imagines their children playing hopscotch in the dust, their laughter ringing amongst the mango and guava trees, echoing in the jasmine-scented breeze. She imagines sharing a life with this man, a simple, uncomplicated life. A life where she is happy, where she owns herself and is not at the beck and call of another, bound to another by duty.

'I would like that very much,' she says.

He kisses her then, their tears mingling, the future tasting of salt.

He takes her to his friend who lives in Koramangala. And then he goes back to the mansion. They have decided that it is best Aarti doesn't know Ram is involved, best that Ram carries on as normal. That way, they will know what to expect, what is going on.

Ram must have called his friend and his wife in advance because they do not to ask any questions. They welcome Vani and feed her, their big-eyed children watching curiously as she pecks at the rice, not really able to eat but not wanting to waste what they have willingly shared, food they can hardly afford.

Afterwards she lies on the mat on the floor beside the woman and her sniffling children, their soft snores filling the meagre space between them. And she does not think of Aarti and what she has asked. She does not. But her dreams are coloured with babies and screaming women who point accusatory fingers at her: *You promised. I gave you everything. Everything.*

The next afternoon, Ram comes to visit. Vani does not ask him how Aarti is. There is no point. He sits with Vani for a bit, both of them glum, and then he goes.

The third day he doesn't come. That night at ten there is a knock at the door. Soft and yet urgent, insistent. Vani has not fallen asleep, listening instead to the others snoring, the children's soft breath inhabiting the mosquito-infested, dream-tinted air, letting the sound crowd out her thoughts, her anxieties at Ram's no-show, knowing something of import must have happened. Ram's friend, who is sleeping on the bench above the rest of the family clustered on the floor, startles awake.

It is Ram. Crowding the small doorway. Apologising to his friend. Ram, his face ashen. Pale. As if he has swallowed a ghost.

Without a word, they move outside into the tiny courtyard, so as not to wake the children. Vani looks at the sleeping family one last time, the children's limbs flung across their mother's body, her outstretched arms their pillow, her sari pallu their blanket.

She knows that she is not coming back.

'I couldn't get away before,' Ram says and his voice is croaky, sodden with tears.

She has been observing this family, the man going to his labourer's job, the woman caring for their children. They work very hard to make ends meet. And yet, Vani notices in the way Ram's friend and his wife look at each other, in the way she serves him more rice before he's even asked, the soft, quiet avowals of affection. Their children are happy and secure. They are a close-knit, quietly content family. All Vani has ever wanted all her life, she realises as she watches them, is this. What this woman has. The freedom to be her own boss in her own little house, the freedom to live her life the way she wants it. The freedom to be. Just be. Not beholden to anyone. Vani wants love like this woman has with this man. No fireworks, no explosions. Just small, day-to-day intimacies. And she wants children. She has always wanted children. She wants to love them like she was loved. She wants them to be the centre of her world, her husband's world, like she was her parents'. She wants a little family and she wants them to be happy.

Ram takes her hand. He touches her fingers one by one, as if memorising them, learning the feel of her hand in his. She breathes his face in, that hooked nose, that strong jaw, that mouth made for smiling. This man she loves, who brings her a measure of peace. This man who knows her, with whom she could have the family she yearns for, the life she wants.

She doesn't want to hear what he has to say. Not just yet. She wants to prolong this moment. She looks at his sombre face and she knows then that she will not get the small, happy family she has dreamed of. Not in her lifetime. Somehow, she knows. Even before Ram says a word.

She knows by the look on his face. Defeated.

She knows because she is bound to Aarti; she was bound the moment Aarti held her when she sobbed, the moment she took Vani's hands and called her 'sister'. She wishes it were possible to go back and whisper caution to her younger self. The timid, impressionable girl she was then, overly awed that this great woman, this supermodel, cared for her. Vani had been tickled that Aarti wanted what she had. The parental love that Vani had taken for granted. The love she had thought every child had as a given. Vani had been pleased to realise she had been special to get such love from her parents. She had been proud.

'She tried to kill herself,' Ram whispers. 'Bhoomi, the girl who does the floors, found her just in time. She was holding some letter in her hand. Some promise you made to each other.'

Aarti wanted what Vani had as a child. She wants what she has now. Vani will never be free.

'The pact,' she whispers.

'She had written another note as well. A note saying she cannot live without you and that is why she took the pills... She is in a critical condition in hospital.'

For one minute, one brief minute, a horrible thought flits through Vani's brain. She curbs it instantly, before the shock of it, the thrill, the forbidden pleasure of it makes its way onto her face. *It would be good all round if she dies.* She looks at Ram and she knows he knows what she is thinking. And yet he loves her. He loves her despite her worst side. Perhaps he loves her because of it. He understands. He is the only one who does.

'They are all searching for you. Sudhir, her parents.' His hold on Vani's hand tightens. 'I had to tell you. I couldn't not.' His voice is drenched in sorrow.

She recalls how she and Aarti used to talk late into the night; how Aarti nursed Vani when she fell ill one time, feeding her soup, talking to her, sitting vigil by her bedside; how she stood up for Vani when one of Aarti's fellow models was rude to Vani; how she has stunned Vani, at times, by her compassion, how she has moved her by her generosity.

'You don't have to go back. Stay here and I will visit when I can. I can't leave them now, they'll suspect something. But once she's better, I will extricate myself. We will move away, far away from all this.'

He loves her. They could have the life she's imagined. The life the family sleeping behind her have. But would they ever be happy when they have begun their life tainted by someone else's unhappiness, coloured by her despair?

As if reading her thoughts, Ram says, once again, his tone urgent, distressed, 'You don't have to.'

Then she will try and kill herself again. And if she succeeds, her death will be on me. The unspoken thought hovers. How can Vani live happily knowing she has caused someone else's life to end? How can she bring children into the world knowing how much Aarti wanted one, thinking, always, *if only I had given her what she wanted...*

'You will do it,' his voice is flat.

Vani nods, her head moving of its own accord on the weary stalk of her neck.

She will do what Aarti wants, like she always has, bending to her will like a sapling dancing to the tunes of a whimsical breeze that cannot quite make up its mind which way to blow.

'I will be waiting after. I love you, Vani, only you. Give her the child, then come to me.'

He leans close and she feels his warm, spiced breath on her cheek, her eyes, feels his lips on hers. She wants to stay here forever. In this man's arms. In this man's embrace that encompasses her. This man who loves her, who has just vowed that he will have her even after she has borne another man's child.

They both know it is not that easy. Vani will give Aarti the child. But Aarti will want more, she will want something else. She will have Vani, own her, possess her until Vani dies. Or…Aarti does.

❄ ❄ ❄

Aarti is a pale replica of herself, a ghost haunting white hospital sheets, sprouting myriad tubes.

Vani takes Aarti's hand. Aarti's eyes, barely there lashes like butterfly wings, flutter.

'Vani?' Her voice is the swish of dust particles. It is the quiet of a flower opening under cover of night, a gift to the dawn. 'Why?'

Vani holds Aarti's hand, her insubstantial, bony, icy hand, and lets the tears fall. She does not know if she is crying for Aarti or for herself, crying for the litter of lost dreams scattering the streets of Bangalore as a devastated Ram transported her silently back to the hospital, back into Aarti's world, back into her life with Aarti as parasite, leech, sucking the lifeblood out of her.

'I will do it,' Vani says, thinking of Ram.

'Marry me,' he had said. 'We will have a family together.'

All she's ever wanted. A family to call her own. Children. Love like she had with her parents. They could have been happy, so happy.

She lets the tears fall in that room reeking of cloying flowers and bitter medicine and crushed hopes, huge sobs that rock her body like a boat in a storm. She sobs like she did that day when Aarti held her and it all began.

This time, no one holds Vani as she sobs. This time, all there is is a smile, Aarti's flimsy lips the soft pink of a summer morning tilting upwards. A suggestion of a smile on the face of a ghost sealing Vani's fate.

Chapter 40
Aarti – Travel Plans

Reverential Silence

It works. Aarti's plan works. They both come running back. The two people who are *her* world, the people *she* loves the most. But, she realises when Vani runs away, it isn't the same the other way round.

When they comprehend how desperate Aarti is, how seriously she wants a child, how her life depends on it, literally, they agree to do it. Both of them. A chastened Sudhir and Vani.

She shares her husband with Vani. Three tries is all it takes. So supremely easy for Vani. Impossible for Aarti. And a baby is created. Nestling within her closest friend, sister and now proven traitor's belly.

Sudhir is just as excited as Aarti knew he would be when it sinks in, finally, that he is going to be a father, responsible for a new being that he has created.

I was right all along, Aarti thinks. *We will be a proper family now,* she thinks.

She will keep them all together by overdosing on pills again if need be, making sure she is found before it is too late, of course. She wants for her child the childhood that Vani enjoyed. And her child will get that. It will have a family, adoring parents and an 'aunt' to look after it.

Sudhir asks after Vani's health, he is attentive to her and just as insistent as Aarti in cajoling Vani to eat plenty of fruit and vegetables, to take vitamins and folic acid. It heartens Aarti to see her husband so excited, so involved. Nevertheless, she watches them together, Vani and Sudhir, but there is nothing there. She knows this. This, at least, she knows.

Aarti takes a break from work, cancels all her modelling and acting contracts. She invites the most notorious gossip amongst the tabloid journalists to tea and drops hints about how her doctor has advised her to take it easy and has recommended bed rest for at least nine months. As she expected, the news of her pregnancy is in all the newspapers and gossip rags the next day. 'Top model and actress Aarti Shetty takes a break from work to have a baby with her husband, actor Sudhir Shetty.' Aarti rubs her flat stomach and smiles, pleased beyond words to see it in print.

This is the best way, she thinks as she hears Vani retch in the bathroom – morning sickness – and come hobbling out, her face the greenish yellow shade of a ripening mango. Vani's belly is thickening and her face is rounder than before.

Aarti looks at her own face in the mirror. The pumping of her abdomen in hospital to get rid of the residue of the sleeping pills she overdosed on has helped immensely. She is the thinnest she has ever been.

This is the best way, she thinks and she hears an echo from the past, her mother saying to her friend, 'I never wanted children. The havoc they cause to the figure.' She flicks recollections of her mother away, but not before the thought that her mother was right flits across her mind. She watches Vani hobble towards her with the teapot, her green face, her expanding girth. *This is definitely the best way all round,* she thinks as Vani pours tea for Aarti, as she cuts up fruit the way Aarti likes, as she covers her mouth when she's finished and rushes to the bathroom again.

Sudhir comes home one day, and from his sheepish expression Aarti knows to expect something that will rock the world she has created so carefully.

'I have to go to London for a shoot,' he says, studying the curtains, looking out of the window, his eyes darting everywhere but in her general direction.

'Don't you care about our child?' she asks, trying to keep her voice on an even keel.

'Of course I do. You know that. It is only for three months.' He smiles that smile that used to charm her once, but only serves to infuriate her now.

'Only three months!' she explodes. 'You will miss the scans; you will miss so many developmental milestones.'

'The baby isn't even here yet!' he yells back, eyes flashing.

'And what message are you giving it by not being there? The baby isn't even here but you are already escaping.'

His shoulders droop. As with every other argument, as he has always done, he walks away.

She cannot leave him alone in London for three months. She will have blonde girls with lithe bodies and great sexual prowess to contend with in addition to the usual: his co-stars and myriad starlets who are always making a play for him in the hope that this will give them a lift up the career ladder. No, it will not do, not when he is on the cusp of becoming a father, settling down. She cannot keep an eye on him from here; she has to go too. But she cannot leave Vani behind. Not after what's happened. She does not want to come home and find that Vani has vanished, taking Aarti's one precious jab at playing families with her.

And so, Aarti tells Vani she is coming with them to London, that they are accompanying Sudhir on a shoot.

'We'll be back before the critical stages, by the time we are six months pregnant.' She is always careful to say 'we'. It is a joint endeavour after all.

Vani nods, her eyes empty. She has been missing something, some spark since she came back from wherever she disappeared to, since she said yes to having the baby. Vani goes through the motions but it is as if the girl Aarti knew and loved isn't there anymore, a vacant shell, a lacklustre robot having taken her place.

Aarti telephones the gossip tabloid journalist, confirms the rumours of her pregnancy. She has been careful not to be photographed in public much, and when she hasn't been able to avoid going out, being seen, she wears loose kaftans and maternity trousers that give the impression of pregnancy, of expanding girth. Aarti informs the journalist that the doctor has given her permission to travel to the UK to accompany Sudhir on his shoot. She asks if it is possible to keep the news quiet, to avoid media coverage until after the baby is born. She promises that if this is the case, this journalist will have first dibs on baby pictures and an exclusive photo shoot with the new family.

A week before they are due to fly, they go for a scan, all three of them, to the discreet private clinic where celebrities have their abortions and their facelifts, where paparazzi are not allowed, and gossip, the whisper of a rumour, is anathema. The pregnancy is twelve weeks in. Vani is strapped onto the bed and a machine moved across her stomach, which is not distended, not yet. And as if by magic, on the screen a picture appears. A blurry tadpole, frantically moving its tiny appendages, squirming and squiggling. The music of the little heartbeat, *glug, glug, glug,* punctures the reverential silence of the room.

Aarti is overwhelmed. Sudhir squeezes her hand and she sees the awe she feels reflected in his eyes. And then, she looks at Vani. Vani is transfixed. Tears fall down her eyes, traverse her cheeks and soak the pillow she is lying on. She is mesmerised, her unblinking gaze devouring the tiny being that shakes its minuscule fists at the air, at them.

Afterwards, on the drive home, Vani is silent as a tombstone, still as a corpse, staring out of the window unblinking, at traffic-clogged, dust-soaked, noisy, jostling

Bangalore. Aarti talks into the heavy, uncomfortable silence, worrying about how much packing still needs to be done, complaining of the heat even though she is ensconced in an air-conditioned car. She muses about the cold in the UK; she hopes the weather will cooperate and Sudhir will get his shoot wrapped up in three months, seeing as it is notoriously rainy there.

'Wish we could take you along, Ram,' Sudhir says, patting Ram's elbow as they step out. 'Doubt we'll get a chauffeur of your calibre there.'

'Thank you, sir,' Ram says, but his voice too is distant, somewhere else.

Vani maintains her deathly silence as if she has taken a vow of muteness, not acknowledging Aarti when she asks Vani to eat her vegetables, not saying a word as she combs Aarti's hair and plaits it, a ritual before bed.

'Wasn't it amazing seeing our baby?' Aarti says, and Vani's reflection in the mirror winces.

Aarti turns, stares at her. Since Vani ran away, Aarti has felt ever so slightly out of control, suddenly finding that there are depths to Vani she cannot fathom, realising that Vani is her own person and not just the acquiescing meek girl she has come to expect.

'What's the matter?' Aarti asks. 'You know you can tell me anything.'

Vani's eyes do not meet Aarti's. Her gaze wavers, it falters.

'Come on, Vani; tell me what's on your mind. We are sisters, remember?'

Vani clears her throat, and one hand, the hand not holding the comb, goes protectively to her stomach, rubbing it gently in concentric circles, as if she is soothing the baby.

Aarti does not like that gesture. It is too proprietary. 'Why are you doing that?' she asks, and the irritation she has been trying to contain colours her voice.

The hand drops to Vani's side. She looks up at Aarti and her eyes are flinty, dark grey like storm clouds reflected on a violent sea. 'I want this baby,' she says.

'Of course you do,' Aarti smiles, relieved. 'We all do.' She turns to the mirror. 'I can't do this without you, Vani. We'll bring the baby up together like your parents brought you up.'

In the mirror, she sees Vani flinch again.

'What is it?' Aarti's voice is rising, she cannot help it. Vani is carrying Aarti's child, she is living in this house like a guest. Aarti has forgiven her for her desertion, has not said a word about how she broke the pact, driving Aarti nearly to death. What more does she want?

'I...I do not want this baby to treat me like a servant, a mere possession. I want this baby to call me Ma, to love me, to acknowledge me as its mother.'

Now she has gone too far. Aarti stands up to her full height and looks down at this girl with her temerity, her cheek. Her mother used to always say, especially when Aarti got too attached to a servant when she was little, 'Give them a little and they want the lot. You have to keep them in their place.' She hasn't thought of her mother in years, she doesn't much care for her mother's opinions, but in this, Aarti realises now, she was right.

'How dare you?' Aarti's voice is a high-pitched squeak. She cannot help it; she is at the end of her tether. 'Look around you. Does any other servant have what you have? You are living in this house with us. I haven't yelled at you, haven't said a thing about you running away, breaking our pact, nearly killing me in the process.'

Vani recoils as if she has been slapped, her face pallid, the colour of ash.

'Everything you are is because of me. *Everything*. And now you want my baby.'

Vani's hand goes to her stomach again. 'It is *my* baby.'

Aarti pulls the hand away. 'The baby is mine and we both know it. You did not want it, remember? You ran away when I asked you to have it. Now stop this nonsense, Vani. It is not good for my nerves.'

She runs to the bathroom and is violently sick, regurgitating the lemon sherbet she has drunk, the papaya she has eaten, retching over and over again. Vani does not come like she usually does; she does not hold Aarti's hair back and rub her shoulders. She turns and walks away, leaving Aarti to her misery.

Alone in the bathroom, Aarti is convulsed with fear. What if Vani runs away like she did before, but this time taking the baby with her? No, she cannot bear that. She cannot.

She runs to Vani's room and finds her lying on the bed, one hand caressing her stomach, tears making tracks down her cheeks and smearing the pillow like they did in the room while the ultrasound was taking place.

She stands over Vani's bed, glowers at her. 'Don't you dare run away again,' she spits out. 'You know Sudhir and I have contacts, influence, money to spare. We will find you. No matter where you hide, whether it is in the deepest corner of the country, we will find you. We would have found you when you ran away last time, if I wasn't almost at my deathbed, thanks to you…' Aarti takes a deep breath, making sure the words have sunk in. Vani's eyes are wide open, sparkling tears staining her profuse lashes. 'If you take my child away from me, I will kill myself and my death will be on you.'

She reaches down and, ignoring Vani's recoiling, lays a proprietary hand on her stomach. 'This baby is mine. Ours. I will share it with you. I am nothing if not generous. But if you run away, we will find you. And you will lose everything. Everything.' She takes a pause, gathers her breath. 'You want this child to call you Ma, but you are not thinking of this child at all, are you?'

She watches Vani's eyes widen, flash ochre with rage.

'Without us, where will you go? How will you feed it, look after it? It will get a great upbringing here, the very best of everything, the world at its feet – and you know it. Do you want it to have a good life or a cursed one, my death hanging over its head?' Aarti pauses and then goes in for the kill. 'A mother always puts her child first. If you do not want to give your child the very best, if you want it to live with the consequences of your actions, your selfish desires, then what kind of a mother are you?'

With that, she walks away, knowing her words have gone to roost.

The next day, Vani brings in Aarti's tea and newspapers, combs Aarti's hair and irons the outfit Aarti is planning to wear, as usual.

'Looks like another sunny day,' she says. 'Shall I finish the packing today? Which outfits do you want to take?' she asks.

And Aarti tells her. They are back to their normal relationship and Aarti is glad. Not a word about the previous night's altercation passes between them.

The following week, they travel to the UK, Aarti wearing a loose kaftan and tucking a shawl inside it to give the impression of a bump, just in case the press turn up despite her request for privacy, she and Sudhir flying business class and Vani economy. Aarti makes sure Vani is ensconced in her window seat, hemmed in by two other passengers, before she makes her way to Sudhir.

Their second month in the UK, Vani comes to her, face glowing. Vani is brimming with joy, beaming with barely suppressed excitement. For a brief moment, the old Vani, the girl Aarti used to know and love, is back.

Vani takes Aarti's hand and places it on her stomach. After a bit, Aarti senses a flutter, like the whisper of wings, the baby talking to her from inside the womb, the baby making her acquaintance. And then they are grinning, falling about on the bed and laughing together, their hands on top of each other on Vani's stomach, feeling the baby dance beneath. And it is like the old times. Just like the old times.

That evening, Sudhir announces that he will have to return to the UK six months after the baby is due.

'We can only shoot in the summer and in the UK, the season only lasts three months: June to August. So we'll have to come back.' He is looking at her apprehensively, worrying his lower lip with his hand.

Aarti goes up to him, rests her head on his chest, listening to his heartbeat and thinking of her baby making its presence felt in another woman's womb. He said 'we'. He said '*we'll* have to come back'.

'Our first outing as a family, already planned,' she laughs and notices a shadow cross Vani's face which has, since she felt the baby move, been happier than Aarti has ever seen it.

Aarti thinks nothing of it.

Chapter 41
Vani – Travel Plans

Bhindi Bhaji

Growing up, Vani had always imagined that the man she slept with would be the man she would spend the rest of her life with, her husband, her destiny. They would grow a family together, grow old together.

Instead, she loses her virginity to Sudhir. Both of them not wanting to be with the other. Doing it because they have to, because the spectre of *her* in the hospital looms, pale, ghostly, almost but not quite of the next world.

Sudhir is gentle. He is kind. But he isn't Vani's.

Vani gets pregnant. A miracle takes root inside of her. She feels her body shift and grow to accommodate a new life. A part of her. How can she bear to share this child? How?

Aarti is everywhere. Her needy face, her grasping hands, laying claim to the one piece of Vani that she desperately, completely, wants just for herself. Vani has shared her dead parents with Aarti. She has shared her happiest memories with her. She has allowed Aarti to borrow her childhood. She has said yes, under duress, to letting Aarti borrow her womb. But how can she stand back and allow Aarti to appropriate her child?

Vani agreed to sharing her child with Aarti when the baby was a concept, but now that it is growing inside her, now that she has seen her child on the screen at the twelve week scan, a scrunched, squirming tadpole, minuscule fisted appendages waving hello, its jiggling, gulping heartbeat filling her being with hope, she cannot do it, she cannot. Vani knows that Aarti will lay claim to her child, have the bigger share, the deciding share, like in their silly, childish pact. That the balance will always shift in Aarti's favour.

Already Aarti has put about in the tabloids that she is having a baby with Sudhir. She flounces about in public wearing loose-fitting clothes and conspicuously ingesting vitamin tablets and folic acid, which she regurgitates later in the privacy of her bathroom. How can Vani bear it if *her* child, the fruit of *her* womb, the child *she* nourished into being, how can she bear it if he/she starts treating her the way Aarti does, like Vani is her favourite dog, a prized possession to order around, to insult and to hurt and then pat on the back to make everything all right again?

Aarti has threatened to kill herself if Vani runs away again. That threat stopped Vani eloping with Ram. It is not enough to stop her now. Vani wants nothing but the best for her child. The life of a runaway, struggling to make ends meet, worrying about getting caught is not what she wants for the precious miracle growing inside of her. But a life of luxury with no heart to it, the life Aarti lives, Vani does not want that for her child either.

This much Vani knows: she doesn't want her child to become like Aarti, treating people like objects, obsessed by image, thinking being sick after every meal is *de rigueur*.

And she doesn't want her child to become the person Vani herself has been up until now either. She doesn't want to subject her child to a life of servility, of dancing to Aarti's tunes, of changing his/her temperament to suit Aarti's quicksilver moods, her imperious commands.

Vani wants her child to have the childhood that she had, unburdened by the trappings of wealth, the noose of fame. She wants to keep her child, bring it up her way. And the only conceivable option, even though it isn't the best one by far, is to run away.

She thinks long and hard about how to do it. And then the answer comes, from a very unlikely source…

When they are in London, Aarti gets a craving for bhindi bhaji. She says she wants the proper bhindi, not the thin dry ones from the supermarket, but the fat green ones available so readily in Bangalore but not in evidence here.

Vani goes in search of them, thinking, *what a waste of time and energy.* Aarti will take one bite and she won't eat any more. Or she will eat and then be sick. What is the point?

After much asking around, Vani finally finds a stall selling the bhindi that Aarti wants and gets talking to the woman running it. The woman asks Vani where she is from.

'Dhonihalli originally, but I live in Bangalore now.'

'I am from Hubli,' the woman says as she weighs the bhindi.

'How long have you been here?' Vani asks.

'Four years,' the woman sighs.

'Ever go back?' Vani queries.

Another deep sigh. 'Can't.' The woman lowers her voice to a whisper, even though she is speaking in Kannada. 'Am here illegally, you see.'

'Ah,' Vani says, and by the time she has left, she has garnered enough details to have the beginnings of a tentative plan.

Vani studies London closely after that, squirreling Tube maps and bus timetables in her luggage, working out train lines, public transport. London – a sprawling metropolis, so many people, all different colours and races, a city where Sudhir and Aarti don't have clout.

'It is a place where one can disappear easily,' the bhindi bhaji vendor had said, her eyes soft as she smiled at Vani, wishing her luck, offering her blessing.

The moment they return to Bangalore, Vani goes to see Ram. He beams when he sees her, his gaze taking in her stomach which is showing, just, and yet the light does not go out of his eyes. He opens his arms and folds her into them and she breathes in his smell, musk and lemon. She has missed him.

Vani has stayed away from him since she agreed to Aarti's request, since Ram ferried her back from his friend's house, both of them quiet in the car, their tears speaking the words they couldn't quite bring themselves to utter. She has stayed away because it would not be fair to continue seeing him when she is sleeping with another man. And after she got pregnant, she stayed away because she was ashamed of carrying another man's child when it is him she loves, even though she knows that he doesn't blame her, he never will. She has stayed away because she is selfish, because seeing him would mean confronting everything she has lost; it would mean aching for a different life and it would be a betrayal of this child, conceived under duress but whom she now loves more than life itself. Seeing him would make her yearn for things best left alone. It would make her regret this child. And she doesn't want to regret this miracle growing inside her, the one wonderful thing in her life.

And Vani has come to see him now because she is selfish. She wants to ask him for help. She has no one else. She is shamelessly using him, exploiting his affection for her. But she is a mother now and she has to put her child first. And so she tells Ram her plan.

'No. You cannot do this to me, go so far away,' he says. 'Come with me. We will run away, be a family.'

He doesn't ask Vani to give up her child. He knows she can't. She won't. He knows she wants this child like she has never wanted anything or anyone, even him. He is condemning himself to the life of a runaway just to be with

Vani. She is touched, she is awed. She cups his beloved face in the palm of her hand, learns its contours with her fingers.

His offer is tempting, tantalising. But she cannot do it to him. Wilfully destroy his life. If they run away, they will always live in fear of being caught. And if they are caught, he will lose his livelihood, nobody will employ him. For what? A fallen woman. A child that isn't his. He is young, handsome, a nice man, a kind man. He deserves what his friend has, the one he took Vani to, the one she stayed with. A harmonious life. A family to love and care for. The family Vani wished for.

'Please,' he says, and he is standing very close, she can feel his breath caressing her face – cinnamon and mint.

She desperately wants to take up his offer. To turn the precious burden of protecting her child and doing the best by it over to him.

But this much she knows: Vani could, perhaps, live with the guilt of Aarti killing herself because of what she has done. But Vani couldn't live with the knowledge that she is destroying the life of the man who has loved her, purely, fiercely, unselfishly.

She has got herself into this situation. It is her job and hers alone to get herself out of it.

And so, she refuses his offer, his proposal. But she does enlist his help.

And when his pleas fall on deaf ears, when he sees that she will not give in, he says, finally, reluctantly, his voice the grey-black of dejection, 'I know people in London. They will help you.'

He loves her enough to agree to help her even if that means she will go to another country a world away, even if it means he will never see Vani again. She is humbled by his love.

And so, it is set in motion.

Hope uncoils in Vani's belly, wrapping itself warmly around her child, warring with fear and worry. Is she doing the best by her baby? She does not know. All she knows is that she cannot share her child. She will not.

❉ ❉ ❉

Her little girl enters the world screaming lustily and she is everything Vani had imagined and more. Vani holds her baby girl in her arms after ten arduous hours of labour and sees in the contours of her daughter's face the silhouettes she has been looking for in the clouds, the visages she has been hunting for in the horizon. In the curve of her daughter's cheek, in the way her lashes fan her cheeks, Vani sees her mother's sleeping face in the moment before waking. In her daughter's stub nose, in the shape of her cherry-bud mouth, Vani sees her father. Tears travel down her face and baptise her newborn and she squints, her mouth opening and rooting for her mother's breast. Vani holds her daughter to her chest, and she can feel her parents smiling down at her, and she promises them and she promises her daughter that she will protect her, that she will love her like she deserves to be loved.

To Vani, her daughter is Diya, meaning 'Light'. She is Vani's guiding light, the person who has brightened her life, showed her the way forward. But Vani doesn't get a say in choosing her child's name. Her daughter is supposedly called Rupa Shetty, a name decided upon by Aarti, a name Vani first hears of when she is asked to keep the birth certificate in the safe with all the other important documents.

Vani's name is not on the birth certificate. For the right amount of money, her child's parents are Aarti and Sudhir Shetty. Vani is a nonentity even though she nurtured Diya in her womb, laboured with her and gave birth to her, even though Vani is the one who nurses her through the night, even though Vani puts her to sleep, far away from her 'mother' as the baby's cries disturb her. Aarti visits with 'her child' a few times a day. She loves her, on her terms, like she has everything and everyone else. And this makes Vani all the more determined to carry through with her plan.

The only thing that makes Vani have second thoughts is Sudhir's obvious joy in his child. He is besotted with his daughter; he is a different man where she is concerned, incredibly patient, utterly tender, spending every minute away from work with her, delighting in her company. But even though the nursery is right next to the master bedroom and Sudhir would like it to stay that way, Aarti has asked Vani to move downstairs with the baby temporarily. It is because, she says, she cannot bear her child to be unhappy. Aarti says it upsets her that the baby is hurting.

'All babies cry,' Vani says. 'It is their way of communicating.'

'Make it stop,' Aarti complains, putting her hands to her ears. 'Take it away.'

To placate the journalists who have been calling non-stop and parking outside the gates of the mansion, Aarti and Sudhir host a celebratory do to introduce their child to the world. Despite Sudhir's urging, Aarti does not allow Vani to attend.

'The baby will not settle without me,' Vani says. She refuses to call her daughter Rupa. To her, she is Diya.

'It will be better all round if Vani attends. There will be noise and flashing cameras; Rupa will be daunted,' Sudhir says.

But Aarti is adamant. 'The baby will be fine for a couple of hours,' she insists.

Vani knows that Aarti does not want her to be present because she fears some enterprising hack might put two and two together and the truth will out.

And so, Vani sits in her room and tries to hold in the milk and tears which flow incessantly from her breasts and eyes as she hears her baby scream non-stop for the three hours that she is separated from her mother and showed off to the world, subjected to flashes and intrusive cameras. And that is the last straw.

When the final journalist has left and an exhausted, sobbing Diya is handed to Vani and promptly stops crying and falls asleep at her breast, when Vani spends the night trying to console a fretful, hiccupping infant who clings to her and sobs in her sleep, who wakes up wailing in remembered bursts of agony the moment Vani disentangles her from her arms and places her in her cot, Vani vows never to be separated from her daughter again, making her mind up once and for all, Sudhir's bond with the child notwithstanding.

Aarti sets about acquiring a passport for the baby in anticipation of the proposed UK trip for Sudhir's shoot. She renews Vani's visa to the UK, along with hers and Sudhir's. Then she gives Vani the passports as is her wont to keep in the safe with the other documents, as Vani knew she would. She has been counting on it.

Vani spirits Aarti's passport and her child's away and passes them on to Ram. He gives them to a man he knows who is an expert at forging passports, who switches Aarti's picture with Vani's. Ram also gives Vani the contact details of the people in the UK with whom she will be staying initially until she finds her feet.

'You can stay with them for as long as you want,' Ram assures her. 'They are very close, almost like family to me. Their children are both grown and settled in the US so they are lonely. They told me that they will be glad of the company.' His eyes glitter and shine. 'Are you sure you want to go through with this?'

She is sure, she tells him, although what she would like more than anything is to give herself over to the relief of his arms, the comfort of having him make the decisions for her, having him look after her and her child.

This couple, these friends of Ram's, own an Indian restaurant in Wembley and Ram has arranged for Vani to work there, pay her way. He also arranges for fake UK passports for Vani and Diya and a false birth certificate for Diya. Vani withdraws the money she has been saving all these years, all the money she has received from Aarti in return for her life of subservience. Ram changes most of it into pounds for her.

Everything is in place. She is nervous, she is worried, she is as ready as she will ever be.

And then, she gets her chance. Sudhir has to go to Mumbai for an awards ceremony. Just for the weekend. Aarti wants to go too; she wants all of them to go.

'You go,' Vani says. 'Is it worth disrupting the baby's routine for two days?' she asks.

Aarti thinks about it. Vani knows that Aarti has found the reality of a baby very different from the idea of one. Babies require a lot of attention; they are not much fun. Aarti cannot stand Diya's tears. The thought of sharing a flight with her, to have no means of escaping her wails even if only for an hour, is more than Aarti can fathom. Vani can see the cogs turning in Aarti's brain, can anticipate the direction Aarti's thoughts are taking. The luxury of having a weekend away with no baby is inviting. The idea of having Sudhir all to herself even more so. Sudhir is too focused on the child; he hardly pays any attention to Aarti. And even though Aarti tries not to let it affect her, Vani can see that it does. Even though Aarti endeavours not to be jealous of the baby, of the time Sudhir patiently devotes to her, she is. Vani can tell. She has always been able to read Aarti's thoughts. Except of course that one time Aarti sprung the decision of Vani having a baby for her.

At this moment, Vani can see that Aarti is thinking of the press. She is anticipating what they might say, whether they will label her a bad mother if she spends a weekend away from her child.

'Every new parent needs a break from their children once in a while, especially parents in the public eye who have the pressures of fame to deal with as well as new parenthood,' Vani says soothingly. 'You need some time for yourselves. The press know this. Ragini, that Bollywood actress, went away recently didn't she? To LA with her husband, if I remember right, leaving their three-week-old baby behind. The press were indulgent.'

The irony that Vani is the new parent is lost on Aarti. She has lied so long to herself as well as to the public that she believes the lie, forgets that Vani is the mother of her child, that Vani is the one who has recently given birth, Vani is the one doing all the caring of the child. Aarti has had people cater to her every need for so long that she forgets to consider anyone else, only thinking of others in relation to herself. Vani is banking on this as she makes her arguments.

She has said the right thing. When she sees the smile grace Aarti's face, Vani knows she has won.

And so Aarti lets Vani convince her.

'It is only for the weekend. I will be back in two days,' Aarti says. She is not worried about Vani running away anymore. Since the baby arrived, she has relaxed her vigilance on Vani, seeing how besotted Vani is with the child. And the thought that Vani might run away with her daughter in tow has not occurred to Aarti, or perhaps it has and she has dismissed it, thinking that Vani would never have the guts…

Ram books a flight for Vani and Diya as soon as it is confirmed that Aarti and Sudhir will definitely be going to Mumbai. He drives them to the airport the very night that Aarti and Sudhir fly to Mumbai.

'Promise me this,' Vani says to Ram, losing herself one last time in his coffee eyes. 'Marry a nice girl. Have a good life.'

He holds Vani close, kisses her on the lips, kisses her child, lets them go. This man who has risked so much for Vani. Who loves her.

She waves goodbye, committing to memory that beloved face, the slumped shoulders, the defeated body that she would have, in a different life, been honoured to own. She does not know what is in store for her and her child on the other side of the barrier, what she is getting herself, getting her child into, and for the briefest of moments she is tempted to go back with this man, back to the life she has been leading; she is tempted to stick with the devil she knows.

And then her daughter moves, she snuggles closer into Vani. Vani looks at her daughter's face, serene in sleep, completely innocent of the circumstances, the drama that prompted her arrival into the world, and she knows that she has to do it. Be strong for her child. Finally do something after years of doing nothing. Stand up for her child and for herself.

She waits trembling as their passports are put under scrutiny. She shivers until the inscrutable man doing the inspection nods, waves her daughter and her through. She has crossed the first hurdle. Now for the next. And the next.

She heaves a sigh as she sits on the plane. She waits for it to take off. Hoping, praying, a part of her expecting policemen to rush onboard and apprehend her. A taste of how it is going to be from now on. Always on her guard, always praying, worrying, running.

The plane takes off, flying Vani and her precious bundle into a new life. She thinks of Aarti coming home to an empty house, going from room to room, calling for Vani, calling for her daughter, her voice increasing in pitch, wobbling at the corners as each room is empty, devoid of the faces she is searching for. She pictures Sudhir looking for his daughter, the only girl he has loved wholly and with abandon, the only girl he has been completely faithful to. She thinks of Aarti taking pills, putting one after another in her mouth. Aarti's face as she was in the hospital, ghastly pale, on the brink of death, looms. Vani holds her daughter close, breathes her in – her scent: talcum powder, milk, new baby. Chasing away the smell of death and doom.

Chapter 42
Aarti – The Aftermath

Waiting

As soon as she steps in the door, Aarti knows.

They find soiled nappies in the bin; they trip over toys – the teething ring, the windup music box, the baby gym, the cuddly bear almost bigger than the baby herself. They find the clothes she was wearing when they waved goodbye to her just two days ago, the Babygro, the little vest and skirt, uncharacteristically discarded on the floor. Normally Vani tidies them away immediately, does a batch of laundry… Vani…

There is a letter on Aarti's nightstand: 'I am sorry. So sorry. I just cannot stand being your possession anymore. And I do not want my child to treat me that way.'

Aarti runs. She sprints through the house calling for her child. The house populated by myriad precious treasures but not the treasure she is looking for; peopled by numerous servants who avert their gaze and try to be unobtrusive, but not the servant she is looking for. The unnervingly silent house undisturbed by the wails of a baby, uninterrupted by the gaiety that accompanies an infant's delighted gurgling. The disconcertingly quiet house, a noiselessness very different from the quiet of a house with a sleeping baby in it, people tiptoeing around so as not to wake it up, watching over it, marvelling at the miracle of its little chest moving up and down, its beautiful face serene, the tiny fisted hands thrown in abandon above its head, its mouth twitching, dancing to the tune of its dreams. The eerily empty house, the air heavy and still.

Waiting.

Waiting for the chaos that is to follow, the questioning of servants who vow they know nothing, who deny allegiance to the traitor amongst them and any knowledge of what she was planning, their faces composed in masks of appropriate concern, unswerving loyalty and unimpeachable honesty.

Waiting for the team of police officers and detectives who will trudge through the house, dragging mud across its scrubbed floors, populating it with a different kind of noise.

Waiting for the flash of bulbs, the gaggle of reporters and journalists who perform a vigil outside the gates.

Waiting for the unexpected sound of a grown man's sobs to reverberate through its walls, to shock its very foundations, a grief like no other, all the more distressing, all the more profound for its rarity. A grown man sitting in a nursery surrounded by the debris of his child's limited time with him, more toys and clothes than the number of days she's been in this world, a grown man reduced to a sniffing snivelling heap, clutching to his face his daughter's clothes, garments that he refuses to allow to be washed, the clothes she had worn when he innocently waved goodbye, not knowing it would be his last, breathing in the last lingering traces of her sweet baby smell and imagining he is holding her, the tears continuing to come, unhindered.

Despite floundering in a quagmire of grief, this shocks Aarti the most, seeing Sudhir go so completely to pieces.

'It is all your fault!' Sudhir yells on one of the interminable dark days after, black as endless night and blending into one another, thick with grief the colour and consistency of sludge.

The detective in charge of finding their child has just called to say that although they are following all leads, they have come up with nothing so far. Aarti is lying in bed, curtains drawn, pillow shielding her swollen, throbbing eyes when Sudhir comes barging in.

'Vani runs away with *my* child and you…you have the temerity to blame *me*?' She screeches at him.

I will kill you, Vani, she thinks, *for doing this to us. When I find you. I will put my hands around your neck and squeeze, until all the breath leaves your body and you go slack as a cloth doll, floppy as a puppet.*

'You caused this.' Sudhir's voice is distorted by anger, unhinged by pain. 'You blackmailed Vani into having Rupa. You blackmailed me into sleeping with her.'

She is too stunned to come up with a retort.

'We brought that innocent child into this world on a whim of yours. And now. And now…' His voice anguished, the colour and texture of a burnt auburn sky bemoaning the setting sun.

'You are a grown man,' she bellows, her voice morphing into a shriek. 'You could have said no.'

'And sit back and allow you to take your life?' Sudhir looks at her, properly looks at her for the first time in days, and his voice is soft as he says, 'I loved you, Aarti, more than I have ever loved anyone.'

Despite her agony, or perhaps because of it, she notes the use of the past tense and it devastates her.

'I loved you. But my love was wasted on you. You only love yourself.' He accused her of this once before – when she told him of her plan, asking him to have a baby with Vani.

'What I did, I did to keep you and Vani with me. You and Vani were my world.' If he can use the past tense, so can she. 'I loved you both so much.'

He shakes his head vigorously, like a Bharatanatyam performer. 'You *needed* me and Vani to fan your ego, to dance to your tunes. You don't love anyone but yourself.'

That again. She cannot bear it, she cannot. She tries to block out his words, fisting her hands and putting them on her ears, rocking back and forth, back and forth, but they nudge in anyway, twirling inside her head like impish devils pointing accusing fingers.

'When, for once, we didn't do what you wanted, you turned on us. You used us. You manipulated us. It's all you know. To use others. To possess them. It is what you learnt from your parents. You do not love Rupa; you don't know what it is to love, truly love, selflessly love. You wanted the child, my child,' his voice trips over a sob but he soldiers on, 'as a possession. So you can surround yourself with people you own, call them your "family", delude yourself that you love them, when they are mere planets revolving around you – the sun in the centre, mere subjects catering to your every whim.'

He pauses, draws in a breath. When he releases it, he is a much smaller, thinner, insubstantial version of himself, not the handsome actor who graces the screens but his shadow, a man who has lost his puff. Literally. 'That was the police commissioner on the phone. There are no leads. Vani has disappeared. We are not going to find them,' his voice bleak, desolate as land devastated by drought, parched and cracked and aching for rain. 'Perhaps it is best to leave Vani to get on with her life. She will raise Rupa well, be a good mother to her.'

Shock silences her, robs her of her voice.

He leans into her and she jerks away. Undone by what he has said, the accusations he has hurled her way.

'Goodbye, Aarti.'

Sudhir leaves and doesn't come back. She waits for him. And waits. Like she waited for Vani to return that fateful day when Aarti asked her to have a baby for her. It is becoming a pattern, this. The people she loves leaving her, disappearing clean from her life.

And so, she does what she did when Vani went away. She arranges the pills she has been collecting meticulously for just such an eventuality (although she never really believed she would need to use them again; she had assumed the threat of taking them once had been enough) by her bedside table, writes a note – again like she did before. But this time she does not arrange for a servant to find her just in time. After all, what has she got to live for? And then she takes the pills. Or tries to.

She can't go through with it. If she dies, Vani will win. Perhaps Vani is hoping for just this – after all, she knows Aarti well enough. Aarti can picture Vani scouring the papers for news of Aarti's demise so she can relax and enjoy her child, flaunt her in public without worry. Aarti will not give her that satisfaction. She will not.

Aarti does not take the pills, saving them instead, with the note – just in case. She flits about the empty rooms of the huge house like she did in her parents' home as a child, lonely once more, alone like she never thought she would be again. She tried, desperately, to protect herself against this very eventuality. She failed.

She roams the rooms – every one reminding her of the hopes and dreams she had weaved for a future that included her, her husband, her child and her friend. She is a ghost, insubstantial, unable to puncture the heavy silence that settles like an interminable sigh. Who is she, without people to define her? She is lost. Hollow.

In desperation, she turns to what she knows best, the gorging on food to fill the abyss and the disgorging after; the comfort derived as she throws up, as her stomach is emptied, her body drained. It is the only time she is able to keep the other pain, the mental pain that pulls her towards a yawning void, at bay. That pain takes second place as her body heaves and shudders, as she regurgitates all the food she has mindlessly eaten in order to forget. The smell of vomit and phenyl briefly dislodging the fog of pain, the purple aura of grief, the reddish yellow stain of loss that trails her. After, she is able to sleep, slip into a black dreamless daze until she wakes and with consciousness comes realisation, the heavy silence of a sombre house doused in mourning – no baby cries, no noise, no laughter, no joy. And the nightmare begins again.

It is her driver, Ram, who calls for medical help. She cannot remember the ride to hospital, the transfer to the exclusive clinic where they coax her back to health with a mixture of firmness and kindness, something she has never previously known. They encourage her to start keeping a food diary and she finds that penning down religiously what she has managed to push past the plug of her throat gives her some measure of comfort, some structure to the day, some way of filling the cavernous hours that stretch before her.

When she returns home from the clinic, having achieved a semblance of sanity, Sudhir visits and for one brief moment she thinks he has come back to her. But he is here to apologise for what he has inadvertently put her through, to inform her that he has moved on.

'I had to leave, Aarti,' he says, wringing his hands. 'Our marriage had been floundering for some time and this was the last straw.'

She is hurt beyond belief. While she has been sinking in the quicksand of depression, he has been 'moving on'. Images of Sudhir with nubile co-stars float before her eyes. She blinks them away. She shows Sudhir the door, does not binge on food like she would have done once, and is disarmingly pleased to write in her diary that she had a chapatti, some vegetables and a mixed fruit salad for supper. She has passed her first test.

Afterwards, she patrols the empty house and thinks: *You did this to me, Vani. You have destroyed my life, taken everything I ever loved from me.*

Her voice of conscience pipes up, softly, 'Her note. Did you read what it said? Perhaps if you had treated her better...'

She shushes it, angrily. *What more could I have done? She has taken my child, everything good in my life. I will find her. I will.*

She calls the police commissioner and finds that the police team searching for Vani has dwindled to two officers. They assure her in progressively weary voices every time she phones that they are doing everything in their power to find her child but that the trail had gone cold.

She calls Sudhir and rails at him for letting things slide. She hires a team of investigators, the very best, to search the length and breadth of the country, to dig Vani out of hiding. After an extensive search, they too come back with nothing. No trace of Vani. It is as if she has disappeared into the ether, taking Aarti's child with her.

How can that slip of a girl outsmart me? She's a mere servant; she's nothing without my generosity, my munificence.

'She is not in India, ma'am,' the investigators inform her.

And hard as it is to believe, to picture shy, diffident Vani abroad, all the evidence seems to point that way. Perhaps Vani decided not to stay in India, after Aarti's threats, aware of the clout Aarti and Sudhir exercised. So where can she have gone?

Aarti tries to put herself in Vani's shoes. She thinks of the shadows that crossed Vani's face every time Aarti said 'my child'. She thinks of the way Vani had said, the day of the scan, 'I want this child,' and the way her face had become an impenetrable mask when Aarti had first laughed and then raged at her. Aarti should have been more careful, she realises now. She grossly underestimated how motherhood would change Vani, how it would give the meek, shy slip of a girl a backbone of steel, how it would compel her to steal what wasn't hers and run away, to start a new life rooted in the sorrow and loss of the sister related to her by friendship.

Where can Vani take a baby?

And then one day, as she is getting money out of the safe, Vani's passport tumbles out. Aarti doesn't think much of it; after all, she herself had actioned Vani's passport and visa for their trip to the UK that... Wait. Frantically, she rummages in the safe for her passport and the baby's but she knows she will not find them. She calls Sudhir and asks him to look among his things, her hand clenched around Vani's passport, flaming orange rage consuming her, thick green bile flooding her mouth with the acrid taste of Vani's treachery, of being taken for a fool.

And thus it begins.

Aarti applies for a new passport and because of her connections, she is able to get one almost immediately. She flies into Heathrow the following week, hires a private investigator, stays a month while the investigator scours London. When no trace turns up of either Vani or Aarti's baby, Aarti asks him to widen the search area, look in the suburbs and the other big cities with thriving Indian populations, knowing that Vani would want to blend in, not stand out. Nothing. No sightings. She retains the investigator even after she goes back, although he costs the earth and a bit, and they search. And search.

Sudhir pays another visit.

'You have your whole life ahead of you, Aarti,' he says, impassioned in a way he hadn't been during the last few years of their married life. 'Go back to work. That is how I got over it.'

She looks in the mirror, at the husk of the woman she has become, the lined face, the bloodshot eyes, and laughs. 'You are joking. Who would want me?'

'I am not joking,' he says. 'All the agencies want you back, I assure you. They keep hounding me to persuade you to give it a try again. They know what you've been through, what you are still going through. Lord knows I've had enough of the press coverage. And now, there's even talk of a movie, did you know that? They are enthralled by a servant having the temerity to steal the child of the "golden couple", leading to the breakdown of our marriage, the ending of your career. My director even had the gall to ask me if I would play the lead! Lord, some days I want to shout the truth from the rooftops.'

She whips her hand out, encircles his wrist like a handcuff. 'Don't you dare!'

'I won't, Aarti, don't you worry. Your secret and your reputation are both safe with me.' His voice bitter as mustard seeds. 'What I will do is stop this movie ever seeing the light of day.' He swallows, rubs a hand across his forehead. 'Anyway, I did not come here to argue with you. I wanted to ask you to stop searching for them, Aarti. Let Vani be. She wants this child. Let her have Rupa.'

'How can you ask me that? Have you forgotten how much you loved Rupa, *your* child? Aren't you angry with Vani?'

'I miss Rupa, of course I do. I miss her every single day. But... Vani will be a good mother to her. Let them be.'

'Don't you want to find your child?'

'I want my child to have a good life. Vani is her mother.' Aarti flinches at this and Sudhir notices. 'Whether you like it or not. Vani has made a choice, to bring Rupa up away from us. I have decided to respect that even though I wish I had known. I wish she had aired her concerns with me. I wish...' He rubs his hand wearily across his eyes again, takes a deep breath. 'I want the best for Rupa. I do not want her to feel hounded, to have to live in fear. Please stop. Don't let the hate destroy your life.'

'She stole the family I wanted. She took *everything* from me.'

'Please. Stop. Let them be. Let them get on with their life.'

'What about *my* life? What about the life she has stolen from *me*?'

Even though she will not admit this even to herself, Aarti *misses* Vani. Vani always brought out the best in Aarti. Vani made Aarti feel better about herself. Compared to dowdy, meek, quiet Vani, Aarti was the superstar she did not quite believe herself to be. In Vani's starry-eyed gaze, in those early days, she could do no wrong.

Without Vani to underline her successes and triumphs, she is nothing. Nobody.

And so, Aarti does not stop. She spends all her time and all her money trying to find them because without Vani and her child, there is no meaning to her life.

PART FIVE

Present Day

New Beginnings

Chapter 43
Aarti

The Colour of Loneliness

This is what I know:

The colour of remorse is blue. Inky blue like the darkest hour of night just before it fades to grey and is streaked dusty pink by the brushstrokes of dawn. It tastes bitter, like morning breath after a night of excess. It is the sensation in your mouth when you've just been sick. It has a charred tang like rice left too long on the stove and forgotten. It feels like an assault, blue-black welts blooming on battered skin. It is the dirty navy of burnt bridges. It is spilt ink on your best dress. It is the smell of lost chances, missed opportunities. It feels desperate. It smacks of failure. That is remorse for you. Failure couched in an armour of regret, a sheath of 'what ifs' and 'if onlys'.

The colour of loneliness, on the other hand, is white. Silvery white like morning mist that evaporates at the slightest whisper of a touch. The doomed arctic white of winter, icicles and frost, its frigid tentacles creeping, skulking, pouncing when you are at your lowest. It is omnipresent; enveloping you in a filmy white halo, igniting aches in you, yearning for the vibrant but elusive cornucopia of company. It tastes of wistfulness, insubstantial, like eating air. It smacks of desperation, the white hangdog smell of longing. It is thick air sagging languidly in a room, populated by laments and cravings, weighted down with melancholy, un-punctured by sound, untouched by laughter, undisturbed by gaiety.

❄ ❄ ❄

The lawyer calls. 'You lied,' he says.

'Why did you lie to me?' her daughter had asked the other day and her heart had stilled.

'I did not lie,' Aarti replies, injecting the colour and texture of ice into her voice. 'Rupa Shetty is my daughter.'

Despite trying her hardest not to, her voice quivers. She looks around the tiny room she is reduced to, the plate of biscuits sitting on the wobbly table representing the hope, the bribe to get her daughter to love her. Her anticipations and dreams for a family like the one Vani had described to her, countless evenings, reduced to this. A girl with Sudhir's passionate eyes and Vani's delicate features looking at her accusingly, suspiciously.

'*I* wanted her. *She* didn't. She ran away when I asked her to have my child.' Her voice trembles, it shudders, it refuses to do her bidding.

Nothing is as it seems, nothing belongs to her, not really. She had wanted the two people whom she loved to stay close to her, always. She had wanted to bind all of them together by means of a child.

She failed.

'The DNA test has proven beyond a doubt that the child is Ms Bhat's. I have the papers right here.' The lawyer's voice is crisp, shiny smooth, like pebbles roasting in the sun.

'I could not have children. I was infertile. It was *my* idea. I wanted the child. It is *my* name on the birth certificate.' The acrid taste of lost hope, disintegrating dreams in her mouth.

'Ah, yes, that. A crime might have been committed there,' the lawyer's voice: pebbles dropping, one after the other. 'Why is there no mention of the surrogate in the birth certificate? In the official documents?'

'The child is mine.' *But she is not here. No one here but me.* Loneliness her only friend, the one that has stuck by her all these years.

'Is there any document where Ms Vani Bhat signed away her maternal rights to you, where she agreed to be the surrogate?'

She closes her eyes, thinks of the pact they made when they were girls with everything ahead of them, the future a gift waiting to be unwrapped, seized, lived to the hilt. The yellowish-grey piece of paper fragile and fraying from overuse. Her signature and Vani's. *We are sisters, bound by a bond thicker than blood. Bound by friendship.*

'No,' her voice barely above a whisper.

'I am sorry, Ms Kumar. This doesn't look good for you. You might have to serve a sentence for perjury. And then there is the matter of having wasted police time and resources searching for a child who is not legally yours, actioning the extradition orders, getting Ms Vani Bhat arrested... For these offences, you will have to pay a hefty fine at the very least. Also, Ms Bhat might bring charges against you...' The pebbles have settled. The voice is soft, quiet like mud, dry and powdery beneath bare feet.

They once danced barefoot on dry mud, she and Vani, she recalls. Vani was shocked that Aarti had never done it, never been barefoot.

'Come on,' she had said, holding Aarti's hand, dragging her along.

Aarti had followed Vani's lead, had dug her heels into the mud, allowed it to swallow her light brown feet, baptise them red with dust, savoured the feeling of warm filth caressing her feet. A sudden spidery flash, a low growl. The heavens had opened, without further warning. And they were wet, dripping, the dust thickening to sludge, squelchy beneath bare feet, oozing from between Aarti's toes, her feet sinking where she stood, mired in soggy earth.

Vani had thrown her head back and laughed, had opened her arms wide and twirled. Aarti had watched this girl in her pink and emerald salwar kameez, a colourful moth, the water falling off her in slanting swirls as she danced in the shimmering curtain of rain.

And Aarti had done the same, offered her face up to the sky, opened her hands and pirouetted in the pouring rain and it had felt wonderful. She had felt free. As if she was throwing away her old self. All the need, the hurt, the long, lonely days spent aching for her parents to notice her. She had opened her mouth to the warm drops kissing her lips and tasting like blessings and she had felt happy.

Happy.

She lies on the bed, closes her eyes, the phone forgotten, the lawyer's voice, 'Ms Kumar? You there?' a distant echo.

Chapter 44
Vani

The Unvarnished Truth

Darling Diya,

You must have heard the results of the DNA test by now.

'Then why,' you must be thinking, 'did they have to arrest my mum? Put us both through all of this. How could Aarti claim I was her daughter?'

In these pages, hopefully, you will find answers to all of your questions. My story and yours. The unvarnished truth.

Looking back, I can see, Diya, that I was weak. Picture this: a young girl, cruelly orphaned, thrust into a big house full of strangers in an alien city. The young mistress of the house – a supermodel, the girl everyone fawns over – extends her the hand of friendship. And she takes it, awed. Amazed. Blown away. She has been chosen. She is special.

I realise now that any time during those years I could have walked away, but I was afraid. I did not know the city, the people. I did not know anyone except Aarti. I believed when she told me I was nothing without her. I believed blindly and stayed put.

When I met Ram, when I started spending time with him, that car our palace, I should have left, run away with him. But I was naïve. I did not identify love when it was staring me in the face.

All those hours Ram and I spent together in that car, we should have woven dreams, populated our future with them. But we stuck to the bounds of propriety and were unhappy separately, alone with our thoughts. Ram told me later that he was garnering the courage to profess his feelings for me. While I, unaware that the comfort I felt with Ram was the blossoming of love, ruminated on how to escape Aarti's friendship that had long since become a noose.

I was unhappy, I felt tied, trapped. And yet, I let myself be bound closer instead of gradually breaking each tie. Instead of slipping away, I slipped further into the net. Aarti told me she couldn't function without me. She told me she would die without me, she showed me, by leading herself to death's door. I believed her.

And then. And then you came along. And everything changed…

You made me grow up finally, my sweet. You transformed me into this person who actually does things instead of thinking about them. You made me pull myself out of the rut I had let myself get sucked into, you gave me gumption, a backbone. You made me into the person I was always capable of being but had been too afraid to become. You gave me the courage to finally bid adieu to my parents, to stop being someone's daughter and someone's servant, someone's friend and someone's sister. You made me a mother. You changed me.

And so I left. I left without looking back. I escaped a life of being a nonentity and entered another life of being another kind of nonentity. But at least here, I had you. At least here I was able to bring you up the way I wanted for thirteen blissful years until my past caught up with me.

Here is a truth: not a day goes by that I haven't felt guilty – not about what I did, but the way I did it. I feel terribly guilty for what I put Aarti and Sudhir through, for denying Sudhir, who loved you so completely, his daughter, for denying you the love of a father and the warmth of a family. I have made so many mistakes, caused so much hurt. At the time, Diya, I could not think of what else to do. I was flailing, lost, backed into a corner. And so, I took you and I ran.

It is only fair, I tell myself, when I am missing you so much that I gag with yearning, longing for one glimpse of you. It is only fair that now I am denied seeing you, being with you for a bit so I get a taste of the pain I doled out to Sudhir and Aarti.

'You have a visitor,' the guard says, unlocking the gate.

It is the lawyer, I think.

My lawyer is busy getting the extradition charges dropped. But he's warned me that I might still face extradition for the possession of false documents.

'What about Diya?' I asked when he told me.

It seems, darling, that you will be eligible for citizenship by virtue of your having lived in the UK for most of your life, since the UK is the only home you know. And since I am your sole guardian and I did what I did out of love for you, my lawyer thinks that if my case comes up for trial before a kind judge, we might be able to swing it so I can live here with you. If not, Diya, if you are willing, after I have served my sentence, we could go live in India for a bit? We could go to my village, perhaps. Stay for a while in the little cottage by the babbling stream where I spent my childhood, see how you like it.

So, I go to see the visitor, thinking it is my lawyer. But it is a girl. A young girl who has shot up in the time I have been gone, slimmed down. The girl I have watched grow and take shape, the girl I have watched come into her own. The girl I am so proud to call my daughter. My girl.

You are here. In front of me. There is a woman with you and she looks at you with affection, and I am happy. She is small and stout and it is obvious that she cares for you.

You hold your hand out, and I take it. I pull you into my arms like I have yearned to do every minute we have been apart. I hold you close and breathe in your smell, basking in the pleasure, the cherished warmth, the familiar beloved comfort of your body. My girl. My baby. My love.

Chapter 45
Aarti

The Colour of Acceptance

The colour of acceptance is yellow. The yellow of daffodils heralding spring and the promise of sunshine. The yellow of new beginnings. The yellow of life budding in trees bare and shorn by an icy winter. It smells like spring. It is the assurance of summer. It is biting into the first ripe mango of the season, yellow juice dribbling down your chin. It is the colour of smiles on kids' faces. It is marigolds nodding, sunflowers waving like old friends. It is the sun thawing a heart frosted over by loneliness, icy with hate and blackened by revenge. It tastes of forgiveness, minty and fresh. It is a clean slate wiped free of past mistakes. It is the sound of laughter, the chatter of birds, a sign that the worst is over, the potential of things to come. It is tentative, it is hopeful – not quite orange, but getting there.

❄ ❄ ❄

Aarti has got her wish. It has taken thirteen years. But she has won. Vani is in prison and will be in there for a while, Aarti's lawyer informs her. Even though the DNA test proved that Vani is Diya's mother, she is serving a sentence for possessing false documents and living illegally in this country.

And yet, Aarti finds that there is no joy, no satisfaction of a job well done, like she had imagined she would feel at the culmination of this quest. There is no happiness.

Lying on the hotel bed, after taking the call from her lawyer, Aarti accepts that she sorely underestimated Vani, like she has been doing for years, ever since she met Vani, in fact. She thought Vani would give up the moment she was detained, that Aarti would grab her child and swan into a brighter future. Aarti had nurtured the fantasy that somehow the child would accept her as her mother – miracles happen don't they? She had hoped for a little Vani to patch the Vani-sized hole in her life. A companion to stave off the loneliness.

But now she admits that she's always known, deep inside, that there was no way Vani would meekly give her child up without a fight, not after she was brave enough to take her daughter and run, despite Aarti's threats, despite what she had to lose.

And even though Aarti had known, deep down, that she would not get Diya/Rupa for herself, she had wanted this to happen. She wanted to teach Vani a lesson, to put Vani through the pain of loss, to punish her for what she did, to show her that she, Aarti, had not given up searching. She wanted Vani to feel hounded, to feel trapped. She wanted Vani to go to prison. She wanted Vani to suffer. All through that was her motive. To penalise Vani for stealing her child, destroying her life.

She hadn't done it out of love for her child.

'Don't you ever think of anyone but yourself?' Vani had asked that fateful day when she ran away for the first time, the day Aarti asked her to have a baby for her.

'It's all you know. To use others. To possess them. You don't know what it is to love, truly love, selflessly love.' Sudhir had accused before he left her for good.

Sudhir...he deserves to know.

She calls him. Tells him she is in London.

He interrupts before she can say anything else. 'Let go, Aarti,' his sigh is immense. 'Give up searching and get on with your life before it runs away from you.'

'She is lovely. Vani has brought her up well, like you said she would,' Aarti says.

A pause and then, his voice awed, barely above an amazed whisper travelling five thousand miles to reach her via a telephone line crackling and sighing like a prickly old woman, 'You found her?'

'Yes.'

Sudhir is remarried now, to his make-up artist, of all people, an ordinary-looking plump woman two years older than Aarti. How Aarti had worried that he was having affairs with his co-stars! How she had envied them their beauty and their youth!

'Does she look like me?' His voice wistful, naked hope threading it.

'She has your eyes.'

'Not a day goes by that I… I miss her so.'

This is the closest Aarti has ever come to having a heart-to-heart with Sudhir, the closest she has come to seeing his soul laid bare in thirteen years.

He has a son with the make-up artist. No daughters apart from the one he lost.

'Will you be seeing her again?' His voice wistful, punctuated by longing, carrying down the crackly line.

'I will come tomorrow,' Diya had promised, but that was before the results of the DNA test came through.

'I…I don't know.' Diya's face looms before Aarti's eyes, the way she stood in Aarti's arms, a little stiff, a little unyielding, the way her eyes, Sudhir's eyes, lit up when she smiled.

'If you do, give her my love.' His voice infinitely sad.

'I am sorry, Sudhir, for the way I was,' Aarti says. 'For what I asked you to do.'

Aarti's apology is thirteen years too late. Diya – the result of what Aarti asked Sudhir to do – staring at Aarti with her father's eyes in this very room, trying to draw the truth from Aarti's depths with the strength of that golden, unwavering gaze, interceding with Aarti on her mother's behalf, never losing the belief that Vani was her mother even after Aarti showed her the birth certificate.

'It's all in the past now.' Sudhir's voice is as soft as snow falling under cover of night, gentle as absolution. 'Have you spoken to her?'

'Of course I spoke with her. She's…'

'No, not Rupa. Have you spoken to Vani?'

A pause. As always with Sudhir, Aarti is blindsided, lost for words.

'She is the one who deserves apologies.'

The click of the connection being aborted, the whine of the ring tone. Only Sudhir has ever dared to speak to Aarti this way. Only him. She feels a pang. For what might have been. If she hadn't come up with her foolhardy plan, if she hadn't persuaded Vani to have a child… Who knows? Perhaps Aarti and Sudhir would still be together. Then Aarti thinks of the fights they used to have. No, they brought out the worst in each other. They always have.

Lying alone on her single bed in an alien country in a run-of-the-mill hotel room populated with old regrets and new memories, she ruminates over Sudhir's words. Thirteen years on and he still manages to surprise her, this man she once loved. He has forgiven Vani, the woman who wronged him, who denied him the daughter he loves, aches for. And now, he is asking Aarti to not only forgive and forget, but to apologise also.

She thinks of Vani, that girl she had loved, who in her mind had been her only family apart from Sudhir, even though, if she is to be completely honest with herself, she never quite thought of Vani as her equal. She loved Vani, but her relationship with her was always slightly derogatory; she treated Vani, she thinks, her cheeks burning, like a favourite pet. She recalls the note Vani had left behind, 'I cannot stand being your possession…'

That had hurt. It had touched a nerve. Had she treated her friend like a possession? *Yes,* her inner voice concurs, the one that used to be so vociferous in the beginning until she shut it up.

Unbidden, the memory of the time Vani had brought the baby in to see her, dressed in a white jumpsuit, looms.

'Why is she wearing that?' Aarti had asked, as soon as she saw the baby. 'I asked you to put her in the pink one.'

Vani's smiling face had ironed out into the empty expression that was so common when she was with Aarti. 'She's changed now and she's sleeping.'

'No,' Aarti had snapped, annoyed that Vani had not dressed Rupa, *her* daughter, in the clothes she had chosen for her. 'Change her. Now. Then bring her back.'

Vani had walked away with the baby without another word and a moment later, the first wails of protest had reached Aarti as the clothes were wrestled off the baby and she awoke from slumber.

'Do you miss her?' Diya had asked in this very room and Aarti had not been lying when she said, 'Every day. I miss Vani every single day.'

She misses the fun they had. The camaraderie they shared. After Aarti came back home that weekend and found no Vani and no child, what she missed most was noise, laughter, companionship. The joy of having a friend to share everything with.

How would Diya/Rupa have turned out if she had lived with her, grown up with Aarti as her mother? What would she, Aarti, have been like as a mother? She cannot bear to think of that. It hurts too much. What is the use of deliberating on what might have been?

This is what she knows: Diya – it is time Aarti started addressing her by the name she prefers, the name Vani chose for her – is lovely. Chubby yes, but that can be rectified. She is kind, well adjusted, fiercely loyal. A credit to Vani. It kills Aarti to admit it, even to herself, but it is the truth.

And now that Aarti is admitting truths, here is another: she, Aarti, had been ill for years.

'Have you gone quite mad?' Sudhir had asked her when she came up with her plan to have Vani create a baby for her.

After her spell at the clinic, Aarti realised that Sudhir's accusation was not as preposterous as it had seemed, that it had a grain of truth in it. She had been messed up, mentally, for a while. Decades of abusing her body had taken their toll. Not only had the bulimia rendered her infertile, it had played havoc with her mind, so she was suspicious, neurotic and not thinking right.

Looking back, she has to admit that perhaps she wouldn't have been the best role model for a child. Sudhir saw that. And Vani. Vani put up with Aarti the best she could, but she would not stand for the same for her child. And so, she ran away. She knew, even though Aarti didn't, that Aarti wouldn't kill herself. That Aarti was stronger than that. She must have known. Even though she was but a slip of a girl, she was wise, was Vani. And brave. What she did, Aarti has to admit, is the bravest thing she can think of. Vani was, she *is* the better mother.

Diya's face swims before her eyes. The daughter she desperately craved for the wrong reasons. The daughter whose arrival caused the rupture of the very things she'd wanted. The daughter because of whom she lost both her best friend and her husband. The daughter she searched for mainly because, *only because*, Vani stole her from Aarti. How dare she? Vani, that mouse. And instead of giving up, Aarti found her purpose in life. To thwart the woman who had thwarted her.

But she is realising, too late, that this is not chess. And Diya is not a pawn. She is her own person. A young girl with her whole life ahead of her.

This should have been about Diya but it has always been about Aarti. Her feelings, her hurt. Her suffering. Her loneliness. What Sudhir said when he left her, the words that hurt her so, was the truth. She has done exactly what her parents did to her: treated everyone else like possessions, the only way she knows. Her mother's face, the day she came into her dressing room, the day she apologised, appears before her eyes.

'At least you have parents,' Vani had said to her softly once during their late night chats, when dogs howled and cats prowled and friends stayed up exchanging confidences and making pacts, one lying on the floor on her mat swatting at mosquitoes that hovered, while the other slept in a king-sized bed with a mosquito cover and wished she had had her friend's childhood and her friend's parents.

'They are horrible to me. You've seen how they are.' Aarti complained.

'They care even though they perhaps cannot show it.' Vani's voice soft in the darkness.

'Pah,' Aarti had laughed, hurt making her voice sound harsher than she intended. 'You don't know what you're talking about. All they care about is the prestige that comes with being parents of the best model in Karnataka.'

'They are alive,' Vani had whispered into the dark smelling strongly of mosquito repellent, thick with memories of her absent parents. 'Appreciate them; make your peace with them, before it is too late.'

'You don't know a thing about my parents,' Aarti had interjected sharply, cutting Vani off.

Now she thinks, *I have travelled across the world in search of a girl on whom I have no proper claim. My parents and I live in the same city. They are alive. They are mine, like Diya will never be.*

Her mother's defeated face that day in that dressing room looms. *I have spent the better part of my life seeking revenge. Perhaps it is time I built bridges instead of breaking them, practised forgiveness instead of multiplying the hurt that has been done to me, perpetrating it further.*

The expression in her mother's eyes the last time Aarti saw her, the naked need supplanted by crushing disappointment, a mask of hurt, hovers. *They have lost their only daughter too.* It comes to her in a flash, the revelation. *They must be desperately lonely. Like me.*

She picks up the phone. Rummages in her address book for her parents' number. Even after all these years, she has kept it. She has.

It rings and rings. Seven rings, ten.

Then, 'Hello?' Her mother's voice, tremulous, plaited through with the ravages of age.

'Amma...' she says, tentatively.

'Aarti!' Joy bursts down the line, piercing the regret-strewn space in that tiny room, dispelling the gloom, cutting through the emptiness. A glimmer of sunshine angles between the chink in the curtains and dances on the white sheets, staining them the sunny yellow of hope, of new beginnings. 'Oh, Aarti, my darling, how *are* you? How have you been?'

'I...' She begins, 'Amma, I...' and bursts into tears.

❋ ❋ ❋

At first, Aarti does not recognise the woman who stands at the door to the Visits Hall accompanied by a prison guard, anxiously scanning the visitors to see who has come to meet her. Vani is smaller than Aarti remembers, her hair is shorter than she remembers and, Aarti realises with a shock, it sports quite a few grey strands. Her face is lined, the lines of a woman older and wiser than Vani. It is weary, mapped out with the cares of the world.

Vani's eyes scan the room, brush over her, then away, then back again, her face doing a double take as recognition dawns. A smile sneaks into her eyes, an involuntary, unguarded, wholesome grin of delight at seeing an old friend, before being abruptly snuffed out as everything that has gone between them, the heft of all the years in between, the weight of the disservice they have each done the other, settles like a mask, a screen.

Aarti remains sitting on the uncomfortable chair in the Visits Hall, with all the other people waiting to visit their relatives, their faces needy, desperate, worried, expectant, and watches Vani approach hesitantly toward her and lower herself gingerly onto the chair opposite.

Somehow, it seems incongruous that this ordinary, slightly shabby woman who looks as if she has been whipped, battered by the years that have passed since Aarti last set eyes on her, has been the subject of Aarti's rage, the target for her loathing, all the hate she's harboured her whole life for the lack of love she's experienced, seeping into the seething loneliness and becoming a toxic cocktail that has been brewing for thirteen years. A residue of that wrath, that hatred, that hurt flares and is doused almost instantly by a glance at the slight woman, weary and stooped sitting across from her. This ragged person is not accountable for all that angst; this woman is not to blame for everything that has gone wrong in Aarti's life – well, not completely at least.

Superimposed in the time-ravaged features of the woman across from her, Aarti catches glimpses of the girl she had counted as family, the girl she once loved. Affection wars with hurt, anger with a yearning for the bond she had shared with the girl hiding within this strange yet infinitely familiar woman before her – a kaleidoscope of emotions.

Aarti wonders what Vani is feeling, what thoughts are coursing through her head. She used to be able to read

Vani like a book, or so she had always assumed with the nonchalance of being the superior in their uneven relationship. What she knows now is that she knew nothing, nothing at all of what was going on in Vani's mind, what she was feeling.

She wants to hug this woman in front of her. She wants to hit Vani, hurt Vani like she hurt her.

She wonders what expression her face is displaying; whether it mirrors Vani's own one of wonder, that of waking from a dream and not being quite sure which world one is in, the dream one or the wakeful one. The years that have ensued since she waved goodbye to Vani and the baby and left for a weekend away in Mumbai sit between then, a shimmering screen of hurt and regrets and loss and what might have been.

Tears fall silently down Vani's cheeks, snaking into her open mouth.

Aarti opens her own mouth and tastes salt and sorrow as she remembers the young girl feverishly sobbing for her parents whom she had held in her arms, Vani's thin body shuddering as it convulsed with grief, reminding Aarti of the baby sparrow that had fallen out of its nest that she had rescued once, the ridged bones of Vani's spine digging into her.

'Aarti,' Vani says, and that one word encompasses their friendship, and the screen of the years in between crumbles with a soft, melancholic sigh.

How they had laughed together late into the night, how Vani had held Aarti while she was being sick, how she had wiped her tears, plaited her hair, nursed her back to health. Her friend. Her sister.

This woman Aarti has loved more than she can imagine. This woman whom she has missed desperately over the years.

Aarti clears her throat of thirteen years of clogged-up sufferings and grievances. 'You devastated me.' She cannot help it. She thinks one thing and says something completely different. Years of habit. Of being the boss. Once again the haughty memsahib. Some habits are hard to break. Argumentative with Sudhir, domineering with Vani. *Stop this. She is not your servant anymore.*

A glint flashes in Vani's eyes, blue-black like oil on the surface of stagnant water, her face hardening like milk curdling. 'You possessed me.'

Despite herself, Aarti is shocked. This is not the Vani she remembers, the meek girl who used to jump to do her bidding. This is the woman she underestimated, who took her child and ran, who has fought for her child even from prison.

'I surrendered my freedom to you, permitted you to play me like a puppet. I allowed you access to my dead parents. I shared my past with you. I sacrificed my future for you. But I did not want you to take my child, the best part of me, the only part of me that was precious, unsullied, *mine*. I was not willing to sacrifice my innocent child on the altar of your whims and fancies, your bulimic delusions.'

Aarti is stung. She did not know Vani harboured such bile. 'You destroyed my future,' she manages at last.

'No. *You* destroyed your future.' Each word is a grenade, precisely aimed, flawlessly executed. 'You had a choice. You could have stopped searching for us, chosen some other innocent girl to have a baby for you. *I* did not have a choice. You gave me no choice.'

'You ran away when I asked you to have her, remember?' Aarti's voice is bilious orange, the colour of the flames causing havoc within her, lit by the ire in Vani's voice, the vitriol of Vani's accusations. Where is the Vani she knows? Where has that gentle girl gone?

'And you made me come back. You trapped me. Bhoomi, the servant who found you when you overdosed on pills told me later how you asked her to come into the room at nine o'clock. Exactly at nine o'clock. You planned it all. You wanted to be found. You made sure I would come back.'

'I loved you.' Aarti does not recognise the cowed, flabbergasted whisper as hers.

'Your love, Aarti…' Vani's voice is pained, bleeding tears. 'It was like feeding scraps to a dog. I did not want that for my child.'

'I still do,' Aarti says, her voice soft.

'Huh?' A question dances upon Vani's face.

'I have missed you, Vani. Yes, I treated you very badly. Yes, I blackmailed you into having a baby. I am sorry. So very sorry. You were my family. You are my family. I love you. I love your child. Your child…'

'Are we quite decided on that then?'

Aarti does not recognise this woman. The sardonic tone does not become Vani. 'Pardon?'

'*My* child? You sure?' Vani's voice is shaking, threaded through with shimmering rage the fiery red of a stormy sky at sunset. 'You always maintained that I was nothing without you, that you gave me everything. And I believed you, the fool that I was. But you...' Vani's voice stumbles, breaks and she gulps, recovers. 'You took everything from me, everything. My freedom, of course – a given. After all, I was a mere servant, sister, pact notwithstanding. My past. You scavenged upon it. Did you think I didn't know that you imagined my parents were yours? That's where the sister idea for the pact came from, isn't it? That is why you did not let me go to my village after that one time – you could not bear the thought of me communing with my dead parents without you. They were *mine*, Aarti. Their memories were all I owned in the world of servitude I found myself in. But you wanted to claim those too. And, as if that was not enough, you wanted my future as well. How would I hope to get married once I had slept with a man who was not my husband, had a child out of wedlock, in a land where women are prized for their purity? Did you think of that?' Vani pauses, takes a breath.

Aarti grips the sides of her chair, too stunned to speak.

'Your love was a noose around my neck, pulled tight if I strayed too far. You took and took and are still taking. Thirteen years later and where's my freedom? I am separated from the one person whom I wanted for myself, whom I was unwilling to share. Thirteen years later and you are still taking.' Vani takes another deep breath, collapses into herself.

Aarti feels very small. True, everything Vani is saying is true.

'She is yours, she always was. You weren't mine to own and neither is she.' And before Aarti can lose her nerve, she plunges right in. 'I have met her.'

Vani looks up, her eyes shining with naked need, the look of a man driven mad by thirst about to be fed water, a look that says, *tell me more about my child*.

And in that moment, Aarti understands. Vani is a mother, like she, Aarti, never will be. Vani loves like her own mother must have done before her: absolutely, selflessly. In that moment, any residual anger, any residual rage dissipates. How can she grudge this mother her child? How can she deny her her daughter? What was she thinking?

'She is lovely,' Aarti says.

'Isn't she just?' Vani's face disintegrates in a flood of tears. 'I miss her.' She stretches her hands to indicate the prison. 'I miss every minute spent away from her.'

'I am sorry,' Aarti says, feeling her face flush. 'I will try my hardest to get you out of this bind. I will talk to my lawyer, see if there is something I can do. I am so sorry.'

Vani's eyes shine. An expression of awe graces her face, shimmering beneath the deluge of tears. 'You have changed.'

'So have you,' Aarti says and Vani smiles, the completely uninhibited, guileless smile Aarti recognises, and Aarti finally sees the girl Vani once was, the girl she loved, shining through this woman's time-mapped features.

'I just met Diya,' Vani says, and her face beams like a car on a dark, deserted road on a blustery night. 'She came to visit just before you. I do not get visitors at all except, occasionally, my lawyer, and then two very special visitors in one day.' She laughs, slightly hysterically. 'She... Diya's grown taller in just a few days, slimmed down. She looks different. I...I want to hold onto her, to capture this moment in time, otherwise it will run away from me and she will be an adult and I will be thinking, where have the years gone? Like you must have thought when you saw her.' A brief pause, then, 'I stole her from you, Aarti, but you know what I wish I could do? You know what would be good? If I could steal time...'

Aarti is surprised by the snort of laughter that bursts out of her. She has forgotten the effect Vani has always had on her. With Vani she could be herself. They could talk about anything, anything at all. She could let her guard down. She could laugh like she did just now. Open-mouthed. Unmindful of appearances, unworried about being judged. And it is saying something, to laugh in these circumstances, in this mirthless room peopled with felons and their tearful relatives, to laugh with the person who has just put Aarti's emotions through the wringer, who has shattered her, assaulted her with her words, her allegations.

She cannot believe that she and Vani are sitting here, talking, as if the intervening years never happened. She cannot believe how much at ease she feels with Vani, despite all that has gone before, despite all that has happened just now. She cannot believe the warmth creeping into her heart, which has been frozen by hatred and the desire for revenge for thirteen years. She cannot believe how light she feels now that she has dislodged the heavy yoke of hate and blame, how weightless, she who is always obsessing about weight and who always feels fat, never mind that her bulimia has been in check for years. She cannot believe how buoyant she feels, how…how peaceful, for the first time in what feels like forever.

'If I could steal time,' Vani says, 'I would do so many things differently. I comprehend, fully now, how you and Sudhir must have felt, to have Diya…Rupa grow up without you. I understood while I was in here, missing her dreadfully.' Her eyes are iridescent with the mascara of tears; glittering with remorse. 'Back then, I was young and felt trapped. I…'

Aarti surprises herself by reaching across and putting her hand on Vani's. This is the other thing she has forgotten – how when with Vani, she always did things out of character, things which amazed her. If Sudhir brought out the worst in her, then Vani always, without question, brought out the best. Her heart thaws completely and the words she has come here to say spill out. 'I am sorry,' she says, 'for what I asked you to do.'

'Without you, I wouldn't have her.' Vani swallows. Then, her voice barely above a whisper, 'I know I hurt you and Sudhir. Not a day has gone by that I haven't regretted the pain I caused…'

'I am the one who has been selfish, Vani, I know that now. I have known for a while but refused to accept it, preferring to wear the veil of hatred, point the finger of blame at you. My motives in searching for Diya weren't exactly pure… I persevered mainly because I wanted to punish you.' The words stick in her throat but she forces them out. 'Truth be told, I wouldn't have been a great mother or a suitable role model for Diya. She is amazing. You have done a good job.'

'She is.' Vani's whole being lights up so that, despite her worn face that appears older than her years, she looks beautiful. 'I was angry with you for a very long time, Aarti. But Diya…she healed me. I thought I had got rid of the anger, the hurt, but seeing you here… I was harsh with you just now, Aarti, but the words have been brewing within me for years. They had to be said.'

Aarti nods once. 'They hurt like mad,' she says. 'But I suppose I deserve them.'

Vani's face is transformed by incredulous amazement, her mouth open in a perfect O of surprise, tears snaking into it.

Aarti reaches across and puts her arms around Vani and they hug, awkwardly at first and then they are laughing and crying and comforting each other like they did once before when it all began.

Later, much later, Vani asks, 'Is Ram still your driver?'

'Yes. The only one left in my employ. Why do you ask?'

Vani is smiling weirdly as she says, her voice slightly shaky, 'No reason. Just remembered him, that's all.'

'You once asked me to make peace with my parents before it was too late,' Aarti says, 'and I have.'

Vani nods, 'I am pleased.'

'They did love me; they just didn't know how to show it.'

'Yes.'

'The same with me. I did love you, you know, Vani.'

Vani nods, her eyes overflowing again. 'I know,' she whispers.

Chapter 46
Diya

Home

Home

Noun: the place where one lives.
Related Words: blood, kin, family.

✼ ✼ ✼

Home is the cradle of my mother's arms. Her voice whispering sweet nothings in my ear. Her head resting on mine. Her tears baptising my hair. Her body propping me up. Her smell of fruit ripening in weak summer sun and sweat. After floundering for so many days, after being lost and lonely, a directionless compass, I have found my bearings. I am home.

'I am sorry,' she whispers, over and over. 'I am sorry you had to undergo this trauma. So very sorry.'

Afterwards, she hands me the letters. Her words to buttress me, keep me company while we wait for the machinery of the law to chug into place, to release her to us – or not for a while, as it may be.

I take the letters back to Farah's, read the words my mother has penned, and I understand. I understand. I know now why she did what she did. I know why she felt she had to run. I know why she worried about telling me. Her guilt. Her fear. Everything makes sense. I am angry at that woman, at Aarti. I am horrified at what she asked my mother to do, what she made her do.

'I hate her,' I say when I see my mother next.

Her eyes widen and she looks at me with all the love in the world. 'Hate narrows a person, Diya. You have a gentle, giving heart. Don't layer it with hate. It makes for a very bitter lining. It will eat you up inside, make you into a smaller person than the one you are capable of being. Forgive her. Let go. It will set you free. Trust me.'

I clench my fingers into fists.

My mother takes my hands in hers and very gently opens my fingers one by one. She cups my chin with her palm, lifts my face up to hers. 'Look at me.'

I do. I look into eyes that are as familiar to me as my own. Eyes that I have woken up to every day of my life except the last few nightmarish days. Eyes bursting with love, the melting chocolate-button gaze.

'She was not in her senses, not completely herself. She had abused her body so much that it messed up her mind. But…if she hadn't asked what she did of me, you wouldn't be here. I am, I will always be grateful to her for giving me you.'

'But, Mum…'

'Diya, she's suffered for it. She has. And she loves you.'

An involuntary snort escapes me. But then I think of the doll sitting in the wardrobe in Farah's house. Aarti's needy face, her gaze fixed on me, drinking me in like a man in a desert who's stumbled upon an oasis. The biscuits in that room soaked in her desperation, reeking of her loneliness. The prison of her scrawny arms holding me captive. The leathery skin stretched like elastic, the silvery bones that ripple just underneath, that play peek-a-boo when she moves.

'She does, Diya.' Mum knows me, knows when to press her advantage. 'She did not know love, did not experience it growing up. And so she loves in the only way she knows how.'

'Mum…'

'It is easy to hate. Much, much harder to forgive. Forgive her, Diya.'

'Have you?' I ask and she smiles.

'I was angry with her for a long time. It soured me inside, the anger. It shrivelled my heart. You saved me, you healed me. You filled my heart with love, chasing away the loathing, the rage. I would look at you, innocent, happy, and think, God has given me this precious gift and instead of thanking Him, I am hating one of his creation, the very person via whose insistence I had you.' She takes a breath. 'When my parents died, when I first went to live with her, I would wonder, *what is the plan in all of this?* Then you came along. And I knew. You are perfect; you have a beautiful, loving, giving heart. And you were created out of all that madness, that discord. I learnt from you, took my cue from you. I threw away the hate, darling – and look, I am so much the happier for it.' A pause. 'She came to see me,' her eyes shimmering.

'She did?'

'I finally spoke my mind after so many years of subservience. Told her how I felt. We cleared the air, apologised to each other.'

'You have nothing to apologise for,' my voice indignant. The prison guard looks our way and I lower it again, bashful.

'She has suffered, my lovely, because of what I did…' A pause, then, 'She said she would speak to her lawyer, use her contacts to try and get me out of this…' Mum lifts her arms to indicate the prison.

'She got you in this situation in the first place!'

'I have you, Diya. Who does she have?' Mum smiles at me, her expression full of love. 'And despite everything, in her own way she loved me, she still loves me. And she loves you. Go to Aarti, make your peace with her.' She looks at me, her eyes glowing, and I revel in her gaze; I bask in the familiar warmth, the comforting fortress of her arms.

And after, I go to visit the woman because of whom I came into this world, the woman because of whom my mother is in prison.

I go because I do not want to hate for the rest of my life. I go because I am too happy to harbour grudges, too happy to feel upset, angry or sad for too long. I go because, even though I am angry with Aarti, for lying, for causing all this, she is also the reason I exist. I go because even though my mother is in prison and Aarti put her there, it has been proven that Vani is my mother and no one can separate us anymore once she gets out after serving her sentence. I go because my mother asked me to and I do not want to deny my mother anything. I go because, despite everything, the overwhelming feeling that skeletal, needy Aarti arouses in me is pity.

Her face lights up when she sees me, naked hope shining out of her eyes like the lone lamp in a dark courtyard, glowing so brightly it hurts to look.

'Why did you lie to me?' I ask and her face crumples.

She sobs and she sobs, the sobs tearing through her bird-like body, rendering her even more fragile, even more breakable. And I hold her and I pat her back. And she looks at me through her tears as if she is memorising me, storing my every feature in some secret corner of her mind for use later.

'Would you like a biscuit?' she manages in between sobs.

And we both smile.

She says she is going back to India in two days, that she will stay with her parents while the court case against her, for claiming me as hers, for not including Mum as the birth mother in my birth certificate, for wasting police time and resources, takes place.

But my mother is in prison for forging documents. Why don't you have to go to prison? I think.

As if she can read my mind, she tells me that things are a bit different in India. She tells me she has contacts in high places, as do her parents. She tells me that with the right amount of money changing hands, she will be able to stay out of jail. She tells me that is how she managed to get the staff in the private clinic where I was born – a discreet establishment where the very rich and very famous go to have their babies out of wedlock or recover from their addictions – to conveniently ignore the fact that the woman who had actually given birth to me was not the woman mentioned in the birth certificate, to sign it and make it official.

She tells me she has spoken to my father (whom she is no longer married to, which is why she goes by Aarti Kumar now and not Aarti Shetty). She tells me he loves me very much and sends all his love. She tells me I have a half-brother who would love to meet me.

'Will you come and visit sometime?' she asks and the need is there again, bright as a lighthouse on a stormy night, guiding wayward ships to shore.

I think of my mother, serving a sentence for living illegally in the UK and for being in possession of false documents. I do not know what is going to happen, what is written in my future.

But I do know this: I will be where my mother is.

Epilogue
Two Years Later
Diya

Barefoot in the Rain

We dance barefoot in the rain, ensnaring warm drops in the wide net of our mouths. We breathe in the muddy scent of freshly ploughed earth; sink our teeth in the bruise-pink flesh of a perfectly ripe guava.

Afterwards, we lie on cane mats under the fruit trees in the courtyard, the piquant air caressing our cheeks and whispering perfumed secrets. We slurp sickly sweet tea from stainless steel tumblers and watch the cows placidly grazing amongst emerald fields, the droplets on the blades of grass sparkling and shimmering in the sudden sunlight breaking through the scowling cover of clouds, the whole world glowing green and gold, dazzling the eye.

We listen to the growl of insects and the chatter of birds in the coconut fronds above us through which dappled honey gold rays inveigle, creating rainbow patterns on the bed of maroon and russet leaves, while the stream warbles over pebbles somewhere below us.

'I can feel them here, Diya,' Mum says, 'my parents. They are smiling down at me, at us. I can hear them in the whistle of the wind. I can feel them in its zesty embrace; they are here, all around us.'

Snuff, the stray mongrel we have adopted, barks, setting off the neighbouring dogs, a cacophony of woofs, a medley of discordant howls heralding visitors.

'They've arrived,' Ram calls from his vantage point – the field he is ploughing, closest to the road – his voice laced with excitement, and as always, Mum's eyes light up at the sound of his voice.

'Ready?' she asks, turning to me, giving me a hug.

It's been two months since she's been out of prison, two months since my mother has been returned to me, every day precious as a dream spun from the gossamer silk of every granted wish. Her eyes sparkle. Her hair – now almost completely grey – resists the confines of her bun and crowds her face. She looks happier than I have ever seen her, and younger, despite the grey hair and the lines busily mapping her face.

The stream gossips along merrily, whispering confidences to the silvery fish darting past. The green scent of leaves and the ripe yellow aroma of decaying fruit, the buzzing of bees and the thick, honeyed sweetness in the air evangelise the promise of good things to come.

'Yes,' I say, as I fall into step beside my mother, my heart somersaulting, performing flips of excitement as I go forth to meet my extended family: Aarti and her parents and, especially, my father, his wife and my stepbrother, for the very first time.

Letter from Renita

First of all, I want to say a huge thank you for choosing *The Stolen Girl*, I hope you enjoyed reading Diya, Vani and Aarti's story just as much as I loved writing it.

If you did enjoy it, I would be forever grateful if you'd **write a review**. I'd love to hear what you think, and it can also help other readers discover one of my books for the first time.

Also, if you'd like to **keep up-to-date with all my latest releases**, just sign up here:

www.bookouture.com/renita-dsilva

Finally, if you liked *The Stolen Girl*, I'm sure that you will love my first two novels, ***Monsoon Memories*** and ***The Forgotten Daughter*** which are both available in paperback and eBook.

Thank you so much for your support – until next time.
Renita.

Printed in Great Britain
by Amazon